P9-EEM-090

Also by the author

NOT A WORD ABOUT NIGHTINGALES

BRIDGEPORT BUS

BEFORE MY TIME

GRACE ABOUNDING

AUTOBIOGRAPHY: FACTS OF LIFE

EXPENSIVE HABITS

A NOVEL BY

MAUREEN
HOWARD

SUMMIT BOOKS
NEW YORK

This novel is a work of fiction. Names, characters, places and incidents are either the product of the author's imagination or are used fictitiously. Any resemblance to actual events or locales or persons, living or dead, is entirely coincidental.

Published by SUMMIT BOOKS
A Division of Simon & Schuster, Inc.
Simon & Schuster Building
1230 Avenue of the Americas
New York, New York 10020
SUMMIT BOOKS and colophon are trademarks of
Simon & Schuster, Inc.

Designed by Susan Brooker/Levavi & Levavi
Manufactured in the United States of America

10 9 8 7 6 5 4 3 2 1

Library of Congress Cataloging in Publication Data

Howard, Maureen, date
Expensive habits

I. Title.
PS3558.08823E9 1986 813'.54 86-5727

ISBN 0-671-50625-0

Thanks to the Ingram Merrill Foundation
for their support
when I began this book.

To Cleo and Gloria,
long may they wave.

I dreamed that I floated at will in the great ether and I saw the world floating also not far off, but diminished to the size of an apple. Then an angel took it in his hand and brought it to me and said: "This must thou eat," and I ate the world.

—Emerson, *Journals*

CONTENTS

WONDER BOOK

Have you watered the rum?
  Yes, Sir.
And sanded the sugar?
  Yes, Sir.
And dusted the pepper?
  Yes, Sir.
Then come up and say your prayers.

—Yankee joke.

GO AND SIN no more. A jingle of brass rings as the priest pulled the little curtain. She was through and had never forgotten the elation as she walked out of the double-sided confessional—there were that many sinners in the world. At least in her parish on a Saturday. So many waiting, you'd think it was a movie line and they'd come for the next show. But there were no movie lines then, back at the Rialto, and what did she know of box office, ratings. Now Margaret would say it was a classic—the confessional, always a hit. Down to the tacky wood surface that stuck to your knees, a bit of a penance to start with, then the revelation, a dramatic unburdening, contrition in the dark. The curtain was small as a puppet theater's she'd sewn many years later for her son and when it was drawn open you had your time, your say. It was queer how the sinner ran the show: that was certainly part of the appeal for Maggie (that girl was a caution), and after the absolution, always given, even when she cheated on a test, rouged her cheeks or filched a dollar from her grandmother's purse—when she was through, she flung back the door of the confessional and walked out heartily sorry, yet high and mighty, as though she'd signed on the dotted line for a good part of God's take.

She is through now, or so they tell her, but she will not listen. Heart giving out. Fine, she can hardly argue with that, but Margaret Flood is furious that they—the doctors, whoever—dare pull the curtain before she is finished. She is accustomed to tough times, hard work, not exactly smilin' through, but to survival. Always special, often improbable, Margaret's disease is fitting in that it is unusual for a woman of her age, off the charts. She will not have it. She sets down an overnight case. Still in her fur coat with the outdoor chill upon it, she stands at her bedroom window overlooking Central Park. She has signed herself out of the hospital against medical advice.

It says that officially, AMA, on a paper she holds in her hand. It says this is the first admission of a forty-five-year-old female, overweight, self-employed, admitted with myocardial infarction, severe intermittent pain. Possible lipid abnormality? There is no one to notify in case of emergency other than her sixteen year old son. It says that her mother suffered a rheumatic heart and yes, died comparatively young. Vital statistics. Well, semi-vital as she sees it. Margaret likes her medical history: it is swift, powerful, establishes the scene. What will transpire is her death. So we have from now to then: we all know that.

She looks out over the city. In the foreground the park is bleak, flat in a hard winter light. The manmade lakes and reservoir still, cold to the eye. She shivers and draws the mink coat around her. The goddamn city. For years she has taken it on, but it resists her: she comes back to it like a homely girl unabashed who will try her charms again and again. At times she gets a nod of recognition, a brief collusive grin. Today New York gives nothing to Margaret Flood. The hospital she's left, far across town—one small chip in a tight frieze of stone and glass—is naturally indifferent to her fate. She puts herself to bed thinking of her mother, a fearful woman who lived behind starched white curtains in a dim room, who shuffled the hall toward kitchen or parlor at a careful pace. Margaret has never been careful, surely never held with family advice, but rest, simple rest eked out her mother's life for years—life in the shadows, bedroom door ajar. It was all they knew then, passivity, digitalis and prayer.

As for fear, it's not her style. She's not timid, scared to death. Her great and memorable efforts have not been along the line of ironing a few shirts, baking yellow cake for supper, calling ineffectually to children—beware, behave, be quiet, be good. If she had the strength she would laugh her broad, theatrical laugh, but the determined exit from the hospital, crawling into her own bed, have taken their toll and all she can manage is a weak smile at the notion that she's gone to such pains to be in no way like her mother and is similarly afflicted, what's more is following the remedy which prolonged that sweet and languorous life.

Bed rest, old as witch hazel and Watkins' Liniment. Ladies and Gentlemen, step right up. Margaret Flood knows how to warm up the audience. See—she is finally taking a spoonful. The bitter tonic sticks in her throat before she swallows it down. Ah, it is beneficial and she sleeps. Her head propped high against the pillows is crowned with artful russet curls that have little to do with her sallow skin, colorless lips, the rough uncertain pull of her breath. Her pale hands, worrying out a dream, fret at the real lace which trims her linen sheets. The lots are empty. The Big Indian Medicine Show has come to town, or something like a circus with death-defying tricks, elixirs and tonics, wads of cotton candy that clot the mouth like cobwebs. The show is over. Nothing—rich plops of horse manure. Nothing left—a few stakes, trampled popcorn, ropes trailing in the dust, a blank street full of houses, houses. When she awakes in the middle of the night, she thinks of Lulu Zazel, the bravest woman in the world, the human cannonball. For years she had kept her program from the Ringling Brothers, Barnum & Bailey Circus (it cost a dollar more) with Madame Zazel's autograph. That was Maggie's idea of a celebrity before she knew the word. Madame threw off her cape. She stood strong and small in her sparkling bathing suit and, taking off her royal crown, tucked her head into a tight golden cap, solemnly bid the folks farewell. Silence. All were hushed and silent. She was shot into the air. The blast was deafening. The whole tent smelled like war and before you knew it there was Lulu waving, smiling, shaking out her blue-black hair, slithering down a rope into the sawdust. No safety net for her.

Now Margaret leaves her bed, gathering scraps, old letters, pictures, clippings—her tools and props. She climbs back to her lair exhausted. How far had she got—yes, to where she's come back home against medical advice, is pleased with the vital statistics but she would flesh that out—a sick woman in her middle years, betrayed by one man, abandoned by another. Her finger puffs out around a plain wedding band. She claims she cannot get it off, not with soap or butter. In case of emergency, her son is the only living soul she loves. A failure then—no, Margaret Flood is a big success. Keep that in—a proven, bona fide star. It's December. Take it from the date on her admission form, but the merchants declared it Christmas a month back. So had the Christians declared it. Her son, who is way ahead of the game, has explained all that . . . if there was a star, if there was a couple fleeing tyranny, wise men crossing the desert, stable, babe, shepherds with spring lambs . . . Come now, it's evident; that it was spring and more likely a comet with a gaseous tail or the atmospheric effect of ice and dust, Aurora—Bethlehem would get our Northern Lights. "It has all been calculated, Mother." She does love his facts: our calendar is four years off and Christmas had been rescheduled with jingle bells, Santa in his snowy scenes to cover up some Roman holiday or unspeakable saturnalia. Calculated it may be, but she loves Christmas trees, the parties, a well-stuffed turkey, grog—but not this year.

This year no holiday. No gloom either: it's just that she sees she won't have time for the perfect Scotch pine (she likes them broad-beamed, chubby) or the painstaking German cookies cut as stars, moons, angels that still please her son. She will be fully occupied with bed rest and one last job she must absolutely finish. Maggie pleases herself, they said. That was not true: Margaret never could please herself. That is what they failed to understand. But now she might as well, now or never. And so begins from memory, getting it down—*Potatoes*—scratching that out: *Whoever reads must understand that if these pages contain a great deal about me, I can only suppose—suppose or hope—it must be because I have something to do with them, and can't be kept out.* Stealing that line from somewhere. She has stolen so many. Forever writing herself in, Margaret is not self-effacing. Nothing could be more apparent, and if you want a sweetheart, long-suffering, modest and demure . . . a heroine who cannot choose between suppose or hope . . . How she wishes she dealt in goods, not words. In her bed, upright, ready for the fray; she is not used to false starts. A mechanical malfunction of the body, the doctors with their machines—Providence, if you will—has taken over. What a swindle—she has paid her dues, but that's not it. At last she comes to the hard little core of her misery, small and painful as a pebble in the shoe: for years that now seem always, she has controlled the plot. "Boy," says Margaret, tearing up her bad notice from the hospital, "they have some nerve."

So, let the story begin with potatoes. A young woman—twenty-four, twenty-five—sits in a restaurant. East Side. French. Uppity maitre d' with an innuendo to his "Mademoiselle." Mademoiselle has come early, to her shame, and sits alone playing with the silverware. She does not know the man she waits for though they have written letters back and forth, a short business correspondence which has taken a cozy turn—"Sincerely yours," to "Best," "Best ever." "Warmly," he has signed his name. She waits for him in her one and only suit, a stiff lavender tweed her husband doesn't like. She has caught the backhanded compliment of the officious Frenchman who can see she is not Mademoiselle at all, but "Madame" would not flatter a young countrywoman come to have lunch alone with a man.

And the look of the place. Cream walls, lace curtains, maids of Brittany sketched in their starched white caps holding poultry and produce. A restaurant so solid there is no pandering to décor, just one brass demijohn with the splay of peach gladiolus to be ignored, she knows, for the food. A famous restaurant. From her corner banquette she's well aware that the lady in the smart feathered toque paying no mind to her salad, the U.N. gang, the Monseigneur cradling his balloon of claret—all know they are at L'Auberge.

Foolishly, she feels out of place as though she's never sat at a good table in the city, only Times Square beaneries or Schrafft's. Foolish, because the young woman is sure that a redheaded waiter across the room was the fellow assigned to serve them dinner on the North Atlantic, her first and only trip, on the *Ile de France.* An arrogant kid who had broken his sullen reserve to thank her husband for their tip in Southampton and declare with a redhead's sudden flush that he would have his American papers soon, his working papers, and he would not be serving them or any other third-class tourists at sea. Now here he is scooping sauce onto a perfect filet of something. Tearing at the L'Auberge matchbook (tricolor, fleur-de-lis), she is watching the fulfillment of a provincial boy's dream. *Hubert,* that was the name, in his black waiter's suit and fresh linen. He is buoyant, professional, without doubt charming to his first-class customers in New York.

Five minutes stretches to the infinity of ten. "If, by any chance, you can meet me in town . . ." "Warmly," the man had signed himself. Now she repeats lines of his letters that have brought her to this humiliating corner. ". . . the feeling on my part that the work you have given me is culturally so vast, yet so revealing that we must talk." By now she has dropped her knife noisily to the tile floor, dined on bread and water like a criminal. Across the room Hubert is flaming kidneys or crepes. Surely he will testify that she should be allowed to sit on with the crumbs in her scratchy lavender suit, the harsh material cut like a man's jacket, the skirt a drab afterthought. He will bear witness that she has stomached *homard, quenelle, baba* on choppy seas. Given his success in America, Hubert will be kind. Though she smiles courageously at the busboy when he deals her a second roll, he is most certainly contemptuous. A quarter to one. Groans of disappointment at the next table: the duck is finished, so *populaire.*

When he came he was no one I could have imagined. An enormous rough-looking man, baldish but with a disorderly halo of patriarchal white hair.

"Philo Pierce."

His voice had a coarse authority, physical as a gruff embrace. Flash of gold crown in a large smile, streak of red suspender under rumpled suit, hitch of trousers, bow tie askew. The maitre d' danced attendance at his elbow, dainty and ineffectual as a chorus boy.

"I am Margaret," using my first name only like a child.

"Of course you are," said Philo Pierce.

It remained part of my story that he reached both hands down to me from his great height, across my crusts and tattered matches and in that gesture so like—oh, the greeting of an old Shakespearean nobleman to a child long lost—in that blessing my glass of ice water toppled.

"So sorry," said maitre d', taking the accident upon himself. In a modulated fuss, I am mopped up and Mr. Pierce provided with a dry cloth and cutlery, the scene launched again.

"Well, Margaret," said Philo Pierce, caressing my plain name as his discovery. Margaret (I am minor royalty) sat across from him in what she now feels is a damn good English suit that will last a lifetime. Madame would like a cocktail? When the menus, wine list, all that was over, we sat in perfect silence, the corner banquette at L'Auberge hovering grandly above the world.

"Margaret," said Philo Pierce, "you have written a wonderful book."

For years I would live off that. I would bury that moment in an excess of unimportant detail—that he drank bourbon straight up, that I was assigned the upholstered bench like a queen while a delicate French chair creaked and squealed under him, that his mouth opened full in a gilded smile, that duck had been saved—ah, for Monsieur Pierce, *le bon caneton en chemise*. He was crudely shaven, knicked and tufted. And that in those days when a man's hair still might have been cropped by the military, his was brushed out over his ears, curled down over his collar. Wild, strong hair that could not have been tended by a barber. Cracked rough hands that looked, to my unpracticed eye, ruined by early hardship—the nails ragged. Close up he was a lost American type, portly and attractive, the big man who built railroads or half a city, the public buildings—library, hospital, schools—endowed with his name.

So, I was to understand I had written a wonderful book

—warm, exhilarating and (he spoke each word gravely with equal intention) sympathetic. How could a young woman fresh from the country know life in generous detail, reach into the past with an accuracy that did move Philo Pierce to pin me to the slippery leather banquette with a fierce look of plain awe at my powers. The wonderful book was, perhaps, too short, left him wanting more. More of the Irish grandfather, say, when that homespun man is courting the prim teacher from New York, and of the schoolmarm yielding to that handsome, unlettered lout, struggling with George Darby's crude demands as well as his accounts. The Romance. My black stable boys, Italian stonecutters—wonderful, but surely among the workers Darby hired there was bad blood, racial slurs and primitive vendettas. Miserable wives and sick children. Cold and hunger. The Tragedy. Darby's grappling for political power with the tight Yankee bigot—that conflict must be heightened to lead, so to speak, up the grand drive to the veranda, the rose garden, the stained-glass windows of the Irishman's manse on the hill. The Triumph.

Part of the L'Auberge story was the offhand, nearly dismissive way in which Philo Pierce put aside Margaret's book as though to relieve us for a while from its wonders. A formulaic exchange between us might have been titled *Personal: Brief Account.* He was married to a good old girl from the South who raised dogs and children out in Bucks County and she'd as soon never set foot in Pennsylvania Station again. God knows she was right, but there was what Pierce modestly referred to as his job. To me, aside from editing a big-think journal (perilous, left wing), orchestrating the prestige of his publishing house (that I now presumed was about to issue my unworthy book), and writing his own wry essays on the flagging culture-at-large, Philo Pierce's job seemed to be Grand Purveyor of American Letters—from a translation of Poe he was getting up

("The French are ape-shit about Poe.") to the particulars of Bill Faulkner's last drinking bout. I, Margaret Flood, lived in New Haven (hardly country) where my husband was a doctor, thoracic surgery, a heart man on the cutting edge, with the beginnings of a practice and a dwindling connection to the Yale hospital.

We returned to the family chronicle (my poor family, before they ran out of steam), a grand story which, for all its wonders, seemed to fail at passionate encounters. I had let dreary reality dictate each lovers' meeting. That Irishman, heroic type, said Pierce—what a pity that I have him stooped, waddling like a comic bear on ice skates, rolling barrels up into a shabby cart at the first sight of his beloved, and she, a sexless lump of wool stepping off a sooty train. Not to mention Mae, their daughter (should she not be set up as a remarkable beauty?)—frail, tubercular Mae trapped in a tenement hall by a limp geezer with shell shock or (I had not made it clear) a debilitating palsy. What a waste. I could only agree that I had missed what my editor called romantic opportunities.

Our ducks were a pretty sight, thick with glaze and a bright slice of orange. "And for Madame," our waiter said. There was a small dish with something burnished, fluted like a confection or birthday surprise. I'll never forgive myself the fearful testing with my fork, my abysmal innocence—"What is it?"

"Duchesse," Pierce said, "Mashed potatoes." Then his raucous laugh: "You ordered mashed potatoes."

Indeed I had, but not my mother's bland dish with careless lumps, crying for butter and salt. And Philo Pierce, gulping his wine, laughed on, reminding me I had written a scene—one of the wonderful scenes—in which Darby sits at the head of his table dishing out mashed potatoes to his children. It is the feast of All Souls and in one portion for a lucky child there will be discovered a prized silver dime.

"The point is to move that foreboding symbol to Mardi Gras," Pierce said. "Lent. Impending doom. Sacrifice—that's something people can get hold of since the war. Put those potatoes right up there with the mother's sorrow, Darby's guilt when the favored son dies."

A stroke so obvious, exactly right, oh, the great man tackling his duck, blotting up sauce with a hunk of bread, had earned his reputation over lunch. Father of raw talent. Director of discreet ambition. Take your humble servant, Margaret, sweltering in tweed, flushed with drink and delicious praise, into the published fold.

I cannot reconstruct our quick, inevitable turn to Joe McCarthy. It was spring of 1954. And I was twenty-four, old enough to know better. I'd like to claim it was Philo Pierce led me down that satisfactory path, a garden path of rehearsed delights. Put history aside. McCarthy was sniggering into the microphones (some took it for a laugh), snorting in a psychotic ventilation for the world to see on our first television sets. For the purpose of this story, the story of my ingenuous lunch, there is no reason why you must know or remember that he was a senator from Wisconsin, Joseph R. McCarthy, the big cheese gone rotten. No short entry on the man, a mean, poor boy who elevated his crude vengeance to a menacing art. No late and lengthy editorials on a penny-ante demagogue who terrified senators and generals, two presidents. Proven liar, embezzler, boozer. No long academic views that, as a victorious and powerful nation, all too predictably we brought forth a foulmouthed bastard to soil us, cut us down to size, let his name become a proper noun, the dirty news of his success rub off on ours.

McCarthy. I brought up McCarthy. Pleased with my apple tart, pleased to be with Philo Pierce perched on my banquette. As the crowd thinned, I said, "Now he is losing, losing in front of our eyes."

"At last," Pierce said, "like a fever breaking."

So we led each other on in a mutual seduction. There is no reason to know McCarthy from Caligula or Robespierre or from a malicious school-board creep lusting for power in the old home town. History is beside the point. What's interesting here is that I brought up Joe McCarthy so that Pierce would be assured I was wonderful. Deploring the senator was easy, a kind of shorthand for thinking and for thinking all the right things. I proposed a wedding of like minds so that we (Pierce and me), raising our moral observation to a new high, we suspected the very pleasure we took in watching our enemy fail. Pierce, of course, had taken a firm stand in *The Sectarian,* early on had scored the senator with lethal wit. Held his own in print. I had voted in one national election and cried bitterly when my man lost, like a kid who has been cheated of honest fun. Ignorant of all political motives, I knew in an instinctive girlish way that Joe McCarthy's infamy was a way to Pierce's heart. "I am Margaret," your good, bright girl.

We drank brandy, lingered. Now Philo Pierce filled the deserted restaurant, a small room it looked, cottagey. A big man out of place in a tea shop, rumbling predictions, no recovery from national dishonor, lighting the cigar presented in the L'Auberge humidor, and again destroyed with laughter at me not knowing, for Christ's sake, the French for mashed potatoes. The waiters stood patiently by empty tables.

Pierce said: "Believe me, Margaret, you have written a wonderful book."

Without, however, a wonderful ending. A reader might feel it discouraging—breadlines and foreclosed mortgages. The great house of the Darbys spiffed up for a Slovak funeral parlor. Somewhat flat, Frank Darby sorting at the post office, a dull failure, last of the line. The slightest twist, ten degrees, would transform the mansion to a gothic ruin and Frank to a proud undefeated soul, an alienated man.

Yes, I saw how hopelessly underimagined my finale was. Most likely I blushed. In those days my complexion was rosy and high. At home I walked to the market. I rode a bike. Ah, that's not it—I felt things then so readily. I have no intention of omitting that young woman in the lavender suit—her pleasant pieface with the almost constant smile (learned), the fluttering Betty Boop eyes (natural), the soft, incomplete look to the wide cheeks and broad chin. Not pretty, just young. No shadows. No contours. It's sentimental to call that girl vulnerable when, in fact, she's all forward charge. There's such an appetite in the way she talks and moves, a touch of greed as I see it now with the unflattering double vision of time. Sidling past her table at the expensive restaurant, a little drunk, she gathers about herself a sturdy false composure.

We, Philo Pierce and Margaret, stride across the room. Terrible to contemplate the dignity of those waiters—*Merci, merci*—who fake their attention and goodwill as, finally, they pass the great man out. Hubert, my Hubert, is a wizened man I've never seen—just a similarity in the lithe maneuvering of plates. On close inspection, his red hair is evenly grizzled with white like the muzzle of an old dog. There is not (how could there be?) even a moment's recognition. The hat-check girl—overblown, mustachioed—yawns in our faces, hands Pierce a battered soft felt hat and a disreputable briefcase sprung at the seams. He stands hitching and humphing in front of the door which reads *egrebuA'L* unmysteriously through a scrim of lace, then swings it wide, a courtier ushering me out into the sun.

Hot, as I recall it, a fluke, one of those last April days that turn to summer, gets the sap running. We walked to Grand Central with our jackets off. A Friday, because Pierce was calling it a day, going out to the wife and dogs, his daughter riding in a gymkhana. That briefcase, well, I believed it to be stuffed with perfect stories, penetrating articles for *The Sectarian,* novels not as wonderful as mine.

Our tongues set loose by wine and heat, we couldn't stop ourselves talking, talking in the sunshine. We fled from the naked expanse of Third Avenue with the El ripped down—and Pierce was surprised that a country girl should miss the rickety dim arches, their spook-house shelter, the racket overhead. Our day accumulated memories like a lover's day: the intimacy of Philo Pierce stopping square in front of Brooks Brothers to say that his shirts had all gone to hell; my superior glance at the Biltmore which already had a flutter of college girls arriving for the weekend lottery of dates. We sobered a bit in the cool of the station, buttoned our jackets primly for the parting, the formal confirmation of an unholy communion.

"Consider that you are under contract, Margaret."

His last glittering smile, then the dear grumpus lumbered down the ramp to his shuttle. I wanted to cry after him—"I will revise. Trust me. The Triumph, the Tragedy. I will revise"—like a young mistress seeing her man out of sight, perhaps losing him forever to the wife and dogs, forever to dripping faucets and unmown lawns in Bucks County, losing him forever to the insatiable demands of our culture.

I revised. I went home to the spare bedroom where I'd set up shop, a fat armchair to swallow me, lamp with scorched shade, and I revised my pages. They were not wonderful; perhaps they were good enough for the first time out, but more likely that story, simply my family's story as I'd heard it, should have ended in a grocery carton with clippings of my engagement announcement and local obituaries, love letters, high school diploma, attempts at occasional verse. I wallow in the possibilities that never were, in the blameless, tranquil life I would surely have lived, if I had not been taken on by Philo Pierce.

Instead, I gave George Darby the full effect of my

grandmother turned coquette, a high-tempered flirtation at a dance swiped from Tolstoy or from Jane Austen or just that ballroom scene that Scarlett steals in *Gone With the Wind.* She is now Myra (Pierce was not happy with my names), the spark plug from Manhattan with jet beads displayed on the low-cut bodice of her gown, the daring of which poor George has never seen. Well she was Mary as we all are more or less—Mollys, Marys, Mary Margaret, Maggies, Peg. We were given to repeating the old names. Minnie. Mae. And none of them had a dress that couldn't go to church, decent and dark, that couldn't be ripped apart and recut next season. Not one of them had an overcoat. They wore wool undervests and shawls. Later, later, they had dancing shoes to ruin their feet and sealskin coats, muffs, galoshes. But when Mary stepped down from the train and saw George Darby it was in the cold slush, wearing her inadequate city shoes, huddled under a dreary plaid, a gray wool rag that I knew, shredded by moths, fifty years after the fact.

Fact is not the point. For the record, for this accounting, I went home the day I met Philo Pierce and on the train, passing the same destroyed industrial towns along the shore that Mary Darby had seen in 1885 when they were blooming, I changed her to Myra, put her in a modish beaver hat, had her look up from her *Atlantic Monthly* out to the Pequonnock Bay where a fellow in a cap with an outsized but fascinating jaw directed his men. Building a breakwater they were, and he, their master, riding them hard up on a big-bummed roan. That would be George Darby who never sat a horse in his life.

She, my grandmother, even as a young woman, had those prominent thyroid eyes, bald eyes with dark, skimpy lids. The peeled-back eyes that caught me breaking off the rhododendron buds, pilfering dimes, sucking her horehound drops. She looked hard at the world whether she liked it or not. My impression is that she accused no one with that involuntary gaze, that her judgment was as gentle as her little mouth and nose that hardly mattered. But Grandma Darby saw me—so never again dig a muddy pit by the cellar door, glut on movie magazines, tuck the peasant blouse tight, tighter, so my nipples, small as cherry pits, might devastate an imaginary beau. It is to be noted that my first perception of a steady moral vision grew from my grandmother's glandular disorder.

At best those terrible eyes may have looked Oriental when she was young, and I recast her as exotic, fetching as some Celts are, gave her the lovely flat face of a Breton. That at least might be true since Ireland—before tribes, before stories—splintered from the continent, drifting to a perverse geographic independence that mocks its everlasting subjugation. A Celt she became in revision, laughing over her ivory fan, dangling a dance card with every waltz taken. In the Knights of Columbus Hall, George Darby approaches. He is in a white winged collar that pinches his thick neck, his feet cramped in a pair of borrowed evening shoes. He removes the dance card from Myra's wrist and, with the slim gold pencil attached, X's out all of her partners.

"I cannot dance," he says.

She's hot with rage: "And by the look of it you cannot write your name."

The setup for a fraudulent scene in which we find this Myra sounding out for him difficult words in *The Catholic Messenger,* the *Sears Catalogue* and other elevating texts. It is the beginning of her control over the big handsome lummox, a subtle ascendancy which is brought into balance one night when she guides his pen in an ill-formed GEOR. Trembling under her touch, he throws aside the copybook and with ink-splotched hands reaches up to her pert little head. Almost cruelly he twists her face to him and for once, shamelessly begging for his kisses, she is blind. For once she closes those see-it-all eyes.

George Darby, the man, wrote a large, open hand, was trained to do so in the public school which he left in the seventh grade in order to support his mother. He read all commercial notices in the local papers—real-estate transactions, commodity reports, shipping news in particular, for he had wanted to sign on to a freighter out of New Haven, to sail away from the rent, the butcher's, grocer's, doctor's bills, from the hacking cough shared by his sisters, the soft sound of a woman's phlegm being dealt with in the middle of the night. He read of raw rubber coming in from Brazil, brass fittings shipped for Spain, of whalebone arriving at the corset factory, bobbins and needles of fine German steel. He composed eloquent letters to the editor on the improvement of sewers and drains and wrote snappy advertisements for George Darby, Carting and Hauling:

No task too small or heavy the load.
We are worth our weight in gold.

We being a half-dead mare and the torn ligaments of my grandfather's back. With that beginning he lived in considerable pain the rest of his life. As a prosperous man he drove home from his office above the City Trust at noon. His wife had a hot dinner for him on the table. Pa, she called him. But at night, in the kitchen, she would first wring out the steaming poultices and lay them on his bare back, so that their children remembered all suppers with the smell of camphor, a penetrating herbal oil mixed with whiffs of stew, fowl, Mary's excellent pies.

Stories that gained in authenticity from the domestic setting but would hardly appeal to the expert sensibility of a Philo Pierce, a man who took me to be raw material like sugar cane and refined me into a small bowl of salable white crystals to draw the ants.

Let me point out that Philo Pierce would not admit to the wonderful book a very white old man, paralyzed:

"Ibber. Ibber," he says, handing over a jar of pennies he has saved. "Give her. Give her," my grandmother translates and I took George Darby's treasure thinking it worth my weight in gold. Deleted, the flannel cloths folded in the linen closet, soft with a churchy medicinal odor, folded away with reverence for a dead ritual. Pa's cloths that were never put to ordinary use, to polish or dust. Or that she, Mary of the great eyes, as an old woman, as I knew her, held her hands up in a shield, a constant gesture, creating a blind, cupping her fragile translucent hands up and around the bulging eyes as though she had seen too much. As though she might direct her last view into a harmless stereopticon slide.

I am glad no Darby was there to see me when I got off the train in New Haven. There was Jack to meet me in his white doctor's suit under an old army jacket, swinging a stethoscope. In those days he wore all the accoutrements of his profession as often as he could, believing there was no time to change before late rounds, night duty, wanting to be called Doctor in all the cheap Italian restaurants near the hospital. He was not a vain man, just proud of his accomplishments, savoring his dedication. It was cool again, the unseasonal summer day past. We went to Mitzi's so Jack could have his veal and peppers with the side dish of plump overcooked spaghetti awash in red sauce that, in truth, we loved.

My day was over. I felt that particularly as I watched my husband eat. My meal was over—*caneton, duchesse*—and I drank watery bargain martinis. This has never been a part of the L'Auberge story, my extraordinary day being over, so it is unembroidered, what I'd now call new material. The evening blurred, seemed unimportant, but it was in the sticky pine booth at Mitzi's I gave my first rendering of Philo Pierce, that portrait that became a set performance.

"Jesus," Jack Flood said, "it sounds like you're in love with the guy."

"I can't believe you said that." Oh, didn't that seem foul to me, Margaret Mary in my ladylike suit, just a rotten thing for Flood to say. Philo Pierce was old, an old man with a bald head, bad teeth. (Pierce, as I work it out, could not have been fifty at the time.) Old, I said, protesting too much. Bald. Stout. We fought that night. I will have to invent our bone of contention—that he could not afford new tires for the car, a decent couch, my reluctance to work in a library or teach high school now that I had written the wonderful book. I was ready for it—some nickel-and-dime battle. Sorry for it.

I'll have to invent because I cannot turn to Johnny Flood. I cannot ask, "Was it tires you couldn't afford, Jack, or was it obvious that I'd gone to New York and come back to you spoiled goods? I cannot give you the satisfaction of being right." True, Pierce did more for young ladies than edit their books. He was famous for it. That night there was no case against me, Jack, but we squabbled. You had to go back to the hospital in any case. The rest I must remember alone, make up alone. I can't put the question to Dr. Flood, a hearty man with impeccably cut white hair who looks as though he spends a good deal of time in the sun, a man in a perfectly tailored suit who stared right at me from the television set, ignoring his interviewer, telling me that he has patched and sewn the human heart in ways unimagined, singling me out of his audience of millions, "There, there, Margaret," he said, though no one else heard, "it is a remarkable organ, resilient, adaptable, spunky to the very end."

Such a wisp when I knew him, long-chested, stringy—like a poet (I thought that one up), turn-of-the-century aesthete. It was appealing in a medical man, and he did read Latin verse, liberal journals, all Hemingway, all Waugh. Somehow stealing the hours. A gawky boy who could not grow into his frame or thicken in the waist. Flood I have called him to sound tough, to introduce my residual pain, but I never did that, not when I knew him. A sandy-haired Jack who leaned into his loping stride all concentration, get ahead. Golden eyebrows that left his eyes unguarded. Hardly a beard, smooth. My "Johnny" an endearment. He would wince, or pretend to, at my "Johnny Flood." Blaring trumpet voluntaries on the old hi-fi when he came home to blow the hospital out of his head.

Finishing his supper at Mitzi's, he said: "I lost Neth. And Mrs. Casey."

I do not need Flood to remind me that I did not hear. More exactly, I did not listen to him. My day was over. I was onto dreaming up an Italian assailant for Mae Darby. Pretty Mae. She would be trapped at the top of the stairs by a tile setter. In the tenement her father owned, with the rent envelopes in her embroidered reticule, stupid Mae would think it was money he wanted. He would taunt her, this Tony, with his sweat, his foreign smell, his cheap gold wedding ring—and throw away his life when he jumped her. So I was off in my calculated pursuit of passion when Jack said he'd lost them, his cases.

The spring of 1954: the last months of his residency, the first of his patients trickling in and he could not yet believe that they died under his care. Death did not transfer readily from the textbooks, the lecture hall, lab, from the edifying rounds with senior physicians. Not to *his* patients. Each time it destroyed him—facing the real family, signing the final papers—cause of death. He was the cause. He felt that like a madness those months when he was going on his own, that if he, Jack Flood, had changed a dose or drained a lung or forced his own fresh blood up a broken down sewer pipe of an artery . . .

He would come home white as his suit and blare the trumpet voluntaries. The few souls he "lost" in New

Haven passed on to the ceremonial music of kings, of jewel-encrusted doges, of joyous grand occasions. I would turn off the voice of our twelve-inch set with the nightly replays of the Select Committee and keep track of Senator McCarthy jeering at four-star generals to Telemann, sucking his spittle at Cabinet members to Purcell, laughing his secret laugh like an outcast in the schoolyard who's got something filthy to tell. I see now that it was fabulous played out before me—the tale of one wicked man coming to an end while a good man rid his mind of a crippling innocence. Taught to heal, my husband was confounded by death. Blaring his loud, loud ceremonial music, Jack Flood looked tender, quivering, pale—a hothouse plant set out to harden off.

He had lost Neth and Mrs. Casey, the names I did not hear then, but will never forget. It was that spring I was discovered by Philo Pierce. Better to have spread myself naked under what seemed to me his ancient body. Far better to have straddled him, ridden him high, knelt to his specified desires—but that is not the game he played with me. Any whore's trick better than to bend to the contours of his stale mind. In the rush of my enchantment, in love with the guy as Jack Flood said, I rewrote my book.

That very night I began shuffling through, marking up my pages. I did not hear Jack come in, but it was no surprise when the trumpets blasted. I did not go to see him white in his white coat, letting his failure at the hospital drain from him until he, the doctor, looked bloodless, newly dead. Neth a faceless name. But Mrs. Casey ran the smoke shop across from Grace New Haven. For forty years, mistrusting all doctors, she sold cigarettes and candy, magazines to the staff. There was no Mr. Casey, no child. A white-haired ogress, tall and stately, with a miraculous constitution, tending the shop twenty hours a day. Silent and severe—the doctors seemed to relish her disapproval, to need a cut from Mrs. Casey before they enjoyed the adulations of their professional day. It was a reproof to several illustrious medical men that she chose Jack Flood, asked him curtly for an appointment when, one day, she sold him Life Savers, funnily enough. It seemed a compliment until, listening to her heart, Jack understood she was long past saving.

I could not revise against the grandeur of that music and went to him, surprised to see that he had turned on Senator McCarthy as though that wordless picture show was necessary to his desperate nights. He smiled, let me sit next to him and when the record ended, Jack said: "I'm glad it went well with that man."

"With Philo Pierce."

"Whoever—"

I deserved that one. "I'm sorry about Mrs. Casey."

"Well, so am I," he said. "They're amused at the hospital. She played me for a fool."

The senator from Wisconsin was waving what appeared to be an empty piece of paper at twenty million people. Facts. His hilarious facts. This time it was the entire military of this country had sold us up to commie spies. Losing in front of our eyes: How right I'd been at lunch to say we were bloodthirsty watching the man feint but not dodge the blows, like a tired fighter, outmaneuvered, outclassed. Jack went to the set, squatted there studying the man's twitches, the erratic breathing, squints, jerk of the head.

"Cirrhosis," he said. "Alcoholic facies." He was a good doctor, my Jack Flood. No trick of Mrs. Casey's nor mockery at Grace New Haven could put him down. Three years later to the day Joe McCarthy died, and I'm sure Dr. Flood never mentioned his brilliant diagnosis to the colleagues who already turned to him on difficult cases with the blank facts of conflicting medical reports.

But I was happy to revise, not to worry out connections, not to work at the mystery of the Darbys and their ordinary life. A good girl, I solved the simple problems—the

Romance, the Tragedy—all for Philo Pierce. What a triumph we were. And I never suspected that he was a dead ringer for my grandfather, the great editor a murky version of George Darby, a grainy blowup against the background of a larger, darker world. Ruthless, charming, successful men—I tagged along. Jack Flood will remember the money I made, like money in a child's tale, a pot of gold, and his wife's picture in the papers, her early prizes. He will remember me transformed to a simpering country girl setting the bars down, leaping the easy hurdles for Philo Pierce. Jack will remember my symptoms and that I never learned to diagnose.

Tell me, Doctor Flood, now that I am dying—oh, I would not play Mrs. Casey's trick on you again—now that I am dying, how many months or days? I must rewrite. I am very quick, accomplished . . . but unlike you, Jack, I never learned to place my failures, so give me the weeks or days, an educated guess. Time to find the original, some uncorrupted text. Now that I am dying and death's the usual thing to you. Only the facts, no trumpet voluntaries, please.

But she is not that quick—no longer. Lethargic, doped with sleep, occasionally the crushing pain wakes her fully. Christmas is passable with a scrawny tree dragged into the bedroom by her son, the turkey roasted to a terrible death by Lourdes, the daily maid. The boy does not live with Margaret, that might be read on the initial report. He lives (she would not call it that) in a moldy basement shop with his father, Pinkham Strong. That is his residence. That is her son's choice, or duty as he sees it.

"Five dollars," he says, stuffing the tree into a wastepaper basket, "and a silk scarf." Rayon, he admits to Margaret, proud of his trade. "It was just one of those sleazy rayon scarves." So she has a tree and this is Bayard setting it up, weighting it with a useless marble obelisk, an iron doorstop. A dunce cap of a tree, listing toward the Park. "How sick are you?" he asks. This is Bayard who wouldn't expect a straight answer, who does not flinch when his mother, pale as a soda cracker, her hair the color of weak tea, attempts to hang the bare limbs of his tree—his tree that looked O.K. on Broadway—with her expensive baubles. This is Margaret's son who, at sixteen, travels in an elongated orbit from father to mother, a terrible and constant trip on the New York subways. A journey of such tension that only Bayard, who has learned to live with great common sense, but one notch above reality, can make it seem a jaunt—effortless, miraculous as a gyroscope upon a string.

"A skinny tree," he says. Nevertheless it is Christmas and his mother, tucked back in her bed, allows that it is natural, feathery and light. She turns her face into the pillow, wipes at her eyes, but she will not cry to think he lives in a damp cement cellar, her son gone underground with a drunk. He stands at the bottom of Margaret's bed, anguished as though his adolescent pranks had brought on his mother's decline. Yet anyone can see he is blameless, the exceptional son. Margaret sees it and lets him go his way, poor little rich boy, to sell his hat or gloves for a second tree he will set up for Pinkham Strong. She is not needy, whining. She has set her course and it does not include telling a sixteen year old boy that his mother will soon be dead.

That would be Maggie, self-punishing in her pride—the time her brother rammed her with the sled, a hard bruise the size of a lemon on her thigh, and she did not limp or even cry when they found her ruined snowsuit hidden in the trash. Or, Miss Margaret Mary, finally invited to the prom as second or third best, taking herself off to the movies alone, walking past the high school where they gathered, hoop skirts under tissue taffeta and tulle, her proposed escort looking quite the gent in a rented tux. Right down State Street she walked to the Rialto in sloppy dungarees, her father's shirttail hanging out. These old stories she has put aside, never had the time to tell.

Taking to her bed, what would they think of her, those brothers she has mortified with her outlandish life? They have long counted her dead. What would Jack think of her behavior against medical advice—that it rang true for Maggie. And Pierce, oh, if he were still around, diminished as she is, she'd get her own back. What would he think of her now? She merited the best table in restaurants, that was the least of it. She knew her potatoes. She has signed a new contract and would love to flaunt it at Philo Pierce, a document more substantial than any of Joe McCarthy's. Only days before the first pain struck, she had ordered filet of sole and a glass of white wine—it being light years ago—the chic of hard liquor and fatty duck. It was the right restaurant that week—not a dowdy old faithful—brass rails, gray carpet, mulberry walls. White freesias and apricot lilies in large crystal vases sat about the room (once a garment-workers' cafeteria) on false marble columns. Beautifully appointed, she was sure of that, as she settled in her Breuer chair. Her editor, new man to her, was fashionable and fussy—Fred Peach. He asked that the ashtray be taken away, objected to an imperceptible smudge on his fork, before he began his canticle of praise to Margaret Flood. Wonderful books, but my, oh my, the thrilling scripts. She was a tested marvel. What he had in mind was what she had in mind.

"I would like to do the Fifties."

"The Fifties!" said Peach. She might have said the Stone Age, Imperial Rome, his squeal of surprise was that unsure.

"Politics," said Margaret. She had made quick work of it —not politics really, nothing to fear, though a shocking story, heroes of the left, men and women who had survived the inquisition. She did not call upon overworked scandals, Nixon, Watergate, just said, "We are ready for heroic types. Those who stood to be counted. Survivors." She brought up Hannah Brandt, Max Gideon, and could see their names still had a draw. Philo Pierce. Ah, she'd hit a nerve—Fred Peach with all the conglomerate money behind him was struck with wonder at the name of the legendary editor. Peach was clever with his fish fork. He had learned that. A thin mustache trembling on his upper lip proved he could grow facial hair. He had done well for himself. The world, his world of publishing, knew his ridiculous name. "Philo Pierce," he said like a long-forgotten prayer. "You would have known him."

"Oh, I knew him. I knew them all." Margaret played her cards. Scandal. Pierce was a randy old goat, a fraud. Perjury. Plagiarism.

"Pierce!" The editor bounced in his chair. Nothing could please this little man more than to bring down the big guys. Fully exposed, Pierce would better him from the grave, laugh to show his gold crowns, snap the red suspenders.

"It's a thick mix," Margaret said, "of treachery and real commitment. There may be bigger names but this is the big story. The women are still alive—Dorothy Schwartz and Hannah Brandt. The closest thing I have to heroes."

"A personal story?" Peach asked. "A testimony?"

Then Margaret showed her hand. Yes, extremely personal, for years she had wanted to get at it—why these people—old commies, old radicals—made her feel too late at the feast. Even in the days when Gideon and Brandt would have been happy to know Margaret Flood, there was something so goddamn special, spectacle or Passion Play, something was over before she began. "What did they *have?*" she begged Peach to tell her, knowing he could not answer. "What is it they had—Masonic rites? Mumbo-jumbo practices? Some secret? They never let on." She knew she'd cut a deal when she said, quite honestly, "They closed me out."

She could not tell her editor's age, he was hers now. Peach's body was curried, plumped like a pillow. His cheeks were buffed and polished. His hair gray, but it hardly counted. She would guess he wasn't let out after dark in the fifties, but that he had a long and important history of being excluded. It was such a bond with Margaret Flood: The words he could never say, she said so bravely—"They closed me out."

What would Pierce think of his protégé: I am Margaret, alert to the main chance. Of course she was Margaret the eternal naïf and she was cunning. The Fifties. It would read like a novel with Saints and Sinners. At last she would get at those illustrious reputations. Peach had ordered a pot of espresso and talked six figures. Sent her the advance. Between now and then, the book would never be written. It was a dead issue. She could hear the guffaw of the great man, smell the bourbon on his breath, "You ordered mashed potatoes."

Closed out. The biggest fool that ever hit the big time. There was a dime-store lock she could have broken. Up in the attic of the stucco house, a two-family house and always the hope, never realized, that her father would do well enough peddling insurance not to rent upstairs. Then they would remodel; they would all have bedrooms and no noise overhead—though her mother could not climb the stairs. The attic was shared, partitioned off by a frame of two-by-fours with dangerous nails sticking out, tacked over with a chicken-wire scrim, a lock she could have broken. They would call to her, "Margaret are you up there?" Moping in the attic, they knew. She would come down filthy with sticky cobwebs in her hair. What was it so entertained her?

Other people's lives. She would look in at a wedding dress, its train pinned up in a yellowed sheet, outgrown tricycles and kiddy cars, rolled carpets, magazines—the treasures of the Finns, McGurks, Keelers—whoever lived upstairs. Closed out from their secrets, tenants who always moved on. At her back the familiar accumulation—postcards, board games, her own baby carriage, a broken Sheffield jug. Her mother's sidesaddle and riding crop. Her father's boater and striped blazer that she was to believe he wore singing grand old songs up on Poli's stage. What can entertain her all those hours? If they had ever really seen her, dusty and glum, they would know she was not entertained. That she wanted to tear at the chicken wire, knock down the partition and walk through like little Fred Peach to the enchantment, the real stuff of other people's lives.

From her bed Margaret can see only a glint of tinsel, a spatter of dry needles. The Christmas tree is gone: she is left to her potatoes: Myra and a dandified George Darby preside at the dining-room table—stately sideboard, double damask, electric sconces, roast beef—all of that. The children—Mae, Francis and young George—are costumed creatures in stiff collars and high-button shoes. A maid comes through the door with a dish of mashed potatoes. She is Patsy with a brogue, straight off the boat, and in this pot of slow molasses provides a blessed ounce of comic relief. Myra, whose instructive dinner-table talk is as much fun as an earache, dishes up the potatoes, explaining that therein she has secreted a dime. Oh, lucky child who bites the coin before the onset of Lent, to have such a treat before that season in which they must fast, reject worldly pleasures, deny the flesh. Oh, lucky Myra, that those children do not pelt her with their napkin rings, hurl the creamed cauliflower at her yattering head.

" 'Tis a vale of tears, Mum," says Patsy while Darby, who has a drop taken, tucks into the roast beef and lets the day's profits run in his head. How carefully Myra has hidden the dime so she will be able to serve it to her favorite, George, her firstborn, her sulky pet. But Patsy, that nuisance, has given the dish a stir and it is Francis, dull Francis, who holds up the coin with an apologetic smile. A slack middle child, he does not understand why his mother is furious, reaching across the lima beans to serve George, her beloved, ill-fated son.

"Sure it's a sign, begorrah, Mum."

Oh, lucky George with his hero's grave waiting for him in Normandy, who will not have to endure the mawkish family fortunes, who can cut and run.

They never did have servants, not to wait on them at table. A neighborhood girl to turn out the closets in spring and beat the carpets. Darby's mother had been an Irish maid with gnarled feet to prove it and sciatica from hauling out a rich man's slops. Mary Darby waited on her own. Once, on All Souls', she polished a dime and stuck it in the mashed potatoes, something they did at home for a bit of luck.

"They'll choke on it," George said, looking down the table at his kids. The three of them sat there destroyed with laughter, their tongues sorting through the mush. "If one of you swallows it," he said, "I suppose you won't find it funny to pass a good ten cents sitting on the throne."

"Pa! It's just something they did on Halloween at home." Mary Darby was glad when Francis found it and put the coin proudly by his plate. Mae was a girl. Young George was spoiled. It was Francis she worried over, no gumption, an unsalted spirit—her priestly son.

Mae said, "They've a bonfire going down at Reichert's."

"You'll not go there," Darby said.

"With my brother."

"You will not go to Reichert's. It is a night for childish games."

He was that strict with her. George went, of course, the

elder son. Windows were broken in the German bakery. A shed burned. White paint thrown at the minister's boy. White paint to clean off young George's shoes. After Mass, his mother was out on the back porch, God save her, working them over with turpentine and boot polish, covering for him always. And when he was dead in the war soon after, she could not help thinking it was the end of their shame, the end of his childish games.

Something they did on Halloween. A fallen-away myth—Lent or All Souls—a farce that only made American children laugh. Remember, she stuck it in the mashed potatoes. Can you remember—a half-dollar, a dime? It is clear that despite my prompting these people cared little for the hocus-pocus of their origins and in this respect they'd say Pierce was right, what use can there be in a boring backward glance?

It ended with potatoes. Margaret Flood peeling them: young, with a show of green to the skin. She cuts the potatoes thin. Nearly translucent, the white rounds fall from her hands as skillfully as the card shark's deal, fanning out in the buttered dish. Onions still milky with cutting. Here she has learned restraint, perhaps in her taste, more likely from years of onion weeping, and she lets the circles lap in spare Olympic Os.

This is the last meal she will cook in New Haven. Tomorrow her husband is off to California, to Stanford, where he will teach and have a laboratory of his own. The date is set for the movers. The house is dismantled. The good china packed. With explicit care Margaret has put aside her papers, her reading chair, her money. It is money she has earned herself, writing a clever book. She does not want to be shipped to California with the dressers and bedding. And though she has not said so, not even to herself, she will never go. It is six o'clock and Jack is saying goodbye to the dumb nurse who has slept with him and worshiped him for at least a year. That Margaret knows. A good-looking girl but with a flat pieface laughably like her own: a Margaret—presumably sexy, uncomplicated, no film in the camera.

The Gruyère is shredded. A pale curl of it hangs at her ear. With both broad hands she dips into the buttery elastic spring of it. The cheese is caught in her rings, under a thumbnail. Wiped on the breast of her apron it sends off the sweet smell of foreign pastures. Again potatoes, onion, cheese. Again and again. The last meal she will cook in New Haven for another couple (the pleasant double pairing of married life), their best friends.

A generous soak of beef broth. With satisfaction Margaret lifts the terra-cotta dish bought at a housewares shop in Tuscany, in Siena one day when they would have paid with their souls to get out of the sun. She slides the dish back into the heated oven, the last meal she will cook for her husband. *Gratin de pomme de terre Savoyard.* Well, that's just scalloped potatoes—in many ways a recipe of accommodation, but an honest effort, safe, a comfort to her then.

It is the New Year. Margaret at death's door: she gets out of her bed to celebrate, walks her room in the dark, stands at the window and watches them waiting in the cold for cabs. So cold in evening slippers, long skirts dragging in the gutter. She hears the doorman's sharp whistle, desperate for a cab. The men wave at the bitter air, beseeching. The hour is ticking away, thirty minutes and it will be Nineteen Seventy-six—too much is made of that. Margaret knows it to be the year in which she will die, though now she is feeling fine what with bed rest, deceptively fine. Manhattan is tricked out in holiday gaud, clean wrap of snow in the Park, diamonds all diamonds tonight. It looks real, close, as though she could reach out and touch it now that she no longer wants it. In the dark she is comfortable, concealed, warm though half naked in her nightgown. As the hour dwindles she is just beginning, old acquaintance not forgot. Jack and her first book. Some history may be to the point if she is to find the young doctor lost in her pages.

In all their finery, the men and women below will not fit in one cab, but the driver is lenient, in the spirit. Margaret is glad they will get to the party, toast and kiss, perhaps watch the big ball descend on Times Square. It is quiet here, not a tick or pop, but she resolves: She will run it all backwards, rewind. Next year she will undo the harm. She will revise. Next year . . . Then it is over with a noiseless light in the sky, unearthly as eclipse. She shuffles to her bed like Father Time though, in truth, she's just beginning, and now turns on the light.

CHILD'S PLAY

"I only took the regular course."
"What was that?" enquired Alice.
"Reeling and Writhing, of course, to begin with," the Mock Turtle replied: "and then the different branches of Arithmetic —Ambition, Distraction, Uglification, and Derision."

—*Alice in Wonderland*

FEBRUARY 14—AS GOOD a day as any to end this affair of the heart. I have been hard at it for some weeks while my reports came in, the entire portfolio on my cardiovascular weakness, before going to Jack Flood. Perhaps akin to faintness of heart: biding my time though I knew from the first look in the first specialist's eye that I'm doomed, need not wait for his careful, do I fear pitying, explication of the printout, the steeplechase blips (sluggish in my case)—the crazed beat of my heart.

I had forgotten the day until a package arrived, a soft brown sack meant for books, and Lourdes spilled out a red satin box on my quilt. Sleek item, dark as a blood-red rose. It is filled with German chocolates which I am forbidden to eat. Love from Fred Peach. One of my creditors. A new man to me, wounded and skittery with a sweet Charlie Chaplin tilt to his head, the sugary smile, but dollar signs reflected in the depths of his black eyes. I owe that man. Love written on a business card—well, why not? They are like paramours, the long list of editors, directors, producers to whom I have given my work. Given myself from time to time. Handmade, criminally expensive chocolates —a good way to die. No one can forbid me sweets or thick blue tenderloin marbled with fat, but I have put myself in training as though I'm to run a marathon or open in a Broadway show. An idle exercise when it's the home stretch, closing night.

My final lap, my curtain call: chocolates, therefore, to Lourdes who will bring them home to her indolent sons, where they will gobble them like penny candy and she will cherish the box. Lourdes who has just now brought in my decaffeinated coffee. She knows something has gone very wrong and is prepared to save my life. She cries over the box of candy and cries again when, after gently knocking, she brings in the scarlet carnations from my son. He can ill afford them. *"Pobrecito,"* Lourdes whispers, turning her broad Indian face to me which even in sorrow remains placid and serene. "Is sooo beaudiful," she says. Wandering the room with flowers, she cries for all that's cruelly spoiled in family life. Then she turns flirtatious and coy, setting the carnations on my bed table, all secret smiles, "Is a boyfren?"

"I have no boyfriend." The little envelope bears the name of a Ukrainian florist shop on the Lower East Side. Lourdes goes round a corner to a dressing room all fitted with scented drawers and shoe racks, satin cases zipped over soft challis, kidskin, Venetian lace. I cannot see her but I know what mischief she's up to and she's singing in Spanish—*"Ay, y-ay y-ay ay"* to cover her rustling in tissue paper and comes out waltzing with a red velvet jacket cut close to the ribs like a matador's. I will not enter her fantasy. I will not rise from my bed to dress for the day or open my mail. I won't answer phone calls, read a headline or take the lacquer tray she brings me with paint pots and wands to put on a face.

"Go home," I say.

"Missus Flood . . ." But I don't listen to her singsong high-pitched "When you gonna? Why you not?" And soon she's off leaving me with the sharp cinnamon smell of hothouse carnations to disturb my work. I hear the vacuum, then the clatter of her polishing and cleaning. Poor Lourdes, *pobrecita,* it's awful for her attending to the perfect rooms of this apartment where no one really lives. I take my freshly scribbled pages from the strongbox where they lie with my medical reports. Next, lock the door—but that's foolish: Lourdes does not read English.

We came from simple people, Jack Flood and I. Provincial people with narrow views: they were not unloving. Not one of them could believe in our divorce. Catholic all around, it was against their way, but more particularly it was a procedure or state they could not imagine, could not get the feel of in those days—as alien as espionage or kiting checks or hiking in Katmandu. I have not seen any of his people in years. For some reason that suits me, I believe them all to be dead. Gone, with their infuriating denial of the facts and queasy disapproval. My own family bore with me for some time—lovers, illegitimate child: Margaret Flood pushed into a paddy wagon or receiving her awards. I became subject matter to them, a name—not daughter, sister, niece. Somewhere my older brother must have the shameful yellow clippings they kept with reverence and a few of my self-justifying letters in which I beg off on their holidays and funerals . . . though at my mother's his plain good features drew up in rubbery contortion when he saw me get out of a queer silver limousine, march up the church steps with Sol Negaly. Sol in cowboy boots and white cashmere coat. My brother winced like it was last week and I was an embarrassment in the school auditorium, reading out my lofty thirteen-year-old prayer for those slain at Pearl Harbor.

Their twinge of exasperation. What now? What now, Margaret Mary? All of them asked it when they did not turn me into an amusement, some distant personality, tainted, glamorous—a character removed to public life. That was easier for all of us. It absolved me and I recall—the late Sixties it was—getting a Christmas card from Jack's mother, who surely deserved to think ill of me, saying she'd seen me (pushing an anarchist line) on her television one night. "Dad was so pleased." And she wrote "Hurrah!!" with exclamation marks. Hurrah. Hurrah.

There were no cheers when I flew to Mexico for the divorce. We had let the marriage trail on while we lived three thousand miles apart. I have kept the old evidence: these bills for a string of good pearls and the cigarette case (Tiffany, no less) to remind me of my festering rage—oh, fakes were good enough for me and where would his little woman in white wear pearls with a platinum-and-diamond clasp (as noted on the receipt)—to the hot pillow joint in West Haven they frequented on coffee breaks, or would she flash the gold case (inscribed with maudlin message) in the bowling alley so near her house?

My anger was real, but only for a while. Humiliated, I wished them bad cess, Jack Flood and his nurse. After he'd gone I drove down to the hospital in the old car he abandoned with me and waited to see her in her spongy white shoes, trot out to the parking lot on ghostly legs after night duty. She looked blanched as well as blank with dark thumbprints under her eyes. She carried a cloth bag with knitting needles poking out. Of course she would knit—hideous afghans, jaunty hats and gloves in the new bright synthetics—filling the hours she kept watch with this womanly task. I know that she never saw me, for I found a spot up above the parking place reserved for staff where, as a visitor, I could quite literally look down on her. She drove a Volkswagen in a dull shrimp color made back then, before they seduced the American market with their pretty bug. Jack had wanted one. I said no Kraut car. I came to believe he'd bought this shrimp for his pale nurse. Decapitated, as she was in my view, I liked to see her wrestle with the shift. Sweet music to me when she stripped the gears. That was all I ever got on her, that she started a car incompetently, choked and sputtered, then wavered turning out into the street. I heard her voice, light and nasal, call to a friend "Good night" though it was morning, and once she had forgotten to unpin her cap which sat askew on a mound of teased blond hair—like a cupcake frill. I had come to witness that she was lonely or in pain, but the nurse was complacent, placid as Lourdes is always. Sometimes drawn from the night's work, sometimes smiling with a gleam of good teeth across the cars to her nursey friends. "Goodnight, Em," they called to her.

I spy with my little eye—Emily Licht: License—Conn. RN 22180 in angelic white with milky broad face, pallid hair: uninteresting Emily who had her affair with a young doctor. Emily exposed, the negative of Margaret Flood. I envisioned floating down from my hideout like a leprechaun or Billy Goat Gruff and asking, "Do you miss my husband?" as if that were the cruelest wit, not to be punctured with a knitting needle. At the very least I wanted to see her fumbling with her keys, slumped over the wheel of her bug, devastated by more than her professional duties, aching for Jack Flood. She was not worthy of the script I wrote for her. After sleepless nights, I mourned behind the dusty bushes of the visitors' parking lot for my doctor, my sandy-haired love who had not, at the time he left for California, learned to look bland as Emily Licht after a night shift of misery. In the cold light of dawn I tracked her, but not for long, really no more than half a dozen times before with my little eye I spied that she was of no great interest to me, the blond nurse with ample tit, no ass to speak of—a peripheral figure, a walk-on. I pricked my flesh with the sight of this woman to beg relief from what seemed a terminal wound—my life.

"The Bay Area is warm and sunny. This season is unnaturally dry. Here sprinkling systems water at night so that all is lush and green next day." I have nothing from those first months but the clumsy letters I received from Jack. He could not manage words, not then, and struck an impersonal tone I did not take to heart. "Many writers live here." As though I gave a damn about writers or green grass. He met a colleague's wife who admired my book. He extolled the advantages of the supermarkets. "Margaret, you have never seen such tender lettuce." Without comment or urging, he included an ad ripped out of *Life,* pushing the speed and safety of the transcontinental jet, still something of a novelty. A military stewardess salutes the snub nose of a chubby plane which looked to me like a bomber—*Sixty Seconds Over Tokyo.*

These letters are dutiful reports, letters home from camp, written by an older boy who'd never say I caught a cold or poison ivy or I am lonely for you after taps. Soon, a spirited pride came through regrets: "On duty Thanksgiving with the footloose bachelors. Sorry, I could not . . ." He was up round the clock writing grant proposals, big bucks to salvage the weary heart. "Gosh, this is a forward-looking team and I am confident . . ." Phone calls were painful to begin with. I remember degrees of pain, have forgotten the drift of lies. I'm fine. Fine. Act natural. This dinner and that trip to see New England, leaves gone, cold. The train to New York. Often. As he might imagine I was sucking olives out of perfect martinis, gorged on seductive lunches. All fine here. And Jack was fine there with this dinner and that trip to see the wharves in Monterey, twisted pines clutching the wild Pacific coast. Only nine o'clock there. Bedtime in New Haven. We checked that out and in those days said, "What a good connection, like being in the next room!" And the money—that was fine, fine. I suppose it was—I have no memory of wanting for food, a winter coat, the rent. He said: "Margaret, you will kill me. I've gone and bought a small Italian car." I would not kill him. That was it exactly; by the end of November, my wounded pride intact, I let on that I didn't care to the killing point if Jack squeezed into a Fiat. "A fascist car," I said, "well, that's a forward-looking team you're on." It was all banter between us—snappy talk, lines out of the old movies we grew up on, but in the movies brittle repartee ends in zany reconciliation, the putt-putt of a honeymoon jalopy, the sophisticated wink of an adorable terrier as the bedroom door swings shut. No, we were to come to a violent Punch-and-Judy end.

My invention, most likely, that I quit spying at the first frost when the marigolds at the back door of the hospital went slimy and brown, when Emily Licht would have covered her white uniform with a long coat and the puff of yellow hair with a knitted contrivance. That rotten car of Flood's had the MD plates but no heater. What was the use of getting up in the dark to see Emily Licht? The rooms of the apartment or flat on Chapel Street are forgotten, just that I was there alone remains—in the upstairs of a large two-family house among the leftover grocery cartons, twine and tape I'd used to pack him up. All gone, what must have been the furniture of young people—Danish chairs, a coffee table with wrought-iron legs. I'd set up in the big kitchen meant for meat-and-potato suppers, home-baked pies. There, on the table looking out over narrow back yards each with its garage, over the old maples and wash lines, there I set up shop. Typewriter, papers, toppling books, eraser crumbs, crusts, butter on the dictionary's spine. Ashes. Ashes. There by the side of the gas stove, I dragged a sturdy cot Jack had bought expecting patients. In that kitchen I worked and slept and ate, closing off the rooms meant for parents and children, for daily life.

One lunch. I went to New York and got teary, confessional, with Philo Pierce. Just once. I was a few minutes late, presumably, for the great man waited for me with half a bourbon gone, and presumably I did my girlish ordering of green beans and got a stunted portion of *haricots verts.* I could see how that might become a routine—pease porridge hot confused with a dainty dish. Margaret never getting it right, with her flustered out-of-town smile at being early or late and then not knowing her brownies from *brulé.* Charming she was, unfashionable, and all the bumbling indicates that her mind was on better things, oh, on more important matters. Coming as she did into the city in her respectable suit and good shoes, return ticket in her purse, coming from a simpler place. By the time I had the one lunch that particular fall with Philo Pierce, I saw how it worked: Margaret coming into the restaurant breathless, eyes smarting with October's sting. The big man rises to kiss her—buss on the cheek being what they did, publishing people, movie and theater people, maybe city people. The bright flush of her ineptitude attractively stains her face. *She* was not of that world, you see, that world of kissing strangers as a prelude to intimacy, or something that passes as intimacy—disclosure. The big man with spotted vest, his eyeglasses taped together, stands to kiss her. He is presiding on the banquette like a magistrate—solid, judicious, Gilbert and Sullivan solemn, the very hang of his jowls solemn, the grand rumbling voice pitched low.

"Poor Margaret. Has it been unbearable?"

The word strikes her as wrong. She has borne loneliness, humiliation. In her wobbly chair she leans toward him, she must present her case: "Unbearable," she says. This is the beginning of her story, after all, which she has borne like flood and fire or like the quarantined scarlet fever of her childhood. She knows she has survived, at least she's off the danger list, but "Unbearable," she says again, ordering a second drink, letting Pierce suggest the crab mornay, letting him cover her little hand with his manly nicotined paw. It is her left hand he caresses, stroking her naked ring finger, that soft dent in her flesh which is the only visible scar of her marriage to Jack Flood.

"Jesus, that is tawdry. With the night nurse," Pierce says.

"So common," says Margaret, beginning the story, not the guarded summary told to her family or the painful fragments of betrayal choked out to young doctors' wives, but the story she will write.

It's a still shot, old black-and-white glossy. None of the figures move; not the large rumpled man who, though he's heard everything, is shocked out of his pomposity, mouth loose, eyes blurred with wonderment like a giant Disney bear looking on a scene that is sweet, ineffably sad; not the young woman who has turned away from her perfect audience, her editor, turned so that she faces us—about to deliver an aside. The ice does not melt. The single rose locked tight in its bud vase. At the next table there is a smooth man, sleek sideburns and white silk tie, poised over skeletal remnants, rack of lamb. The young woman is about to say, "Gosh! I will write *Maggie Runs Amuck.*" The surprise bulb flashes over her head with a Little Orphan Annie *aperçu* or with the fresh interior monologue of Nancy, the comic strip kid she resembles, flat-faced Nancy full of tricks.

I was ahead of Philo Pierce by a good hour: main course, salad and dessert. The moment I approach is unbearable. As we talked of "other things" I knew I'd exploit Jack, and that in my hesitation step, my reluctance with raw truth, Pierce would feel that he had suggested it. We were a good match.

Jump to a shot of our success. Here—the interview in *Vogue,* best of places, in which I say Philo is mentor, friend, magician. Pierce can draw the story from me, lead me to its troubling depths. The book is *Child's Play,* "The unmasking of American ambition, the harsh private fable that lies under the surface innocence of our postwar success." The interview concludes with a flourish of overstatement: "It is a woman's book, written by the new woman George Bernard Shaw . . . the courageous woman we will look to with the dual charm of purpose and feminine . . ." Hi-dee-ho—and there we are: Maggie Flood in pearls and page boy, trying with the demure collar to look like Grace Kelly, a class act: Pierce, tidied up by the publicity department, is right beside me, behind an empty plate at our cozy, much-frequented L'Auberge. It is hardly shameful to me that we share the page with the Duke of Bedford, thriving now that he's let the rabble into Woburn Abbey. On the overleaf, Samuel Beckett: he does not pretend to be anybody—his open eyes, his sweater, his withered cheek. Beckett's own mouth clamped shut, unsmiling, unembarrassed over the silly caption: his hit play of 1957 is in for the long run.

I can't bear the inception of *Child's Play* so I flip ahead to the amusing picture. I have managed it thus over the years. Now I have little heart for these acrobatic leaps. That awful day weights me: I am playing a hick come late, misorder beans, spill what I want of my sad story. Vamping an old roué, toying with the button on my blouse. I'll soon be stripping in public, strutting the ramp, all bumps and grinds. It is only to be imagined, my rising from that first still shot to compose myself in the ladies room (pink flamingos stalk through incongruous water lilies), the carcass of lamb removed from the neighboring table, fading rose, bottle of Graves upended in the wine cooler. At the end of the meal I am sure Pierce said, sonorous and deep: "It is a woman's struggle." The word destiny used, I'm afraid it was my female destiny implied. If through these encrusted arteries the blood might rise, I'd blush to admit we were on to a good thing. And so the walk to Grand Central, the reckless kiss, his hand around my waist under the violet tweed jacket, my head dropped for an instant on his breast pocket bulging with glasses, pens, a handkerchief stiff and gray. The sexual acknowledgment was a lapse on both our parts. Bow to the ladies. Now curtsy low. Pierce wanted no dalliance with me. And my excitement lay back in the unbearable moment at the restaurant when I contracted with myself to write a revenge tragedy, to make an insupportable thesis of my marriage to Jack Flood.

Out of bed, I steal to the bookcase. It's been weeks since I've let Lourdes tend to my room. Under a film of dust the leather-bound books are lifeless, losing their value even as décor. I can't think when I bought this rosewood cabinet with neoclassic columns and installed its cargo of forgotten titles. I know there is a copy of that cursed book, the work that sealed and notarized the end of a marriage. It lies discarded on the bottom shelf behind a dish of shells and silk-soft beach glass that once pleased me, its binding faded under a tattery jacket. Myself again, in the Princess outfit, such a haughty girl, wasn't that the point, so young to be so wise. Her face too large it bleeds off the book. On the front a gold wedding band circles the medical caduceus, the snakes entwine so gently it seems a magic wand. *Child's Play* spelled out in a garland like letters of an alphabet book that will introduce our singsong rhymes. I am afraid Lourdes will find me now as the book cracks open scattering shards of amber glue. By some sorcery she'll find me without slippers on the cold floor.

"Is walkin' aroun' in summer. Is winder, Missus." (Pantomime shivers.) "Why you not . . . ?" Dress. Eat. Phone. At the foot of the bed Lourdes stands pat, her white uniform mostly covered by a man's mock-collegiate sweater, one of many rejected gifts to her mock-collegiate son. My slippers are moved a fraction of an inch closer to the bed, my robe flapped about to no purpose, the carnations briskly rearranged. "Is some one give you, you say theng you. Too much you say theng you?" She kicks the wire to the telephone but does not dare replug the jack that will connect me to the world, scolding, scolding, and I must agree to soup and one of the *latino* salads (garbanzo beans with soft canned fruit) before she leaves me to my work—*Child's Play:*

In a small city park a young man and his girl face each other on a swing, a two-seater meant for kids. Slung from squealing chains, the diminutive benches collapse and open, collapse again, their grown knees whacking, thumping. She's on top. He's on top. Her laughter mounts to a happy hysteria until he rises to show her how far he can take it—the limit. He pumps and pumps until they are horizontal, now right, now left, silently pressed together in the cold clear air. Oil drums and factories of the port of New Haven, now right: now left, the University, encrusted dome of Woolsey Hall, Harkness spire. Aerial artists, there is a fleeting ecstasy in the split second of their levitation. Then a cry, a sharp animal yelp from a primordial world outside their bliss, but the swing will not stop at once and the girl screams again.

It is the girl who yelped like a dog, her hand crushed in an accident that might have been foreseen. She jumps from the punishing swing, stumbling across the frozen earth, dancing crazily around the slides and seesaws. Her husband (he is her young husband) corners her under a maze of pipes, the jungle gym. She beats against him, dancing still, then kicks at the big steel toes of his army boots. He locks her to him in an expert maneuver and she is calm, no tears at all as he leads her to a bench and takes the injured hand in his. Three fingertips are bleached and flat.

She stomps furiously with her feet to beat the pain. "Oh, Tim, make them pop up again."

"Nothing broken." He is golden, firm of jaw. In the winter sunlight his close-cut military hair glints with streaks of fire. High, intelligent brow above clear blue eyes steady as the cloudless sky above New Haven. As he examines her hand—the angry dents rising—Tim Healy is hero, doctor, her soon-to-be doctor, three months to graduation. And Jane, his apple-cheeked wife with black unruly locks, pretending she's a tomboy, Jane is his patient. He takes a pocketknife and quickly cuts through the battered nails, easing the blood out. "My first operation."

She looks at his hands that are miraculously unstained, like the perfect hands of Jesus Christ upon his Sacred Heart—soft, long, white—the hands of a surgeon she thinks all aglow. When he tells her the extremities are full of nerves thus the god-awful pain, Jane Healy says, "I'm tough," as she will have to be, a doctor's wife. He guides her along in her post-operative state, past the innocent swing they both condemn, out of the empty park, downhill, down Boulevard to home.

Nothing worse than the slight mangling of Jane's fingers has happened to them. A flat tire, an encounter with bad shrimp cannot compare. Now, as he kisses the hurt away at a stoplight, it seems they've had a first scrape with Daddy Death, though Tim, who wears an army jacket, has heard a master sergeant with his jaw blown off howl his last command

and seen soldiers with arms and legs jointed backward like the limbs of pliable dolls, innumerable Saturday-night wounds in Emergency, a steering wheel sliced half through a man. But this is his darling and it's a hell of a note on the one afternoon he's gone to meet Jane at her job, walked to get the hospital smell out of his nostrils, the diagnostic jargon out of his head. Jane begins to dance again with pain and runs past the old two-family houses and the Texaco station like a toy hacienda which once, though the Healys would not know this, marked the city limits. He catches up, sees the stinging tears in her eyes. "From the wind," she says. "I'm tough." Together they run through the chain-link fence onto the asphalt lane, down the row of army barracks to R, which is their home.

Their fate is sealed: with this small accident in the playground begins their injury to one another, their carelessness. Tim and Jane with their names from a first-grade reader enter their cardboard rooms in the medical students' ghetto. It is temporary, with cast-off furniture, many of their wedding presents still nesting in boxes. Only the firm bedspring and mattress have come from a department store, top of the line, intended to endure the long energetic assault of their love.

When Tim works late at the hospital, when she is not collecting fines and checking out books at a branch library, Jane studies the real-estate pages of the *New Haven Register.* She calls landlords asking the size of bedrooms and parking facilities, if the stove is electric or gas. It's almost a sure thing that her husband will be invited to stay on at the hospital for his residency. They want a solid half-house on a pleasant street, shade trees, wide lawns, the paperboy on his bike, a few dignified old people, a place that has not changed. They want a side entrance where Tim can hang out his shingle, cheerful office, a desk of oiled teak at which they see Dr. Healy turning to his patients with good news. They want a lot, these two —sure things—and Jane Healy has made the quest for the ideal house her hobby: It makes it possible for her to spend the nights alone in this nasty barracks. Thin partitions stake out bedroom, kitchen, bath. In an effort to make a home, other wives have bought watery paints—pastel yellows and greens, chalky blues—that soak into the fiberboard. Some have made curtains and bright pillows, even knocked together bookcases to the amazement of their studious husbands. It is not that Jane is unhappy with her lot that makes her phone "sunny, fireplace, near University" or "spacious three-bedroom" inquiring after shower stalls and cross ventilation, it's that the barracks is not her lot. Not their lot, the Healys feel.

Never to be said, not while Tim studies in the bare living room or she reads under a shadeless lamp, but they won't give in to this prefab shell by half a domestic inch. The difference is felt. It is observed that Jane is the only wife who works, goes out to the library for miserable pay, but goes each day into the world. It is heard, their silence in the barracks where the walls are paper-thin, where voices raised in accusation travel clear and distinct, where abandoned wives laugh foolishly together on weekends, where babies cry. There are babies on all sides sending out alarms morning and night. The Healys are quiet, without phonograph or radio. Living on the first floor in R, a corner apartment, no one can hear their box spring and good mattress whomp the wall as Tim swings into the final strokes of his coming. No one can hear Jane's soft moan or the release of her (sometimes) plaintive cry. The Healys can hear the Gwertzes grinding it out above. Two or three times a night before Lou's final exams and Beverly, who is a screamer, rooting for him.

The quiet Healys, alone, do not have a baby, no milk deliveries at dawn, clatter of diaper pail, scent of talcum masking baby odors, the wash strung everywhere, teething toys and chewed animals strewn on the linoleum. It cannot be that they are juiceless, programmed to have children when it will be economically proper and just. They are funny of an evening, get drunk upon occasion, abhor the medical school's politics, groan at lewd professional jokes. But they leave so completely to go back to R with their Woolworth window shades and no place comfortable to sit. You cannot fault them, though Tim's masterful jaw, the cropped gold curls, the eyes like a pure blue base solution, are hard to take.

Cracks are made about Healy being destined for gynecology, a Park Avenue practice. His classmates are not saints and find it somehow offensive that this man never told them he was awarded a Silver Star in the Pacific, that he comes from ignorant working people though he is effortlessly bright.

What does he see in her? It's Jane's queerness that saves them from a damnable perfection. Blue gooseflesh knees in Bermuda shorts on weekends; shooting baskets at an imaginary hoop, always something wrong with her—collar awry, button off, hem out, smudged like a negligent schoolgirl—or boy. Why he puts up with her Dinty Moore Stew and canned corned beef, pizza from De Angelos? Not a carpet or a curtain. There is no child. Coming and going with a sack of books from her library, reading all night it seems from the lamp burning in cubbyhole R. Writing—that is lightly dismissed—she has turned out a few articles, fillers, for the *Register* on Igor Sikorsky and his peacetime helicopter, on the demise of Connecticut oyster beds, witchcraft in West Haven. The sight of her striding off to work, even the money Jane has saved so that the Healys will sail to Europe third class after graduation, is not enviable to the women in the barracks. A stranger among them, though she picks up their babies, listens to their gossip and—like every one of them—worships the doctor she has married. Jane lives apart.

She's only a major irritant once or twice a year when there is an obligatory dance and Mrs. Healy appears all perfume, décolletage (the figure is not that boyish) and waltzes expertly in high heels with an extremely important Viennese professor of rheumatology. She drinks wine, not whiskey, and is enchanted, bending to Herr Doktor's words. Unconscious of her transformation, she plays with the false pearls on her creamy breast. Would she be less sorely resented if her neighbors knew that the old professor is past lechery, fakes that gleam in his eye as he talks to the beautiful young thing of no more than White Russians he has known or oyster beds in France?

How easily it becomes Jane's story, no doubt of that, the woman's story. Pierce tagged it, an early specimen of the genre. I timed it, I believe I knew this each day I wrote in the garret I created out of an acceptable home. A fierce story, a partisan story from the first scene of Jane's injury on the teeter-totter swing. It was a time of great domestic revival: Welcome home, get on with it. Get on with that version of home that never was a clear mandate before the war. Get on with a retouched memory of families huddled around the radio—what a hoot, Amos 'n' Andy, Fibber McGee, Fred Allen with the harmless racial jokes. *Oooh, Mrs. Nussbaum! You were expecting maybe Too-ra-loo-ra Bankhead?* Dad and Mom pulled up to the speaker, attending to Franklin Roosevelt, first media star and still the best. Get on with American life, Amuricun, and the comfort of a president who said that—Amuricun and nucalur. The building of the little houses row on row and babies issued as though they'd just been perfected along with Scotch Tape and Technicolor. Babies back on the market. Reliable Plymouths and Chevies. This is the world Doctor Healy and his wife will inhabit. A time when virginity is overpraised, staging a comeback, though both the hymen and the family car are threatened by imported notions picked up overseas. Certainly Jane passed for a virgin when she married Tim and they have decided it will be the roomy half-house for starters with professional office before they can afford the two-door Chevrolet.

It was peacetime in the barracks where the graduate students live in a semblance of hardship, where the Healys alone can afford their slight immaturity. It is not his fault that Tim is favored above his classmates, every teacher's pet. But she is idle (though she earns the little paycheck), free to mash her finger in a playground, ride an ancient Raleigh bike. Her hair is all cut off to make her an Italian urchin begging in the streets of Naples and she's clever enough to wonder at the perverse masculine fashion and the contradiction implied when she hooks herself into the Merry Widow corset that prepares her waist and breasts to receive the stiff cocktail dress in which she will waltz and accept the gallantry of the old Viennese professor.

That is Jane's affliction. She does think too much, even as she listens to Beverly Gwertz and Ginny Fusco, very much the doctors' wives, talk about naturally getting their tubes tied after four kids. She thinks of the word naturally, and from her distance she says, "Suppose there was an epidemic. Suppose a disaster and your children . . ." Jane thinks of Louis Gwertz shipped out of Cracow with his mother, as they well know, shipped to an unknown cousin in London. It is said a large family of brothers and sisters, the father—all dead. By quick conversion, she asks, "Haven't you seen the gravestones in old cemeteries with dreadful lists? Sara, two weeks. Seth, three days. A dozen children gone, a couple of survivors."

Well, that was Jane Healy's turn of mind, suggesting dead babies to young mothers. Then not really listening to them on the decline of infant mortality and partial hysterectomies . . . Ginny Fusco whose second child shows large as a long watermelon under her smock is plain bewildered. Beverly, bragging and complaining, launches into the lusty workout she will get during her husband's final exams: "Lou says, leave in the playpen, take out the crib." To her credit Jane thinks that is one of the worst things she has ever heard, like the easy-care fabrics now in the stores—useful and ugly.

She is winning: I'm not won. Not as I read her story many years later. What does it gain this creature of my making, this cleaned-up version of myself, that she can outwit the Ginnys and Beverlys on their homey turf? How can they, with their vaguely comic names, their meager household budgets, devotion to the patriarchal hearth, their getting on with it, be so easily, so unsympathetically put down? And by this yearning, dissatisfied chit of a girl? Questions I never asked myself as I drew my heroine with deliberate strokes. Jane towers over the barracks with a crooked smile, little shading, no cross-hatching of experience to give her depth. Ill-proportioned, Jane Healy dominates the narrative of her marriage like a naughty child who manages to get, any which way, all the attention. The husband is necessarily dwarfed. One feels early on that his actorish good looks, his cool intelligence and gentlemanly demeanor entitle him to lesser billing.

• • •

Vase and carnations topple when I hurl the book across the room in a wild pitch. Lourdes mops up. How efficiently she changes the sheets, then sets me back among my pillows. "Gonna be beddar." By this time in the day she does not bully me. Not a stricture in my chest nor the much-touted shot of pain down the arm, nothing to show for my ailing heart. The red carnations, those few not beheaded, loll about the rim of the big vase. "Lucky," she says to me and then, "Nize. Nize boy," with her hearts-and-flowers grin. Adoring all male children, Lourdes will drag home the nightly six-packs to her swaggering sons and if they lift the package from her weary arms call that her valentine.

As she picks up my books, the backs of her legs are strong and shapely. Lourdes came to me, it seems as if she chose me after Bayard left, when I'd come to live alone. A blessing—I was without my history and I have never known her origin, her age. Impassive Mayan face, hands split and scarred with work. Those legs are young. She cannot be, God help us, forty years old. The dust jacket, much smoothed and patted, is returned to *Child's Play*. I'm glad to see it's torn right through the flap that recommends it as a small enduring classic. "Sooo beaudiful," says Lourdes, showing me the picture of Margaret Flood, Miss Priss with the knowing eye, every trace of her growing pains airbrushed away. "Why you not . . . ?" she begins about my straggly hair, a white stripe showing at the part like the markings of an old coon. "When you gonna . . . ?" She gently plucks at my dirty nightdress to exhibit a brown splotch of tea.

Too late in the day for recriminations: "Go home." As I look at this good woman with thick black hair and heavy skull, I can't imagine how we ever got into this skirmish that masks our affection.

"I fix dinner," Lourdes says, knowing that the next day

she will find the chop or chicken breast with wilted vegetables uneaten, a cold reproach.

The spine is broken—with a will of its own my book flips open to the end of doomsday begun on that damn swing. They are in bed. Jane and Tim on their Beautyrest Elite. She is sucking her mangled fingertips like a cat for the cure of it. He slips her flannel gown down over her shoulders. The wind whips through the open seams of the barracks. Her breasts are round and upright with large pink aureoles he cannot see in the dark. He feels the firm ducts leading up from her pectorals to the armpits, the birthmark above her left rib, a pigmented naevus, and her nipples which square off like erasers, she says, the kind you stick on the end of pencils. This self-deprecating turn of phrase her husband discounts as shyness. Jane has been quiet all evening, reading as usual but taking herself off early to bed—one of the few nights Tim has been home. Now she lies under her husband. He is careful, stroking down her sides and into the *symphysis pubis,* a laying on of hands. She spreads herself to him and with her good hand thrusts his buttocks down hard to her body, thinking this is his way, a man's way of making her feel . . . of healing. This is his comfort and she takes him to the hilt, yelping with pleasure. Still big after coming, Tim lies on her and then she sees that all the while she has held up her wounded hand in a Girl Scout pledge. No feeling in the fingers, but a sharp pulsing up through her arm. Jane knows to suffer in silence or he'll read her chapter and verse on the median nerve and the peculiarities of referred pain.

Ahead of the game, isn't she? Your move. Then jump, jump, jump across the board. I win. Turn, turn on—second car, new furniture, Tim's appointment comes through. And always the head work: her summary view of the recession, of housing projects, the comic gift of Marilyn Monroe. Dinner with Jane is like a flip through last week's *Time* in the dentist's office. Not an ordinary wife, she becomes an ordinary civics teacher, informative on Elvis, Levittown, aftermath of Suez, Negro boycotts. Jane has subjects and it is this last, a bus boycott, that frees her from the branch library and takes her South on her first grown-up assignment. I do not blame Tim Healy, accused at each heedless, hardtack meal of narrow careerism by the narrator of *Child's Play.* The poor fellow rushes to the arms of Dolly Panik (big ass, sunken chest). They meet at an emergency tonsillectomy. Who would deny him the comfort of casual tit given the hard lessons he must learn at home, or an after-hours steak with willing, homely Doll, given the unpardonable things Jane has done to him with frozen food and tuna fish. With unaccustomed ease Tim pats his nurse on the rump as she draws his instruments from the sterilizer. "Hands off, Doc," says Doll, artless, inviting.

Pity poor Jane! No: there is a noble savage in the woodpile. Her blood is quickened by a militant broad-chested chap, described as "honey-hued," "cocoa-tinged," who stops midway in a rousing paragraph on the indomitable agrarian Negro to throw Jane "a dusky glance." I pray that Lourdes may enter with a last-minute crisis in the scouring or waxing department, but there's no reprieve and nothing to redeem the daring interracial sequence. As a period piece it is no more interesting than a temperance pamphlet written by a repressed spinster in a parsonage. Calvin (that is the gentleman's name) speaks in Biblical cadence, long patches that would send anyone but Jane to sleep in the pew.

Turn, turn on. At last, on a country road that follows the old Natchez Trace, they are thrown together by an automotive problem. Calvin, having spent much time perfecting his rhetoric, is a lousy mechanic. It is a balmy night with the beat, beat of the cicada, the sweet smell of some night-blooming flower as they find their way along a footpath in the woods for they dare not stay on the road with every backwater town on the alert for the slightest provocation. When a mossy bank presents itself in the moonlight, our Calvin and Jane do not see the dusting of floury stars; they do not hear soft night hoots or the involuntary flutter of a sleeping heron's wings. They talk. It is insufferable. By the shallow swamp, they talk of their racial and sexual destinies.

With an unexpected remnant of self-respect, Jane says, "Take me."

"And stoke the myth of the black boy's power?"

Turn, turn on past their labored self-denial (it lasts till dawn) to their parting at the edge of a lazy courthouse town, where, screened by a weeping willow, they do kiss at last, at least. Back in New Haven midst the trivia of medical get-ahead, Jane dreams repeatedly of Calvin's dedication. He appears to her (it is Calvin, certainly) in Shakespearean garb as lordly bus-driver-triumphant. Freedom stalks the endless aisle—gum wrappers, exhaust fumes, a black leather glove—freedom as a floating, terrible anxiety. There is no way her legs or arms, her heavy body, can move from her seat in the rear of Calvin's bus.

Turn to Jane discovering Dolly Panik, discovering the giddy scent of lily of the valley on Tim's clothes, a dead blond hair, lipstick streak, motel receipts—all the paraphernalia of a routine affair. She is shocked at the degree to which she cares and cannot sort her own disgrace from Tim's defacement of their newly furnished apartment and their old love in barren R. In a frenzied pursuit of evidence (remember, she has just investigated man's inhumanity to man), she comes across a report—measurements, graphs, tabulations, results—hidden between shirt cardboards that are hidden under a large suitcase not used since their voyage on the *Ile de France.* This is Tim's work on bacterial endocarditis in the *ductus arteriosus,* the very paper that procured his first grant. Indeed, this is the copy she had typed in duplicate with her erasures, the faintly crossed t's of her Smith-Corona in every "tissue," "transplant," at the end of each "heart."

Now she's off and running, half dressed, bare-legged in scruffy slippers—block after block through a dirty haze settled on the city that morning, past the cemetery, its horrendous red stone gates the color of New Haven clay, obelisks and granite blocks all poking through soiled lumps of fog. At the hospital she waits with a distressed family, silently weeping parents and a sorrowful little girl who cuts pies and cakes out of *McCall's.*

"You are waiting?" the mother asks.

"I am waiting for my husband to come down from surgery," Jane says with a sudden fear it might be Tim up there sliced open, his flesh clamped back from a gaping wound.

When he steps off the elevator in his scrub suit, Timothy Healy does not see his wife next to the crying family until he is half through his happy announcement and the father is hugging the child with the scissors, the mother crossing herself in little methodical taps—forehead breast breast, forehead breast breast. Cupping his hand around Dolly Panik's rump, the green doctor could not imagine a scene with his wife at all, never mind playing it in the pediatric waiting room, playing it in front of joyous strangers whose baby he has snatched from death.

"If it's about the nurse," Tim says, "that's nothing."

"Screw her. Well, that's what you've been doing." Jane doesn't crack a smile. It is then he notices the damp papers in her hand, his paper on congenital heart disease as first written, before he nudged the findings ever so slightly in order to make perfectly sure of his NIH grant.

"Bless you. Bless you," the mother says in a general way to the Healys before the family is led offstage by a mechanical attendant. The dim light slanting through venetian blinds chops off Tim's nose, amputates his arm raised in a pleading oratorical gesture. To Jane he looks like the statue of a forgotten Roman emperor, idealized in art, corrupt in life.

Skip twenty pages of Tim's breast-beating and Jane's recriminations—she is right, always right—to a seedy high-domed railroad station in Philadelphia, prelude to the abortion scene. How Philo Pierce did admire the abortion. A flurry of letters from Madison Avenue to New Haven encouraged me to "search the hearts of betrayed women." How brave we felt. How prescient of my editor to goad me on to that shocking moment when Jane stretches out in a filthy office, trusts her body to a bald, blinking man with thick fingers, a jolly man aping the manner of an old GP. "Little lady. Now, now, little lady," he says. And all this: the cold forceps, the cruel probe, the life dragged from her into an irrigation pan with less pain than an ear lanced in childhood sickness before the bitter green horse pills, penicillin—all this to walk unburdened into an uncertain future. Her freedom: Philo Pierce saw that it justified this needlessly ugly scene. Her liberation from a servile role she never played. Her disobedience, if you will—I will call it that for she is headstrong as one of those willful girls, Antigone or Judith, who beg for our praise as they race toward their predictable doom.

The last we see of our heroine—she is surely that: Jane does not rat on Tim Healy or drag his infidelity into a court of law—she's swinging: a solo performance. It's on her final tour, the glider in the playground. She's had her last look at the flat expanse of New Haven Green with the borders of diseased elms, at the agreeable gargoyles on Berkeley College, on Saybrook, the old medical school no bigger than a rectory, less fine, like a merchant's solid house, but good enough for the guesswork of a dubious science. As though she is leaving campus, not a life, she's walked past the *Register* to feel once more the twinge of tenderness for this gritty place where she filed her first stories. Jane has hiked out to the barracks for an outside shot of cubbyhole R, where a woman's crisp white curtains flutter in the breeze. Scenes of childhood. Now gently swinging. Her steady view of sandbox and slides. Blessed sunshine, early June. Kids squabbling, pushing, ganging up—friends, some of them, with secret pacts, clever rules to bind them. They do not much notice the woman in their swing, nobody's mother, a thin woman ogling them like Olive Oyl on morning cartoons. They do not see her caress her knobbled fingers as she wonders at the careless intensity of their play.

"I go now." Lourdes turns on the lamps. She's come too late. I can read about the Healys in the dark not missing one false detail. "I go now." She does not fuss over me, lets me wallow in the trail of old letters and new blood tests that litter my quilt. She is in her fake fur, glossy black as a Labrador retriever. An orange hat in the popcorn stitch covers her black hair. She stands a bit taller in her boots, but lopsided, weighted with her purse and shopping bag. The tip of the red candy box pokes through the oddments of cosmetics, curlers, alternate costumes she hauls back and forth each day. Good night. We are through with each other: it's a draw. She is hoping to catch the express train, the token in her palm. What will she feed the louts who wait at home for her to serve them? She knows or thinks she knows, it is simple faith, that I'll be in my bed still unwashed and crazy in the morning.

"Goo nide." Is so cuckoo, Missus Flood.

I do miss her when she's gone, unfairly, like a sick child whose mother must leave on a practical errand. Damn her black eyes, her abracadabra kit. I miss Lourdes at this moment more than I miss my son. More sharply tonight for there it is—the dedication of *Child's Play.* "For Philo Pierce." In boldface for the world to see how desperate I am to want their love—editor or maid with whom I've made my commercial arrangements.

Strange, the land outside my room. At the doorsill my knees tremble. Turn back. Shoulders hunched to protect me, toddle to the bathroom. My sink and tub, my toilet, very grand, privileged being Margaret Flood's. The pee runs warm, plentiful and clear as it has these days when I check on any sign as if my heart will molt or weep on the surface like a wound. I feel fit, rested, strong. Steady now, I step, why quite sprightly, into the hall. What's left of the winter day, a hopeless fading, casts its light on the floor like small rugs all slipped aside. A series of doors, beyond them windows. My route takes me out to the public rooms. Behind me the closed door. My son's room closed—it might as well be sealed off, scene of an uninvestigated crime. It might bear again his warning with skull and crossbones—DO NOT ENTER: the unenforceable order of a child. It is not, in any case, on the agenda.

Here the room where she worked, never to be touched. Half glass of water next to the silver pillbox with the last medication that did not quiet her nerves, a cup of forbidden coffee evaporated to powdery dregs. Books in no order—Plato, Tolstoy side by side with *Anne of Green Gables, Kidnapped, Van Loon's Lives* and best-sellers of the Fifties (the early competition) all read so long ago. The globe in its walnut stand is Sixteenth Century, miscalculated axle, purely decorative. The Indies, the old Holy Roman Empire, whole continents float unformed in their oceans as if suspended in amniotic fluid. To the left, very neatly, encyclopedias, atlas, thesaurus, dictionary, Bartlett's—the world at a glance. Her work: novels, scripts, reportage—here every scrap of it leather bound. She could not abide an overhead light, so like a store in the public mall. The reading chair and desk are picked out in pools of light. A theatrical spot on the typewriter, its bright beam strikes off the silent machine, a corpse under its plastic cover. The half page as she left it: generous note to one of her fans. Photos: tailcoats, ocean liner, guitar, peace rally, beach, bikini—Bel Air, Woodstock, Cannes, White House. You might play a party game with these pictures of men and women inhabiting their fame, patron saints of the post-Christian world. She is conspicuously absent from the photographs as though the central figure in a Dutch portrait was left out. All we have is background—roll of Bicentennial stamps, mug of sharp pencils, erasing fluid. Tools of her trade, all with their great significance.

Pass on to the dining room. Here you can almost see her at the head of the table delivering down its length one of the stories . . . oh, if you have heard the one about running into Cary Grant in Abercrombie & Fitch or Cartier-Bresson leaving his camera behind, a simple Leica, in her apartment, never mind, you will love the variations, the control over her material which she has always had to large degree but the delivery is perfected now with elegant stops, interesting choices as to gesture with napkin or crystal, catching the eye of a guest (editor, critic, politician) with a little off-center smile, complicit as a wink. The chandelier dims. That's a Hockney next to the Hogarth and the sideboard—claw feet and Georgian pulls—a mongrel from the set of *Playtime,* stolen from the old Warner Brothers lot. The dinner—it's all offhand to indicate no pretensions, the plain fare passed around by Lourdes who wears a hospital aide's uniform for the occasion and looks forward to the long cab ride home, a special treat.

Living room nearly expired. Sofas and chairs roam the floor, shift in the eerie light. Tables misty with the glint of wax are fixed in place. Display cabinets: shards and implements. The searchlight of a night watchman moves across the wall, over a swollen urn, ficus, palm—and plays on the stalk of a lamp with fringed peony head. Who lives here? Polishes the brass, sets the pillows straight? I have lived like this in a landscape of doors and windows, watched the ceiling float marvelously overhead, before. Once before. When unclear as morning scum on the eyes. I stumble, so to speak, upon the big ashtray stolen from the *Ile de France* —clunky, chipped, mended with telltale glue. Lourdes does not think it fit for Margaret Flood's living room. It is mine, stuffed between sweaters in a suitcase after an agonizing moral dilemma. The decision to take it from the Trianon Lounge was solely mine. A prize on our coffee table in New Haven.

It was in New Haven I lived like this, holed up, a nervy

animal, urgent with some purpose. At first it was survival, my kitchen lair fitted out for the hard season. It was then the other rooms receded. Phantasmagoric, they sat at their distance, a broken chair or drawer forgotten in the void. What had I to do with bedrooms or living rooms or whole blank cubicles in which to dine? I guess it's on the house tour: that kitchen on Chapel Street, all of my life drawn into an ungainly upstairs kitchen with the sink on high legs, my desk by the gas stove, iron cot blocking the pantry door and the prewar refrigerator, temperamental in its menopause, sweating and groaning, then perking up with a girlish whine. Here, I had already launched the nurse, declared her the dumb blond, but crass, demanding. This was not the first young doctor, etc.; and that sweet sawbones reduced to caricature, dewy-eyed, feeling his oats, lusting after a bit of fame, not yet depraved . . . The *Ile de France* ashtray by my typewriter. Stubbing out cigarettes in the eye of the French Line logo, I was on a tear.

"What? Are you crazy?" Jack Flood shouted. He did come back, of course, after our long-distance calls and his youthful letters from the Golden State. He came across the continent to see if it was true that he had left me behind. He stood in what little space he could find by the kitchen window where I'd set my reading chair, swallowing hard, poking a finger in his ear, half deaf from the plane ride, so shouting at me, "Are you crazy?"

"I suppose I am."

"What's that?"

"I am crazy," I said loud and clear.

He walked the empty rooms complaining that there was no furniture. Well, how could there be—all that was bundled up and gone, sitting in his Spanish revival apartment with a courtyard, he said, and every morning the smell of eucalyptus trees. He was a person from California, Jack Flood, my husband smoothed with sunshine, coppery brown. (On the beach in Hammonasset he had burned sore red, blistered, peeled: he deplored the sun.) His clothes had a festive air, houndstooth or glen plaid, blue slacks, pale blue. He wore soft leather shoes. Back east, he said that, back east it was dullish and beside the point whatever he'd wear. Now he stood different, draped against the window frame, hands looped in his pockets, charming me, and I thought how little time he'd given to charming me. Partly what had changed was his size, full chest and the new bulge of his thighs from lap upon lap in some faculty pool. Partly it was the fair eyebrows that showed up now against the burnished alien's skin. Mostly it was the attitude, the easy argument, no edge to his grievance with me. Now his soft smile, now his concern: damn his soul, three months out of my sight and Jack Flood was relaxed. It was seductive, just the look of him yawning to pop his ears and the talk of his research casual, even anecdotal, of his lab and the medical conference in New York that had paid his fare back east. That smarted. I thought—oh, I did think—that he had come to get me and that smarted.

I said: "This is a business trip, then?"

"Now, Maggie—"

"Two birds with one stone."

"You were always sensible," he said, wooing me. Sensitive . . . sensual. I heard him: "You were sensible," and then he flicked the return on my ancient Smith-Corona, a high-set office model. It was my prize. He had bought it for me secondhand. And when he got the roller centered, all doctorly and scientific, he said: "Pack it up, Maggie." He meant my work. It's easy to see there was a slight in that. Pack it up. But I knew he had come to get me and all I felt was a swelling of happiness, so feverish it must have showed, mottling my throat, a bright burning in my eyes. I was safe home. Rescued. Claimed.

"I could never part with that typewriter." So flustered that I spoke now of my unwavering love for the swayback chair. Jack came round to light the cigarette I fondled slowly as though I was thinking about his proposition, as though I might not know my mind about him, might not care. The miniature box of matches out of his pocket was from their motel on US I, a skip from the hospital to jump a nurse. As he leaned to me in the fancy coat of a traveling man, he smelled of her, and there, stuck to his spiffy lapel, was the inevitable long strand of golden hair. I slapped at the matches and they scrambled over my desk like pick-up sticks. "Two birds with one stone," I said.

"You have no bed for me." His voice was loud and distant as though projected through a megaphone. Neatly he gathered up the matches, all their little red heads facing up in the box, and set the box beside my typewriter. Jack never smoked. He was right—there was no place for him in my kitchen on the single cot.

"Margaret, you are my wife." I saw that he wanted me with the sleek Scandinavian headboard and the good saucepans. I saw that he expected me, that he'd never let on to them, whoever they were with their dead of night sprinklers and eucalyptus, smug with relaxation, that I was to pack the typewriter and papers (my personal belongings) and appear with him, pale but wifely and complaisant, by the side of the pool. I saw that I had not been taken seriously and that broke my heart more than a peroxide blonde, more than his waiting for a free ride back east, back home. I saw what I wanted to. The hunkered-in, camp-out kitchen was my defiant house. That seemed the worst to him and he shouted: "You have no furniture." Very angry it sounded as though I was a curiosity, a woman without breasts or womb.

Then he smiled. The pressure on his ears had popped again and we finished our scene in a quiet chummy sorrow, a closeout, a reprise.

"Yes," I said, "I suppose it was an awful business to set up all those lamps and tables by yourself. Did anything break?"

"No," Jack said. "It was a perfect move."

"It seems so." We spoke of furniture and I was glad I'd sent it on. He asked after the car, the car I'd used to play girl detective in a plot with no mystery. The car was running. So it ended that last time in New Haven and he gave me a quick pat on the shoulder, friendly encouragement he might give to a patient. Some animal defense set up in me, clever as endorphin. *The music playing so nonchalant.* Now I think of how we smiled our faces off—his teeth too white set in the newly bronzed coat of California skin. *Good morning Mister Sunshine, you brighten up my day* . . . something, something *by my window* . . . something *in your way.*

When I was alone the hurt came on, an everlasting pain delayed during our easy parting. I rocked and keened and cried out to the empty rooms. I wailed at the wintery backyards, at the cruel sight of the neighbors' clothes frozen on the line, at harmless cats and garbage pails. Exhausted, I lay on my cot and with spare invalid gestures put hand to head, hand to heart, head to wall. I never slept and rose at the end of the day to see the cell I had made for my life. On the next block early Christmas greens twisted with blue lights had grown up the balustrade of a two-family house: funereal—it set me off again. A weary sobbing was all I had left. Then, or soon, I bled. It was unexpected, excessive, terrifying. The withered corpus luteum, that hospitable richness of my body shed, shucked off the children. I bled away all the children I might have with Jack Flood in a miraculous miscarriage. I mourned them.

Soon, very soon, in a day or so, I went to my typewriter and stared at the tough old platen that I would further punish with my story. If I'd never been prompted by Philo Pierce, I would have written *Child's Play,* though at the time it had no shape or name. I tapped their motel matches, shook them like a rattle, set the box upright, prominent—a cheap trick to goad me to bitter words and fancies, my only consolation, having lost the game.

"It's not the first time I've elected solitary confinement." This is said to my son.

"I've never seen you in such a mess, not for years." I wonder, not for years would mean when he was ten or maybe way back when he was eight and which of many messes—political, professional, personal—might he refer to.

Bayard Bidwell Strong. If a mother may say, he's the best-looking boy in his class and verifiably the smartest. Precocious, yet nothing in his manner suggests a mind untimely ripe. In his school jacket and flannels Baby is irresistible. I should not call him Baby—I do.

"Those were long-stem carnations," he says, "a dozen."

"We had an accident. They are lovely still. Costly, I know."

"I traded Mr. Zak a striped suit out of a Buffalo department store. Good fit, shoulder pads, old-Europa double-breasted slouch."

"Clever."

"I live by my wits." He settles on a straight-back chair to interrogate me. This is not a sweetheart's visit. My secret admirer is a weary man of sixteen. Drained by his father's nonsense, he must now put up with me. Baby's hair falls at a beguiling angle on his forehead, thick dark hair like mine once; long face, quality nose, eyes steady like his father's once. His look, not disapproving, is dark. I hate that hard acceptance in him, borne without malice or self-pity. I'm extravagant about Bayard . . . oh, that hardly covers my offense: wanting, not my kid, but the surface glint of his perfection when, as a little boy, he read Hamlet and Kipling and Spider-Man all in one day . . . wanting, in league with his father, Pinkham Strong, his soccer trophy and Egyptology, his cultures labeled and breeding in tea-cups on an abandoned breakfast tray. Patter of Cole Porter songs, celestial calculations, model of Da Vinci's bicycle, Woodrow Wilson buff, Mick Jagger fan. He knew how to please us. We were greedy, flamboyant people. Twinkle Bayard—and our boy would shine. An entertaining worldly little man. Shine like Mamma. Shine like Pa, but call us Margaret and Pinky, not affected as we saw it in a three-year-old, but lively, man to man. I never sat on a back stoop and watched him worry his tricycle over a puddle. On the side of his bathtub yes, his rosy penis dancing with the ducks . . . too often I let a hired woman wrap him up and carry him warm and moist to bed, though I never abandoned him, happy and stupefied, in front of television. I am looking for a natural moment, just once when I did not stage the chocolate chip cookies, once when I screamed—"Go play, Baby. Go outside and play." I haven't found it yet. I wanted Bayard . . . an accomplishment, bound and gilt-edged, a slim volume to make up for all the rest. It is a crime, this tired young gent sending me flowers, working his jaw at me in strict self-control. When we talk it's smart, defensive, a crime, and I pull under my covers like a petulant child.

"The phone is unplugged," he says with the slow deliberation of a prosecutor. "There are two cartons of mail placed, presumably by Lourdes, in front of the oven. Perhaps she means to roast them, since you have no intention of reading letters or paying your bills. The new editor, the dapper fellow, has come down to the shop. The tax man, fatso with the intaglio ring, has come down to the shop. An angry woman with a brogue comes daily."

"That's the knitter, Baby. She's finished my sweater."

"Wonderful. On the phone we have a television personage with a mush-mouthed drawl and a real aggressive woman from Sarah Lawrence. On the phone constantly, Mother. Pinky can't bear the fuss."

"What can Pinky bear?"

"He is fragile to me, spineless to you."

"Oh, I'd never say spineless. I'd say your father just lost his starch."

"Pick the words, Mother. I take the fast train after school and run down the block to see if he's alive."

"You haven't given up soccer?"

"No time for games."

Bayard loves soccer. His calves are thick and muscular like mine once and he's swift, so swift below the knees you know he isn't thinking in his brilliant head.

"With the shop I have no time for games." He begins to pace at the bottom of my bed. The shop—he stiffens at the name—is called Golden Oldies, not a bad choice, but cute and sinister given his father's life gone to dross within. No time for fun, running from the subway to sell racks of hideous clothes imbued with the stains and odors of strangers. Silk with dry rot, moth-eaten bathrobes, peach nightgowns, funky jeweled sweaters, queer evening cloaks, indecent miniskirts. Previously owned. And Baby doing his math between customers or screening out the prattle of Pinkham Strong, who is gathering his family history, cultural detritus, poring over ancient marriage certificates, ledgers flocked with mold—as though in the seal of Trinity Church, the price of molasses in 1843, a contract to dredge Kill Van Kull he will find that the world was sound, safe as brownstones and railroad shares, before it all fell down.

"It's a damn shame you have to give up soccer."

"It's all a shame," he says with a wistful smile. "It's a shame my father doesn't work for a bank or a brokerage house or sell appliances like Grossman's old man. Write beer commercials like Malone's. It's a shame, but I can't think of anyone but my mother who would have electrocardiograms draped over the bed like party streamers."

"Let's send this rubble to the archives."

"How sick are you?" he asks.

His shoulders square off like his father's once. "Do you need anything from your room, Bayard? Your calculator or the chess set? Don't you want your lovely telescope?"

"How sick are you?" pulling the quilt down from my chin with a fatherly hand.

And I lie. After all the years, I lie convincingly. Did he

ever know me to be anything but in the pink, sturdy—go ahead and say it—fat and sassy? It is more a retreat that I've devised. The world is too much with me. "Bayard, don't laugh at me." I leap out of bed in a show of good health and off we go to the kitchen, where there's a little hen browned with its bonny legs trussed in, resting on the decreed bed of Lourdes' yellow rice, the ever present beans. I watch my son eat—one of the great pleasures—and with motherly perseverance find him a beer.

He cannot speak of his charge, his father in the old-clothes shop, a man who is wasting away, wasting his days, but there's an edge of masked anger at the both of us as Baby tells me that florigraphy, he scores that word, florigraphy was Victorian bullshit, quite appropriate to an arrogant age that revered science as its very own. I wonder if he has a girl—no time for games—how he looks at the women coming in the shop, measuring skirts against their hips. Studying breasts and waistlines to further identify the species, is he expert only as to cut and size.

"So the deluded quacks," he says, "classified ferns and flowers in a kind of prepsychology. Daffodils mean best regards. Petunias—don't despair. A lot of crap. Red carnations—my poor heart aches." He can't speak of Pinky. He tells me Grossman's father is getting him a used stove, good as new, a nice change from the hot plate. Grossman will need a white jacket for the prom. He tells me Canadian quarters work in an uptown stile at Union Square. Malone can get him a fake ID. I can't say that I am dying. It seems enough for a boy to go home (it's a hideout, a malignant basement shop) and do his calculus while begging his crazy father to shush about the popish tendencies of the General Theological Seminary, to shush about the demolition of the Astor Place Opera House, to shut up about Walt Whitman stalking New York Hospital and go to bed.

"The lovely telescope," he says, "is a toy."

"Very expensive."

"Nothing personal, Mother. Expensive—the rig I want to build will take near-infrared measurements of the intensity of light from variable stars, if you care to know what's expensive."

"Let me—come on, Bayard, just for once?"

"He cannot bear it anymore, taking money from you."

"To hell with what Pinky can bear. Tell him you found it in the pocket of an old mink coat. Don't laugh with your mouth full. And use the napkin next to your plate."

At the door in a formal chesterfield with velvet collar (golden oldie, indeed), his hair flopped, my lord, he's tall, superior thrust to his Protestant chin, he looks like a young man who is about to attend, unwillingly, all the debutante balls—like his father once. His cheeks, unshaven, are smooth as a girl's. Now you see it, now you don't—my valentine is palmed, the check that will buy my son the stars or the groceries. A kiss for his terrible mother, the fierce woman who does not even bear his name.

"You'll not be bothered down at the shop with my business. I'm thinking of going south. I'm leaving town." He doesn't trust me, but sees that it's practical to take my word, a necessary solution: his mother is somewhat demented this season, but on the whole larger than life, robust, so perfectly fine. After, after I hear the elevator doors close on him, I wish he would stay and build his real telescope, figure out my medical conundrums, talk man talk with the doctors, restrain Lourdes in papayas and beans. Sit by me with your busted carnations between us, their spiced fading . . . and listen, Baby. You may be the only adult I know. No. Give it up, Maggie, you want your kid to sleep in his own bed where he belongs, not this glorified young man to tuck you in and listen to the unraveling of your stories. . . . As bad as you make yourself out to be—oh, they are the true and annotated version, no lovely, lilting Scheherazade, but the unforgiveable truth about your mother, Bayard, and, God willing, she'll tell it to the end.

After the woman's story was out and had collected its first round of applause, Jack Flood came with no rights. He came as an intruder. In town for yet another medical convention, he set up our appointment by way of a cancellation. He could fit me in. I was by this time living in New York. In this place. He remarked upon the rooms, their ample furnishings, reluctant to see me in this grand setting. "Such nice chairs," he said, or tables, though chairs I would imagine, nice chairs, Margaret—as we sat down.

"Well, yes, if you bless a single iron cot and makeshift desk they multiply like loaves and fishes. They improve." It was after the divorce. Jack had by that time met the suitable wife, daughter of his chief of staff at Johns Hopkins. A girl who played tennis, sailed in Chesapeake Bay, who—not burdened with particular interests—had studied French in Switzerland. A girl who worshipped Daddy and would pass what she could of that on to Jack, my husband being both Dr. Success and to her an older man. It was after the divorce he came . . . indeed, he had married with some urgency. I had, at his request, stopped in El Paso on my way to California. The divorce was a travel agent's dream—flight, motel, spiv lawyer across the border in Juarez, three meals by a cheerless pool in the Fiesta Lounge. The package included young women like myself brought together in bitterness and agitation. I sat apart from them eating a safe omelet, projecting respectable sorrow, but I felt dutiful in this, my last accommodation to Johnny Flood. All their talk—these women dressed for the big day as though it was a bridge party—was what he said and she said, my mother said, then he said. In my dull aphasia, a neutral I'd shifted into as I sipped a margarita (warm, but on the house) . . . I could not recall the terms of the argument, what he said or I said.

By the time of the divorce I was going to California to be with Sol Negaly and rewrite my inept treatment of *Child's Play,* shamelessly discarding half a roundtrip ticket and the tearful ride back to New York with these disenfranchised women. Margaret Flood—I would keep the name—going to lie in the first king-size bed she'd ever seen, to share a joint rolled by Sol's houseboy, to smoke it down—then like a geisha I would slowly, formally reach for the gold roach clip and offer to that hairy, audacious, God help me, powerful man the last drag with my obedient hand. I was going to Los Angeles to learn the movieland patois of hard bargains and immediate pleasure with more purpose, I knew, than Jack Flood's betrothed ever had, reciting her schoolgirl French in Lausanne.

That was the divorce, and all I had to do was get out of Juarez and mail some papers to Dr. Flood, sealed and stamped. It was after that he came to me in New York. Yes, after my mother died and I had gone to the funeral with Sol Negaly, who wore that swaggering coat the color of heavy cream, shocking among my family in mourning, and his silver limo was gaudy driving out to the cemetery in the funeral cortege. I did that on the day they lowered my mother in the ground and I threw a rose on her coffin, its tight head landing with a soft thump, cinematic gesture—not our custom at all. That I came with Sol Negaly, my director, was pure bravado . . . and I presume even my aunts, my brothers especially, knew that he was my lover as though we lay before them in St. Michael's Cemetery debauched on the king-size bed. My father turned from me—it was the only time. Such disrespect, the sunglasses—Sol and me in shades on that gray New England day. Coming from our world, we . . . I could not look these good people in the eye. If they wanted a black sheep, well . . . my mother did not need their prayers when they had me. That was galling, but I was a clown, outrageous to upstage them, to protect myself from them, from their show of faith, by coming with Sol Negaly. To my mother's funeral, coming from my world. And Sol's Haitian chauffeur in his New York livery, standing well to the side of familiar faces, cops and firemen off duty—pallbearers and the man who drove the hearse for Hennessey. I'm sure I cried behind my glasses for I believe I loved my mother as well as pitied her—that was Maggie; but Sol, the white coat thrown over his shoulders Italian style, the chauffeur in brass buttons with more aplomb than old Hennessey with his fluttering embalmer's hands—that was pure Margaret Flood.

It was after that, Jack came to me from Hopkins and now that he was east again and had taken a well-bred lady for his wife, he wore tweed with decorative leather patches at the elbows, heavy English brogans, foulard, a vest. I remember a professorial pipe, a reaming and stuffing of that prop and Dr. Flood's solemnity, sucking but not smoking. My irreverence in recalling to him his California garb, wondering if he moved on to a Texas teaching hospital would he sport chaps, a ten-gallon hat.

"This is a serious business, Margaret."

"How's that?"

"That muckraking book of yours."

Sitting comfortably on the proceeds of *Child's Play,* I had not revised my critical opinion. My laurels were still fresh. I wanted to say it seemed a while back—he said and she said—that placed me in an odd kitchen cell in New Haven. Forgotten issues had set me to flush the anger from me with a brutal plot, to wash our dirty linen in public, but I couldn't get a word in edgewise. His scolding would not give way to discourse.

I had formulated, said Jack hissing air through the stem of his pipe, a ludicrous version of our marriage. Did I understand the humiliation brought upon him and those we lived among—trusted colleagues and dear friends—not to mention the dishonor visited upon the entire medical profession? "I have long sought this day, Margaret, and dreaded it." Lord, I would have dreaded it, too, if I had imagined Jack scowling at me and speaking his mind in such fusty prose. I once knew a skinny intern who read his favorite Latin poets, and listen, he'd say, to this verse he found just swell. Listen —this line of Petronius sounds like a hush, a whispering stream. Now he said colleagues and dear friends, those we lived among, etc. Those we lived among were not happy to find themselves mocked in my smutty book and so forth, getting to the point that I was pitiably inaccurate (fortunate for him), something of a laughingstock *re:* medical details. *Re:* he said bringing his brow low. Those eyebrows had remained a redhead's but his coarse-cropped hair was going early white. *Re:* medical details, I didn't know my tibia from toenail clippings. He thanked God for small favors. My ignorance was one of them. I had set out to destroy his professional life. What had I imagined—oh, he put it to me—when I scrawled a cockamamie story about cooking the evidence in his laboratory reports? Had I not known he would be investigated, every paper he'd ever written come under review (here a tweedy, self-effacing shrug), even his sound work on the vestigial artery, his breakthrough? Thanks to a vindictive woman, childish, irresponsible, he'd been denied one of his grants. A pause. Much spittle shaken from the pipe, strict rapping of its bowl.

"I am to blame then for innumerable heart attacks? Go, little book, you're as good as a seizure. Is that it, Jack? My story delayed your cure?"

"It's no laughing matter."

"No, indeed, if my cavorting stops the progress of medical science. I'm a menace to mankind."

"Margaret, I have been exonerated." Looking into the hollow of the pipe, he said: "It has been extremely painful to my wife."

It was then I threw the pillow, just a chintzy pillow, bounced it off his august head and he let fly the shreds of filthy tobacco that smelled like hell's apple pie and I threw my drink, for we were most certainly having the civilized drink, and I wet the foulard, ice cubes in the twill crotch. It was the fight we'd never had—exciting to us. Our voices squawked—bitch, bastard, prick—simple satisfying words new-minted in our innocent mouths. Whack, whack with the pillow and the French Line ashtray skimmed at me like a stone. No laughing matter . . . my mobcap awry, whack, and his stick thump, thump, hidden behind his Punchinello back. The domestic comedy that children love, that children love to see in a theater where it is not home, where they can squeal with delight at every slap, whack, thump. It is allowed in parks and playgrounds, a laughing matter after all. After all the years sucked up, sodden and decomposed, from the muddy river of forgetfulness . . . why had I not cherished this scene, kept the memory alive in story and song? Maggie Flood at the campfire or strumming my legend at the foot of a laird's throne. In those days we had large cigarette lighters, heavy as rocks, that must sit upon low tables. Lighters often, not always, functional, of silver or semiprecious stone. Mine was malachite and I raised it to defend myself. He said, "Tell me then that you did not kill my child." I was silent. "Tell me that you did not. Can you imagine what people think of me leaving you in that condition? Can you imagine?" I lowered my Ronson lighter, disarmed. I could imagine that I'd done him some mischief. I was silent. "Tell me, Margaret." But I would not answer. I would not tell the real story. My silence was loud and triumphant, as soothing as trumpet voluntaries. He left quietly, tucking his pipe apparatus away, girding himself in a British greatcoat, sourly swinging a Donegal cap. On his talented cutting hand Jack was wearing a gold wedding band, and he used to say to me what sort of sissy would wear a wedding ring, what sort of man.

Trusted colleagues and dear friends: it must be said that Jack Flood's final visit came after the book's success but before the release of the movie. On the screen *Child's Play (Playtime)* may have pleased him, if he saw it. The lives of those Healys are considerably softened: his amorous adventure is not actual infidelity, her prick of social concern acceptably blunted. Will Desdemona wake with a crick in her neck? Camille's lungs clear up? Salome attach the head? Does Rhett come back to Scarlett? All the questions we must not ask of good endings we can fairly ask of the unresolved, sentimental write-off, the tepid possibilities given at the end of the film to Tim and Jane.

It must be said—the Sol Negaly affair was over, a business deal in retrospect. But by the time Jack came to this apartment I'd met Pinkham Strong and without question he was in my mind like a distant radio that plays on with dance tunes. He was always present from the day I met him—oh, not here with the furniture, but in the breathing, walking, waking, sleeping subtext. A man I'd met, easy and strong, a straight arrow. The air between us was clear-mown pasture though not virgin land. It was after I'd met Pinky that Dr. Flood came to me to file his complaints and I don't know why I kept that lighter for by that time I'd given up smoking to please Pinkham Strong. As though it was all new we were holding off from each other. Pinky and Miss Margaret, we were genuinely courting. In less than a year I had our son, but I am confident, trusted colleagues and dear friends, though we had signed away our souls we had not bedded then.

The book was dedicated to Philo Pierce. It was after Flood naturally. Long before Pinkham Strong. The lady in transit, yet the woman's book is dedicated to a man. Impoverished: "To Philo Pierce with gratitude." Stiff as the complimentary close. True enough, gratitude for my published name. I had stayed with Philo Pierce, traded my private life for this public one. I could not dedicate the book "in awe." I stood in awe of the huge untidy man, one girl clapping at the end of his wise stories when I should have thought myself a woman grown. I sat in awe with the food and wine set before us and honestly did not know that table, that service played its part in a daily routine. Wise story. Wiser girls.

Philo Pierce had been somewhere I could never go. To war. Not a combatant or sideline medic, to the grand war in conference rooms. London and Paris: meetings of the gods, a sphere beyond top secret. I never asked how Pierce (with teeth and hair), a glorious sight in his colonel's uniform, stumbled into publishing, that sweet protectorate. He had been, it was only hinted at, in a Communist cell at Yale, later position meetings in Greenwich Village went on far into the night. I never asked how Pierce, so eloquent during the McCarthy years, marched in the front lines without a wound. He knew—I believe he led me to those people who closed me out—Max Gideon, Dorothy Schwartz, Hannah Brandt—old Lefties with their glory and their fame. A grand cotillion, gold rush, Waterloo—something had happened. Look in through the chicken wire, catch the glitz of all their emblems—forbidden to you, a little Catholic girl, as are the Knights of Pythias, Maccabees, Nobles of the Mystic Shrine. Look in, Miss Flood, that may be your vantage point, your favorite view. Listen, Margaret Mary, but you'll never understand. When had I listened to my father (there's the sad connection), my father still at it in his Mutual Insurance Agency, bland as processed cheese, neat widower in dark downtown suits. When had I listened with anything but restless sighs to his stories. Sure, he almost made the minor leagues and he sang, who'd care to believe it, at Poli's and the Lyric as the sun went down on vaudeville. *Sally's in my Alley. Kiss Me, Kiss Me Again.* And my mother, tell me—the dainty braided whip, the sidesaddle, show me her splintered crop, the brass tip gone—my mother rode in a musty divided skirt, a dented derby hat.

Look. Here I am with Philo Pierce in *Vogue.* I call that rapt attention. What can I be hearing? Perhaps in an overview he is explaining the onanistic implications of the Hula hoop, resuscitating the Hungarian revolution, still crying over the Supreme Court, after all that unfortunate fuss, telling us that the House Un-American Activities Committee was a three dollar bill in the first place. "The treachery of it, Margaret. You will never know such suffering." I did not ask, just listened, but there is much I didn't hear, swallowed with a gulp of bourbon, choked back with his catarrh.

Or is it Philo Pierce listening to me (I learned so fast), listening as I made reference to my thoughty article (worthy of Jane Healy), my consideration of bugs and blobs in the horror movies of the Fifties, that exposed our titillating fear of invasion. Asking—why did we need that? The shivers and shakes? Proclaim, Miss Know-It-All, don't listen. So sure that I answered with a question: Why call boo from the closet? For heaven's sake, when we were snug and warm?

Imagine: it cannot be known that Lourdes is in her tenement. A five-room, counting bath and eat-in kitchen. She takes the small room as her own and there she sets out her things, pulling out sweaters, warm stockings, slippers, gat-toothed combs from her shopping bag, discovering shattered water biscuits and a gibbous moon of yellow cheese that rocks on the dresser. Midnight. It is the end of her day. Express train. Shop. Home. Cook. Clean. Midnight. Every windowsill and cupboard clean. Manny's clothes, dropped in a slovenly trail when she comes in the door (his hands do not function to pick up socks and underwear) now all washed, hung to dry. Pepe's motor, a greasy skeleton disgorging bolts, gears, pins, she has gathered on a field of newspaper. In the small room with her bag—nail polish, a chiffon scarf flaked with gold, a large useful safety pin and what she's looking for—the silver butter knives. Outside, the gunshot and sirens of television. Manny and Pepe are finishing the box of German chocolates along with their beer. A red satin box, beautiful. She will keep it here. They are watching, as they do every night, the police running and shooting, police crouching. It is often slick and wet with flashing lights when she steps out in her nightie to say her *buenas noches.* They do not turn. They are watching. All winter she is glad the boys will be home, not in the street. She brings them beer. As soon as the weather turns they go down there, down on the block. That is where Manny is troubled by the woman, *hija de puta.* That is where Pepe stole the fat man's car. But it is cold, raining February and her boys are finishing the valentine with the last of the last six-pack of beer.

She breathes on the silver butter knives and shines them

on the tail of her blouse, a blouse of Missus Flood, soft velour. Soon, in her nightie, real silk of Missus Flood, so long she looks like a child in Mamma's clothes, in this fine dress-up, she steps out to say good night. The police are running under bright palmettos. Often when she steps out the police are under these trees or by a bush of flowers that remind her of home. "Gooo Ni-i-ide," she says in English, stretching the foreign vowels. They do not turn. She thinks it is Manny who says something though, something comes to her like a spring squeaking in the couch. In her small room again, she packs her bag—all but the silver knives. On the dresser she lights a candle, white paraffin poured in a red glass, votive light from the *botánica.* Its flame spits at the ceiling, then calms to a sputter. All else is dark. Flat Indian cheeks, square chin are picked out in scarlet flashes as though she is wearing paint or splashes of fresh blood. She takes off her wig and sets it on a faceless head, smoothing, petting the thick black pelt—always she must be kind. Her own head is sparsely tufted as a baby bird's, downy white with blue scalp patches.

Pepe: she puts out his picture. It is beautiful color taken at Gimbel's studio in his blue Easter suit to send home, a boy of fourteen then, and he is smiling, ay, smiling and his eyes are clear, eyes bright and quick as beetles then and she sets out the little silver spoons, coffee spoons that go with the little cups at Missus Flood she put for company in the living room. All around Pepe's head a fan of silver spoons. Manny: she sets out his picture. It is bigger, glossy black-and-white. His cap and gown. The shadow of a swinging tassel crosses his face. At Lincoln Center with high school diploma. Looking good. Looking at her borrowed camera. She had bought black-and-white, the wrong film. Manny—sullen, suffering the graduation shot. Shiny and handsome, going to City College for a while with books and papers in a pack, and looking at

Manny she forgets all the days he lay in bed and smoked or sat on the couch watching the police running or just went down there, down the block where that daughter of a whore got him. All around Manny in his cap and gown —it was maroon, you cannot see—she places soup spoons. They are important like her son with big round bowls that catch the flame. His head is round and large, she knows for brains. A painful birth. Help me, Jesus. And the spoons Missus Flood used three, four times when she made white soup for people who come. Missus Flood: she puts out her picture. It is creased and cut. She has picked it from the wastebasket. Missus Flood is looking good out of doors in a place with high brown grass. She is looking happy with sunglasses and easy clothes, all made up and hair nice and on her brown shoulder the hand of a man. It is Missus Flood who has cut off the man and she is just looking well, not with her lip curled or face squeezed, just well out of doors. Around Missus Flood she lays the butter knives. These go above the plate, down the table pat, pat, a straight line. The silver knives are so flat around the photo, they do not catch the light. Lourdes shudders, for this final halo has no body: it is unspirited as tin.

Praying then that Pepe will work in the auto supply full time, that he will not steal motors and lights—headlights, taillights under his bed—and that he will work at Exxon, his eyes clear, or just work at all. Thank you, Jesus. Praying that Manny would not go down there, down the block with that woman and the black, black child. Three years now, a jumpy kid, a monkey girl with dry wrinkled skin. It was not Manny's with a narrow head, dangling legs and arms so thin. Cross herself and kiss the spoon that Manny would come home with books. She would not touch his papers. That Manny would wear the jacket bought for college. Thank you, Jesus. He would not watch so late and lay all day heavy in his bed.

Then for Missus Flood, praying she will not die, praying

she would be nice again and wash, comb and dye her hair, talk on the phone, walk to the fancy kitchen and cook, crying over onions, slapping the beautiful roast like a baby in the palm of her hand. That she have people come again with candles and fruit, then Lourdes will bring back the silver. Thank you, Jesus. Praying Missus Flood will wear her lady clothes, rise from her bed. Cross herself and say, Baby you come back from where it is you go. Come back to the nice room dusted with all your toys. The candle guts out noiselessly, the wick drowned in a pool of paraffin. Smell of damp churches, of crypts, of playing in ancient ruins. Lourdes at her prayers is cold in the silk nightie. All is dark, but a light now enters through the curtain in her small room, one shaft of streetlight that glints off the silver, all but the butter knives. No, Jesus. Please, Jesus. She takes it as a sign.

I don't feel a thing, no tug or skip, not tired, not even tired. Confident that I won't pass on unshriven, I call for the car, leave a sizable check. Baby will pay my bills: that's not good of me. Imagine: I cannot know, Bayard Bidwell Strong dealing firmly with my accountant and the phone company. No time for soccer, paying Lourdes and running from the subway to the shop of rags he now calls home. Imagine Pinkham Strong, my husband, lost in the dedication of a cornerstone—New Trinity Church, Ascension Day, 1859, scorching an old dress shirt to hang on a rack with dead finery . . . or cheering as the first troops (Irish American) leave the city for the South. . . . "Let 'em bring their pavin' stones. We boys is sociable with pavin' stones." The bravery of it, while Pinky sips aged Scotch with never a mind who pays, sorting through Joan Crawford jackets and junk jewelry, washing out Depression dresses, poor housewives' dresses to be worn by feminist poets and cute Barnard girls . . . the nation mourns, so I imagine Pinky mourns Lincoln's death and notes the weepers, black bunting all down Broadway.

I pack the medical reports, the photos, canceled passports, books and scripts, indictments and lavish praise: the material of Margaret Flood. There's no system, no guide . . . through me the Way into the Woeful City and so forth, coherent if not consoling, a place all designated for Eternal Pain. I'm just going to my doctor. This time I'll pay him, not with silence. Would I have given up the book, my woman's book, to have him? An unfair question. Yes, the sunglasses and Sol, that was cruel about my mother's funeral, but I swear I never knew it at the time. I dress, then undress to wash, letting my arms and legs steep in a warm scented tub as though I have all the time in the world. Calm, not even tired, I eat a mess out of the refrigerator —gray meat, rice and beans. All that luggage by the elevator . . . he comes to mind. With all that luggage, it looks as though I'm sailing on the *Ile de France,* sailing with my summer dresses and high-heeled shoes. No appointment, but I'll find him in his office. Jack, I'll pay you with our story. Give me borrowed time, six months the way they do in bogus movies. Fair trade-off. Take it, Johnny. Take the rewrite—it's a true story, heartless and unkind.

DEADLINE

It's lovely to live on a raft. We had the sky, up there, all speckled with stars, and we used to lay on our backs and look up at them, and discuss about whether they was made, or only just happened; I judged it would take too long to *make* so many. Jim said the moon could a *laid* them; well, that looked kind of reasonable, so I didn't say nothing against it, because I've seen a frog lay most as many, so of course it could be done. We used to watch the stars that fell, too, and see them streak down. Jim allowed they'd got spoiled and was hove out of the nest.

—*Huckleberry Finn*

"YOU DIDN'T KNOW her." Moving into a spot of sun, the woman says, "You didn't know her." The light coming from behind is kind, an early blessing that smooths the bright cap of her hair, leaves her face in shadow. A girl perhaps, not a woman—in pleats that lie flat on her stomach and narrow hips; breast buds under a Fair Isle sweater. She repeats with satisfaction: "You really didn't know who she was."

"I knew." The man looks down at a circular which he tears in half, shuffles through a stack of mail until he comes upon a blue overseas airletter. "I felt I knew her, but not who she was." It's not the first time she has the story from him. There is that distance between them of father and daughter, that air of her waiting while he attends to business, of her eliciting what she already knows as a reassurance and of his patience in the comforting reply.

"But she knew you. Right away."

"The moment she set eyes on me."

"In the cafeteria . . ." This is meant to lead the story on, but suddenly two children appear cutting her words off with the quick smack of their book bags against the stair rail—two blond girls, identically, sensibly dressed. Now it is apparent we are in a hallway. The morning light seeps in from beveled glass panes set on either side of a heavy wooden door. Hall table, hall lamp, umbrella stand—all of this expensive and ordinary. Hall mirror aiming at Chippendale: colonial brass chandelier, its white frosted bulbs off at the switch. Carpet, doormat, wallpaper in a mindless quibble between assertive yellow and reluctant green. The girls are on the verge, thirteen and fifteen, Tweedledum sisters with little gold hoops in their ears and veils of golden hair to swish back from their healthy faces as they wait. Silent, presumptuous girls who look up at their father across the entrance hall, familiar terrain. They look up to him as their royalty privileged to pay their bills on the hall table, the large well-suited gentleman who protects them with his distinguished name.

The older of the two, an inch broader and taller, flips her hair—"You going away?"

"No, Princess. I'm cutting school today."

But her father, John Sarsfield Flood, does not explain further—why he is not at the hospital or in the laboratory or on his way to Houston or Minneapolis. The politics of his family life shifted long ago into solitary, uncomplicated positions. Separate, not equal. The girls are Dr. Flood's family, three modern graces, lean, muscular—socially and athletically astute. It's unusual for him to meet up with them in the morning before school or tennis and he cannot remember when—way back, the day he first watched them playing in the sunporch, their Ping-Pong volley ruined as he came into the room—an intruder. He has watched the three of them ride bicycles and horses, sail and swim. They are Jack Flood's girls.

The door swings open to a chilly winter sun. The long blond hair whips about. On the verge, the children's faces are like two creamy buds that will soon open. Their mother, who keeps her hair a matching gold, walks out into the light. She is brown, softly withered, elfin. The green glass of her eyes shines with unreflected contentment as she buttons her duffle coat and moves into the day with her schoolgirls, shopping lists, car keys, racquet.

"In the cafeteria," she says to herself in a rehearsal of the story she will tell during the morning to this friend or that—"Jack coming up with his tray in the public cafeteria, avoiding the staff room, and he really did not know who the woman was."

He sits on the hall chair, a chair he has not noticed, padded in birds pecking pineapples. One of her accommodations so that the older girl, who is popular, can take long adolescent phone calls downstairs on her line. Some years ago he was in the house alone before he joined them in Bermuda. In her playskirt his wife was at least taller, their mother by a head, her hair as God made it, dead-level brown. He had been alone in the house, before he could get away—that was his line always. Office, lab—how could he abandon the team of men and women awaiting him at dawn, masked, turbaned like an ancient sect. By their eyes he knew them. Or turn from the subject waiting on the table, bubbling and bleeping humankind. Induced to sleep, his patients did not dream, yet he often wondered, unmedically, if the last stray fear cut off by the quick caress of anesthesia—stopped dead while he clipped and trimmed around the injured heart—might resume. If, spliced and primed, building to a healthy beat, unmonitored—the same old fear clicked on.

It was that one time alone in the house that set him

against anything like solitude on Shady Lane. The first time alone as he remembered it, though that could not be accurate. A Sunday night, awaiting the week's operations, Dr. Flood thought of them, his girls browning in the sun, floating in the clearest blue water, paradise provided. Swirling a snifter of brandy, he had entered the empty living room where he took up a book, Ovid—the *Metamorphoses.* It was a resolve sorely neglected—to go back to his Latin which had been such a satisfying game. *"I propose—I intend—to speak or tell of bodies transformed to figures—"* he took a wild guess and pushed on—*"of bodies transformed into shapes of different kind."*

He had settled into the biggest chair. Papa chair not much in use, upright and toughly pebbled as a daisy's center, that color too, but the walls a soft creamery butter, the reflection of buttercups under the chin, the couch strewn with leaves, full summer green. Dr. Flood rose, the *Metamorphoses* dropping on the smooth turf of carpet, and strode directly to the windows pulling the drapes against the winter night—canaries in golden cages slept or sang among garlands of lumpy green pears and pale grapes. Defeated by the early evidence, he stole through the rooms of his wife's freshly sodded house, a bewildered man in a tartan bathrobe and stiff Christmas slippers in which he had never relaxed. All was glade and sunshine, Edenlike. The dining room mossy, kitchen in limey bloom, lemon pots, herbaceous tea towels.

He pitied her narrow spectrum, this woman he had married, infatuated with her confident social manner and small accomplishments of French and tennis and with her name, Ginger. Now Ginger Flood. When she was no more than a schoolgirl herself, he had taken her from her father's house, a doctor's house where she had been set in motion to become his wife. Thinking he had wiped the slate clean of his first marriage to a woman who had scored his soul with her energy and an unrelenting love, he had admired his Ginger for her simplicity that lay so close to the surface under a country club gloss. Uncritical of his late hours and what had been his large ambition, she tended to him nicely, but managed always to suit herself. A privileged only child, Ginger withdrew comfortably to her pursuits—the little blond girls, the best of houses in Roland Park, her winter vacations and the shingled summer place at St. Michael's near her family's on the Eastern Shore. Marla, Pearl, now Fay—black women got off the bus at the corner and hiked up the hill, came in through the back door to help her. She had never asked him for anything extravagant, just her continuing life. Ginger, the name was no longer piquant, and he knew that in her steady self-absorption she would never change.

She is terribly decent: she is sweet: he held to that idea for dear life as he stooped into the powder room Ginger had caused to be built under the stairs. His head bent to the slope where the wallpaper entangled him in fronds and broad-leaf tropical plants. A rain forest. The stream of his urine struck angrily against the side of the green toilet. Toppling the wastebasket embossed with an undergrowth of fern, he washed his hands and threw the yellow soap back onto its lily pad—a bespeckled frog balanced coyly on the rim. Hands reeking of yellow scent, he rubbed them down his sides rather than sully her guest towels—bobbing daffodils.

He could find no way in which he had been so negligent or cruel to his wife that it warranted his humiliation with the ridiculous flora and fauna of this house. Perhaps his colleagues found him pitiable. Did the neighbors laugh after the Christmas drink? It came to his mind clear and large as a slide projected in the lecture hall—her Christmas tree bearing ripe pears, golden apples, and he did not imagine gilded bananas—no. Was he a discernable fool to his students who came for beer and Ginger's mild chili? Or had they joined him in not seeing? And suddenly the generosity of his friends overwhelmed him. It was such a small thing, really, gold and green—a surface irritation or a visual folly. So far as he knew, no one considered his wife a sorry case.

His Ginger wanting her house to flower and grow, it indicated, clearly, a slight derangement, a harmless, even endearing, aberration. Still, something might be done—a gentle remedy sought, short of psychiatric. Dr. Flood dared not think of the rooms above where he slept and showered and considerately made love to his wife, where he said good night to the girls who lay in their separate bowers. Of Ginger's bed of yellow roses and daisy bath, he could not think, nor of his own verdant room—late calls and early surgery had decreed the affectionate end of a strict marriage bed. Merely daffy, she was not mad: he had been color-blind, and was, at that moment, a doctor without a prescription. The brandy went directly to his head. He set it aside, closing his eyes to the welcome rosy sting on his retina, thinking in layman's terms that something must be done.

After a three-hour bypass in the morning, Jack Flood canceled his teaching rounds and drove to a furniture store he'd seen a thousand times on his route to the hospital. A pretty warehouse of a place, pillars and cornices affixed, inside soft music playing. A young man in a three-piece suit trailed him through half-rooms with false windows and doors, elaborate mantels, the flicker of cold logs glowing. He was shocked to see that a blue sofa cost twelve hundred dollars and the price of a velvet wing chair was slashed to four ninety-five. Dr. Flood did not find what he wanted. He looked up at a beige wall unit, a vast arrangement of trick panels and doors that hovered above him oppressively and at a number of plummy, purple cubes that hugged low to the floor. The clerk asked his color scheme. He made no reply, then he spotted the red chair, its surface tight and glistening, the bright color of oxygenated blood in the aorta. The young man jerked the chair into its three positions of coercive relaxation and said, contemptuously: "It's our most popular line."

Dr. Flood took out his checkbook. He did not try the tough red vinyl seat or read the tag exhorting the virtues of the Strato-Lounge. The clerk said: "I wouldn't mix it with colonial."

That very evening the chair was delivered. Bulbous and imposing, it sat in Ginger's living room like a swollen berry, taut as a blood blister. Or a positive stain. To Jack Flood the red chair was a reasonable choice, not a retaliation but the beginning of a sly cure he would effect, dose by clever dose. Each night that week he slid onto the seat of the lounge, alert, head propped to read as though his own body must lend itself to this experiment in color modification. His book, his chair, his attention to Ginger's problem ended a long established affair with the head nurse in pediatrics. Ovid was tough going, twenty years since he had considered himself a Latinist in New Haven and he took up a translation quite readily to help him along: *"There was no sun in those days to provide the world with light, no crescent moon ever filling out her horns: the earth was not poised in the enveloping air, balanced there by its own weight. . . ."* And the doctor felt it was a pleasure to read of the universe beginning and some of the old tales of gods turned to trees, to bears, to stone; that he was himself quite different, sprung back in the red chair, weighting it with his presence, his authority—husband and father come home to the duties of family life.

But when he saw them in Bermuda, three happy girls pedaling toward him, their golden knees and shoulders in the island sun—yes, like candied ginger—he was filled with shame. In the hotel his wife laid out the sweaters and kilts she had bought for herself at the duty-free shops and he could do nothing against her happiness. All these fine woolen clothes were in the fated shades, the color of real money, green and gold, which she had never earned. Not a dollar in her life. It was the first time he had thought of this and he felt strangely responsible as though she were his child and he had passed a flaw into the genetic structure of his kin. Awaiting his approval, she held a bottle-green sweater to her breast.

He said: "I ordered a chair for my office and by mistake they delivered it to the house."

"How stupid," Ginger said. "What sort of chair?"

"For my patients," Jack Flood said. "It's an ugly therapeutic device."

Since his failure with the red chair he had avoided being alone in the house. Each winter when his girls went off to restore themselves in the sun, he found a warm bed to share in one or another woman's apartment—an arrangement which could be resumed in the summer when his family moved down to the shore. He was the best man at Johns Hopkins with medical Latin, but he put aside his Ovid and never found time to open it again.

An exception in every way, this morning when we find the doctor loitering in the front hall, studying the postmark on his airmail letter. The characters are Chinese and, as always, meaningless to him, yet he fancies they are differently arranged this time, the string of them longer. He admires the stamp—happy worker with a sheaf of wheat—fine engraving. The letter from China this morning is a gift of the gods. He is avoiding the hospital and the work he claims to love. Avoiding Margaret Flood.

Yes, he had known her. In the cafeteria a woman had turned to him—a sick woman with a white patch on her head, pale cheeks, inflamed eyes. He had known she was extremely important to him before he had known she was Margaret.

She said: "You were always one for rice pudding."

He had looked at his tray—guilty, unbelieving. In the hospital he ate pudding and pie, a slice of chocolate cake. Ginger, to give her credit, did not hold with desserts.

But it was Maggie, in gray sack and shawl. Like an ancient druid she had come for him. He had always known she was not finished with him yet. In a quick maneuver with a twenty-dollar bill she paid for his tea and pudding, then conducted him to a nest she had made of papers and bags. Full of an invalid's false energy. He had seen it often —an urgency about dying. Hallucinatory, she launched a series of lunatic orders having to do with a baby and her car which had broken down on the Beltway, then proceeded to deliver a rundown on her disease—cardiomegaly—which sounded to Jack Flood as though she had translated the diagnosis to palmistry or divination. Without a stethoscope he could sense the disorderly heart, off beat, jazzy as a drummer's riff. Extensive damage. In a remarkably controlled and charming appeal, she begged him to oversee her end.

Maggie, the russet dye grown out to her temples, she might be wearing the white veil of a Catholic schoolgirl. Mocking, irreverent still. "Dr. Deluge," she said, "don't you look fine. Better than yourself on television. To think you are settled all this while on the Bay, Jack, like an old blue oyster."

It was the crabs were blue in Chesapeake Bay. He did not correct her. She was the unhealthy color of a sad mollusk, gray-white and puffy her moonface. If he had pressed his finger to her wide zygomata, the dent of it would live on in her cheek. Mechanical edema. The public room was sharp with ammonia, being mopped for the evening meal and here she was, tasting his pudding— "Needs cinnamon," she said—licking his spoon, beshawled and fringed, a sorceress in the bag of gray wool he could see was something splendid, a thousand dollars of sackcloth and ashes. A slight thread of violet ran through the material matching the bruised flesh under her eyes. He had known he must see her photograph in bookshops, her name in print, but he had never figured how she would appear to him live.

She said: "So—you tell me how long I have, then grant me a bit longer. I'll make it worth your while."

He began to speak in his lecturer's voice, "A doctor does not. Only under extreme circumstances . . ." but the subject matter was charged with her unethical presence, ". . . in the examination of a patient he feels and listens to the body."

"Does he?"

"Despite the machines," Jack said.

"Then it's still a laying on of hands?"

"Ah, for Christ sake, Margaret, I can't treat you. You're family."

She laughed, a wild hoot. The attendants and lingering visitors turned to them, to the corner where she'd set up camp, imperial with her papers and distinguished shopping bags, a mink coat fanned on the linoleum floor.

"I couldn't touch you," he said, taking her wasted hand to his starched white coat in a plea for reason. Then softly, as a faltering joke, "Certainly not charge you."

"I am very badly off," she said. "Money is no object." She rose. They looked an operatic pair. Her hand clasped to his chest. The white-haired lover beseeching the gray-robed lady who spoke loudly, "Cross." No, it was not cross alone—cross-purposes. "We are still at cross-purposes." He remembered Margaret's strong familiar voice and exactly what she said to him before she fell in a swoon to the cafeteria floor.

Well, she had checked herself into the hospital, smart woman. She was stabilized—he was in the thick of it.

"*That* Margaret Flood?" an intern in CCU had asked him.

"Yes, she was my wife."

His early marriage had never been a secret, yet Ginger was visibly upset: "I hope this will be kept from the girls." As though he had betrayed her with a sick woman. Yes, it might be an item in the Baltimore papers—she was Margaret Flood. And Ginger shook her little head as though she could not understand what had come upon them in her flowering home—some blight. He noted that a nervous twitch, quite uncontrollable, passed over her face at such unpleasantness.

It was then he said: "At first I didn't know her," which quieted Ginger and made him feel rotten, like Peter in the courtyard, denying Christ. But it was only Margaret's name he lied about. When the woman turned to him over the rice pudding, he sensed they were one flesh. Jack Flood had not looked at the medical records she dragged about with her. Willful, eccentric—she knew there was perfectly good medicine in New York. This morning they would do a workup: perhaps it was not hopeful. He must get to the hospital and find the best man to attend her. His wife. His impossible wife.

Jack Flood's attachment to Margaret is still in effect, the scattered particles of his emotion now within range of her draw. So he dawdles, alone in a big suburban house, shuffling the bills. He does not put his doctor's beeper in his pocket or the plastic card that admits him to the reserved parking lot at the hospital. Instead he takes his airmail letter and tucks it safely inside his suit jacket where he keeps his passport when he travels to conferences in Zurich and Milan. The crinkle of the paper whispers over his heart as he makes ready. Staring straight into a botanical print (yellow loosestrife), he massages his breast pocket, listening to his letter from China. It is a talisman or lucky charm to get him through the day.

In the spring of 1970, he had received his first letter from Yin-Li. It was full of praise for an article Jack had published years ago, outdated medicine read as precious contraband. Addressed to John Sarsfield Flood, smuggled out of China, somehow the letter arrived at Ballymore, Sadi Lane. The postmark was Hong Kong. Yin-Li was a urologist, his English flawed only by his prepositions. Since 1949 he had been allowed to work in the laundry of a farm cooperative, but an arthritic condition prevented him from carrying the heavy caldrons of hot water and he was now fortunate to be "at a southerly province" where he "kept after the books" of a bicycle factory.

Reading the letter, Jack had felt the specific cruelty of the Chinese doctor's fate. Felt is operative: he'd been on to Stalinist terrors, gulags, camps; ranked Hungary, Czechoslovakia, Poland as tragedies; signed petitions at the University against our use of napalm; but he placed that world of public terrors at a distance, as far away as blown-off limbs and faces he'd seen as a kid in the Medical Corps. He deplored the radical Catholic element—much of it initiating in a scrubby back street of Baltimore, and as a professor of surgery let it be known that the childish despoiling of draft cards with pig's blood, slaughterhouse shock, had no bearing on human suffering and would not end our humiliation in Vietnam. One night, watching the Democratic Convention in 1968, he had been mortified to catch sight of his former wife screaming slogans like a banshee, a dead weight dragged across police lines in Chicago. Mortified but silent. Though he knew Margaret's position to be fully justified, certainly no crime, he could not buy her rage and sorrow as a dissident living in a state of siege. It was Yin-Li's happy letter, a little parable of grateful acceptance under tyranny, finding him out so mysteriously in Ballymore that at last brought such intolerable matters home.

The Chinese doctor, now bookkeeper, had no complaints. Having showered Dr. Flood with praise, he told his own story modestly and ended with a rhapsodic evocation of the Big Ten. Yin-Li was a graduate of the University of Minnesota and he had loved our football, traveled freely to Ann Arbor, Michigan and Bloomington, Indiana, once to South Bend to see Minnesota at Notre Dame. The Golden Gophers had licked the Fighting Irish "at a field goal in downpouring rain." Jack figured it was in the Thirties, when football was still unprofessional, a heroic college game. It sounded like the play of emperors in the letter from China, a memory unfolded with reverence—warm lap robes, colorful pennants, and a heartfelt allegiance almost beyond recall.

And so John Sarsfield Flood treasured Yin-Li's letters, kept them in his office under lock and key as testimony to his feelings. Reading them over he did feel a shame for all recent history as though history was an imposing public statue defaced with a mustache and witless obscene words, and that feeling gave way to a more general melancholy about the short span of years since an educated foreigner could cheer his team in a midwestern stadium without finding us foolish or himself shallow: the quick roll of time had reduced the Chinese doctor to an outcast sending a note in a bottle to a stranger just to say here I am. I am here. I am here.

It came down to a personal view: Jack Flood imagined himself stirring vats of workers' clothes in a scalding solution of animal fat and lye, or seated on a high stool recording Communist sprockets and handlebars for hordes of bicycles riding, riding in unison around a monstrous square under the benevolent porcine smile of Chairman Mao. He imagined twenty years of forgetting the mechanics and chemistry of the body and whatever one knew of modern medical techniques: twenty years without his professional accomplishments and, yes, the honors which defined his name. But in fact, the deprivations of Yin-Li's life were not conceivable to him and Jack Flood was sorry, as a good doctor and a decent sort, that in this matter of political tyranny his feelings had finally been triggered only by reference to himself.

There was no return address on the first letter from China, nor on the half dozen that followed sent through from Bangkok and Taiwan, until 1972 when Richard Nixon and his wife went to eat bird's-nest soup and admire the Great Wall. The rapprochement of great nations exonerated Yin-Li, shipped him back to his native Peking. At the age of sixty he ministered to the common ailments of children and was placed in the household of a minor bureaucrat, his only surviving son. Then Dr. Flood did write to his friend with news of urology and enclosed clippings from the sports page of the Cornhuskers and the Irish trounced by the mighty Golden Gophers. He thought it was not safe to ask the Chinese doctor why he wrote to Sadi Lane or by what route he came by "Sarsfield," his peculiar and unused middle name.

Yin-Li was weary and arthritic, but he wrote of his declining health with such dignity that his letters seemed full of good cheer. Jack talked of going to China. A few American doctors were invited on our first cultural missions and he looked into that, but when the offer came he turned it down saying he had just picked up major funding from the Heart, Lung and Blood Institute. He could not think of his trip to visit Yin-Li as a professional jaunt. Several of Ginger's friends who pursued expensive tours had been to China and it surprised him when his wife said that if she could take the girls to Hawaii first, she'd travel on with him if he must visit a rusty doctor he never even met on the far side of the world. Jack Flood wanted Yin-Li above all men to respect him apart from the medical honors—and going to Peking with Ginger, roasted in Maui, trussed in the inevitable gold and green purchases from the South Sea Isles, would never do. Now he wanders through the queer chromatics of her indoor garden, avoiding a difficult patient at the hospital.

Avoiding Margaret, that's the truth of it, and her assault upon his feelings. He never thought to see her, to see her growing old and ill. She had come for him and bought him tasteless pudding. Hell, he knew her. Now she is hooked up in CCU. His poor defiant Margaret who always had a sure hand with the cinnamon. Jack Flood leaves the house without a hat or overcoat, his white hair puffs crazily in the wind. Let's think of him now, our eminent heart surgeon, as befuddled Job. After he has faced the music, he plans to read whatever the Chinese doctor says about the daily miracle of inoculations at the children's clinic, the fine mattress he sleeps on at his son's, and the old man—for Yin-Li is old beyond his years—will thank him most graciously for the latest paper he has sent "upon" a laser beam that can zap a kidney stone like a magic wand. When he reaches the hospital Margaret is sedated so that as he smooths the mottled hair back from her temples, holds her cold hand, examining the white welted scar on a distorted finger, it seems to the attending nurse that Dr. Flood is only finding a weak pulse. That he resumes his professional stance.

A hospital room is a gray area planned for recovery or death, wired for entertainment or life-sustaining gear, a room for transients who use it during the long hours of healing or dying, either way facing their mortality. Margaret Flood doesn't know whether she's coming or going. Having written flamboyantly of her approaching death, she entered the hospital in a drama and lives on quietly, a peaceful day-by-day existence, subjecting her body to further tests. Deep breathing and coughing to prepare her lungs for open heart surgery, she sits on the side of her high bed, feet dangling in woolly pink slippers. Scrubbed plain, she chooses to wear a hospital gown and the loose cotton kimono that is issued to men or women who do not bring their own bathrobes from home. Her radio plays homogenized show tunes in which no instrument can be distinguished—soft, dithery music of the sort not really heard in hotel lobbies. And Margaret smiles.

"She's not a difficult patient." Bayard says this with some surprise. He stands in the doorway with Dr. Flood who has just come by.

Jack says: "She's a darling. She sleeps like a baby, flatters the nurse."

"Don't talk about me."

"You have been so good, Mother."

"I've not gone simple, Bayard." But she has. In many ways Margaret has changed since the day in mid-February when she expired on the cafeteria floor. She obeys her doctor, a serious young man who has served in the Peace Corps, listening to his every word, asking him only for further information—what material will he use to tie off the arteries he severs, does he graft or patch, how long will he poke around at the cooled heart cut off from the life of her body? He's the doctor Jack has chosen, a talented surgeon with no bedside manner, just finished his training. Ingenuous, the way in which he says straight out that he is Dr. Flood's protégé. His name is Newman and he looks it with only the vestiges of his past about him, one pierced ear like a handsome sailor and longish hair. By way of consolation he tells her of the incurables he came across in West Africa: babies with rackety little rib cages—too apathetic to hold out a hand for a proffered toy; as though modern medicine never was—river blindness, dengue fever, actual elephantiasis and leprosy lingering in the bush.

Margaret knows that Dr. Newman means to please her with his stories: so much human suffering must make her glad that she's a good risk. As for the idealistic young man playing at Dr. Schweitzer, he could not wait to come back to the civilized world and turn his attention to heart disease. So much has been accomplished in the field and he had failed with ignorance and despair. An early age to take measure of yourself, but Margaret sees that at thirty-five or six he believes he has chosen the profitable course. She listens to all Dr. Newman says with a childlike trust. He allows her to sit up for hours with her feeding tray adjusted so that it forms a useful desk. As long as she is not excited. Not in the least, says Margaret, if you can believe her, and writes—she will never say what, though the nurses ask repeatedly. They are all for a hot love story or for murder, incest and with what they have seen in the hospital full of good tips. They never guess as they deal out her medication, tuck her into bed, how patient she is, listening amiably when one of them says: "Honest, Mrs. Flood, if you want to write my story . . ." or, "My husband—there's a character!" Margaret doesn't say their stories are of no use, she has enough material to last the rest of her days.

Not allowed a typewriter—she cherishes this and other limitations—lights out, coughing and breathing exercises, bland food, slow stimulating walks. She writes in a blank book her son buys for her, letting her sentences slant up and down the pages until she trains herself to a neat and legible flow of words. Often she's tired and, like her mother in the old days, gives in to little naps.

Dr. Newman (in daily consultation with Jack Flood) detects further deterioration to the heart valve and continues to tell her his horror stories of Africa while the night nurse says, "You wouldn't believe my father. You could put him in your book." Bayard comes on a Trailways bus still in his school clothes. She will see no one else. His rumpled trousers and soiled shirts trouble her. The lining of his blazer is ripped and she begs round the corridor for needle and thread.

It was only after Baby came the first weekend that she asked for the tranquilizer along with her last round of pills. At all other times she sleeps through long dreamless nights, but her son lingers as an after-image. She sees him still, flopped in the visitor's chair doing his homework, mumbling, laughing at intervals. He always talked to himself as a child, chattering along, not in any way nutty or disturbed. Pinky said it was to be expected: Bayard liked to speak to the smartest person in the room. Now, it seems to Margaret a lonely discourse like watching a boy feint and dodge in an empty playground and kick his triumphant goal all by himself.

He came when she first fell at Jack Flood's feet and arrives every weekend. She's delighted when he pushes in the door of her room and unslings his knapsack, though she tries to assume her old discourteous voice. "Stay home," she tells him and again when it is time for his bus, "You hear me now, stay home."

Home gives a tilt to her new equilibrium—her son who lives in that dank basement with clothes from dead times and Pinkham, in a mist of Johnnie Walker, making out his file cards on the founding members of the Century Club. Home—her empty and elegant spaces with Lourdes coming in to air, wash and dust. A sorrowful and distant place; with her loss of energy there is nothing she can effect there. Once she laughed so uproariously at news of home that she gasped and sputtered. A nurse ran in to apply the oxygen mask. She was still laughing or floating when revived: Lourdes, yes Lourdes, tends to Pinky down at Golden Oldies while Baby sits by his mother's bed.

Bayard was offended: "Well, she's on the payroll. It seemed sensible to me."

"Sensible," his mother whispered, "it's inspired." She lay back on her pillows exhausted. "I wonder how he'll like fried bananas with his rice and beans?"

Events are dealing themselves out. Margaret seems to herself a docile spectator taking up her blank book which she has nearly filled, page after page, though her story is not complete. When Dr. Newman schedules her operation it will put an end to her work, then she'll write "to be continued" and pick it up again, another day. In the Atlas Garage, her car waits for a flywheel—a new part for an old body, the damndest thing. Oh, that even got to Charlie Newman and he comes by to check her ignition or her carburetor in his humorless way.

One morning soon after her dramatic arrival at the hospital, Jack came into her room. The light of a gray winter dawn joined the pale gray walls. He was on his way to surgery and would not take the parcel she held out to him, so she set up an appointment in which Dr. Flood was officially summoned to her room. With Bayard standing witness, she delivered a small speech. "These papers are yours," she said to Jack, but no matter how clearly she explained he would not understand that the parcel did not hold a will and testament, documents entrusted to him in the eventuality . . .

"Now, Mother," Bayard said.

"I don't intend to die. Not yet."

Jack told her again she was a good prospect and a fighter. At that moment she was tired, not scrappy. "None of your back talk"—she closed her eyes—"just read what's there, Johnny." And she entered a shallow sleep that sent them away. It's out of her hands—she had bargained for time: it was granted but it is only time out. The clock is set to run again, to run against her when she's mended. Though she feels she will never be the same or herself fully, she can't regret it. An extraordinary serenity has come upon her, even now before they cut her chest and patch her heart. Out of her hands, attended by technicians, wheeled to other clean gray rooms—she is a likely subject. Her motor chugging along, ho-ho, for Dr. Newman who has discovered her resilience, the plucky shafts and pistons of her working parts.

So it doesn't matter to her, now or later—when Jack Flood reads the final version of their story. Back in New

York, she had worked with a frenzy to set the record straight, as though she were ripping out the seams of her life. Now she has a sense of time meted out decorously, choices decreasing—what matter the costume as the curtain falls. A pull to essentials, the tug of old values, a shortening of lines. She is transformed: made to live the good life for a few weeks, she's a different animal. Delicate, but easy now as a young woman who might have nothing to do but sit on the front porch and move languidly from hammock to rail to rocking chair. In white. In her long white hospital robe with her blank book held to her breast like a girl's diary. With proper sleep and medication her skin has tightened, returning the high cheekbones to her face. All the diets of the past—vats of yogurt, crates of grapefruit, tricks played on her body with erratic denial—never reduced her to the lean creature who graces the hospital corridor. That is Mrs. Flood who steps so lightly in and out of the ward distributing flowers that arrive for her most every day, who strolls to the chilly solarium making it seem a sunny piazza, passing out, with a shy smile, some of her containment.

There's nothing she wants, living under benign supervision. Her only request a haircut, and that she entrusts to a pretty chubette, a volunteer who comes round with a trolley of magazines and gift-shop trinkets. The girl has a head of glorious black hair that she twists and turns into a baroque crown to counter her matronly bosom and waddling behind. Her lashes and brows are glossy with makeup, her lids emerald, her mouth drawn with fine brushwork. She confesses, with a natural blush, that she wants to be a beautician after high school. Margaret says: "Then cut my hair." The damaged locks, wilted and dried, fall to the floor like dead brown petals. The fat girl, not Margaret, cries.

"No one will punish you," Margaret says. She takes up a hand mirror to show that she's pleased. Shorn close as a novice or a prisoner: spare and unworldly, the haircut gives her past the lie. The hair that had shown white against the red-brown dye is steely, a good gray, but the fat girl continues to weep as though she has mutilated Mrs. Flood and will not stop until Margaret agrees to buy a pair of cheap earrings and a pot of sticky rouge from her trolley to restore her womanhood. She knows the girl cries for her own confusions, the battle staged between her large unattractive body and her sweet come-on face. Jack and Bayard take to the haircut. Her son, gallant for his age, says she's far out.

On the day of the haircut, Margaret allows herself one indulgence—in her blank book she writes:

Today I have cut my hair and I am forty-six years old. My son is in New York and I am glad he has forgotten my birthday. Jack has not come. I am in for repairs. As it turns out my disease is ordinary, just peculiar to my gender, so that I am not a true curiosity when the teaching doctors do their rounds with a flock of students eager for some novelty. The reformed exhibitionist, not even an exhibit. In the beginning I begged Newman for a heart transplant, but I'm ordinary. He did not take me seriously. I said, I want a miracle. He said they were not yet safe. Some are—not walking on water, but multiplying loaves and fishes. Only imagine: the excitement of waiting for someone else to die, a cliffhanger, not this rest-home preparation. A stranger would die, auto accident or suicide, man or woman, good or bad, but with a healthy heart—type A. The iced heart flown to Baltimore, met at the airport like a dignitary. The clock running. Others in line with needier bodies, worthier lives, but I am chosen. The hollow body in the operating theater is mine. The moment of death technically defied. Organ affixed. A dream interlude—I am a mythic beast, griffin or gargoyle—screwy evolution. No, I rise again as man or woman, doctor, lawyer, heathen chief or just myself with that most sentient organ of a stranger, falling in love with scoundrels, hand over thrilled new heart I salute the flag. But that has the makings of a story and in the time allotted only the necessary stories are allowed. I have cut my hair and look like a sinner. A hundred years ago it would have been disfiguring. Bayard's wrong, today it is not even bold.

And having written she crosses out all but the first line which marks her birthday.

Only Dr. Newman is flustered by Margaret as a mendicant, beginning a flirtation with her from that day. "What have they done to you?" His awkward instincts tell him she's kind of sexy with her cropped gray head. He looks long at Margaret's chart, then says, "Blood pressure good, Mrs. Flood. You're a wow."

Bayard sits on a broken stool in the Atlas Garage reading *Scientific American*. He feels funny with the mechanics working away in their greasy parkas. They bend with dirty rags into the body of cars and call to each other for tools. Two kids who look about to burst lift something up into the body of a station wagon, straining and grunting. He never felt funny on the subway reading about quasars or auroras next to people in their *Daily News* bubbles. He never minds going up front in the shop with his schoolwork when girls come in to pick through the dresses or that they laugh at him stuck in his books, but he feels like a creep in the Atlas Garage reading about the Crab Nebula, its glowing orange filaments caught in a white cloud of electrons—and like a total nerd in his gentleman's coat with the velvet collar. Chances are, the broken stool will shatter, dumping him into the black puddle with its rainbow of oil. Bayard rises and drifts back and forth on a shore of grime. Fan belts and hubcaps and something that looks like one of his mother's mousse tins hang on the garage wall. So does the picture of a redhead with her ass in the air. "The March wind doth blow!" Has blown her scant clothing to reveal a bare bottom, legs spread, a rosy orifice. Her head twists round like a dog about to nip its tail. She wears a white lacy garter with shamrocks. Bayard's mother is Irish and goes on about it, incorporating phrases from the old country she has never seen, assuming a lilt she is not entitled to. He no longer blames her, but he has always disliked her very good ear. The Irish lass winks at him from her calendar and he fancies the young mechanics laugh in his direction.

Bayard Strong could address every man in the Atlas Garage on the history and principle of the combustion engine, but he cannot drive a car. Today his mother's Corvette is finished. He has arrived with a cashier's check from her bank in New York—eight hundred and forty dollars. A nice old guy, the boss, said, "You can take her out anytime."

Bayard stood with the keys dangling, "I don't have a license."

"I mean just to move her"—the old guy pointed out to the parking area—"until your father comes."

Bayard cannot drive: he waits for Dr. Flood, who is not his father. One by one the men come and stand by the vintage convertible, swiping the big fenders with a cloth, touching the chrome trim, paying their respects. "Some baby," a black man says and though he smiles at Bayard, the boy feels mockery in his remark. They all know he can't drive and that he's showing off with *Scientific American.* He is wearing pale chamois gloves which he sticks in the pockets of his dress coat. Though it is cold, he will not sit in his mother's car.

He hates the big red Corvette that is older than he is by a year. "The quintessential American car—" he can hear her say that. The way she speaks, making every observation a pronouncement, grand story to follow: The day she bought the Corvette with big bucks from a script or contract. Marching into a showroom out in Queens with his father. She had just met Pinkham Strong—in love, then falling in love with the car. Bayard has never been to Queens, except to airports. The mechanics cannot keep their eyes off the convertible and the black man opens the door to fiddle with a knob on the dashboard. From where Bayard stands he can see the man stroking the seat one last time.

He remembers sleeping on the back seat when he was a kid—the leather smell and the slippery sweat along the back of his bare legs, driving with his parents up to the house in Vermont, his mother at the wheel, waking to the sound of their hushed, hard voices . . . the silence, then, very low, the radio turned on. The canvas roof like a tent clamped over them.

The boss comes over, a long thin man with a heavy belly slung on his middle and big hornrim glasses that give him a scholarly air. "The doctor called in. He's running late." The kid looks cold to him in his fancy clothes, thin shoes. The boy's hands are stiff and spotless against the dark coat. "You want to wait in the office?"

"No thanks," Bayard says. He knows the old guy is trying to be nice. "I'll wait in the car." Behind the wheel he touches the shift, puts the key in the ignition. He is not sure which pedal is clutch or brake. It's not much warmer, but he has the illusion that no matter how often the men look they won't see him. He is hidden under the canvas roof and safe. With his parents, in the past few years with his mother only, he had always fallen for the moment when the latches were released, the button pressed and the top began to rise in the single motion of a large cat stretching and folding itself in another place. A magic that faded fast when they were exposed. Margaret Flood and her family for all the world to see. He hated driving up to the hardware store or the IGA—showing off in their showoff car. The long red hood swells in front of him, the fenders rounded to each side, crowned with silver tits. *"I will not sleep—"* Bayard talks to himself, a soothing habit—*"I will not dream."* The brave resistance of a boy who feels funny looking out at the men in navy blue work clothes who go about their business in the Atlas Garage.

Though hidden, he is not safe. He is very tired: the trip on the bus with all he must keep in mind—having already been to his mother's lawyer at Paul, Weiss and taken Lourdes' pay down to the shop and bought his father's weekend whiskey—ordered it, for they will not sell it to Bayard in the liquor store. And left Lourdes the telephone numbers—doctor, emergency, precinct, name of the old-clothes dealers who get a discount, and a note; they are low on summer suits—anything linen, rayon if not faded or yellowed and looks like—he has attached pictures of Donald O'Connor and Sydney Greenstreet and, thinking it might bridge the cultural gap, a South of the Border shot of Elvis in a big boxy tux before his army days. A good thing, too, since Lourdes cannot read. He does not sleep in the Atlas Garage though the Late Late Show had played in his motel room not far from the hospital, the set turned on for company until three o'clock. Fully awake, with Cokes and a club sandwich ordered up, cartons of shrimp fried rice, pork with snow peas, in an orgy of what he takes to be freedom from hospital and home, he read of the mysterious transformation of the Vela Pulsar in 1969, a reversal in the star's behavior, a speeding up and a more rapid slowing down. Without the slightest warning.

Not understanding the calculation of the star's density, nor the stages of compression, he played with some figures on the back of his Trinity notebook. It was beyond him, but a pleasure to think about. As some young men might think about when they'd fly a plane, make a million, make a girl, Bayard Strong thinks about the time to come when he will make ingenious speculations on the neutron star. His own telescope is abandoned, what with Pinky and his mother. It was 1969 when he first noticed the stars—not the Milky Way, North Star, Cassiopeia in the sky that his father pointed out to him imprecisely and too often, but the vast cosmology with life, heat, density, movement wrapped around him.

In Vermont—that was where the universe was visible to him. At night, lying out on the flat lawn beyond the badminton net, the red rear of the Corvette protruding from the barn, the light curtains fluttering with the moths against the screen of an upstairs window where his mother worked. His father in Washington or New York, coming on weekends as though he commuted to the war. So it was, lying out by himself, bored with easy collections of wildflowers and Indian heads, that he discovered, without text or instructor, the phenomena of Northern Lights, the surprisingly long seconds to observe a falling star. Until he was wet and chilled with night dew, he watched like a sailor for movement or signs in the heavens. He took the sky as his to study because it was distant and difficult. Then his parents could not say, "Baby has classified the Appalachian umbels. Baby has identified a Ticonderoga shard." Though that must have occurred to him later, not when he was nine years old and it could not be Vela, that particolored star he claimed was his that whole summer in Vermont. He came to dream or half believe it was Vela that he'd seen with the naked eye, but that was like one of his mother's stories, clearly untrue.

Bayard is asleep by the time Dr. Flood taps on the windshield. He sits up smartly: on the back of a battered van now parked in front of him it says: "I'd rather be sailing."

The bright boy and the doctor: they are a formal pair. Neither one lets on how peculiar it is that he should come to know the other through Margaret Flood's diseased heart. They had existed as untroubling shadows, but to the boy it seems impossible that his mother could have been married to this gentle, flourishing surgeon, unless she was quiet, sweet-natured long ago—the way she is now in the hospital—but he supposes that her forever carrying on had driven the doctor away.

Bayard's own father had been a match for Maggie Flood until he took off and turned up drunk, burnt out and silent. Growing up the boy listened to his parents argue—they loved the sport of it. He knew that as a child, had listened to their voices rising, locking, then breaking off in a defeated sigh or victorious laugh. The good old days of prolonged combat over a recipe or a matter of great principle were noisy, but when the real split came it was quick, without a sound. Pinky walked. It was supposed to be political, some cloak-and-dagger business of his father's left over from the war; Bayard knew that it was private though his mother never told him why this last dispute was fatal, outside their raucous game. Two years later his father had called him and in a hoarse plea begged him to come down to St. Mark's Place. Pinkham Strong, by that time a shaky alcoholic who rarely saw the light of day, did not recognize his own tall son. Hands trembling over yellowed newspaper, he looked up at Bayard in the dim shop and said, "May I help you?"

The doctor drives slowly along the streets of Baltimore, adjusting to the spread and weighted glide of the old car. The boy watches closely—the layout of the shift, the moment of braking, throwing out the clutch. The wipers push down against the slush, then up, accelerating to a carefree swish. The boy's hatred of the convertible has made him assume contempt for cars in general. Automotive fantasy he calls it at school, listening to his friends' tales of shooting stoplights, cruising down Columbus Avenue, big-time races on the Brooklyn Bridge. In what seems a lost age he can imagine his mother applauding his snotty attitude rather grandly, "Baby does not drive a car."

"You've turned on the parking lights," Bayard says approvingly and could die of it, such a dope. He cannot imagine his mother married to this surgeon with silver hair and good new clothes. He wants to thank him for all the trouble but it will sound like that means taking on his mother and he means picking up the car. Instead he blurts out a long speech on the Vela Pulsar. Dr. Flood attempts a few smart questions.

The worldly bright boy saddens Jack Flood, fills him with remorse and guilt he knows should not be his. Bayard Strong was a bastard, born out of wedlock, Maggie's love child. The old fashioned phrase is right for this extraordinary kid and the melodrama of his life, not of his making. Strong had not bothered to wrap up the legal affairs of a forgotten society marriage when Margaret Flood fell for him, "Head over heels in love." That was pointed out to Jack Flood in a gossip column: he did not believe them to be Maggie's words. An unwed mother was still a shocker in those days but the happy couple were soon splashily wed. Margaret and Strong (weak product of old family he looked to Jack) ran through a shower of rice, swinging this pretty boy between them, their baby son. Down proper Episcopalian church steps to wedded bliss. Poor kid. Jack supposed you could adjust to such beginnings or repair them like congenital defects, but the boy seems permanently injured with slick hard tissue grown over the wounds. And not like a boy at all, as though he must disdain the youth he never got. Between the father and the mother what choice has he, except to preen the gaudy feathers of his intelligence.

Jack drives to a garage near the hospital where he has arranged to billet the preposterous Corvette. "Pull up the emergency brake," he says kindly to Bayard and gives a good many tips on locking up and checking the lights.

Then it's his turn to feel foolish, overly instructive, worse than foolish when he leaves the boy off with his *Scientific American* at Margaret's gray door. It's a damn shame he can't take the kid home. That would set Ginger twitching, would be painful all around: furthermore, he can't imagine Bayard pressed into small talk with his girls, or the nervous bright boy spewing out astronomy to his Peter Pan wife.

The night before Margaret's operation Jack Flood stays in his office. Not unusual, but it involves calling Ginger and each time he hears her disappointment. She speaks of the meal that has been cooked or the party they will miss, always saying, "Oh, gosh, I hope there is nothing wrong." He works in a hospital: there is always something wrong. Even when he's tied up with some woman, his wife's innocence troubles Jack—to think Ginger inhabits happy valley where all things must be right. On this night, the night before the operation, he hears an especially plaintive "Oh, gosh, etc.," and is sure the twitch, of which she is completely unaware, has bleeped across her face. She has been nerved up since the day his first wife collapsed at his feet. Ginger thinks the incident disgraceful, a continuing scandal as though the sick woman is displayed on her front lawn, a woman, she is quick to tell her friends, so transformed by age and illness that Jack did not know who she was. Above all, she finds the presence of Margaret in her husband's cardiac unit strange—Ginger uses that word for all discomfiting things she cannot abide. It is strange for Margaret Flood to be in Baltimore and in Ginger's book that is worse than wrong, it is worst of all.

"There's nothing wrong," he tells her, and that night it's true. He's reviewed all Margaret's tests. A terrible history: enlarging plaque on the right coronary artery with little collateral circulation, cardiac dilatation, considerable damage to the heart itself. He trusts Charlie Newman absolutely to do the job. The young doctor is gifted and he is not that young after all the years of training. He has not only the skill but wonderment at his profession which Jack had once, which could have made him great. Nothing is wrong exactly, but he has not devoted himself to writing the continuing grant proposals, a process that has not gotten easier over twenty years. Tedious, exacting, necessary —all of the data at his fingertips, fed into the computer by his staff. The blank eye of the monitor looks on while students and lab assistants depend upon him for their apartments, tuition, unpaid-for vacations and cars. Not to mention a populace afflicted with arrhythmia, thousands upon thousands of sufferers he does not actually think of as he writes the deadly prose that continues to support his work.

He has looked at, but not read, his latest letter from Yin-Li, looked to make sure the old man is alive, not read the expected news of head lice, a roseola epidemic or received the doctor's gratitude for the last packet of medical journals and *Sports Illustrated.* It is the night before Margaret's operation. He opens the letter from China. The paper, greenish this time, seems extremely exotic. Yin-Li is taken from his son's house. He has been driven in a Mercedes-Benz to a banquet where he is much honored with flowers and speeches praising his contribution to medicine in the People's Republic. An enlarged photo of himself taken from the University of Minnesota yearbook hangs behind the head table along with pictures of other doctors, chemists, mathematicians—all men of science— who have grown old not practicing their professions. Indeed, some of the honors are posthumous and only the photographs attend the feast. It is a tiring ceremony and Yin-Li finds himself dozing, wishing for the long ride home, the good Western mattress at his son's house that is spread for him with flannel sheets.

"It is with pleasure I pass my honors on you," he writes

to Dr. Flood, "who have achieved which . . ." This night Jack cannot read another word of the old man's unremitting praise. It is the night before Margaret's open heart surgery. He has spent countless nights before surgery. He is not operating—with Newman he's gone over the territory of her vessels and pumps plotting the next day's invasion. There will be no untoward surprises. Predictably safe, but he does not say to himself she's home free. It has been strange these past weeks, stranger than Ginger's pale fears, foreign and all out of context, his attachment to Margaret. It is not love and nothing will come of it, but it's his reading, a distinct murmur between the beats, that she is his only wife. He takes up the envelope she gave him with such formality, an official act in the presence of her son. He believes it to be the distribution of her worldly goods; if he knows Margaret, a striking will, inventive testament. What Jack takes out of the envelope seems to have no legality to it, not strictly speaking. It is a story or a confession. He wonders about the nature of what he is reading and comes to believe it is a history of his marriage to Margaret Flood. His name is used and he can hear her voice, not the even-tempered voice of the invalid being shaved and washed tonight with an antibacterial soap, not the harangue of the wild woman who fell half dead at his feet, but that old voice. That old voice as she could play it, bright and high as a penny whistle or low and resonant with a serious beat. He hears what she has written on the page, but he does not know these people anymore. It is from such a distance that he reads of their troubles, they affect him as pure fiction.

He no longer reads fiction. Only on airplanes he will read a thriller. The stuff of novels and stories is close to the material which Jack Flood deals with, the human stuff that could surround each enlarged heart or deflated lung if he would let it. Margaret's line of work is different. He understands that she is so passionately in pursuit of the story she does not see to what extent she makes it up. What began as their history—an accuracy of time, place, visual detail—has collapsed into an imaginative form. He believes she is too hard on herself. Yet, her cause is vengeful. Now he reads fast to see what will happen. The husband is an idiot. He detects a comic version of himself—the young doctor with changeable costumes, but what of it? As for the infidelity, he has always been a womanizer, drawn a bit compulsively to female flesh. This fellow with his one raunchy nurse seems terribly inept.

Still, it is a painful story as she tells it, for in the pipe-sucking caricature of Jack Flood, he recognizes the ambitious man who is no more. Here Margaret cuts deep, exposes . . . she cannot know that in this pompous, over-achieving medic she prefigures Dr. John Sarsfield Flood, honored friend of Yin-Li, who has hoed a narrow row, found an easy berth. Whatever else might truly and tritely be said of his reputation, he is a good surgeon, not as good as Newman will become. First-year students believe his austerity sets them impossibly high standards, but it is only innocents like Charlie Newman who don't quite get his number in the end. Once he had thought his research a significant contribution; for a long time he's seen it as a piece of unremarkable sky fit into a cloudy puzzle. Once he rode on the back of big men who supported him; now he recommends the promising without looking at their work—not closely. There are men and women under him who suspect that as a man of science he's a talking head, an impressive fraud. It has never troubled Jack Flood that he is useful, established, prominent, though tonight he would diagnose it as a progressive disease.

Reading to the end of Margaret's story, he thinks: but I have forgotten our arguments; but I have forgiven us both—we were so damn young. There is no shock in her Hollywood romance with Sol Negaly or in her childish behavior at her mother's funeral—yesterday's tattle. He could not place that devilish fatso Philo Pierce, but he knows it is the bright boy who makes him feel contemptuous of Pinkham Strong. That neglected boy, this very night alone in a motel, missing school so that he might wait in the recovery unit by his mother's bed. When she came to, Bayard would be a sight for sore eyes. He does envy Margaret that.

Their story sealed back into the envelope, he locks it in the empty file with the letters from China. The accumulation of his research is stored, mute in the computer. Not a man who allows loose ends, professionally speaking, yet it was in just such a mood that he wandered to the cafeteria three, four weeks ago, chose rice pudding and there was Margaret. On a Thursday, that would bring it to twenty-five days. As he walks out of his office into the corridor which doesn't tell him night from day, he can hear her sorting out the time scheme of their marriage and divorce —historical reconstruction. What is it she wants from him? Absolution? He is only a surgeon. Exoneration? He is not a government commission empowered to blow up her picture, an out-of-date photo of a simple girl, and reinstate her with an official speech. *Good night, Doctor. Good night, Dr. Flood.* He does not hear them as he heads out the door. In the sting of the March wind he hears the old voice, the old voice with its lethal and loving inflections, praising him, entrusting him with her life. It was Maggie's voice in New Haven calling to him in their upstairs flat, calling out above the celebration of trumpets that for the likes of Johnny Flood there were no limits to the world at all.

The clerk is suspicious of the white-haired man who asks for the dandy New York boy. Up in Bayard's room they swivel in low club chairs on either side of a double bed. On television the Washington Bullets lead at half-time. A large pizza box flaps open on the dresser, nothing left but one cold slice which Bayard covers with a paper napkin in the manner of a host tidying the house. He turns off the set. "I was good at soccer."

His visitor says: "I never found time for sports." Two old-timers of an age, Jack Flood tells that as a boy in his poor parochial school there was no playground, no organized games. "I believe your grandfather, that is your mother's father, played baseball."

"I never met him," Bayard says. There is a silence in which the boy thinks of his mother in a baby carriage, a brown photo on her desk in Vermont. She is a round baby in a bonnet placed at the side of a raw cement house. An unidentified man stands with a shovel next to a sapling. You cannot see his face in the shadow of his straw hat. Dr. Flood remembers a lean man, an insurance agent, reticent, almost apologetic, handing him two hundred dollars as a wedding present. Neither one of them knows if Margaret's father is alive or dead.

It is noon by the time they wheel her down. Her son is brought in to watch her steady breathing. She lies pale and small, hooked up under the white sheet. Dr. Newman loses his cool and embraces Bayard—"It was a hell of a mess in there"—with these hearty words offering the boy his congratulations.

"Thank you." Bayard cannot think what else to say. He sees that the doctor's ear is pierced not once but twice under his longish hair.

"She's better than ever," Newman says.

Much later she moves, then hears, then sees. It is like dusk, but she sees Baby. "I'm glad you've come. School?" she whispers and wanting to make herself known, she says with great effort, "School," clearly to her son.

Bayard shoots the bolt on his motel room, a cheap pin on a frail chain. The room is a confusion of last night's soda cans, food cartons, rumpled sheets. He got up at dawn to watch his mother wheel off to her operation. Born with decent instincts, the boy is a throwback to the aristocratic Strongs or to his unknown grandfather, the insurance man. A nurse had given him the mink coat, shopping bags, his mother's blank book as he left the hospital. It is policy. Bayard understands and now drags his burden to a clear spot across the littered room. A shoe falls out and he throws it back in with the letters and clippings gone yellow and flaky at the bend. *My mother* comes to his mind, just the words. Her impractical Italian shoes worn to drive the Corvette to Baltimore, her bag dress, the rich dark smell of her fur coat—my mother. He opens the blank book, blank no more. Full of her words. It was hard enough to be her child: he had listened to her all his life, her voice with its scales and elaborate modulations, but he has never read her stories, not one word. We know that the boy has listened with pleasure to his mother's plain, unaffected talk in her recent illness, but now he throws the book back in with the shoes and bundled dress and lies on the bed fully clothed, sleeping almost at once, entering the dream of her depleted body, prone and whitely moving. He speaks where the knot of his tie rides his throat, the words gag, ga, gla, gla. It is fair for us to assume that Bayard is glad. He cries out, wildly glad his mother is alive as he joins her steady breathing.

Dr. Flood watches her sleeping. He finds her mostly sleeping. Once Newman arrives and before Jack can turn away shows him the cut. It is a beautiful incision. To the left and just above her breast there is the tail end of the birthmark he remembers. He comes to watch her sleeping. On St. Patrick's Day he sports a green carnation. She catches him in the doorway and gives him a doped-up smile. "Aren't we a couple of Micks," she says. When Margaret is coughing and breathing to keep the fluid from settling in her lungs, the nurses tease, "You have a boyfriend." They don't mean Bayard or young Charlie Newman. They mean Dr. Flood.

From afar he watches the aides walk her to the solarium, cautiously shuffling her along. He loves her spirit. He loves her frailty. There is more blood than he likes in her urine. She is running a temperature. It is not his case, but all Margaret's bodily functions are extraordinary to him, and her past—her work and her life—are unexceptional now that she has entered the pure world of the sick. He has lost all professional detachment. It is similar to the business with Yin-Li—his feelings have taken a quantum leap. When he finally comes to face her, Margaret's eyes glitter with the pain of breathing, "It isn't like the dress rehearsal," she says. As the days of her recovery go by, Jack Flood recalls almost nothing of their history, what he still thinks of as her will and testament, only this: that Margaret has kept alive her picture of him as a feisty young man who intended to hold off death. Again, his reading is personal: that is how he has edited her text.

Margaret Flood sleeps and eats, laughs painfully. She asks for little attention. She does not fret about Lourdes' pay or feel responsible to her editor—has only the vaguest idea what she was up to with Fred Peach, an assignment she procured. Centered on some literary scandal of the exhausted past, no, it was political—all that about Hannah Brandt, a rich self-styled radical who made her feel two feet tall and something shocking, that would be sexual . . . in any case, a willed, a made-up book. Every day she thanks the doctors, both Newman and Flood, thinking that Charlie is smart but Jack has saved her. All her things are gone—her papers and the blank book. It is policy. She never asks about them. So there is this flaw in the execution of Margaret's plan: Jack Flood does not read her correctly, her son not at all. For days she lives only within her body, fed and drained, feverish, drugged. In a state resembling infancy, Margaret touches water, sees lights, toddles the geography of bed and corridor. She has forgotten her crimes as well as her cause. There is no place in her reduced circumstances for mink coat, fine underclothes, fabulous car, no place for the baggage of old letters, old tales—grievance or triumph. Survival time. Possessions and history scrapped. She owns a name tag and her scars. She has acquired a metal wire which binds her cracked rib. Her blank book is missing and she doesn't give a fig.

One morning when Bayard comes, she says, "I must sell that car. It's costly and pretentious." He has just begun to admire the Corvette, but his mother says, "We need something efficient." He doesn't know who "we" is and can't quite trust the picture of his reconstructed mother with short gray hair, driving a compact car with a permanent lid. Yes, in giving up the vintage car, Margaret further divests herself, but it remains to be seen if in giving up her fierce demands on life she has given up her voice. She has surely discovered that the plot goes on without her. To Jack Flood who is looking for a miracle, she is changed utterly, but to her bright boy there is still the question he might almost put this way: Will his mother continue to be this nice but unfamiliar lady, blessed with the vision of her own mortality, or revert to Margaret Flood?

In a clearing by the tuxedos, Pinky lights the kerosene stove. The smell reminds him of a large shingle house on an island his people owned, had owned, the whole island off the coast of Maine. It reminds him of a fishing camp on Lake Michigan, or First Army headquarters in Neuilly and of a journalists' bunker in Saigon. It does not remind him of the house in Vermont when they first bought it, before Margaret had the two big chimneys pointed, installed a wood stove in the kitchen and then called in the electric company to engineer a heating system for a house never used in winter. Nothing would remind Pinky of

Vermont. That place is cut out of him like a piece of shrapnel: four years have cauterized the wound. He would not recall the jacked-up barn with its stone foundation, the persistent smell of animal that dominated the gas and oil fumes of his gentleman's tractor and of his wife's jazzy car. Margaret's Japanese maple, the landscape gardener's ornamental yew and ivy beds no farmer would tolerate. No memory of the flat lawn created for games where he first kicked a soccer ball into the knobbly knees of his astonished son. No recall of the view, at its best from the back bedroom window where he looked out on a whole range of worn green mountains, soft-edged, almost blue in the morning, a sweep of country without electric lines or telephone poles, the blacktop road in the valley hidden by a stand of lilacs. She had wanted a balcony to eat her breakfast on, as if over the hills of Umbria—some trip she had taken on the *Ile de France:* that would never come to Pinky's mind. And it was not Italy, it was Vermont, where the settlers built to the dirt road, not the view. In fact, an old kerosene stove was scrapped within days of their arrival, not good enough to bestow upon the workmen tearing layers of linoleum off a plank chestnut floor. So there was that pungent smell haunting the farmhouse parlor always, but it is lost to Pinky as he turns down the flame on his gleaming enamel stove set in a peaceful campground, the racks of tuxedos like a sleeping army drawn around. For Pinkham Strong, Vermont is no more.

The shop is warm and dry. Lourdes has bought this stove, the woman who takes charge when his son is away, coming one day under the burden of a large carton, staggering down the steps with her hat and black hair tilted. She had ordered the clearing, not by the evening dresses or fluttery scarves, but within the rows of hard black dinner jackets with metallic lapels. "Is here. Here is safe, is lookin' good."

He awaits her now, looking over racks of used clothes,

over the counter she has installed with a razzle-dazzle display of junk jewelry, to the wet sidewalk where he can see only legs, feet, bicycle wheels, dogs. The shop is below ground. He is very tall, Lincolnesque, with gangly limbs, his joints articulated through shabby gray pants and stretched-out sweater. He runs his long fingers back through a head of lifeless white hair as though to ready himself for an occasion, but the big loop of his jaw is white with stubble, the collar of his shirt is limp and dirty. There is something left of the face in a fine nose and high forehead with prominent bumps of knowledge, though Pinkham Strong has begun to resemble the bums, so often handsome men, who inhabit the sidewalks of the Bowery a few blocks down. He has no age to guess at other than alcoholic. Though he looks with some hope to the front of the shop where the Spanish woman (that is how he names Lourdes) will come with her bags and lively babble, it is a dead short hope, like wanting the next drink that will not long sustain him. At last he sees her little white boots all carved like a cowgirl's, then the fuzzy coat flanked by her important bags, finally the kind brown face that accepts him. Not that he cares or seeks approval even from the Spanish woman: Pinky's will is strong as an old regular who needs a shot; he will get what he wants in any case.

"Is terrible day," Lourdes says, shaking her plastic rain bonnet clear of the beaded sweaters she has positioned for their glitter and beauty close to the door. "Is terrible rain." Terrible it may be, but her singsong complaints are entirely happy. She comes into the clearing with the stove, licks a finger and taps the hot lid proudly. "See?" she asks as though she is dealing with a child. "Is very nize, Pingy?" To Lourdes he is a child and naturally she calls him Pingy. He is her ward, another boy, but he is also an old man. *Is old, old,* she says to herself because she well remembers Mrs. Flood from the beauty parlor in long dresses when the people came. Not understanding the state from which

Pinkham Strong has fallen, she thinks of sick old men in her village who married young girls. Lourdes would not believe it possible that four years ago this besotted wraith was an acceptable ten years older than his wife, with flesh on his bones, the glow of a sportsman, not the ruddy shine of broken capillaries staining his sunken cheeks. Unless by some magic, by some curse—that is what she truly thinks, but tucks that thought away like something stolen in the bottom of her purse. She puts a kettle on the top of the kerosene stove all the while telling—it is the morning incantation—what she cooked and washed and ironed last night. Today she is planning to get Pinky's filthy shirt off him, to make him bathe. A packet of razor blades and a pristine toothbrush complete her plot.

He has already settled behind the army coats and is at work when she brings him his coffee which she has laced (cheating) with only a half jigger of Scotch. "Ay, ay." She mops her brow, fans herself. "You sweat, Pingy, phew. Phew."

Trembling for the first hit of the day, he does not hear the Spanish woman. The coffee sloshes as he swings round to a file where he draws out a card: "Draft Riots July 13, 1863. Conscription of Irish and German laborers. *Rich procure substitutes—$300.* Militia occupy Gramercy Park. Negro lynched in Carmine Street. Sacking of Brooks Brothers Clothiers at Catherine and Cherry Streets. Proposed defense of Union League Club with muskets." The card is written in a hand so small its information might be coded. For a long while Pinkham Strong studies this entry in his complex system of names, dates, events, places that bear somehow on his family or on the lively reconstruction in his head—like a miniature city—of their sorely forgotten world.

The Spanish woman is singing one of her two or three songs that sound so alike, sorting a box of Hawaiian shirts in the tropical clime of the stove. A rainy day, at first no one will come, later there will be customers driven out by the dreary end of winter to try on some fantasy or just get out of the damp in this underground shop. *Linda-O Linda-O'Day* it sounds like she's singing as she sews a button onto a hibiscus petal. After a while she calls, "How you dune, Pingy?" And he calls back from behind the army coats, "I'm doing O.K." He unclips a green bakelite fountain pen from his soiled shirt pocket—it's a Wahl-Eversharp with gold trim that might well be an artifact in Golden Oldies—unscrews the cap and writes: "To avoid death at Chickamauga, at Chattanooga, three hundred dollars. Paddy in his Brooks Brothers finery follows Sherman to the sea." Well pleased with himself, he closes the pen, files the card between Delano and Dred Scott under D. There is no clue in this further notation on the Draft Riots to the attitude of Pinkham Strong. It would be presumptuous to fill in "a mere" three hundred dollars, to read contempt into his "Paddy," for he might mean that it was noble not to fight and the thick Irish were fools. He might mean the rich man was a coward and the Mick a lovable rascal marching through Georgia in his stolen haberdashery. That Life is all? Or Victory? There is no way of knowing from his grizzled drunk's smile, air of a job well done, what he considers just. No story: whether it is a particular Strong who bought out his conscription or a Bidwell who fell on Lookout Mountain in Tennessee, whether, in fact, some poor hod carrier without a job followed Sherman on the long march singing in Erse "The Minstrel Boy to the War Has Gone" and that Ireland must be free.

It is ten o'clock. The rain, coming down fast, finds an old clay pipe that leads to a gully, then to a cast-iron drain directly in front of the shop door, an arrangement that worked when the cellar was a kitchen and laundry for the private house above, when deliveries came down the steps but in at a sensible side door. In a time before "golden oldies," when worn clothes were mended, then given to the servants or the orphans of the parish, the indigent as well as the deserving poor. Now the first customers come through the puddle over the clogged drain traipsing sooty water in on Lourdes' clean floor. Two young girls and she can tell they should be in school, playing around and laughing like their books, all soaking, were the funniest things in the world. Two pretty girls who will get in trouble like Pepe with the truant officer coming to her door—then he stopped laughing and pretended he was scared. Manny went to high school, went to college she thinks proudly: her thought stops there.

With their wet fingers and dripping hair, the girls are at her evening gowns, rudely touching. Lourdes can tell they have no money. Passing the time, they choose black velvet, midnight blue satin. Before they can crush the material to their wet coats, she rushes at them. "Is *espenseeve* dresses," she says, but they are bold girls who go on laughing. She can hear them still in the dressing room behind her flowered curtain, can see underneath as they throw down their books and plaid skirts. From her sewing basket she picks out the scissors and stands sentinel. She hears Pinky go to the hot plate where he will pour a second cup of coffee to disguise his second shot. The two girls spring out of the dressing room lost in their silliness, until they spot themselves in the big mirror Lourdes has hung on the crumbling cellar wall. They are suddenly grave, facing themselves in make-believe dresses. Blue Satin smooths her flat little belly; Black Velvet holds her hand demurely to her undeveloped breast. Each caught in a private dream. Very pretty girls, Lourdes knows they will get in trouble. Clowning again, they pack up and leave, splashing through the doorway puddle. They have not even bought a dollar bracelet which she displays with gloves and beads on a whirligig tree to catch the eye.

The day picks up in kerchiefs and scarves, two army raincoats. If only she had hats. Lourdes thinks it is a pity and the next dealer that comes through she is going to ask. For weather and style she likes a hat. Now that she is in the fashion business, that is how she thinks of her work at Golden Oldies—she is in the fashion business and must choose what the trade will wear. She believes it will be vests and hats. She is happy making Pinky's bed (slept *on,* not in), cooking his dinner which she has brought from her neighborhood—tasty pork sausage to go with rice and *frijoles negros.* He does not listen to the Spanish woman about the morning sales, about how she will fatten him up, about Manny and Pepe and the hooks she must sew back on a blue satin gown. He pays her no mind when she says, "Phew. Phew, Pingy." It is comic the way she holds her nose to tell him he is sour.

Yes, he remembers "Stinky Pinky" back in boarding school, but he does not pay attention when the Spanish woman says, "When you gonna?" He is writing out new cards: "Columbia School of Mines, Winter Garden (Edwin Booth as Hamlet), Brevoort House, Major Anderson and his command stationed at Number 2 Great Jones Street." And so forth, turning this day to a record of places, the map of his New York spread in front of him, a pale green plan of Manhattan folded out of the City Registry, 1861, with the layout of blocks and parks, opera houses and clubs, streetcar lines which he knows by heart from Twenty-third Street to Fulton Pier, which he can see as though he were surveying it all from Trinity Church tower. His world with the recent acquisition of cast-iron buildings, the ferryboat crossing the Narrows from Brooklyn Heights.

It is a busy household with the bell above the door ringing: mid-afternoon brings sunshine and with it students in blue jeans and winter jackets to buy a loose shirt or printed skirt that hold promise of spring. Lourdes singing only when the customers are gone. Very professional in her new work, she is pinning on price tags, marking up every petticoat and camisole, all lacy underthings. "Baby is *givin'* away," she says crossly, and pronouncing on the season and its style, chatters on. He does not listen to the Spanish woman, but when Pinky hears the door tinkle and believes that she is gone, he rises from his desk, by this time unsteady on his feet. Old New York tears at a fold as he sets his drink down. He comes forward to meet a young woman with a baby sleeping on her back. The woman steps clear of him instinctively and is out the door, the child's head bobbing helplessly as she runs upstairs into the light. Pinkham Strong looks at the tin ceiling, at an odd buckling that he is sure blocks the dumbwaiter on which the servants sent fresh oysters and glistening blancmange up to the family dining room and later pulled it down with the dirty plates.

Lourdes is scraping his dinner into the plastic garbage pail. She is doomed to serve people who pay not to eat her food, or to watch her food devoured by sons who do not pay their way. The kitchen is terrible. Baby knows his schoolwork, not how to clean. She has scoured every inch, dusted with roach powder into all the cracks. Electric wires hang about her in a dangerous tangle, the floor is spongy, a gritty seepage collects under the sink. "Is terrible, terrible"—the back of the shop where, with half a turn, she can take in Pinky's bed, Bayard's cot behind a folding screen and the obscure glass door to the bathroom. "Crazy, is sooo crazy," she says of the bathroom in the same way she says it of Missus Flood, but she will not say it of her Pingy. *Help me, Jesus.* She believes him to be truly mad and to speak it is a curse.

"My dear lady," he says. That is the beginning of his fancy talk. Now he will want her to run out for the bottle, calling her his *señorita,* but she will not.

"Phew, phew," she says and pushes by him to the bathroom, where she runs hot water out of a spigot through a dry rubber hose into a claw-foot tub. The cold water she gets from the sink and transfers it in a pail. "Sooo crazy," she says, being careful to speak only of the pocked porcelain surface, the corroded drain.

"Señora?" he pleads. Determined, she puts out his razor, his shaving soap and old boar's-hair brush.

Happy in the clearing by the kerosene stove where she irons and mends, Lourdes has hidden the new bottle of Johnnie Walker. She sews false labels—Made in England, Harris Tweed, I. Magnin, I.J. Fox—into suits that remind her of Easter. Now and again she takes a Magic Marker from a Don Diego cigar box and touches up a buttonhole or stain, an artist in the fashion business. If only she had hats. Going to Mass with Manny and Pepe on Easter (she is thinking some years back), all three of them wore hats. The kerosene stove smells like the paraffin candles she lights at home praying to Jesus. It reminds her of the clinic, a tin structure under the palms, a cold morning in the mountains, of waiting in line with little sores or no big toothache just to get warm by the stove. The smell reassures her of steam heating up in her five-room, but it does not bother her with a picture of Manny on a downer still lying in bed.

"Theng you, Jesus," she says out loud, in English. The bottle is under a pile of Spanish shawls. *Señorita, Sēnora* he calls her when he needs it, but will not get it today till he is clean. It is a quiet time. The lengthening days bring them after work, men as well as women, and they buy something a little fancy, heading out for the evening or maybe to put away. Showing a pink negligee to a gentleman who has put down his briefcase, she displays its breadth. Lourdes knows he will wear it and seeing his narrow shoulders tells him "is sooo beaudiful for the girlfren, for the wive." She is in the fashion business.

With a rude suck the bathwater runs away. Pinkham Strong does not look at his body. In the crazed mirror he sees what he wants to see. His head, long and thin, with the pronounced jaw, a thin flop of hair which he combs back from his gleaming forehead. The hot water has brought a glow to his skin—not the end of the world. Alert to his need, trembling, he lathers his brush. For the first time that day he thinks of Bayard, who would have given him an inch of booze in the tooth glass and not required that he shave at all. The Spanish woman is tough. She is sewing a creamy silk label into a beige tent coat with push-up sleeves: Higbee & Co., Cleveland, Ohio. *Linda-O, Linda-O'Day.*

"Pingee, Pingee." Her solemn Indian face is lit with delight.

"Señora." He bows, then stands at attention, a diplomat with no mission in a double-breasted pin-striped suit. He has chosen a black and silver mourning tie. One cheek is meaty, his chin near destroyed, but the scent of old lavender is fresh and lively, overbidding the kerosene. "Well, well," he says, inquiring into the day's receipts. Oh, she has the true knack, a discernible talent, winning ways, exquisite taste—in sum, a flair. She has already succumbed, before he gets to asking, "How are those fine boys, *señora?*" Lourdes produces the bottle from under the tangle of shawls. Today he is clean. Tomorrow she will make him eat.

Help me, Jesus. In front of the bureau she kneels, candle lit. She has set out the pictures of Manny, Pepe, Missus Flood and the Trinity School seal for Baby (a decal—three gold crosses on a field of blue, eternal conundrum: Father, Son, and Holy Ghost, but it is only the son she prays to; her figure of intercession is a good smart boy). Help them, Jesus. There is no picture of Pingy, nor would she want his image, believing it is bad to capture madness with the camera. *Pobrecito.* With the naked eye she sees that he is drunk and crazy. Help him, Jesus.

As always, she is kind, but it is Lourdes she needs the help for. Manny has been gone for three days. In the shop where she is so happy, she does not think—Manny is gone. Overwhelming as an earthquake or influenza in her village —Manny gone. She continues to cook and mend, to count her subway tokens, care for Pingy. All day she is calm as a woman routinely drawing water from a well. All day she has kept the hard part of her knowing away. Now is the time for weeping. She is kneeling. Only the flickering light on the ceiling and the glossy black hair of her wig draped on its faceless head are visible as she raises her sorrowful eyes to heaven. Jesus, Manny is gone with Missus Flood silver she promise to take back. He is not down on the block. She would be glad to find him (crossing herself) with the *puta* and the filthy child. He is gone with dozens of spoons and the butter knives. Ah, that Pepe knows where is Manny she is sure, where is the silver, but he shouts above the racket of police and guns, "I work for a living." *Sí,* Pepe is at Exxon. She has washed his greasy clothes and the terrible stuff she has got off Pingy, brought home in a separate smelly bag. She has ironed a sky blue shirt printed with airplanes and clouds, the best of the Hawaiian lot. It is ready for Manny if he come in the door.

Lourdes knows that Jesus is listening and has this to tell him: that she does not want Missus Flood to die just to cover for Manny and the silver though that may be what Jesus has in mind. Missus Flood is recovering she has been told, but she does not believe it—many weeks in the hands of doctors, off in a place with no family (Baby she discounts and actually thinks of the comfort she takes in her own boys). All is very clouded, all cannot be well. No, she prays for Missus Flood, dead or alive, and that she fatten Pingy, Pepe stay at Exxon. The sorrow and the fright ebb in Lourdes' telling. She strikes a hard bargain: if Manny come, if doctors mend, if steam come up. Thank you,

Jesus. If Jesus keep her in the fashion business, she will put a wooden tree by the jewelry case and make up silver in no time selling hats.

With a drunk's clever turn of mind, Pinkham Strong draws a blank. He does not observe when his son packs up to go away or that it is then the Spanish woman comes with a brightly flowered overnight case and stays. All the while Margaret is breathing easier. Despite his mother's endorsement of his brilliance, Bayard has dropped behind in his studies. His attendance at school is spotty. The faculty advisor knows it's not drugs or girls with Bayard Strong, but the boy is unwilling to submit to the sticky conversation labeled "Trouble at Home." Though it is unthinkable, he has fallen apart on a calculus test. How could it be otherwise, nursing his parents, paying their bills, selling old clothes? He has come to hate the worn garments pawed with such reverence by Lourdes. He lets her skip whatever the duties in his mother's empty apartment and scurry down the steps of Golden Oldies each day with her proprietary air.

The scene is idyllic. Pinkham Strong both washed and fed. He has just entered the protest of Vander Poel and Suydam over the proposed billiard room in the Century Club as well as the guest list at the William Astors', March 19, 1863—General George McClellan present. Lourdes is singing as she sews a thousand silvery paillettes onto the bodice of a tea-rose gown. In his cubbyhole, Bayard reads for social studies in an abridged Machiavelli, "The Morals of the Prince: Cruelty and Clemency and Whether it is Better to Be Loved or Feared." He is tucked up under a lap robe. Though the stove blazes out front, he does not get the good of it. Under his cot Bayard has stuffed his mother's belongings, the mink coat far out of sight pinned with a sign from his motel room—DO NOT DISTURB. Margaret's gray sack dress (he knows it is Lourdes' greed for business) has already disappeared. The bell tinkles above the shop door. Bayard thinks Machiavelli is hot stuff and he underlines: *Men have less hesitation in offending a man who is loved than one who is feared . . . fear is accompanied by the dread of punishment which never relaxes.*

"Baby"—Lourdes peeks around the screen, her eyes big as coat buttons—"come. You come," she says in a fearful whisper. "Is funny man."

Indeed, it is a funny man and Lourdes, who stakes out shoplifters and desperate junkies, withdraws behind an arras of evening wraps from Margaret Flood's editor—very neat, sewn out of mousy gray flannel like a toy, muzzle and whiskers atremble, adorable soft belly. All pearly gray with wee foreshortened limbs, a derby hat, a boutonniere. He is funny, but smiling up at Bayard he exposes rodent teeth, sharp and small. It is about the manuscript he's come. The boy has dealt with him before. They have gone through the song and dance about his mother's health. "I cannot contemplate the loss," the little man has said with dewy eyes, seeing Margaret Flood laid out on a bier, flanked by irretrievable sacks of his gold.

"Ah, ah," Fred Peach sighs, a prick of relief, hearing that she is well.

Bayard can't stand the guy, the ferrety look of his thumbtack eyes: "She may have a relapse."

"No, no, dear boy!"

"Yes," Bayard says, watching the whiskers tweak, the soft pit-pat of a silk handkerchief upon the mousy brow. "The doctors say it is touch and go."

"The loss. I cannot estimate the loss." (Including the flowers sent to Baltimore. Baltimore!) It is outrageous—the lunches early on, wining and dining Margaret Flood, the large advance. He dare not calculate. The woman has deceived him, she is well past her prime. A disreputable woman. All women deceive him. It was humiliating to present himself in this sweltering rag shop. "We have a contract," he says, coming at the boy in a fierce hippety-hop. "Is there nothing to show?" he cries. "Nothing?"

The guy looks to Bayard like he'll split his seams. "Nothing, Mr. Peach." He had not remembered the editor's name, Fred Peach. Then, taking pity, Bayard thinks of his mother's blank book.

"No. No. No." Mr. Peach's dismay brings Lourdes to the jewelry counter with her largest scissors raised. Pinky is upset, coming with dignity from his littered desk as though from the Astors' dinner table, round the military coats to observe the rabble, one roly-poly pearl-gray man. *Mr. Peach,* it is not a name he knows. Peck or Pack—some alteration from the German. There was a Colonel Patch, trustee of Cooper Union, but that was much later, lost in the Spanish-American War. Even the spectacle of Pinkham Strong flushed with drink does not startle poor Peach out of his wrath as he flips through Margaret's work. These are the ramblings of a sick woman, useless to him. He foresees a dreary legal battle to restore his funds, but he cannot save face. Shrewd of her to get his cash when death was at her door. Dishonest bitch, plotting with these loons.

Quite drawn together, what there is of his chin held high, he sniffs the kerosene. The book is handed back to Bayard like a slice of inferior cheese, and tail tucked, ears down, he scrambles off. Up in the street the fumes of Golden Oldies cling to Fred Peach. He brushes and wipes, discards the tainted flower in his buttonhole which now brings back the stench of an army barracks, a sergeant pulling the sheets off him and something so vile said—an unforgivable scene.

And so we see it's this pudgy, comical man that leads Margaret's son to put Machiavelli aside and finally open her book. He has thought of the Medici prince as a schoolboy rather like himself being handed the real scoop, a kid who needs to toughen up, and . . . well, he's flattered, quite taken when he reads it, his mother's opening line:

To Bayard Bidwell Strong—

VAS YOU DERE, SCHARLEY?

Baron Münchhausen, a radio comic, did his routine with a killing accent—high Viennese Jewish or indefinite Middle Europa, just the way he talked English made me laugh. His material was based on absurdly intricate stories of self-justification. His final quip, addressed to some poor dupe of an interlocutor—Vas you dere, Scharrrley?—cut two ways. So you don't believe me? (Vas you dere?) I should take your word? (Vas you dere?) A no-win situation to the delight of the radio audience. Charming, ever glib, the Baron was harassed by modern life, skeptical but ultimately a successful con man. I am not good at his game. I play both the comic and the straight, putting it to myself, his famous line: I was there, Baron. You believe it, I was there.

I no longer hold with decades, neat packages of time. You proved it once, fighting the siege of Fort Sumter with toy soldiers, you told your father the date was March, 1861. The stock market crash, '29. It never works out—Diamond Jim Brady first meets Lillian Russell, Fitzgerald arrives in Paris—Gay Nineties, Roaring Twenties are like figures in a budget rounded off to the convenient zero.

History is not accommodating. For easy parlance we push it around, though you know as well as any one of us life is rough, raggedy, so tattered we need to smooth it at the edges. I use the Sixties to contain our story and to ease me a little, ease my song.

Your very history supports my notion: born in '60, conceived in '59. Born before your father and I married. We took pride in that. From the beginnning you were called upon to serve us, as an infant to testify to our passion and our mighty disregard of the conventions. Baby, we just never let you be. We swung you between us as we entered the extravagant time. Dancing and singing pop tunes, on a holiday which we thought to be exclusive, a party for high steppers that ended in a brawl.

Newsreels level events, all real, to a show. You cannot know what newsreels were. Television reruns, black and white footage of FDR with Stalin and Churchill, Al Capone skulking on the courthouse steps, Lucky Lindy swathed in ticker tape cannot convey our weekly expectation or our pleasure in the March of Time that preceded the feature film. Double feature. Movie not film. You see, I quickly play a shell game with the facts. I was a kid and remember only the foul smell of the red plush seats from which I must have viewed our Allied leaders seated next to Roosevelt, the only President I knew. I did not know they sat diplomatically, out of courtesy to a dying man. The other images of problematic heroes I have appropriated, taken out of storage for this occasion. The Eyes and Ears of the World, indeed; they were never fresh to me, firsthand—only replays at the Rialto with the stale kiss of nostalgia upon them then. Bayard, I wasn't there.

In our own time, I can show you clips of your father as a respectable public servant on his business to the White House and your mother, an aging flower child, marching in sweet protest to Central Park, but the film is faded, hardly intelligible, like a silent that is brittle and badly spliced. Blank frames, too, but we were there. And the filler—the time I lived through with Pinkham Strong had long sequences of that—amusement that ceased to amuse. Those newsreels you have never seen relieved the somber tone of "On the Home Front . . . And With Our Boys Abroad" with tra-la-la-la . . . a unicyclists' convention, the Dionne Quintuplets, seals fishing through the ice, live poultry on an Easter hat. Tra-la.

A FINE ROMANCE

This tale is fantastic now. It may not be to you. He was the handsomest man. Before I knew his name I thought of him.

I didn't want to know who he was, the dark stranger across a terrace or at the other end of a table. Before I knew his name I thought, I dreamed of him and don't you know I was in the right places, that I sought them out. Your father made right places. He had an overbred ruthless way, coming late, then leaving in the middle. That pleased: yes, that he stopped by at all. Coming from London. Going to a duck blind. Sailing for Bremen, taken on as crew. Somebody's aide, coming from a NATO conference. Going on safari. The handsomest man, older by ten years than your Ma.

Pinky, the ridiculous society name, a prep school name, went directly to my heart. I played a girl to that boy. I do not believe your father's background seduced me. You have all that class if you ever feel the need of it—a clever Huguenot exile married the Dutch governor's daughter and what came of it—the judges, a college president, congressmen, two mayors of the city of New York, a real witch, more missionaries to the heathen than you can turn on a spit, and one explorer at the South Pole with Admiral Byrd. The financiers, less showy—kept it going, now and again someone had to do a little work. Though it was mostly Chief Delegate of the American Committee . . . Austro-Hungarian Embassy, French Equatorial Africa and so forth which may prove nice for you, but I never gave a damn. Your father might have been high mafia or riffraff nobility like Baron Münchhausen, for all I cared. Pinkham Strong carried the world with him—what he wanted of it. Grand, he seemed to me, and careless of the rules. I mined the narrow vein of my success, learning as I went along—the next move. My ambition was enchanting: he saw me as fearless and innocent—an original. I was his equal though I came from genteel peasant stock. It was a trade-off—my energy for his ease. This is not the Romance I intended, Baby. You may read it as dispassionate and summary. From this distance it may be a tale too hard to tell.

I won't die, not this time. What I tell you now is what I planned to say when I was on my way. I had worked myself up to the grand finale, already savoring the fact that I would have the last word. That much is taken from me. Begging for time, I got more than I bargained for. You may wonder, did I need to have death's bright angel deliver a warrant before

I told you our romantic story—my raw purpose for his feckless grace. That's looking through the wrong end of your telescope to find warts on the face of the moon. He was the handsomest man. There is no way to put it to a child. Lovers . . . insatiable . . . the isle we occupied was new, green, sunny without our histories or any further consequences. I liked being plain to his beauty. If you look at what's left in the album, where I have not snipped him out, you will see we were the handsome couple, that while I carried you I looked better than I did in all my life. Better than I do now in this late blooming my illness lends me. Full to brimming—I was, or would be, Pinky's wife.

It was not necessary to be Margaret Flood. Your father needed my name. That was the first scratch on the lens, so faint we did not see it. It wasn't that he'd married up, Pinkham Van Vliet Strong wedded to Miss Flood née Lynch. My maiden name was Lynch. You know the bare bones, circumstances of my birth; two-family house, failing mother, honest clerkly dad. I've never had the skill for their decent and ordinary story.

It was Margaret Flood he needed. She'd made a name—Strong had not. He lived, as I hope you never will, under the burden of a name that's made. All belated revelation. Your father was a floater, insubstantial, and he believed the world knew. There was nothing wrong with the handsome man needing me up front—good corporations, running mates and tennis partners are built on that one. It was no shame.

You are in pajamas with flat duck feet. In the distance you hear the general murmur and canned laughter of our guests. Escaping from your nurse, you slip into the pantry where you pour your father's uncorked wine into paper party cups. You enter the living room with a Mickey Mouse tray. Two cups of wine are balanced far from your small grasp, out on Mickey's ears. You are padding across the room to your father when the rubbery web of your foot catches on the rug. The red wine spills down the leg of a Famous Author and onto the pink satin shoe of the Senator's Wife. I say (because I must) in a company voice that you are a naughty, naughty boy. Sensing my real approval and your father's control of the room, you flap your ugly tray about and will not take your cue. Bayard, you will neither cry for us or say you're sorry.

MONEY TALKS

The Republic had come again: we were charting our course. Oh, yes indeed, like Jefferson and Adams, plotting it out upon the virgin land. We could not read the surveyor's instruments, but the Romance—it was there. Your father, think of it, Bayard, was rebuilding slums. There was to be warmth and light, Shakespeare and the beat of African drums. Teenagers performing *Faust* to early electric keyboard. No one hungry. No one sick. Your mother wrapped in a slave's headcloth above a bastard dashiki. French champagne with grits. See the good of it before you laugh at us. Or before you think playing Caius Caesar exporting culture to the Goths in Brooklyn was a society boy's job. Poorly paid, but well employed, your father was not boasting when he told me he was the only man on the project who knew that Bedford-Stuyvesant was bought from the Canarsie Indians for a few muskets and middling beer.

The legendary family. He had no real money. It's your family and when some old cousin died, then Pinky would be rescued by a small annuity or trust. Club dues and the tailor paid. It's well for you that time has gone. I had worked so hard that I admired his casual, expensive ways. It was like watching an effortless serve come at me after I'd practiced for hours against the backboard. I had worked so hard and worked then, locked into my chosen name.

At first I never left you to go farther than my study. I'd come from my typewriter three or four times a morning to watch you play under the cool eyes of a nursemaid. We made too much of you. The abacus strapped to your crib. Magnifying apparatus from Design Research dangled over your unfocused baby eyes. Sorry. Prisms and spectrums, the jade and ivory stones of your Chinese counting game sat on your toy shelf. Your dull wooden choochoo, a learning device you could not push over the thick, safe carpet we placed on your floor, yet given your great talents we recklessly denied you training wheels, water wings. I'm sorry.

You are a small boy in an art gallery. We are drinking cheap wine in a bare room full of people who occasionally look out into a courtyard stacked with blue tires. Truck, bicycle, auto—and what must be the chubby tires of tricycles. All are sprayed a sharp cerulean blue. A hundred people jabbering in a blank room. When I turn, you are out in the blue tires. When we all turn, you are climbing a hill of tires, jumping, bouncing, rolling tires until you have made a refuse heap. A brilliant judgment, Bayard—you're the show.

Too many parties. The house in Vermont, no escape for Ms. Flood and her consort, Pinkham Strong. What a Babel in Pownal Valley—the first wave of dissident poets, Hispanic dancers. Economists—I've never met such talky men. You will recall that often we were twelve at table. On the sun porch I could feed another ten. The local inn prospered with us. Exotic people demanding gumbo, mineral waters, one hundred proof vodka, Ukrainian borscht. Excessive times. Five years later we would eat nothing but local corn chowder, fritters drenched in Grade A maple syrup, sickly-sweet zucchini bread—the zucchinis big as billy clubs, grown at home.

(Today I have cut my hair and I am forty-six years old.)

I wrote for Philo Pierce. He's dead and there is no reason why you should ever know his name. Retreating upstairs in Vermont, I worked like a farmer who must milk, feed pigs, get in the hay during the high jinks of the village fair. I produced a hefty academic exercise, a sexual romp, purporting to be an Eighteenth-Century novel. Pierce was a ringmaster, harrumphing dramaturge, and he had elicited my pastiche to coincide with what he called the rise of the professorial class. I can hear him from the great beyond—"Margaret, what we are experiencing is . . ." I would then experience what he had in mind. I am like the cuckoo who brings her eggs to other bird's nests, where they take on the color and speckles, every aspect of a stranger's eggs. Miraculous counterfeit: it's that big book that made me respectable. Hard going, but frivolous; all those forced pages of *The Balfour Chronicle* are surely forgotten. Use it to prop windows or hold open the door when you need fresh air. Dead weight, though I do not count it among my literary crimes.

I read to you until my voice went dry. At a party, wriggling to a dance or making conversation with a third world wife, I'd think—Oh, I didn't read to Baby. Greek mythology and Russian folk tales. And the puppet theater with exquisite little sets . . . The Frog Prince, Aladdin for which we found the miniature brass lamp . . . Scaramouche, Three Little Pigs . . . the original Flemish version. The ambition of it always, you will recall.

DUNGEONS AND DRAGONS

Pressing need, the same—to tell you though I am not dying. Paced, monitored, agitation not allowed. I am tired of my own athletic breathing. Not to go on would be sinful, a paltry release: when you find someone else takes the blame for your dent in the fender, then silence is nasty. Steady, careful just to tell, no *mea culpa* or bravado—they will not get me these innings.

Think of a diorama, Baby, the one you made with dinosaurs and elk wired to papier-mâché scrub and rock, in which you gave no demarcation to the ages, just the gradual greening of the cold world to welcome emergent man. Turn to the Sixties, you will not find a single event—protest, music festival, act of war—where you can observe your parents' transformation. Stripped of our raiment, piece by piece, we dressed like laborers and gypsies. People hidden in the farmhouse attic, people prowling the apartment in the night. The People—one of our words—and the intricate and endless plotting. Our intensity woke you through the floorboards. And the magic spells—tomatoes and herbs in the rose garden, your father's claret and aged whiskey turned to jug wine in a year. Pinky tired of his utopia, the Brooklyn Renaissance no longer in the public eye. The sharp tongue is habitual, forgive me. I clatter over the deeper stuff of love and pain to keep to the romantic story.

Remember him as the gentleman revolutionary who didn't want a war. Vietnam was the best of times for Pinkham Strong, the one time he was clearly beyond me. I packed his bags with clean handkerchiefs and little comforts, stiff upper lip as though I was the wife of a soldier. I waited for his key in the lock, for the phone call at any hour. Our coded speech, don't mock us, was precious to us then: "You have mowed the lawn?" "*No,* I have watered the roses." An assurance or warning? The system is lost. "The clouds are heavy." "*Here* the sky is bright." We believed the phone was tapped, but I don't know if we were like kids with Dick Tracy kits, tin cans strung at the end of soft white string stolen from Mamma's drawer.

We did our best. Don't pity us. Personal history, Bayard, personal disappointment—his country done him wrong. I testify that your father was dedicated, angry, angrier than the kids he traveled with. He had always held with the past, with the lot of them—Bidwells, Van Vliets, Sturdevants, Strongs. And all those missionaries, statesmen, teachers of teachers begot a big bully that disgraced him. Your father took it personal as though he had a Junior League cousin hacking up undernourished Asians or one of the stupid Bidwells scourged the pathetic drifters that roamed the land. Leaving his work shirt and bandana at home, he went from speech to speech, to the people, now his people, displaying himself as a patrician in the good suits and silk braces natural to his kind. From riot to riot, clutched fist held high, chanting the people's slogans in his upper-crust drawl. An imposing figure above the mob, untouchable. It was me they whacked with truncheons the first time out.

So, I give you a hero in your father, his name in lights at last, his ministry, his validation. He sailed assorted fugitives in on a sloop at Santa Barbara. He stood blinded in the searchlight of a pickup truck full of locals who threw red paint on the house of Pinkham Strong. Salt in the sugar bowl, molasses in the gas tank. In the bottom of a basket, garden snakes writhe under Farmer Brown's apples. It was a time of many tricks. Remember him coming home to us in New York and the split-second talk of your schoolwork or my head cold —before the doorbell and the meetings and the damn phone started up again—whoopee we're all gonna die and all the sallow girls in love with him. Droopy girls. Unhealthy children. He was their handsome man, but there was nothing left of him. He looked perfect and hazy as a holy card of Our Savior—pastel, embalmed. And when the blessed smile fell on me—well, I was yesterday's mashed potatoes.

The correct line—one of our phrases—I believe there was one about your father's higher calling and I refused to take it. This is merely personal, Bayard, but I began to lose track of his departures and the intricate family squabbles that undermined our cause. The cloying smell of counterculture musk on his clothes stuck in my craw. I wish that you were crazy now, girl crazy, car crazy—that you smoked dope in the empty lot on Ninety-first Street or damaged your eardrums with cruel music, that you fucked up or flunked out. Mother and Pinky—hard acts to follow. I wish you sullen, intolerable, crazy now, because your father's notorious adolescence came at fifty and, believe me, there was no romance in that at all.

Alone in the apartment, you and I. An interminable winter Sunday. Dry-nostril heat. On the other side of the world your father has flown in a helicopter with a graduate student from Berkeley who adores him. A smashing Marxist in expensive khaki, she sees no contradiction in her feminist jargon and the fact that she would gladly lick your father's L. L. Bean boots. They have flown over an opium field in Laos with an American officer, a saboteur. His name is Ray Nickel. Nickel is spilling the beans to your father. We are a nation of dope peddlers: that's heroin on the hoof down there, our issue. There will be no telephone call, no *watered* roses, *heavy* clouds. Now it is the middle of the night in Southeast Asia in a hut or honky-tonk hotel gauzy with mosquito netting I can only imagine from movies of a previous war.

You are well occupied as always. For me the day goes on and on. You have read what you fancy in the *Times* and are busy in your room with stamps or coins or butterflies. So I think, but I do not think much. Only that there will be no call. I will not be allowed to reply to your father, in the middle of our New York winter, "I have mowed the lawn." I am will-less, disoriented, a woman alone with her boy. Leveled to type, I have no name, no purpose to get me through Sunday. It is just past two o'clock here. Middle of the night somewhere. You are fully occupied, your dark head bent over pieces of construction paper which you are neatly taping into homemade envelopes, red, blue, yellow folders with little tabs like grown-up files. I sit on your bed though I know you do not want me in your room. Minutes of slow time go by until I see that you are organizing the leaflets and broadsides and purply sheets that lie in confusion on your father's desk. I reach for the folders against your silent protest. You have printed on each one in round open letters:

Riot Technique
Acid, Skag, B.T.'s, etc.
Mutilation—Civilian

With no plan in my head, I push you out the door. Stuffed into our winter coats, I drag you down the stairwell, not waiting for the elevator. Out in the air we race down the pavement as though we have a mission, you and I, train to catch, urgent message. Down the blocks to the Museum of Natural History which is your haunt. No words. In a show of my authority or my anger, I pull you sideways into a barren park before you can run up the steps past Theodore Roosevelt and inside to your brontosaurus pal. I pay for two tickets at the Hayden Planetarium as though we had run down the avenue just to make this three o'clock show. The gorgeous night engulfs us. Music of the spheres. We Three Kings. The Star of Bethlehem. The other side of the sky, nineteen hundred and seventy years ago. It is the Christmas show. By some miscalculation you have never been to the Planetarium and you breathe audible sighs of wonder. Transported. Out of danger in the night, your father lies in the comic-strip buzz of his snores, protected by Ray Nickel, an officer who has repeatedly jettisoned his matériel, just dropped the lethal stuff behind enemy lines like sacks of harmless rice or mail pouches. Pinky lies safe in a tropical swelter. At the foot of his cot a guardian angel stands, the Marxist femme fatale—armed, wearing her gold Patek Philippe, good pearls, slung with her nifty Hasselblad—traveling companion to Jesus Christ.

We track an eastern star that leads across the desert. The overenunciated speech of a narrator repeats the Christmas Story before he reveals the truer mysteries of light, weight, time. You have left me—just the shell of a boy at my side, still in muffler and cap, sweating with excitement. The helicopter sweeps low over the blazing red poppies, opium fields of the Meo tribe where American personnel protect the lush harvest. The officer, Ray Nickel, shouts above the propeller noise to your father, names of the United States agents who help General Vang Pao bring the evil produce to market and distribute it to our troops, our bummed-out boys. With her reconnaissance lens, the princess from Berkeley snaps the guards, getting the USMC identification number stamped above their pockets. You have left me for the Star of Wonder, now you tell me it's a gaseous neutron mass at best, low on the horizon over Judea, bright and to the unschooled eyes of rough shepherds movable. When the lights go up we buy a real brass sextant and an atlas of the sky. We never speak of your war files. We never speak of that day at all.

I am deep-breathing, Bayard, as though on a fine morning and I'm just standing out on the back porch in Vermont. Practicing for the new life. Tomorrow or the next day they'll cut. It is necessary to crack bone, to divide the sternum which connects to the rib cage. A thin sack envelops the heart. Dr. Newman has injected miraculous threads into my arteries and filmed their adventures—surely the best scripts I've ever written. An honest performance, no faking this one. Breathing religiously. Like the catheter that invades my veins, I have searched for routes to tell this story about your father and mother. Newsreels, romance, history—stops and starts lie littered about the sickbed. Bayard, it's a medieval tale. I did not think of King Arthur that I read to you or legends of the Holy Grail, but that's it—just like Charlie Newman scouting the last clear path to the ailing heart, I find my way. What I have here is the material of a decade (more or less), the old stories of knightly *virtu,* quest of the novice with its many trials in a godless world. The great populist cycle available to all of us—perhaps beginning with the arrival of the Beatles at Kennedy International Airport on February 7, 1964—the *matière* they call it in scholarly pursuit, a neat system, the *matière* of the war years as I tell it in my adaptation—which laughably enough is termed the *sens.*

MAJOR MOTION PICTURE

Margaret Flood on the ramparts, incidental to Margaret Flood the impresario. Theater, it was all theater. My play—well it was *Medea,* poor old thing, done as a prolonged raspberry at the audience. Those poor folks who'd paid their money deserved a good ragging on the abuse of power, naked bodies assaulting them from scaffolds, whipping down apelike through a forest of ropes and bright klieg lights. A dumb show, grunts and howls, stolen lines—the text reduced to a glob of spit. What a tribute that you slept through all rehearsals. Bayard, what remarkable good sense.

My movie—less muddled under the direction of Sol Negaly, a strutting, cocksure man you may remember, Sol, who can co-opt talent and sincerity with so much charm you don't know it's happening until the profit tumbles in. Sol, with his shark's tooth strung on a gold chain, nesting in the ruff of his chest, his breast puffed out about to warble. His gift of sniffing out originality to nourish his ordinary mind. The success at hand obscuring all discriminations. Don't remember us with our honors, me and Sol and a frumpy inspired actress who has dropped out of sight. Far better you remember our rundown on the times—*Dreamland*—which so easily reviled our country and patronized the lower, lower-middle, middle classes.

Come into the screening room, Bayard, and we'll run it off with its neat sound track of wangy-twangy music, its belly laugh at old women in leisure costumes, its inaccurate use of regional language, its slick surface of turnpike culture, all weighted with the frail plot of a hick who makes it into the big time. Like your mother, Baby.

—O.K., Miss Cantor, take it from the top.
—Cander.
—O.K., little lady, you want to sing or not?

No different than a hundred show-biz movies. Sally Cander belts it out for the whole U.S. of A. and for our boys at the front who look farm fresh running out of their quaint straw huts to greet her and a Bob Hope look-alike. Run it off, Bayard, though you've suffered it a dozen times. Notice what Sol and I were up to—pride cometh before a fall, the system (we made millions) corrupts. Sol imagined Sally's rise to stardom and subsequent fall from grace a perfect paradigm for the state of the nation. I knew that we must also have her discarded sweetheart come home from the war with a dainty Oriental wife.

—Say, ain't you Sally Cander? (Dumbstruck, she looks at the injured vet, a whole world of hometown love and laughter die, the trade-off for her fame.) —Gosh, I almose wooden know ya!
—I'd know you, Bud.

Her punishment must be complete, I saw that. The audience wanted it, a big movie house full of kids who wanted to be told they were naughty, greedy, but only neighborhood toughs who must be tongue-lashed. There's some unnatural history here, Bayard: we wanted to be told that we were out of line altogether, swaggering. Like our Sally this whole damn country was too big for its boots.

We felt better going out into the night to our city streets or parked cars in the mall, each of us still in the movie's dream, the lingering sense of oneself chastened, for that moment ready to wander in the shadow of our heroine, who is alone, humbled, forging through a field of timothy grass back home in schoolhouse valley. For that moment, Bayard, before the headlights go on or the bus belches at the next corner, to walk that field alone to the solace of the buttonball tree, there to sit on a bare hillock and to sing—no backup, no mike suspended in the branches:

—O.K., Miss Cantor.
—Cander.
—O.K., you want to sing or not?
—I been ridin' high and on a roll . . .

Run it off. Every time Sol cried at that girl in her thoughtful solitude out in poky Okieland and he cried again holding his bullet-head prize. "I had a vision": it is on record he said that. Oh, he was not the worst man, Sol Negaly, just hopelessly sentimental, a professional believer in each of his lives. He understood himself to be quite the radical while we were making *Dreamland* which you will now find about as abrasive as a Western, as chancey as a Thriller. His vision—I'll admit to a touch of genius in Sol—dissolves Sally under the tree, stripped to her a cappella heartbreak (the end, as it were, of our American winning streak), to Sally in Shea Stadium, Madison Square Garden, Hollywood Bowl—going through her routines with mechanical precision—makeup heavy, electronics heavy, gowns elaborate. Cut from song to song to song—I would never have risked his finale of the heroine, heartless and fully empowered, manipulating the crowd. Too close to the bone. But Sol Negaly called it right, the reprimand of his ending lasted all the way to the bar or the ice-cream shop, if not all the way home. *I've been high, well on a roll. Believe me livin', believe me lovin' without you takes a toll.*

Dear me, I was there with Sol and the actress who was so convincing, soon forgotten. I am still breathing, not going to be punished for a harmless movie, not going to die. I can barely remember the pain that brought me down, the classic heart-attack rag, old story. Pain remote as the time we lived through, your father and I. And you.

You take your telescope up to the roof. I have bribed the elevator man to let you out onto a sooty, tarmacked terrace. There you set up with manuals and charts, but the filth of the city is dense. When, at times, you penetrate the smog only cloud cover is visible. You pack it up and come down.

In the doorway of the dining room you stand with your tripod aimed at us . . . it is the one time. Your father, speaking as though in an auditorium, again, yet again using the quote Ms. Neiman Marxist has found for him in Mr. Justice Holmes: "The best test of truth is the power of thought to get itself accepted in the competition of the market." The cultured voice resounds at his diminished audience. Sol, in fringed buckskin, not the worst of men, takes Holmes' proposition as a personal compliment. Professor of film (once moral philosopher) is duly impressed. A pretty girl or two, camp followers, shiver with emotion in the candelight. You say: "Why don't we live in Vermont?" You stand in the door and pick us off with your M-16 tripod and an angry glare. "Why can't we live out of this shit," you say. It is the one time you defy us. We say it is a shame, children pressed to violence. We offer you our apple tart, your father's port. It is the terrible disorder, life devalued. We say it is pollution, it's the war. Often you must have found us unconvincing, but that is the only time you called us to account.

Old material, folk wisdom—the young or idiotic talking smart. Out of the mouths of babes . . . and time closing in—that too. You have till Whitsun, till cock crow, till sparrow fart. Queen Mag, you have till daybreak. I saw that when Newman came in. With Jack Flood, his mentor (ethically off my case), but here today in a starched white coat, yet another soft silk tie, his shirt cuffs gleaming with polished silver links. He is the only doctor who does not slouch about in a scrub suit. Official presence—not so much as a how-de-do. Livestock to them, a couple of cowboys. Mumbles, inarticulate signals. They will wash, shave, bind me. Tonight, they will put me to sleep. I write to a deadline, that's fine, you see, Bayard, it's the professional thing to do. End of our story almost: me and your father—war, conspiracy, commerce, fashion and its gains. Let's not call it the Sixties, my sense of it packaged like a decade. Time running. Narrow time.

• • •

It is bitter cold now in the brownstone basement. Huddled on his cot, Bayard feels that his fingers are stiff before he sees that they are blue. He has read his mother's words as closely and slowly as an article he cannot grasp on space-time geometry. Some time back the bell tinkled over the door, the dead bolt shot with authority. Now he dashes out to the shop as though to confront a terror. It is deathly quiet and cold. Dark, too. The lamp on his father's desk, hidden by the rack of officers' coats, throws a dim ellipse on the pressed-tin ceiling. The stove has died. Fumbling with the wick and matches, he relights it. Apparently it is night. He turns the flame low. Time running. The first thing he sees is Lourdes' coat, a fuzzy manmade fur worn at the cuffs and collar to its cloth hide. The coat is on the chair where she throws it each day, flanks it with her bags, hat, boots. But Lourdes has gone home. The coat is a lonely cadaver. He knows at once that she has worn the monkey fur and sure enough, when he looks through the molting Persian lambs, the moutons and muskrats, it is gone. For weeks she has been admiring herself in the full-length mirror, hiding the coat from customers. The long fur of the thumbless African monkey hanging like human hair, black as the dead dry black of Lourdes' hair which Bayard suspects is a wig. He wishes he had seen her with her bumpy orange tam, the white high-heeled boots, the bags of mysterious loot—in that real fur coat as she headed for the subway on Astor Place.

He wishes, really, that his mother had caught sight of her. His mother would hoot, but later would speak of Lourdes in the sleek old monkey fur with humor and great affection. A good story. He misses his mother. He would say that tonight, and though she is a far nicer person, quiet, always reasonable in her hospital gown, he misses her carrying on. That was simpler: he was used to her stories with their elaborations and stylish epigrams and her voice rising with deliberation as she departed farther from the truth. Now Bayard turns on an intense small light above the cashbox. The metal box is cold to his touch though it has been swathed in a scarf which Lourdes believes will deceive any crafty thief. He counts ninety-seven dollars, not bad for a rainy day when the city is waiting for spring. A weekday. Time running. As he records the ninety-seven dollars in a ledger which he keeps faithfully, it occurs to him that Lourdes has stolen the coat, stolen the grizzly coat which she has priced above all others. Or borrowed. Surely, she will return it tomorrow, but only after he has gone off to school. School that lately seems beside the point. It is a pity that renting out the basement shop, he cannot get a key to the house above. He would like to go up on the roof and get on with his studies. It is the last quarter of the moon—Jupiter coming into Pisces low in the sky. Beyond the narrow shaft of lamplight, the shop looms gray and black—bright gowns and summer shirts, the dazzle of beads and buckles, dappled plumage—all sucked colorless by the dark. A dispirited line of headless dancing girls, a hunched file of foot soldiers without feet, the uninhabited wares of Golden Oldies. Bottomless, topless horrors to Bayard. His mother is nearly well. She is stitched together neatly in Baltimore. He misses her, Margaret Flood, but as she was. He is not sure that he likes the uncertain woman in the blank book who can't find the story she must tell.

Now Bayard wraps the cashbox in its scarf. It looks obvious and important in Lourdes' secret place. He moves through the racks to his father's desk. Pinky is asleep, Scotch glass empty, his limp silver hair just inches from his dinner plate. Taking his father's head in his hands, he arranges him gently in an upright position and swivels the chair. The bloodless face with lips clamped taut is smooth as a plaster death mask, the real dead face of Alexander Hamilton his parents could not tear him from in the

Smithsonian. He lifts his father, now light as an armful of kindling, and carries him the few steps to bed. Then, with due reverence, he closes the City Registry (1865), stacks the file cards of the day, clears the uneaten meal and empty glass away.

He returns to Machiavelli, a shrewd guy, and is rightly taken with the game plan for his boy. He marks the text: *A prince therefore who desires to maintain himself must learn to be not always good, but to be so or not as necessity may require.* Nice work, but Bayard Strong is not a Sixteenth-Century Italian nobleman. He mistrusts his own kindness, his patience which, in his dealings with Pinky and his mother—cleaning up their messes—displays his weakness to the world. Guilty that he has forgotten his mother's birthday early in March, he feels there is something soft about him and for this he blames his parents. All that talk when he was little, all that time spent on the proposition it was a sin not to care about the poor and blacks, federal furniture, injustice, good wine and homemade bread. Not to care about the people—a sin. So he reads his homework loving every slippery turn prescribed for the prince. He's tired, but not hungry. Often he forgets to eat. Just as he is about to put out his light and sleep, Bayard sees the blank book, his last assignment.

Well, he is cursed with his goodness. There are only a few pages left and the story is addressed to him, though it's queer reading about his mother's marriage and a kid named Bayard. Written not on her deathbed, but on the eve of a perfectly executed operation that has made her well, it is a peculiar gift that has come to him by chance. So far the blank book seems like an ill-chosen shirt or sweater that doesn't quite suit him. Though he must be polite, once again he's exasperated with his mother: he cannot understand what the hell it is she's got to tell.

CLOCK WIPE

The day your school was over we drove up to the house. It was like old times, the car stuffed with our summer clothes, soccer balls, espresso machine, books we could not live without. When we stopped at the good diner in Great Barrington, you hid your telescope under blankets and sweaters. Pinky had bought an impressive canvas bag full of tennis gear. It was like the beginning of summer should be, had been, but not one of us said it was odd. I figure it had been six years since we made an easy getaway and perhaps you did not remember coming to Vermont while the late daffodils were out in town and all up the hill approaching the trees were tender, pale green, the road muddy, still wounded with frost heaves and then the house with at least one shutter flung loose, torn winter branches to be picked off the lawn. So much to do—before us the long stretch of summer and no one said a word, but we all found it odd.

Your father did not have one meeting or trip on the agenda. On the night we arrived a congenial inquiry from the *Boston Globe* flustered him. Was the movement virtually over? He had signed to write a book without much thought, because that is done after a war, a life, a scandal. A public hangnail got you a respectable contract at that time. He was to reconsider the great days of a populist insurrection, deliver valedictions, sign off before he knew he was finished. Your father was unemployed.

We began at once with a plumb line and a sack of lime, marking off a tennis court on the ruins of my vegetable garden. We woke to the bulldozer putting our gentrified mark upon the land. The court's professional specifications thrilled us. We would have the Har-Tru surface and a row of Russian olives to hide the chain-link fence. Of course, neither you nor I, Bayard, had ever held a racquet in our hand. The days were still cool. Only the noise of our workmen and the thump as all morning your father served a bucket of balls against the barn. A van of kids came by who had worked with him during the student uprising in New Haven and sharing our table they laughed at the old hard-line slogans, sitar music, guerrilla costumes—not cruelly, not cynically—as a tribute to Pinky, already seeing him as their favorite high school teacher, not quite believing the dear old geezer wasn't gone.

So quiet a time, as I said, it seemed peculiar. I wrote habitually—something, then drove to small towns in desperate need of a jelly cabinet, came home with a tulip quilt, a hooked rug, a hideous spittoon. You were to start Trinity in the fall and we worried, Pinky and I, at your perfection, at our self-sufficient man with all his learning, all his fine containment, kicking an imaginary goal into the lilacs. You mumbled, kindly and reasonably, to yourself and for the first time we worried uselessly as parents do.

I took housewifely pleasure in early suppers, then the three of us scoured the kitchen clean. So we began the summer. Each night we watched Watergate with a big fire blazing, a rerun of the day. And you kept a speckled notebook with the cast of characters: Special Prosecutor, House Judiciary Committee Counsel, Deputy Assistant to the President for National Security Affairs. Pinky said at this rate you would be a lawyer, but each night at the appointed hour you put on your windbreaker and went out back devoutly to observe your stars.

Your father and I watch the Watergate hearings. It is a swell show. (The night nurse has come in twice with the sleeping pill. I beg for time.) It's a knockout with pretty wives, ambitious young men, more than we could have hoped—the Nixon White House a bunch of thugs, Kiwanis Club honchos —breaking and entering, bribery, racial slurs. We are pleased to observe there is not a gentleman among them. We sit together by the fire and when you come in to say good night you smile on us. It is a queer detail, but I think your father holds my hand. We are watching cops and robbers. We have routed the enemy, almost stopped a war. And at that time I do not think of long ago, of watching political trials with Jack Flood, a television extravaganza, Bayard, with a delayed resolution. I do not recall the past satisfactions, I am so hooked on the current show. Perhaps I had become an aged, breathless child of the Sixties, that decade I ran to keep up with, and I disregarded history, any instructive parallel, any warning. It was later I thought of sitting with young Dr. Flood and all those years after with your father, in front of television sets. We are right-minded, victorious in our ascendancy, watching and watching with a nation that, in the long run, only wants to be entertained.

The phone rang in the hall, as it will in awful drawing room comedies. The set played on. I did not hear your father's voice. The phone set down. I found him up at our bedroom window facing the ridge of hills, black in the moonlight, and when he turned to me, the spirit of the man was gone.

"They got Nickel."

"Who?" I did not remember the helicopter pilot, his rank or name.

"They killed Ray Nickel," he said and pushed by me. Then he was packing the tennis bag and the moment was, in its determined way, like old times.

"Your good shirts are in New York," I said like a fool. He turned to our view again and for a long while looked down on the back lawn where you worked with your telescope. He took in the room, touched the post of our bed. He never looked at me. "I am no better than those liars on television." Then, with a broken voice, he said, "It was an illusion, Margaret." With dead eyes, Pinkham Strong was on the move and he walked downstairs, out the front door, pausing only for a bottle of Scotch. I drove the route to town and back with the big flashlight. The next day and the next there was no trace of him in the woods.

Well, well—we have a spy story. Regard, here come the State Police with bloodhounds that sniff your father's dirty underwear with their livery snouts. The troopers inquire as to his habits, the medical history of his family, color of his eyes. I need not remind you of the hoopla—our slow Vermont workmen grading and tamping the tennis court while I received members of the press, the old radical gang, the FBI, expensive lawyers anxious for the case, if case there was

—an open-ended wake. The excitement surrounding his disappearance was inappropriate, even gay. . . . Did he drink? A little. He used to, often . . . as for cards, the horses, women, I swore he never played. They say that in Chicago once . . . how quickly we sidled up to the past tense, though as far as we knew, Daddy had only run away. Espionage is clumsy, dull, peripheral. Yes, he shot his mouth off. It was one of his good bits in the last round of speeches—the helicopter scene, our own men prisoners in an opium den, inglorious General Issue. Naturally, he bore witness to the sweep of poppies as though further proof were needed of our imperial corruption. Did I think this Ray Nickel, Colonel Nickel, was murdered by our side, A? Their side, B? Could we speculate about drug traffic—C? Did I believe Pinkham Strong feared retaliation? In our accelerated times, cops and robbers playing in the background, nobody listened when I asked my question—"What was my husband into?" Nobody gave a damn by the time we got to D.

The nurse stands at my door, a defenseless white lamb with the sleeping pill, no problem for me. I call, ingeniously, for a Bible. That does it, Miss Flood will make her peace with the merciful Lord before they wheel her down.

I believe that I am left to find the answer, not to make sense of A,B,C. Why get lost in that plot?

He said: "It was an illusion, Margaret." To Pinkham Strong was the illusion his fleeting political power, the heroic days when he was adjutant to no one? All the material of those times—the blood, guts and bloat of revolution, dead roses, heavy skies, correct line, camaraderie? The victory at hand. I admit that, for me, the feeling roused by the cause was greater than the cause, but I believe your father had overdrawn his credit, or invested in an enterprise . . . that he, and maybe his friend, the turncoat colonel, had written themselves lead roles in a quest they didn't understand. Watch as the phony replaces the genuine: Betrayin' your pal, defendin' your honor, rustlin' cattle for the good guys, I guess that stuff remains man to man. And we were small potatoes not worthy of his confidence, though you may say your father is a gentleman who keeps his counsel. To tell you the truth, Bayard, I'd say it was the Hardy Boys, all right—shades of James Bond and a good installment, but the Feds were pretty quick about it, happy to close your father's file. Or, an illusion, addressing the line to me before he ducked out, did he speak of our forgotten lust and its residual romance, our exalted food and wine, our high-flown pass at family life, grand Gaggia espresso machine, the Hogarth, the Hockney, fine proletarian etchings by John Sloane? Apartment, house, convertible, his son puttering in the cold moonlight, his industrious wife. Walked out on that, waltzed out, more precisely, as he always had, Pinky walked into the next adventure. Sure, I take it personal in my adaptation, that's the only sense I make of it, and let there be no illusions, Scharley, I was there.

The Bible (oh, it is predictable) comes with a priest. A dumpy slow fellow, his voice soft as a marshmallow like Elmer Fudd, asks if I want to confess. No Father, it would take us the night. Please, the good book, Father, just a peek at the Psalms. This he accepts as my secular fervor and he is standing now in an embarrassed silence while I copy you my passage—

My heart overflows with a godly theme:
My tongue is like the pen of a ready scribe.
You are the fairest of the sons of men—

And so on, Bayard,

Anointed with the oil of gladness,
Your robes are fragrant, etc.
The queen takes her place at your right hand,
arrayed in gold of Ophir—

Quickly now, through this wedding song,

Instead of your father shall be your sons.
I will cause your name to be celebrated in all generations;
Therefore the people will praise you for ever and ever.

Though it is my dearest wish I cannot write the likes of that for you. I cannot predict wonders for you or wax eloquent, based on the slim chance I may die. I can only sweep and tidy, set my house in order. The poor priest waits for his Bible and I'm not even a likely penitent. Forgive me, Father. He raises his hand for the blessing and seeing my dismissive smile scratches air.

I turn to the end of what may be a plain domestic story. All summer long we stayed in Vermont, you and I. I think we hoped he would come back for the tennis court, the lively new surface spanking, Har-Tru green. You will remember the hours teaching yourself to serve. And that I carried on with unexpected dignity, silent for once, the war widow without a folded flag. Trembling chin, wounded eyes—that parlor pink, that dilettante, that handsome man had reduced us to an illusion. I never said your father was a coward, but he walked out on the disappointing present. All I have to give you is our rowdy past. In those lost newsreels a big circle divided the screen into wedges like a good old pie—baseball, chorus girls, nonsense, history—all playing at once and then, starting with the hour hand at twelve, they erased the screen in a clock wipe. Now you see it, now you don't. Call it the Sixties—we were not altogether wonderful, but it wasn't an illusion, Bayard. You were there.

I am breathing, breathing out to the resilient bottom of my lungs. The nurse is whispering the restful name of a sleeping pill. She smells of smooth almond. Her hand is cool. She is softly pleading. You are with me in a music studio, not thrilled as other kids might be by the control booth, sound equipment, movie star, or by Sol Negaly in the trim dark beard of the young Sigmund Freud. Across the room you read, decorous in the terrible noise. I sit with my legs crossed, white lizard boots, a suede miniskirt riding high on the plump roll of my bare thigh. You hop through the tangle of cables and pull off your navy blue sweater which you tuck neatly around me to cover my shame. Thank you, Bayard.

I am tired, naturally, but take my medicine. Finished, the family saga or the great events for which I could not find a mode. Every night I'd say, "See you in the morning, Baby." Our casual signing off. Doesn't that sound fantastic now? "See you in the morning." Well, it rang true in our romantic past.

• • •

By the time he closes the blank book, Bayard's hunger is acute and he's happy to find stale jelly doughnuts and a quart of orange juice which he drinks from the carton. It is Lourdes' belief that sugar brings Pinky around. Now he brushes his teeth and puts on enormous flannel pajamas he has found in with a lot of Norfolk jackets and tweedy plus fours. Halfway to sleep he rises from his cot to set the alarm. He likes his mother's story when she sounds like Margaret Flood, when she is funny and tough about Pinky, less when she apologizes and makes herself a clown. It is a wonder to him that he has a live grandfather named Lynch. What happened to the girl photographer, ice princess? He has always thought it likely his parents came apart . . . yes, Bayard pins it on that hard-edged girl. Apparently his mother never noticed that he made a point of misbehaving whenever Sol, the greaser, surfaced. As for Nickel and his father, maybe the Colonel used him for a cover. At least she's right, no agents stake out Golden Oldies. Even the way she tells it, Pinky was out of his depth. His role must have been fairly incidental, for he could sure enough be found. And was found, she knows that story. And that Pinky had been on the sauce that year. How he turned up, she knows that story, in some rich guy's house in Aspen, then Bermuda—all right, into the next adventure. Though he always knew his father was a careless man, she's right again, it didn't dull the pain. But this time his father didn't quite pull through intact and pure.

Bayard understands that his mother must use him in her work, but does wish she would stop about the telescope, at least not make him whimsical as Mickey Mouse performing sorcery in a wizard's hat. It was not at the Planetarium he first saw the stars. It was in Vermont. But he supposes it's fair play and he'll stand witness to her story, though she's left out the wads of tear-damp Kleenex that littered her room, the wail of "Pinky"—he could hear it in the night. As for their revolution—he never would laugh at them—only once he could have killed whoever sprung the hemispheres to hide a fat bag of marijuana in his Rand McNally globe. But it all remains a myth the way she tells it, doesn't prove a thing, the Sixties. It's most of his life, the life so far in which he is no street-smart prince, just a plaything of the gods.

Bayard Strong sleeps, haunted by his reading. He misses his mother. She is well in Baltimore and appears sweeping the Pownal Valley kitchen, loud and flashy in gold of Ophir. Pinky, at the prow of a pirate ship, sails up the Hudson on whitecaps of cocaine. In various shapes his parents possess him through the night. They are arguing over salad greens in the front seat of the car. He loves his wretched father who cheats to win at tennis. As the family politics begin to break up, he favors Pinky like a stiff neck. Yet he is breathing, still breathing the cold air dutifully, time running, and listening to his mother's voice until it's dawn.

KILL FEE

Peace, be still, for there is nothing revealed
that cannot be hidden away.

—Sean O'Casey, *Mirror in My House*

LOURDES IS NOT happy on this fine day—blue sky and sunshine of false spring, gutters running with black snowmelt as she makes her way to the subway. A single grocery bag drags down the steps, tears at the turnstile and she crumples it under her arm as though it is no better than a threadbare garment she could never hope to sell. On the AA train—not where Lourdes wants to be—with the sheep faces, the heavy-lidded eyes heading for the day's wages without a bleat, she begins a sad discourse with herself—"Is killin' me." She strokes the black fur which hangs from her sleeves, crosses her feet daintily as she sits among the workers on the double A. On the Lexington is much better people—is bankers, lawyers, nurses getting off at very good hospital—and like herself, women in the fashion business. This is mostly untrue, but her anger distorts the good weather above ground and the ordinary double A crowd into one grim landscape. She covers the brown bag with a large crocodile purse and draws herself away from the dull mass, low types.

It's killing Lourdes that she must go to the apartment to wash and dust—make ready for Mrs. Flood. No Lexington train with its professional clientele. No Golden Oldies. When she ascends into the light at Eighty-sixth Street, her pride is struck another blow—two cleaning women who work in the neighborhood greet her as their long-lost chum. AA or D train people with uniforms and work shoes stuffed in shopping bags, their hand-me-down coats and cast-off scarves so terrible, terrible as they amble along in the bright April sun. Lourdes hurries down the blocks all business with her French crocodile purse (Hermès, ca. 1925), the brown paper bag seeping oil spots through its rumpled folds. Ay—a little sob escapes her. She dabs her eyes, enters the lobby, makes it past the doorman without a word, but *"Sí,"* she says to Orlando in the elevator, *"Sí,* is true. Is Missus Flood is comin' home."

Unused tables and chairs attend the emptiness. The whole place is stale. The very carpet under Lourdes' feet lies too flat: a paisley shawl over a couch is thrown in studied disarray, though no one has tucked up to read in the lamplight—the set done to perfection, play canceled. Lourdes fills the room with sighs, visits the bathrooms and closets, the books, books, books terrible to dust, mirrors dim and Missus Flood pictures dulled under a gray scrim. X—Lourdes marks on a photo of Sol Negaly and Margaret in cowboy hats—on location in Texas, pretending it is Mississippi. X—she marks, an evil sign, and rubs it out for shame. There, in the corner of the picture, sits Baby as a boy in short pants—reading hard, a fat book balanced on his knees.

The refrigerator stinks. The flour tin is alive with tiny black bugs—ay—by this time she would have mended and ironed a fragile georgette blouse—thirty, forty dollars—

with pussy cat bow and angel wing sleeves. Saks Fifth Avenue. No song in her heart as she finally gives in to her fate, flings her coat and hat on a front-hall chair and goes to the broom closet, clunks out the usual—mop, pail, dustpan—and draws on her rubber gloves. It is now Lourdes opens her greasy brown paper bag and produces a screwdriver, spanner wrench, prickly metal file. They are Pepe's tools she has swiped this morning. With these fierce instruments she digs and pokes and gouges the back door, jimmying the lock half free. Is lookin' very good in the bright kitchen light where she has destroyed the plate around the knob and permanently sprung an upper bolt—like very bad men, the worst of thieves has broken in Missus Flood apartment. *Mira, mira*—the silver is gone! In the dining room she topples a candlestick against a cut glass bowl, sets the portrait of a tight-lipped old dame on its ear: a Strong or Bidwell, her raw nose and red disapproving eyes fasten on a ceiling cobweb. Chairs pushed this way and that, two of them lie with legs intertwined in a dead embrace.

Lourdes surveys her artistry which suggests very bad men stealing silver. Wearing her rubber gloves, she pulls out the drawers of the sideboard and throws damask napkins right and left, but the dinner knives and forks of all sizes are still in place. These she scoops up, and off she runs to her crocodile purse as though, in fact, she is pursued, thinking craftily that thieves would not take only the spoons, the little butter knives, thinking the dog will bark, the tires screech in the driveway, hearing on Manny and Pepe's television the alarms and sirens sound. Turning one last time on the threshold of the dining room, she sees it is perfect, this havoc. Crossing herself once, twice, is very scary—Help me, Jesus. Thieves have been in Missus Flood house and when she come in to clean—is Missus Flood alive and comin' home—Thank you, Jesus—the door all broke . . . the candles . . . is good linen napkin. . . . She is chill with fear and cannot stir. No, she will not step in the dining room where they have been, already believing her story, where they have chipped a glass bowl is Missus Flood put fruit, put ice cream.

Turning from the scene of the crime, Lourdes rattles her bucket, discovers her cache of scouring pads and detergents under the sink. Soon she is singing to the rhythmic swish of her mop. Windows sparkle, tables shine. It is not in her nature to stay unhappy all day long and the old satisfaction returns—making Missus Flood house so nize, so nize. Clean sheets. Little soaps. Down in the supermarket grabbing rice, bananas, soup—she buys a splotched philodendron and a spiky snake plant, indestructible as the scrub flora of her childhood. For welcome, is Missus Flood is comin' home.

It is still light as she heads for the AA, her crocodile purse heavy with the knives and forks she has so cleverly removed, the stained paper bag with Pepe's tools crushed under her arm. The days are longer, but the sun is cold. The hatless men and women, tricked by the weather report into light coats, hunch their shoulders against the wind that sweeps across the park. Lourdes walks proud in her monkey fur coat, a gentleman's fedora tilted on her stiff wig, full of energy, a woman who never tires, full of plans. She must find her way back to the Lexington line and the profitable days, the pleasurable days at Golden Oldies. Pingy run the business in the groun'. Stiff with drink—ay, she knows him, stumbling around her racks to turn the sign—CLOSED—at midday, his ink-stained fingers shaking as he locks the door.

But locks do not enter Lourdes' head as she dusts her own clean apartment, not even when she replaces the screwdriver, wrench, file just where she got them in the bathtub among the shafts and bearings of Pepe's dismantled transmission. Loose bolts, scarred wood, thick paint chips never come to mind as she locks the door of her own room shut and lights the vigil candle to pray. The knives and forks are lethal on the dresser, arranged in a jagged pattern, dog's teeth set in a maze. Dangerous in the flickering light, meant to tear and prick flesh and tonight she does not, Help her, Jesus, invent a correspondence of silver implement to photograph of Manny or Pepe, Missus Flood or to the most recent addition—a shot of Pingy helping Robert Kennedy break ground in Brooklyn. No, she closes her eyes and draws a finger through the labyrinth of silver asking—will Pepe stay at Exxon? Will Missus Flood dress nice and leave her bed? And so forth—her petitions being answered as her finger finds its way free of tines and blades. Thank you, Jesus. Swallowing back her tears, she comes at last to Manny. Where is Manny? Why he go off, down on the block with, ay-ay . . . ? (That thought of the filthy woman, etc., unfinished.) When he gonna come home and rest in bed all day? Slowly, she traces her path to the Lord's blessing, but her finger is trapped by a sharp prong and the sleek cutting edge of a knife. Tears wash down her face and she blows out the candle. In the dark she crosses herself many times and lowers her grizzled head, praying away bad signs. If Manny come, she will clean for Missus Flood and give up the fashion business, so help her Jesus. She gathers the treacherous silver and throws it in her dresser, covering it with slippery underwear.

At last she sleeps, each breath a sigh, as a small dark body follows her down the block, a shade or child, and she confronts a heap of clothes in Missus Flood refrigerator, all torn and frayed, to be mended, labeled, priced. In Missus Flood buggy kitchen where her hands are covered with sawdust and metal filings, she will save Manny from bad women. See, she offers by way of explanation—this dented candlestick, this sliver of glass in bloody ice cream. See, bad men have done. Reality never enters the dream: for in her mad concentration, all Lourdes' damage—

scraping, prying, gouging—was on the inside of the kitchen door. It would be a poor, indeed demented thief who could not have turned the latch and simply walked out with his loot, free to the world.

Margaret laughs. Her amusement, at most anything, is merry, unpredictable. She's lively, come up against the clutter of rugs and chairs. After her gray room, the hospital room, after the long drive from Baltimore sealed into the back seat of a limousine, it all seems overwrought, needlessly complex. Bayard follows her from room to room. "Tired?" he asks.

Apparently not. His mother laughs, stroking the keys of her typewriter. Well, he is tired, having watched her sleep through the boring miles of Delaware and New Jersey, her feet propped on the jump seat, having walked her around gas stations so she will not clot. He is hungry—one pit stop for a hamburger has whet his appetite after days of not eating. He understands his mother's euphoria: as they entered the apartment, Lourdes stood at attention in her white uniform, the old retainer, until she gave way to frightened cries of "Missus Flood!" His mother has risen from the dead.

Margaret is giddy. "Just look at the books. Dear God, all this stuff." It's peculiar—household and habitation—more than foreign, as she looks into the dining room and listens to Lourdes' exotic story of the thieves. Plural thieves. Dented candlestick. Bayard rights the portrait of his ancestor, the woman's stern watery eyes disdainful of Lourdes' tears. A chip in the Waterford bowl! "Good heavens," says Margaret, "the breakdown of civilization as we know it." And laughs again, "Oh, the silver. They made off with the silver, did they? What matter, we'll dip into the pot with our fingers like savages." Now she would like to lie down, but will not say so, confronted with Lourdes' detailed account of bad men and what she say to Jesus and what she tell the super. Margaret pulls on the door of the sideboard to show her interest in this terrible robbery. The stitches in her chest quicken with pain. From its hiding place she takes a silver child, a naked babe, dimples in his knees and buttocks—a showoff, straining to hold a large bowl in one hand, his bumptious curls and penis tarnished blue-black. "Isn't he hideous?" Margaret says, putting her cherub down abruptly: he's heavier than she remembers. "He's worth a fortune," she tells Bayard, "if you like that kind of thing." Now she is fading fast, but must be led to the back door to check out the disaster, thinking patiently, all the while, that somewhere in this confusion of rooms there is a bed.

Not her bed: she's not about to connect to this place. Tucked in, with her dose of Inderal, she cannot sleep. It is way past her bedtime in the hospital, or way before. Bayard is in his room at last, where he belongs—a motherly notion, though she is not connected here. Lourdes, a turnkey, has been shipped down to the rag shop this evening to oversee the half-ration of Scotch. Night shift in the pokey. We are all in our cells too late, Margaret Flood thinks. The damage is done.

Her elation has ebbed quickly. All she could do—to thank Lourdes who came stealing into this bedroom with that silly dish—the damned angel, *putto,* whoever he is, his sweet ass polished within an inch of its life. "Is beaudiful, sooo beaudiful." Yes, yes, Margaret supposed it must be. Like gourds scooped out for ceremonial bowls or bones in the nose, beautiful to the beholder, this precious babe serving a godless company. No longer her company—the feast of a people she might record, a society in which the elders sat around this device in candlelight and ate their food with silver implements, but must never touch the fruit, nuts, flowers offered in this child's bowl—a display of pure excess. Repellent custom.

After the weeks of cheerful healing, Margaret cries. She

misses the hospital routine, the sampling and testing, charting of her body's progress. Her plain room. This place is disorderly, garish. She turns off the lamp by her bed. There, it is better with the colors gone, easier to weep in the dark. That flatware was Pinky's, heavy chased silver, bought by the Strong grandmother when a bride on the grand tour. Fish forks and big knives in the English fashion. Margaret Flood cries about the loss—not the silver—the terrible loss. Suppose Pinky wants his silver. Suppose he is ever well enough to come wanting his silver. That will be the day. Her cheeks are raw with salt tears. She has forgotten to take her anticoagulant and will not now, in her exhaustion. Breaking faith with Dr. Newman, with Jack Flood who kissed her into the limousine. Breaking faith with the world, a rotten custodian of the Strong silver. She yearns for the cool metal of her hospital bed, for the sharp smell of yellow soap in the sheets, the thin counterpane boiled and bleached free of disease and further back to the days of an almost miraculous safety when she was hooked up, her new blood visible, running bright and thin in tubes. Her tears are inevitable, tears of the living: now, like the rest of us, she must go it alone.

Bayard punches his pillow, draws up his knees. It's been a while—a couple of years—since he's slept in his room. The bed is too small. He pulls the mattress down on the floor, but now he is fully awake. "Shee-it," his mumbling begins, a good boy's attempt at a foul mouth. He sits at his desk wrenched sideways—the kneehole is for a child—and turning through a notebook with the calculus he's lost track of, Bayard begins to draw the face of a girl, over and over, spiral hair, ear studs, Kewpie-bow mouth. He draws poorly and the googly-eyed girl on the page is nothing like the smooth creature he thinks of, has thought of, since he entered his room. She is a Trinity girl, a senior with long hair, tiger-streaked out of a bottle. No one approves of this Suki, but she is an instant celebrity in the private school set—their courtesan, their music-hall star. With very little effort she is outrageous, defying the dress code with blue jeans, strutting on down with a flask of white wine in her knapsack, popping her birth-control pills in the lunchroom. Suki (Sarah Moss) is the girl who will always be remembered in her high school incarnation, sexually ten blocks ahead of the pack. It is unfortunate that Bayard thinks of her, but she's the obvious choice for his fantasies, so long delayed. Bayard the Innocent, a tender morsel on Suki's full plate. Bayard the Pure. Though his mother has overestimated his genius, she's right about his looks, that beguiling flop of jet black hair on the high forehead . . . her Baby with fine arched brows, thoroughbred nose and jaw. Not quite what is current, an idealized male beauty that has to do with tender heroes, good wars. In 1976 Bayard Strong might model dinner jackets, might play in revivals of happy musical comedies, top hat and tails.

Given the fact that he could have most any girl, he picks Suki as he draws hillocks in his notebook and nipples them with a swirl, long pointed dugs out of the *National Geographic,* nothing like the impertinent knockers she sports —braless, breathless, her shirt stretched tight as though she is forever running against the wind. He remembers her on the coldest days of winter, dashing across Columbus Avenue with her coat off, to set something up with the fact guys in a seductive whisper and then, because her reputation claims she is a tramp, coming on to him—"You going to do my algebra? Call me up. We'll do algebra."

That was some months ago. Bayard now writes her phone number over and under each tit. That, at least, he has right, but not much else. Gone the bright boy, star gazer, dearest of sons. Slave to the flesh, he steals out to the kitchen phone, low and bestial as one of Lourdes' thieves. Suki will do algebra.

"Do you know what time it is?" Dr. Moss, a psychiatrist, contains his rage professionally. This is not a patient round the bend, just some kid with the juices running.

It is twelve o'clock and even Suki has turned off the lascivious flow for the day—"For Chrissake, Bayard." But Suki's last grade on an algebra test was 49, so she manages to say she'll let him do her quadratic equations. Bayard the Untouchable. At his place, Bayard says, with his mother sick it's really like no one home. He thinks of his mother sacked out in the limo. She is easily exhausted and will be dead to the world by tomorrow afternoon. At the same moment in which Suki Moss gives a soft guttural consent, Bayard gets the message as though it were writ large and posted on the kitchen door. Lourdes has mucked up that paint, pried at the lock. An inside job. It fits with the fur coat, more recently the hats she has ripped off from Golden Oldies, shocking, a true crime, but the fact that he will have Suki, that willing girl, in his room is what's immediate, disturbing. His room is a kid's room. He tears the pictures of astronauts off the wall, hides his telescope, but he leaves the cornball paperweight of the moon—"One giant leap for mankind." The mattress is better on the floor. They will do quadratic equations.

"Fuck," Bayard says gently, talking to himself, the old habit, though this time his voice speaks to another with streaked hair, big breasts—half Suki Moss, half Fiji tribeswoman. He speaks to this vision he has willed into his arms, pulled down, down to him in an incantation of words he has never used—cunt and pussy—placed awkwardly in simple sentences. His penis is hot and hard, poking through his pajamas which are printed with the stripes and numbers of a Yankee star. Kid's pajamas. He strips them off as the scene plays, his scene in which this girl is not tainted, not poured into jeans caressing her crotch, not ready to put out . . . she becomes a reluctant maiden under his demanding gaze, the insistence of his touch, inside, inside where she is hotter still and he whispers his small obscenities into the ivory ear eliciting her awakened desire as she holds him in her consuming warmth before he spends himself impatiently, too soon.

Bayard lies limp, silent, pleased with his accomplishment. He remembers to pull the blanket over him before he sleeps—Good Boy—he gives some further thought to the battered kitchen door and stolen silver, whether it would be better or worse for his mother to know in her condition. He does not consider that tomorrow's arrangement with Suki Moss takes priority over his trip downtown to see what's up with Pinky, what's going down. Better Lourdes keep his father in line. Bayard the Cruel. He is such a novice at deception, at self-justification, he can't imagine he betrays his parents with selfish dreams.

Eight in the morning, Margaret answers the phone. "Dear God," she says to Bayard, "that was my accountant. First day home." It's easy—his heading off to school, her settling to a forbidden cup of coffee, not much different than coming back to the apartment after the long summer in Vermont. Air and a little life, decent house plants needed. By the time Lourdes arrives on the double A, Missus Flood is ordering a veal roast. By ten o'clock Margaret understands by way of mournful ay-ays and long, loving descriptions of beaudiful, beaudiful gowns, that this faithful scamp in a maid's uniform wants to be with the old clothes and her Pingy in the basement. "Ashame, ashame—Help me, Jesus." By eleven o'clock she has dried Lourdes' guilty tears and packed her off to Golden Oldies. "Thank you, Jesus." Thank *me,* Margaret has in mind to say, but Lourdes is already transported, stuffing her bags, adjusting her fedora with much good news of Pepe at Exxon, Manny on nice trip, sort of vacation, and her own adventures with a batch of pink dye successfully applied to a stained dressing gown.

But Margaret doesn't believe she's in great shape until

she calls Fred Peach and charms him. She tries to care about the Fifties and it almost comes, a reflex, jerk of enthusiasm, but only says she'll honor their agreement. She will write him a honey of a book, Peach says, a great cultural document, provocative and wise—already writing jacket copy—"final disclosures, insidious cover-ups that continue to poison the political climate of our time. . . ." One hand on the cool veal roast, very pink and pretty, Margaret hardly listens to her editor . . . a little rosemary and bay, throw in a glass of white wine. Peach says go for the names, hang in there with celebrity—he must run to lunch—and, naturally, the scandal. Margaret, patched and cleaned, still on antibiotics, cannot be sure, but thinks that her honey of a book was about a couple of minor saints toward the tail end of moral times. Dotty and Hannah as she has come to call them. Peach is eating at a North Italian restaurant that does extraordinary things with fennel and cream. Cream is not on Margaret's list. She has never liked fennel. "Naturally, the scandal?" Margaret asks.

Peach lets out a prissy little laugh, "What went on between those women . . . Come on, Miss Flood. Come on now, no holds barred." Lean meat and fish are recommended: as she wraps the veal back into its paper, it looks to her such an innocent thing.

Proving something, she sits at her typewriter as though it is prescribed and retrieves a scene, stored throughout her illness. It comes back complete—the first meeting of two young women, neither of them pretty. Wit and raw ambition. According to Margaret's notes the year is 1938, probably October, the end of October when both of them had articles running in the same left wing reviews. There will have to be a good deal of setting up and sorting out "left wing," but for now she has Dorothy Schwartz and Hannah Brandt taking measure of each other at *The New Alliance.* They have just been introduced by Max Gideon, a heavyset fellow with a gravel voice. Most likely . . . it is at most likely, constructed from tapes and letters: Margaret's heart attack cut short the interviews. From photographs: the dingy office of *The New Alliance* is correct and she is moderately secure about late October. Max is already sleeping with one or both of them, for sure.

It goes well—Margaret Flood sees these women wearing hats and gloves, prim collars and pumps, the puritanical working girl costume good radicals held to. A style affected by Hannah Brandt, wealthy, German Jewish, who has given away her sealskin coat, her tea gowns and taken some trouble to buy a cheap suede purse at Hearn's on Fourteenth Street. It crocks off on her white gloves: it smuts her large nose nicely as though she's just up from the coal mines. Dotty Schwartz's stockings are darned. Her mother, who works in a sweatshop, has made her skimpy shirtwaist out of stolen remnants. The live wire at *New Alliance,* Dotty is scrappy, full of gags. Today she is subdued, obviously outclassed by Hannah Brandt. Hannah, speaking in the faintly British accent she has learned from nannies, is extolling the virtues of a proletarian poetess she proposes to put on the tramcar to Parnassus. This has been established—that at their first meeting she held in her hand a sheaf of poems by a tubercular schoolteacher she has just discovered at the Workmen's Circle.

Margaret now reads this woman's work. It appeared in issues of *Dynamo, New Masses, The Anvil* and, of course, *The New Alliance.* An old-book dealer has rounded these up for Miss Flood months ago. The type and stock, the aggressive modern layout of these journals is dated. Printed a mere forty years ago, the pages are more distant from this day's sensibility than Victorian postcards or the craze for any advertisement vaguely Art Nouveau. The verse of Tanya Grass seems to be without a shred of talent, devoid of song and imagery, dead on the page under the heavy pall of a collective insight. The poor and downtrodden are canonized, oppressed workers noble—to a woman, to a man.

Bilge water in tenement sinks, garbage, gangrene, dung —all called upon to invest each line with its purpose— become poetic catchwords like beauty, nature, love. *O tempora, O mores.* Strident, not moving—editorial policy. Slavs, Italians, Jews huddle, retch, shiver, cough, expire in a bourgeois world so unfeeling, so decayed. . . . There is one poem of Tanya's which, in the light of history, amuses Margaret—the title at least: "Poverty Comes to the Kennedys." Yes, the poor Irish, don't forget them: Margaret laughs. She can't redeem the poetry of Tanya Grass, but she has not come to mock, not this time.

In this quiet room, her study it was called, well-appointed place, she's restored to her work. Her work seems a privilege she must not abuse, precious as the tough pump of her heart. This book is about grand men and women—flawed, perhaps fallen, but gods in their day. Once gods to Margaret Flood. Here familiar techniques fail her, the cutting and trimming that has set her style. For the resurrection of her mind there has been no exercise—breathing or walking. The first scene, which she has done at a clip on the first day, is wrong, all wrong. She has made Dotty and Hannah into quick sketches, radical groupies of the Thirties. Taken from exuberant WPA etchings or from old movies, old Broadway plays, she has set them against each other in a Depression comedy that will be full of bright bitchy talk. It is wrong. Margaret knows it. She's tired, so tired and finds no true or even useful story turning through the photos and clippings. As she strokes the covers of the radical magazines touching their reality, she hears a titter in the hall, a thud. The front door—Bayard. The high pitch of a girl's fawning laugh and she rushes from her desk as though to the scene of an accident, only to catch the backside of her son as he closes his door against her.

It's sharp as a slap across the face. The muffled sounds and outbursts are somehow her intrusion, her disgrace: Margaret runs to her bed. In fact, Bayard and Suki Moss have thrown down their book bags and are engaged in empty tattle, the usual tales out of school. They open Intermediate Algebra while Margaret cowers. Her heart clatters—this will happen: she has been advised. Hasn't she also known her son must go his way? After being closeted with his mother in the hospital room, the dark enclosure of the limousine, isn't it hopeful, meet and just that Bayard stake his claim to female flesh? She has prescribed it. Her heart beats, loud and painless. Her cheeks smart, blood whooshes in her ears. Through the thick walls of the old apartment there is nothing to be heard as Bayard takes Suki through linear equations for the third time. Suki is not dumb, but endlessly distracted, toying with paperclips, inking her name on Bayard's boyhood desk. Now that he has her in his lair, they sit at a distance from each other. "Pay attention," he says. She pouts, sticks out the tip of her luscious pink tongue.

While Margaret tosses on her bed at the tragedy of it—he is her only son—makes up nonsense: the temptation, the corruption of Bayard. It's too soon, this place with separate cubbyholes. Her private room at the hospital was invaded night and day by men and women with a shared purpose. At the civil hour of five o'clock they brought her supper. Her blood's not thick enough for this. She prowls by Bayard's closed door, then clunks the dining room chairs. Margaret, never known to sing, singing—"Drink to me only with thine eyes," as though it were a proclamation of war announced by the town crier. "And I will pledge with mine." "Mine," an accusation, rings through the hall. Her incision aches like a devil's stitch. Bayard and Suki stand amazed before her, an open textbook held between them.

"We thought you were asleep," the boy says.

"That's right," says Margaret. Her bitter look bounces off the slick surface of the girl. "I've had a lovely nap."

Thus begins a pattern of deception: wiles and stratagems each afternoon. Loud arrivals, appalling silence, doors opened and closed in a farce of slams and petty clicks. The three principals steal through the apartment as though it is mined. At five or five-thirty, they declare a daily truce. In two weeks' time Suki gets a smashing 65 on her division of polynomials. Then she pays Bayard off, undressing and instructing him. The further treachery of a phonograph is introduced into the game. The Stones, the Grateful Dead play while Suki Moss pulls Bayard to her on the mattress and nibbles down his body to the crotch, her oral exercises just like it says in their book. This is a trip, screwing Baby Strong while his famous mother does this repressed, this masochistic shtick crawling the apartment.

In two weeks Margaret claims she is inured though, let's observe, she is unable to write on about Dotty, Hannah and Max. She attempts terminology, a glossary: Marxist, Marxist-Leninist, Industrial Workers of the World, Fellow Traveler, Trotskyite, National Students League, Popular Front, early anti-Stalinist and late, Democratic Centralism, Paris Commune, Marx-Engels Institute, but falls apart on Liberal—a thick unshapely fog, with pockets of clarity, a flicker of retreating light. The cardiologist in New York does not much like Miss Flood. She is a defector. She has run away to Maryland and has the cheek to tell this illustrious man that in high school young lovers drove to Elkton, Maryland—it was famous—to elope. Her apology tastes dry, unfunny as cold toast. The doctor says, "Going to try us again, Margaret?" before he confirms the steady chug of her heart. She walks up to Broadway or sits in the Park at the hour after school when Bayard brings Suki to his room, but she is drawn back to the apartment to listen for the cree-cree of hinges, the insidious titter, an obscene quiet that precedes the daily selection of Mick or Keith getting it off with the band.

"The thirst, that from the soule doth rise, doth aske a drinke divine," Margaret sings, returning Suki's bold stare, her son's defiance. Now she sees her bright boy turned stupid, his lies transparent. She does not buy the story that he is going to Goldman's, Malone's, the library after supper or that he is spelling off Lourdes down at Golden Oldies. She cannot abide Suki, the girl comes equipped with musk sacs. At lunch, one testing of the big world, Margaret tries this on—"Bayard finally has a girl, the Trinity trollop. Not pretty, but she secretes a perfume —it's called Spore." She gets the laugh and winces. Not a style she values anymore, bread-and-circus popularity. Easy as setting Dotty and Hannah against each other, reducing Max, their lover, to a cut-rate Don Juan.

Sex—unavoidable as death and taxes. Margaret lies on her bed waiting for the affront of a door slam. Shuffling, laughter, cree of hinge. Intermediate Algebra in a pig's eye. She fears the musk, the spore, all sex—the shunting off of poor Dotty when Hannah bought Gideon his magazine; Jack with his nurses' corps; Pinky on his Sixties pedestal—The Father of Us All. She fears, equally, that she's lost it.

The quiet time in the afternoon sequence: Margaret gets up and undresses, taking off her blue shirt, a skirt that hangs loose on her narrow frame, her slip and warm tights, her bra, recommended by Dr. Newman to ride above her incision. Each morning she dresses. It is best, they say, not to hang about in nightclothes. They say loose garments, a regular life, treat yourself nice. Margaret has bought a silk shirt the color of purple-blue iris. She has never worn bright blue or anything insistent on its color like this slithery stuff which she now holds to her cold breasts. She goes to the bedroom window, snaps up the shade, throws the shirt from her, exposing herself to Manhattan. Fifteen floors up, no one can see, but she offers herself, that is what she feels, a woman forty-six years old offering herself to the bare trees, reservoir, snake of traffic, skyline—cold slice of Einstein Tower, motherly dome of the Guggenheim. For the price of a genuine Cuban cigar? Any offers? No one can see the merchandise, but she feels stripped to the city, daring, freakish. Nipples tight, gooseflesh mottling her arms and thighs. What you see is what you get. This perky muff, Ladies and Gentlemen, this dusky pubic pelt belies the cropped gray head. Original mole, the plump new scar. Scars—her left leg is gashed from calf to thigh where Charlie Newman pulled out the useful tubing of her saphenous vein. Recuperating sexuality—if you can walk three blocks, climb two flights of stairs . . . Margaret looks at her cold white toes and fingers, holds her small belly still bloated with anesthesia. What am I bid? This amazing little lady, a mere forty, forty-six years of age. That is her fancy: she is a barker in a sideshow displaying her wares to the whole damn city. Her good working body shows itself in the window. She can take five blocks at a clip, spring up three flights of stairs. When the music from Bayard's room starts, she is mortified. She runs for cover as though the cops have caught her hooch show operating without a license. The beat of that music is mad.

Half dressed, in bare feet, inviting further shame, she calls Jack Flood. Yes, she wants him paged.

"Margaret," he says with concern.

She is grateful. It is only that she wanted to hear him speak her name. "I didn't want to call you at home." That is not what she wanted to say . . . oh, that the man in New York has upped the Inderal. Wrong again. "Could someone down there sell the car?" she asks. "Not you, Jack. A man at that garage?" It is a matter to which she's given no real thought and Jack, off-balance, tells some story about Ginger and the girls going down to St. Michael's to open the house so that this weekend he's got a conference, something on.

"Someone on," Margaret says and can pick out the technician who she had seen robed and masked like an Arab woman, following Dr. Flood around the recovery room with big black eyes. It is just the Inderal she's called about, though Newman wrote the prescription—yes, the car and to say that Bayard has this slut, this older girl.

"Good for him," Jack says. "We didn't start that young."

That evening Margaret looks in the phone book, calls Golden Oldies to see if her son has lied to her again. The phone rings and rings. A man answers.

"Who's calling? Who's calling?" It is Pinky's voice, familiar though slurred. In the background Margaret hears the lilting complaint of his adoring Lourdes. "Who's calling," Pinky asks sharply, with an authority he can still muster. It is the first time she has heard her husband speak in four years.

"Margaret," she breathes and hangs up the phone. She is reminded of calling a boy in high school, the divine suffering that followed, the sweet torture that he might not even know her name. And then, without a moment's hesitation, she dials her father, the same number as in her childhood without the area code, dials again and says, "Tell me, how did Mother die?"

Ned Lynch, who is always pleasantly surprised to hear from Margaret, first asks if she is well. It is such a soft man's voice with no hurry to it, no demand, she could listen forever to her father. His very sentences are neat and calm.

"How did Mother die? It was pneumonia, Margaret. You remember." But she did not; how her mother had gone out on a damp day to the clothesline. Ned Lynch says, "She hung out a wash and when she came back in lay down feverish."

"Not the heart?"

"No, that was an old problem," says Ned and asks, "What's this for, Maggie?"

"It's not for anything." Sad, useless information, Margaret says, "Thanks, Dad."

In the morning she is able to work, no longer troubled by Suki or Bayard. Their drama seems a risky business: she is blessed with a careful life. They say there will be setbacks. She's made her peace with death, why not its sexy shadow. Listen, she is breathing—it's technical, a matter of control, of continuity, getting down to real work. So Dotty, Hannah and Max come clear to her: they are not made to gesture and proclaim from a glossary of terms within a trumped up script. They no longer live in clippings, gossip, obituaries, in Margaret's further reading of their forgotten articles and books, but as her history, her own reported life.

When I was young but not so young that I can excuse myself, I was taken to dinner at the house of Hannah Brandt. I was presented. She took no notice of me: I was not offended. At that time I was delighted to see whatever I could of the great world. I believed there was such a place, that it was out there and important.

The dinner at Hannah's (or Mrs. Gideon as the servants called her) did not disappoint me. I think it was the first time I tasted Belgian endive in a perfectly dressed salad. An appropriate memory: to this day I don't know if I like either the elusive bitterness of endive or Hannah Brandt. That does not alter in the least my initial admiration for the woman and her blanched-out greens. It's not a dodge to record the table before I attempt to recapture the talk which I did not begin to understand—not then, perhaps not now. But the long oval table was Sheraton, I believe, with delicate legs, inlaid work in pale tulip or satinwood that swept the rim to define the area we played in. They played in.

The shells of our mussels and clams were thrown into large China export bowls. Slurping and dunking the soup shut them up—perhaps by design. Gideon, the size of Papa Bear, grizzly in a rumpled work shirt, splotched tie, the elbows of his soft tweed jacket frayed. Dotty Schwartz wore serviceable black, much costume jewelry, and flaunted her young lover—a graduate student, greasy, high as an old trout, proud of it—who had just returned from the Sorbonne to put us New York frumps down with news of France. She looked to me brave, a decorated widow in order of the scabrous pearl, brooch of ruby paste—a flyweight seated at Gideon's right—tense, ready to defend herself. By my side—Philo Pierce, my editor, my guide: a married man, he was to my amazement showing me the town. That was proper, according to their rules. That it was, in fact, proper would have shocked them. If I had crunched and swallowed my shells down to prove it, so help me God, no one that night would have believed I wasn't sleeping my way into their midst with Philo Pierce. We had arrived late and Pierce had hardly poured himself a swig of bourbon when we were led in to dinner by Hannah. There was an air throughout the meal of the first act being over, something essential had gone on. That's my view of it always. I may be wrong.

I remember coarse manners all around, and the first words Hannah spoke in reply to a rude remark: "I always serve shellfish to Jews." She sat at the head of the table, beaky and handsome as a senator, complete in her power as any celebrated man, but all in velvet cut for the cleavage, a spray of diamonds pinned to her breast. She gave us salad and cheese in the French manner, then a most delectable Linzertorte. Though presented by a black woman in uniform, I had the impression that Hannah, Mrs. Gideon, was dishing up our food. When the meal was over she rang a bell and cried, "Send in Sabu." The boy appeared—an Oriental of thirty or sixty or fifteen—ever-smiling, all in white with a snap bow tie.

Still eating with his fingers, Gideon said: "Tell him it tastes like *mandelbrot.*"

Hannah shouted this compliment at Sabu, then turned to Dotty's lover, "Try Spanish on him or a little Arabic. He's from North Africa. I have to watch him like a hawk or we get coriander in the stew." So graceful, cultivated—his bobbing and nodding.

Reversal of servants and masters: Gideon and Philo Pierce sucking away at their teeth, the graduate student shrouded in the stink of Gaulois, playing dead to Dotty's constant taps of praise. I should beg pardon, setting down this dinner, beginning with Hannah Brandt's style when I'm after substance, but it's only now I can see that Hannah and Gideon had become Park Avenue liberals with too many haughty, furious stands . . . that, always embarrassed by her money, she played the fool. I'm on safe ground seeing that Brandt (it's O.K. using her last name) was never successful as a woman of the people, a role that didn't mix well with grande dame. But they were my gods among the dirty dishes and stained napkins they would leave to others. Stars in the moral drama of their time, they begot me. That dinner table a primal scene and I could no more figure their use of each other in rough argument than a child can admit the cries and moans, poor Ma pinned to the mattress.

Drinking Hennessy V.S.O.P. in the living room, they were perfect. To be fair—Hannah presiding in her wing chair, setting the subjects, was duchess and headmistress, fixing us in her world with the eagle eye. Her world, indeed—the Brandts had bought her the whole show. The money was respectable, investment banking, so it was unfortunate that she'd gone public with that overbearing manner and with her agitated articles made Hannah Brandt a name. It was a name to me, you bet, and I was amazed to hear her husband's practiced grumbling cut her down. To discover Philo Pierce to be a nervous imitation of our proletarian host, down to the frayed jacket, the tough-stuff editorials parroted in his *Sectarian,* even the crude table manners of our savage Max. To turn from the pathetic sight of Dotty—she was fifty at the time—pressing her graduate student's thigh as he nattered on about Camus and Sartre. I could not tell whether their talk was brilliant or no better than town gossip—Jackson Pollock's drinking, a lousy biography of Henry James, Adlai Stevenson's sex life—but to be fair they were snappy, charge and countercharge, the drawing room dialectic, that was their game. To be fair, I never really knew them and loved every crumb thrown my way that evening, even the fact that they more or less dismissed me, and that as a woman of the world I might have to see my idols sported feet of clay.

Margaret's happy. Now Margaret is home. Let Suki have Bayard. Let Lourdes have Golden Oldies and Pinky to boot. Let the women in hospitable white, the long parade of ruined vestal virgins, have Jack Flood. She has Hannah and Max. She has the whole history of the American Communist Party flowering in her head. That's the grand route she takes after her first shot at that dinner table, the indecipherable codes and signs of an evening that she thinks, after all these years, she may at last have right. She has gone back to search Gideon out at twenty, a baby Marxist who taught himself to read English, falling to sleep over Shakespeare in the public library, making his way through all thirty-eight plays. Hannah at Bryn Mawr in disfiguring spectacles and white kid pumps, marching with the National Woman's Party, a triumphant suffragette. Dotty in prison overnight, having kicked one of New York's finest in a Textile Workers' brawl. She has Philo Pierce. At last Margaret Flood has an angle on that preposterous man, scurrilous womanizer, windy arbiter of taste—Philo, a beefy mamma's boy at Yale whose only distinction was one tenor solo—yes, tenor—with the choral society and a close attachment to the Anglican chaplain. The park buds out. Soft rain greens up the sheep meadow, the muddy baseball diamonds. From the fifteenth floor Margaret predicts a glorious spring. A spring for lovers—let them have it. When her son is not in his school blazer, he's got up in destroyed denim like one of those aging guys in the Grateful Dead. To prove himself or his mettle to the restless Suki, Bayard has trashed his room. Margaret works through their sexed-up silence and their music. She has the Great Depression, Stalin's treachery, the rise of fascism, the Spanish civil war and she has not even approached the portentous meeting of Hannah and Dotty choosing their weapons over the poetry of Tanya Grass. The apartment is a ruin without Lourdes, but Margaret is home. She has a world of material, a lifetime of work when poor Mrs. Grogan comes to the door.

When poor Mrs. Grogan comes to the door, Orlando stands guard by his elevator to see if this threadbare woman with her parcel is a danger. Poor Mrs. Grogan, her face scooped in a long sorrowful spoon, would like to be paid for the sweater she's knit. It is an Irish sweater ordered by Mrs. Flood six months ago and she has dealt with the likes before who'd have her pick the pattern, buy the wool and chisel out on the sweater, never mind wasting the Lord's good time and Mrs. Grogan's. Mrs. Grogan draws her colorless lips into a thin white line. All is quite changed from a sharp day in November when she measured Mrs. Flood. Mrs. Flood has nothing to her and looks pitiful, a scrap of a boy.

Mrs. Grogan undoes her parcel, folding back the paper with care, winding her string. She is proud of her work, and the sweater, a pullover, has turned out a winner, its stitches sly as a riddle, what her people, she says lightheartedly, call a fairy's curse. But it does not please Mrs. Grogan to hand the sweater, rich with the smell of sheep's wool, over to Margaret Flood. She has knit for these women who diet, who aim to look one of the lads, and the sweater hangs off this starved creature by a mile.

"Wonderful," says Margaret.

"I take a good measure," says Mrs. Grogan, "and I say it doesn't fit."

"Wonderful," Margaret runs her finger down a cable.

"That," says Mrs. Grogan crossly, "is the root of Mall's tree and that the braid of Deirdre. There, the martyr's trellis." Mrs. Flood runs off to get a fat wallet and counts out far more than the knitter is due. "And here upon the arm," says Mrs. Grogan, softening, "is the chain of Breon fashioned in the lover's rope." She names her stitches for the likes of Mrs. Flood who fancy Gaelic names and tales. None of it is true.

"Will you knit for my son?" asks Margaret.

When Mrs. Grogan looks upon the disgraceful sight of Bayard's room, she will not step inside. No more than she'd jig with hooligans and bandits. Turning from the torn curtains, charred desk top, tangle of filthy sheets and half-stuffed pallet on the floor, with a string and her eye she measures his old pajamas. Fine house, indeed, shantytown. This woman should have neither chick nor child, thinks Mrs. Grogan as she heads to the door: the carpet needs sweeping, dull brass, flowers on the hall table expired in their slime. "It will not be long," says Mrs. Grogan, "you've hit the slack of the year." She does not like the looks of her handiwork hanging off Mrs. Flood whose small frame of sticks and bones looks blooming but unlucky as a sprig of hawthorn brought inside. She does not want to knit for this woman's boy, nevertheless Mrs. Grogan says, "Your pattern is Moran," setting the shoulder straight on Mrs. Flood's pullover with little joy. She will give full value. Woman or man, they like the grim stories in her Irish patter about the fishermen's sweaters, art of Aran, where each family had its given stitches so the swollen bodies could be identified when they washed up from the sea. "They'd take you for Moran."

"I was born Lynch," says Margaret.

"Well, they wouldn't take you for it," says poor Mrs.

Grogan, put-upon, needy, string in her purse. Money in her purse, too, and she gives her customer the gift of a bloodless laugh. "Lynch, Flood, whoever, they'd bury you Moran."

Margaret loves her sweater. It suits her for the park where she takes the air. She wears it always, watching the dogs run free, children herded to the playground as she walks a brisk mile to service her heart, increasing the pace each day. Only then can she switch off her love affair with Dotty and Hannah, the tangled burden of their histories which for Margaret sets the course, demanding and sweet. She loves the oily animal smell that seeps from the wool if the day is misty or the bench she rests on damp, and Mrs. Grogan, a sketch with her dour legends, was funny as a crutch. Margaret thinks of the knitter and of long ago when Jack started with the knitting nurse—all that rage for a woman she'd never see again. Perhaps Suki Moss will be such a weightless memory for Bayard. The girl has scored 85 on square roots and radicals and will soon be moving out of his life—a minor character, Margaret hopes, suspects. Philo Pierce, Fred Peach—to be grouped at the end of the credits. Editors, knitters, young doctor, teenage vamp, night nurse. An excess of fury at the girl in New Haven—Emily. A matter of proportion, good sense: keepers, messengers, watchmen, ghosts. It was Pinky got it wrong with that double agent. It was Pinky wrote himself large into some grandiose plot, made much of the Colonel's death to lend incident to his unaccomplished, nameless summer days: the exercise of building that tennis court bordered on despair. But it was not easy, she granted him that, to distinguish top billing from bit part. She has Dotty and Hannah in her head. On a first-name basis. The satisfaction that Dotty, despite her record, gets security clearance to write a mountain of secret memos at the Department of Civilian Defense. Hannah, with her lousy German but stunning connections, covers the Nuremberg trials. She sees these strong women clearer than her own mother who dared no more than hang out the wash, whose features had blurred early on in the haze of sickroom and half days. And Gideon's New Yawk accent, hysterical in its anti-bourgeois, anti-fascist tirades, she hears better than the soothing glottal voice of her father, the insurance man she now talks to on the phone. Her parents, who should be central, it was as if those blameless people had discreetly gone away.

Sitting on a favorite bench she sees branches soften overhead, the first horsefly of the season. When she's early she sees the same class of black and Hispanic children with their teacher. They share one magnifying glass, studying buds. They draw in their notebooks. Little kids, nine or ten—they dance, tumble down slopes and are called to attention again. Look! Look here! This downy stalk, tough calyx, prickle—it will develop and then . . . then they run off, not held by miracles, squat in front of Margaret in a singsong pact:

> Doggy Doggy Diamond, step right up,
> Not because you're dirty,
> Not because you're clean,
> Just because you kissed a girl
> Behind a magazine.

Look here! Then this bud will be slick, fleshed out, uncurling in its progress, next week if you are good. If you are bad—the dull, airless classroom. If you are good the grass will grow, tree blossom. Poor kids, it's not their fault and hardly science—an outing, pass at nature, sketch of time. These last good weeks in April, Margaret, a happy outcast, hits her bench each sunny day of Bayard's rutting season. She lives in her big sweater. It collects a past of soil and spots, but she thinks it would be a crime against God and Grogan to wash the oils out.

• • •

The suburbs thin down to neglected farmland waiting the invasion. Developers' signs are up picturing Bayview and Liberty Gardens, unbuilt condominiums already draped in wisteria and creeper. Rich fields spreading from the Susquehanna: "This fruitful and delightsome land"; more beautiful to Captain John Smith's eye than Europe, Asia, Africa. Jack Flood is with his daughter Lily, tooling along, top down, in the old Corvette. Their day, warm and sunny as they want it. And the adventure is not that they are driving Margaret's car to market like prize cattle. No, it wasn't easy for Jack to peel off his younger daughter who is stuck in the shallow undertow with Ginger and Rose. Not easy for Lily to jump free. We might think her Pro Keds weighted with stones and Jack has had that feeling of nauseous immobility as in a dream, his hand reaching out to Lily, tip of their fingers meeting—no godly act of creation—in the nightmare's touch, an incomplete grasp. It has been a conscious gesture to snatch her to his life. Lily, who has turned fourteen, seems *only* fourteen to her father, not set in the ways of Ginger and Rose, a pale imitation of their Country Day style. He has made this observation thinking of Bayard Strong, the bright boy, son he never had. That kid's loyalty to Margaret has made him want to claim Lily as his own. He sees her shoes untied, hair tangled, the slouch she affects of cool reluctance as she trails her mother and Rose.

Lily is opaque, silent at the dinner table, her behavior just in bounds. These bounds are set by Ginger Flood and have to do with niceness, with nothing being strange. We know that in his house Jack doesn't break the rules, but he's been watching Lily in the last few weeks, seen her popping off her braces, skimming bottle caps, yawning at dry crab cakes (a family recipe of no distinction), sneering at her mother's anemic diet ice cream. His older daughter is lost to him: she has cut her hair so that down the living room, across the lawn—as she moves, as she speaks—well, he can't tell Rose from Ginger. But he has caught Lily in the pantry gagging, an exaggerated mime, at the sight of a bakery cake Ginger has ordered for the school sale, a pasteboard lemony object decorated with sappy flowers and gelatinous leaves, all green and gold. There is hope for Lily, so Jack thinks, and calls out to her as they swing off the highway. She is off in the radio's song and the wind wipes out his words.

The Corvette rides broad on the back country road. Jack Flood brakes at the slightest curve. He sets Lily to reading the mailboxes, now few and far between. Two miles past the Aberdeen power line, where it is supposed to be, they find it—Plunket, with its flag up, a dirt drive within a glossy boxwood hedge and a child's drawing of a house, no bigger than two sash windows on either side of a front door. Mr. and Mrs. Plunket run out to greet the Corvette whooping like kids at a birthday pony. All aglow, Mr. Plunket takes the wheel from Dr. Flood and drives right past the little house. Behind a screen of cedars there lies a long stone barn. Jack and Lily trot after Mrs. Plunket, small-waisted, snub-nosed, so adorable you'd take her for a girl. The Corvette glides up a ramp onto the blocks prepared for it, next to a Futuramic 88 and a couple of '57 Bel Airs.

"Holy cow." Mr. Plunket blushes. Large and boyish, he clamps a loving paw on Mrs. Plunket's head, "She's got the original taillights."

"She's better than when we seen her down in Bal'more," says Mrs. Plunket to Lily. "We been waitin' for the day. I guess your Daddy will miss this baby."

The men attend to business—registration, title—and have a bit of trouble with corroded bolts that wed Margaret's New York license plate to the big back end of what is now the Plunkets' car. Lily is taken by the little lady to the dark end of the barn. "That's your cruiser," says Mrs. Plunket, "all mahogany. That's a Nineteen Thirty-five Matthews and this here with the teak deck is 'Forty-Two, custom-built Chris-Craft, last year before the war."

Lily Flood understands that she must not touch the boats, but admire them. In the dim light she begins to see that they are rare and wonderfully made. Sitting up in its cradle, each boat is equipped with a ladder so she can climb up to see the polished brass fittings, the original canvas cushions and, in the Matthews ("Sweet Sue"), the chrome flask and green celluloid cocktail glasses that spring out from a nifty bar. Turning, she catches the window. It is beyond her father and Mr. Plunket, a high arched window, perfectly articulated like a scallop shell. The sun shines down from it in strong heavenly rays. Heavenly to Lily up on her ladder who sees the window straight on. The fierce light obliterates her father, Mr. Plunket and his fat old cars. The wooden roof, high as a gymnasium, solemn as a church, is ribbed and trussed with beams, some of them round tree trunks with the bark peeled off. The stone barn is the best place Lily's seen.

"You could take your girl out for a spin in this sweetheart." Mr. Plunket fondles the Corvette. "Park her in front of the malt shop. You could run up to Bal'more after the prom. You could make out in this baby."

Jack and his daughter are driven to the bus station in Havre de Grace in a beat-up station wagon, an unremarkable model. "I could drive you folks up home."

"No problem," Jack says. As he waves them off, Mrs. Plunket cuddles up to the driver as though she's on a date in their homely car.

"Holy cow," Lily laughs. Her upper lip catches on her braces—painful, but she laughs and laughs. In the privacy of their Trailways bus seat, her father lets her count the money. The Plunkets, kids with a vintage piggy bank, have paid cash. Ben Franklin on the hundreds which supplement eight one-thousand-dollar bills. "Grover Cleveland?"

Lily asks. Jack Flood watches the unused farms turn to suburbs, then the rim of slums become his city. Lily is silent as they pass projects, neat row houses, neighborhoods she's never seen. Overprivileged, this is her first big bus except for school trips to Washington, Williamsburg, boring Fort McHenry. Jack holds his hand over the roll in his pocket; so much cash—the Plunkets cannot deal in laundered money, nearly ten grand—Margaret's. She was always good at money. She will like to think of the Plunkets' Hall of Fame as the last stop for her car. Out the bus window it's a grand day, sunny because they deserve it—their day. The early azaleas and cherry trees are muted by the tinted safety glass. Jack's daughter seems closed to him now. Brooding, Lily sucks an end of hair, then turns to her father with a dreamy air. "What's a malt shop?"

Lourdes finds Manny on the couch—watching, as though he's never been away. "What's to eat?" He lifts the beer in his hand in a niggardly salute, a gesture so endearing to his mother she takes it for tender kisses, his arms around her in a prodigal's embrace. Manny is home. She feasts her eyes upon him—ay, thin, his clothes no good. His rich oily skin mottled, powdery and dry. It is an occasion for chicken, sausage, pork, rice and beans which Lourdes, though she hustles to the store and back, does not get on the table till after nine o'clock—Help me, Jesus. And almost forgets to set a place for Pepe, never mind herself. Guava jelly, instant flan. Manny is come home. Middle of the program and her boys wheel in the television not to miss the bad woman with money. Where has Manny been? This bad woman lie to the policeman before he chase her up the mountain, tires whining, music fast. Lourdes is mostly watching Manny, something funny with his face. She cannot eat for happiness though he is lookin' wrong. Is skinny, longer? His head was always big and broad.

The rich woman's car sails out into the void. The policeman—is hansome, old, old, wore out like Pingy—screeches to a predictable halt. The hills are shaley and arid with insignificant growth, harsh and ragged as Lourdes' country. "Sooo beaudiful," she says as the woman is consumed in flame. It is very late when she finishes the pots and pans. Pepe's plate is clean. Manny not touch his food. This she attributes to his run-down condition, terrible meals on his trip, terrible. Manny's trip has taken hold: she has him on buses and planes traveling the country she has never seen—America. It is a capital city with palm trees at the airport, little hill towns where they bring in the cocoa, sugarcane, bananas, a media composite of swift highways and mighty forests, front porches with bay windows and rockers, green lawns, public buildings with flags and fountains like Lincoln Center. Not even the Lexington line, it is America all above ground and a great satisfaction to Lourdes, that Manny has traveled. Thank you, Jesus.

Lighting her candle to pray, she does not arrange a pattern of stolen silver. She flips all photos down, leaving only the picture of Manny with fat cheeks and full lips in his maroon mortarboard. As she begins to pray, the glow of the candle is steady. No omens in the paraffin pool, no predictions in a flicker as she succumbs to her spell of help and thanks. Manny has seen the world and becomes to his mother the son of a Spanish grandee, sent out on a quest and when he is rested, when he is well, then he will tell Lourdes his story. That pleases her and she skips to the end of the tale, a fireside tale in which Manny—or any wandering child, always male—is much improved by experience but comes home to stay. Thank you, Jesus. Sorting through old themes like cartons of rags, she finds what serves and discards the trials of the road, the testing of Manny (his skin is ashen, dry), for the more familiar story of her own unworthiness. Manny has been cast away by her coming and going to work, left to his own devices when a smart and growing boy. Lourdes opens the trade: she will give up the pleasures of the shop. She has failed him. She must prove herself, clean half a day at Missus Flood or any lady and come home—if Manny stay. It's all she can bear, help her, Jesus, to give up Pingy, Golden Oldies, her career. No one can enter Lourdes' cosmology: the candle is steady as a light bulb, assuring her course of self-sacrifice. She will be home to listen to Manny's stories. Through her neglect he is sad, so sad he sleep all day. In the unwavering light Lourdes sees for the first time that her son is no longer a promising college boy and help her, help her, she prays—*pobrecito,* his head is not funny or long: Manny is losing his hair.

Sol Negaly is listening to *Lohengrin,* Hitler's favorite opera. The Heldentenor is singing in the marriage chamber—"Farewell, my lovely. Farewell, my wife, the Holy Grail must rule my life." The music fills the empty white space of the loft and swells on to its swollen Wagnerian finale. Sol's eyes are closed. He is laid out on a huge white bed. Margaret stands above him. He has not heard her knock or Tina let her in. He is wearing a silk bathrobe loosely tied over his naked body which is dusted with talcum powder. Sol's sweet as a baby down to his ruddy balls. When he gets the sense of someone—Margaret, Tina—standing there, he puts his fingers to his lips directing silence: Get this leitmotif. A little reverence, this is art.

The loft is bare. Margaret can comprehend it only as four, maybe five times the size of her living room. Bed, TV, refrigerator, phone—all Sol ever needs. Speakers hung from the ceiling and one small domestic corner with books, clothes, glasses set neatly on the floor. Lohengrin marches to his higher calling. Sol comes back to unartistic life.

"Jesus," he says to Margaret, "where you been?"

She chooses not to reveal her illness to Sol half naked

and, running for cover, talks about her work—Dotty, Hannah and Max.

"It's a great look," Sol says, meaning Margaret with gray hair, specter-thin, the Irish sweater swinging loose over an ancient tweed skirt. He gives her the Hollywood clinch, big love-up, sexy gaze into the eyes, left to the body, right to the chin. "Do you know who this is?" he asks Tina. Tina waits for her instruction. "This is Margaret Flood. That's who this is."

Tina is a miniature, perfect replica of a grown woman, made smaller still by black. All in black—high boots, jodhpurs, black scout shirt. Tina's something else in the white loft, only a glint of silver buckle and tiny gold death's-head on her collar. Margaret walks away from Sol's spiel—Who is Margaret Flood? The admiring rundown on her life and times sounds like an obituary. She walks the length of the loft and looks at New Jersey, Statue of Liberty, Verrazano Bridge, mouth of the Hudson, landfill in the Narrows. This is her first time out beyond her exercise in the park and, taking it slowly, one gossipy lunch, but the big man's in town. She's glad Sol Negaly, an old lover, has not come to her apartment where he might detect the remains of her invalid life. Returning his call, she has been directed to come to him, to this new setup at the very tip of Manhattan. The view, yes, but turning back to the big white space she's afraid. Tina is massaging Sol's back. Margaret knows he is still on about her books, scripts, prizes, her past, the words pounded out of him. She does not want to cross to their corner, enter their story. She's trapped, panic flutters through her, useless hand to her heart. No place to hide, no back entrance or fire door latched. An unreasonable fear she ascribes to all this light and begins her journey across the terrifying expanse of floor.

They call to her, Tina and Sol Negaly, to come join them on their bed, for they are man and wife. Margaret has missed the news. Sol has married this mite of a girl. She has seen, but missed, the insignia on Tina's shirt, a Nazi device and the Order of the Iron Cross which hangs on her very white neck.

"Iron Cross, Second Class," Tina says. She puts on steel-rimmed glasses. "Himmler wore these crazy pince-nez." Heinrich Himmler: she identifies him for Margaret as Reichsfuehrer SS.

As it turns out, Tina's costume is legitimized. "I'm making the Nazi movie," Sol says. "I thought it was time."

"No," Margaret says.

"*Dreamland, Playtime*—haven't I always been right?"

"No," Margaret says.

"No—what's no? I get the civil rights, Vietnam—the big picture. You wrote the script."

That shuts Margaret up.

"What's the argument?" Sol opens the refrigerator which is full of champagne. "I brought you down here to meet my wife." They toast the future. As it turns out, in a few days the bridal couple are off. Sol's shooting in Spain, the hills above Barcelona being remarkably similar to the forest near Paderborn where the SS trained.

"In ancient Westphalia," says Tina. "See, Himmler had this school built for eleven million marks. On the ruins of this monastery, the castle of Wewelsburg."

"Get this kid," Sol says. "Research. She's learning the business."

"What Himmler had in mind was very exclusive, very elite, along the order of Jesuits—you know, religious." Tina shows Margaret her buckle, a silver name plate from Wewelsburg where each SS lad had his own chair in imitation of the Knights Templar. "Actually, Himmler was very thrifty," Tina says. "He lived on his salary. He drove his own car."

"Will you get this kid?" Sol pops another Moët Chandon. "I found her in a garage band in Pasadena. She's wearing a dog collar, spiked mitts, a swastika."

"I'm lead guitar in White Bread. What's a swastika? Some goofy bent cross," Tina says, *"Hakenkreuz,"* and gets a kiss from her old man. It happens there's a whole nation of kids out there Sol Negaly is going to educate. It's the big enchilada and Sol advises Margaret on the budget, the stars.

Himmler is Tina's idea: "Hitler's too much. Anyway Heinrich's interesting, an intellectual. He played historical charades about like Napoleon, Genghis Khan. He was into archeology, astrology, you know, mysticism. It's something you can relate to like the Sixties. He had this thing about Tibet."

"No more." Margaret covers her glass. A nightmare, Sol's scholarly child bride. She's a stickler for authenticity and shows Margaret a still they'll run the titles on, the German Eagle over the zeppelin field in Nuremberg, designed by Albert Speer.

"Docudrama," Sol says. "I'm going in and out of real footage. You see, there's this element of truth. Himmler adopted two blond boys, Polish brothers he found in Minsk."

"Spare me the plot," Margaret says.

"What's wrong?" Sol lashes in his bathrobe. "You have a heart condition, a bypass, doesn't mean you write off your friends." So, she's been researched. Sol has his scout and he dismisses Tina to her corner. Orders her off the set. "You write out Pinky. What the hell is your husband doing in that basement drinking himself to death?"

"He walked on me," Margaret says. "He walked out."

"Do you know who you are?" Sol asks. "You are married to Pinkham Strong. You and Pinky, hell—" Sol presents Pinky and Margaret, scenario of the golden days, workup of the handsome radical, the talented adoring wife. Sol gets the magic. A director who can draw sensitive performances out of dull actors, he brings Margaret to tears and she's ready for the take. "Priceless. What you had left them breathless, yearning. You walked and talked that guy. He was Jesus Christ. Now you want some cheesy domestic drama. What are you—a hick with the little white gloves and your pride in the change purse? Some old lady with jewels in the vault? You want to talk priceless, Mrs. Strong? You want to break my heart with this nonsense any longer? Margaret and Pinky—" Sol flips his hand at the prospect of his little wife—lint, a gnat. Poor Tina reading up on the Gestapo is a frippery: Sol's marriage budgeted in. "What's the argument?" he asks though Margaret has not said a word. "You ought to go see him," Sol says. "You ought to go down to that dump and see what's left of Pinkham Strong."

"I support him," Margaret says.

"You take out the checkbook." Sol wipes her tears with his manicured hand. He is not a thoroughly bad man as Margaret Flood has come to see him. "I know that trick with the checkbook," Sol says.

In the next scene they are watching the sun fade over Jersey, guzzling champagne, on top of the world. Tina shows Margaret the type they'll use to run the credits, Germanic Fraktur.

"Get this kid," Sol says. Margaret, drunk and weepy, can't rise to the occasion when Tina Negaly dips into her treasures of the Third Reich and comes up with a picture. It is a watercolor of the Haufbrauhaus am Platzl in Munich by young Adolf Hitler—bland, sweetly tinted and precise. Docudrama, Sol will cut from Der Fuehrer's sentimental work to the classy Wewelsburg set. Margaret is breathing deep breaths that restore her. Tina drops a sheet of tissue paper over the malign painting, puts it back in a folder with infinite care. Margaret breathes deep and says, "Who gets the girl?"

"What?" Sol asks.

"That's what the movie's about, Sol. Who gets the girl.

Two blond brothers. Are they twins? That's a bit hokey. Two blond boys, one of them good, one of them bad. The naughty boy's a Nazi and the other, in the goodness of his heart, only pretends. A couple of young bucks with silver nameplates on their chairs. Goody is older and remembers the Holy Mass in Minsk, the Polish Easter eggs hidden under his father's chair, the last loaf of bread his mother bought which is left on the table though she has disappeared. The fortunate rescue of the boys by our Himmler."

"Something like that," Sol Negaly says. The hair on his chest is white, talcum worn off, defenseless in his silk bathrobe, effete.

Margaret is at the door. "Or the boys get separated—that's the ticket. Innocent blond boys, one brought along in the ways of the merry prankster, Heinrich—the other presumed dead for a docu shot of Dachau, actual footage of the camp. In fact, the good boy returns, a simple American soldier. The brothers stalk each other around Whatsisburg in a First Army Jeep and the SS Mercedes-Benz."

"You're not well," Sol says. Tina has slipped behind Margaret, kicked the police lock, unbolted the door. "She'll get you a cab."

"No," Margaret speaks directly to Tina, only to Tina, in an urgent hush, "get back to your homework, but if you are going to learn this business, remember it is a simple business and you had better use Jewish blood."

"Yeah," Tina says, "the mother." She stands sassy in her boots, showing Margaret the door.

"That's the way," Margaret says heartily. "This is an important film. Kill the good brother."

"You're sick," Sol says. The light behind him is cold, blue-white; without the sun, dark patches roam the empty loft.

"I should never have come," Margaret says softly, apologetically. "I should never have walked across that floor."

She lets Sol Negaly lead her to the freight elevator and not surprisingly he gives her the show-biz kiss and hug.

"Take care."

"I will," says Margaret as she is carted off. More in sorrow than anger, she cries out behind the closed doors, "Think about it. Who gets the girl?"

"Some friend," Tina says.

Which does not please Sol. "Put on something decent," he says. They are going out to dinner. They always go out to dinner. He switches on *Lohengrin* before he takes the next shower. Margaret is right. Not a bad afternoon: kill the good brother, but you got to take it easy. The Nazi can't get the girl.

Rush hour, as it turns out, and Margaret who has transported herself at once to the reasonable world of Dotty and Hannah, specifically Max's break with Philo Pierce, is stuck in traffic heading for the Lincoln Tunnel. An expensive ride home, worth her life to get out of that loft. Not that she dismisses the scene: Sol with the child in attendance; Tina will haunt her. It's a problem she sets for herself in the cab, to consider why it was necessary for Max Gideon to denounce Philo Pierce. Because Max for all the ideology dished out in the Thirties, dealt with real politics, even if it was another hair split along Trotskyite lines. Like mumbling forgotten rosary beads, Margaret goes over this material . . . and Pierce who had always been above the fray, spread himself thin with the publishing, gentleman's articles, diddled with his magazine. The man of culture, an umpire calling the shots in an endless, unwinnable game. The radio in the car tells Margaret that she's sitting in a traffic jam, even as the meter runs. An authenticated moment Tina might value in her docudrama. She could have told Tina, if not the Holocaust, use God in the end—all occasions invite his mercies, even a rotten script. Tina with her corner of expertise. Hitler was a vegetarian, his shirts made of silk. *Snow White and the Seven Dwarfs* was his favorite film. Himmler's masseur, this King Kong double agent, was a pretty good guy.

At home Bayard waits in his blazer and a new school tie. He has tidied up his room. For weeks he has not known if his mother was alive. "I worried about you," he says.

It is apparent to Margaret that Suki has thrown him over. They eat supper in the kitchen. Stabbing a chicken breast, Bayard thinks of the silver, family silver. Lourdes has stolen that stuff and he should say, but Lourdes has been useful to him looking after Pinky during the weeks of his sweet tortured spring. Tomorrow or the next day he will say it. Now his agony consumes him. His sighs punctuate a melancholy silence. There will be no occasion in his life for silver. Bayard suffers, drinks a milk glass full of wine, his heartbreak no less real being the first time, not made easier by soulful gestures: he tousles his hair, rejects a dish of his favorite ice cream.

Finally, Margaret says: "Sol Negaly's in town. I went down there."

"Where?" Bayard asks tragically.

"He's in a loft." She describes the view, the champagne, but she does not get on to Tina or the movie to be made in Spain. She asks, "How is your father?" She has never asked that and has to repeat it. "How is he, down at the store?"

"Fine."

"No, he isn't fine," Margaret says ever so gently, "and you haven't been there."

Which reminds Bayard of Suki—why he hasn't been with Pinky—and he flings off his tie, tears at his collar until he looks quite Byronic. "I know it isn't your business," his mother says, "but after school, tomorrow or the next day, I'd like you to go down."

Sol was not fair about the checkbook. Pinky had ditched

her, sailed off to the call of the Dark Plots, the upper regions of trombones and divided violins—yah, the higher calling. Tina had explained. You have to get in his brainbox, Hitler thought he *was* this pure knight and he would like save this blond princess and then save the world. His favorite opera, he could recite all the acts of *Lohengrin,* every word. Tina wasn't kidding. It was very personal—Hitler had this cute blond mother. She was supportive. Sol listened to Wagner to get him in the mood. For what—Tina, the big enchilada, the Holy Grail.

Margaret cannot forget tiny Tina, her corolla of white-yellow hair. California Aryan. How the SS had this squad, night riders who only worked in fog. I mean it was very romantic. Sol, the director—better he left Tina in the garage band trigged out in Nazi gear, just plain outrageous with spiked mitts and what's a swastika. Charade of violence. Sol, the matchmaker, shaming her back to Pinky. "Do you know who you are, Margaret? You are married to Pinkham Strong." Sol had produced the loft, light, harbor view, heightened emotion . . . the whole afternoon. Pretty romantic.

Bayard has left his door open to display his misery, his brave resignation. Life is a rotten business: thank God his youth is gone. She knows not to enter, to only look in. He sits with an unopened book, very straight in a low kiddy chair. Margaret knows not to smile. "See you in the morning."

"Perhaps," Bayard says.

From back, far back, from grammar school, she remembers a pretty nun who did not like Margaret Lynch . . . does not like that smart little girl, calls her in front of the class, says cruelly, "A little learning is a dangerous thing."

O.K. Tina has her orders. It is a waste of money. Big waste of time. She has rented this van which frankly she cannot drive and will probably kill herself. Her feet dangle above the pedals. It is so New York they did not have an automatic. She called around. A city she could do without. Uptight. Sol is like filled with this hostile energy, pushing Tina with his dopy plans. Garbage. The streets are garbage. You come out of lunch with this backer, eighty-dollar bottle of wine, and there's the black death bags. They serve it for dessert. Shit. You are walking in shit. "What a beautiful day!"—they never stop about the spring on some crummy cold day. The seasons are not Tina's thing. What's the big deal? Spring—it's so New York. Sunshine—whee! They have this lo-cal sunshine looks like you purchased it with coupons. She is heading across Fourteenth Street which is O.K.—wa-wa-wa-wonderful—total sleaze. You would know they have no radio in the van. What would Tina give for any dopey music they play on any soft-porn station in New York, any doodly old rock 'n' roll with D.A. haircuts. Folk, I mean Tina would listen to fern bar folk, to Tony Bennett, Palm Springs Liberace. She's had it to the gigi with Wagner. All velly, velly intereschting—it must be a gas when that swan comes on stage. Howdy! I am a handsome stranger. You don't know my name.

O.K., you are not supposed to make a left. Tina's from out of town. What's it, a crime? Grinding in third. Anxiety time. What she hates about New York is the *Weltanschauung*. Schauung not Schlong. Sol is off sex in New York among other things. He's old Mister Hold-my-Oscar-before-it-gets-cold. Mistah Dignity and won't go to clubs. Well, you better believe in L. A. he does the clubs. Where else Daddy Warbucks find Tina? The circuit—that's where, ripping her licks. On hard body guitar. Und thank you, Herr Negaly, is rescue little blondie from ignorance. Miss Tina-No-Talent. She'll see about that. You want to know NAtional SoZIalist, Clausewitz, Volk. Will you get this kid? You want to talk bunker. Himmler with the tarot cards. Der Fuehrer was a monorchid—yeah, one lonely testicle, one freaky ball.

Tina parks at a hydrant in front of the shop. Sol's out of his mind. Hello, garbage! Hello, ticky-tack! Hello—oh, I'ma Tina Negaly. We make-ah da film. Talk Chico Marx—issah nize place. O.K., Tina has her lines: Gosh, you do have the uniforms, exactly as my husband said. Oh, I am so delighted, just look at these treasures. Tina is dealing with this little Conchita, this funny old Mex. Fatigues and air corps jackets in lovely olive drab. These epaulets are super! Walking shorts, drill trousers—I'll take it, I'll take the lot. Yeah, you got tweenie scouts, I mean if you got blue and gold I'll take the high school band. No. No *mira!* the undies, the top hat, the creepy chiffon. Kee-mo-sabe? We are making this movie. Better thank Sol. What Tina wouldn't give to be out of this city. *Mira!* Even in spic they all talk New York. No wanna the gloves. No wanna the hat. "Hello. I am Tina, Mrs. Negaly."

"Mrs. Negaly, of course, my dear."

He's like this very old, old with the makeup job Gregory Peck. My dear, Tina has forgotten her lines. I mean, Dr. Kildare, whoever, you want to look at my chest? It is kinky how she likes this old guy. How she hated his wife. Sol's got some friends.

"Tell me, Tina—it is Tina? About the excellent idea you have for the films."

Well, it is Tina with her mouth shut. It is Tina brought to heel by courtly Pinkham Strong. It is Tina sitting with her hands folded around her knees. Well, Sol is making this film. It is about—Tina is twisting her wedding ring—well, good and evil. She is telling it all to Raymond Massey, Jimmy Stewart. About two handsome blond boys Heinrich Himmler found in Minsk. All the way to the end.

"I was attached to the United States Strategic Bombing Service," Pinky says. "Eisenhower's staff—a curious group assessing the damage. The rubble was still smoking when they brought the defeated officers in."

"Wow," Tina says. It's romantic. You want to believe this old guy with the shakes met those big Nazis after the war.

Ja wohl. Tonto's waiting on the trail ahead. Tell me another. Tell me again. O.K. she believes it. She believes *Lassie* and *Father Knows Best.* She takes out the envelope with Sol's big fat check. And they're running out of this basement and into the van. Conchita is a worker. She carries a load. *Mira*—the overseas caps. What the hell. Thank you, Jesus.

"Thank you, Tina. Will you give my best regards to Sol?"

Tina is misty. She is kissing Walter Cronkite. She is getting the holy waters or something from Lourdes. Yeah, Lourdes. You better believe it, she's bought half the shop. She is driving away in the big shift-ass van. Five thousand dollars. Sol must be nuts. Does it come out of budget? Who's running this show? Tina is burned. New York is the pits, red lights and arrows—one way to hell. Sol must be stoned. No way, not in New York. What Tina wouldn't give for party time. No way—Mistah Film Macher, buggin' his eyes out like old Orson Welles. Cin-ee-mah Man, got neat ol' John Huston down on the mat. She's heading west. Who would believe that is a river. That is a bomb site. Warehouses, whores—one big bag of garbage. Forty-sixth Street. The Salvation Army. She's got the khaki, she's called around. Tina unloads the whole mess with these pasted-up winos, throws it like trash into their bins. Don't thank Tina. Thank Jesus or Sol. Freaky cold sun. Tina puts on this G.I. jacket, not from her war. Broad shoulders, it looks kind of dikey and nice. She rolls up the sleeves. Some pricey getup, five thousand dollars plus the cost of the van.

Oh, please, *Lohengrin* back at the ranch. Down the elevator shaft comes the wedding march. Tina has never seen an opera. She has this book with pictures of the nuptial chamber. Elsa is some big Mamma, always a blonde. The lovers are left to caress, but not for long does their bliss last. It blows Tina's mind. They don't even make out. *Elsa, ich liebe dich. Dich* not dick. That poor guy. He never even unbuckles his sword. Tina is rising in the big freight elevator. Slowly, slowly—it's grunting and grinding. O.K., plunge to her death, she's sick of New York, of Sol in the city. She married in sunshine, her Daddy Walt Disney. Here, in New York, he's a confidence man. Tina is stuck, sealed in the elevator, pushing the switches, banging the door. She screams with the music—there is no beat. Tina's had Wagner up the gazoo. What Tina wouldn't give to be bending the notes. White Bread—any old gig, wounding the air, just beating it up. She sits in exhaustion. Sol will not hear her cry out till the end of the act. She is quiet. Like she is sick of being quiet and polite to all Sol's backers and friends. Watch Tina make nice. She takes her orders and this very day pulled a charity scam. It's a big waste of money, he'll drink it up. She's learning the business: SS sewn up by peons in Spain: helmets, machine guns, First Army costumes rented in Madrid. Tina, go to your corner. She'll see about that. Ach, isht der crescendo, da tuba, da trumpets—in vich ve hear the angry cry uf hatred, der raving uf revenge, der piercing cry uf luff and the ecstasy uf adoration. Yah, isch sprechen Franz Liszt. Well, Tina would like to see special effects, how they sail this swan on stage. These real doves flap over Lohengrin's head. She would like to see opera. Now she is moving—cranking and grinding. Whee! Tina ascends.

In the expense book, she writes down the price of the van. She is wearing her pince-nez. Authentic, like she told Mr. Strong. Himmler's glasses ordered from Weird-O in Cherman Detroit. Cost an arm and a leg. I mean Heinrich Himmler's glasses. She never told anyone, but she told Mr. Strong—property of the Reichsfuehrer SS balanced on her nose. So? So Tina believes Minnie and Mickey, *The Flintstones* and *Star Trek.* No smart mouth on Tina. He took her for real. Mr. Strong. You better believe he listened to Tina. It was worth five thousand dollars to give a parting kiss to the gentleman. Tina gets a rush—Mr. Strong.

• • •

"Is cute," Lourdes says. "Is so small." She is describing the angel who descended on Golden Oldies. From nowhere she came, so tiny, so white in such a big truck. Though Lourdes stands eye to eye with Tina, she has made her a wee creature, a hop-o'-my-thumb who can bathe in a dewdrop—this little body, at most a size four, from heaven with gossamer hair.

Manny rises from the couch and turns the volume down, the quiet time, only the news and weather report enacted on the screen. Lourdes, just home from work, is uncharacteristically sitting in the living room. With his eyes closed, Manny listens to his mother. With his hand he makes a sharp tilting gesture and Pepe goes to the refrigerator, serves Manny his beer. On she goes, mostly in Spanish, about a kid who bought up all the army clothes. In English, Lourdes says "movie" and "fi thousan' dollar." She repeats these words many times, a response in her litany of praise. It is her good fortune that the movie takes place in a war.

What she is recounting to her boys is a miracle and her testimony includes all details of a routine day at Golden Oldies which set off the supernatural event. Lourdes had just washed the lunch plates, put everything away tight from the roaches. Pinky is writing at his desk. She has him in good pants, a shirt fresh laundered. As though Jesus himself has slipped her a message, she has cheated on his Scotch that day and just come out front when the bell rings heralding the little angel. The only word for Tina. Angel with fi thousan' dollar. Lourdes begins her story again with alternate details, blissful, as though she's won the lottery and is interviewed for the whole world to see.

"What do you have to do to get something to eat around here?" Manny says.

Lourdes does not move at once. Extraordinary—she sits on, reviewing the day. Her black eyes glisten. She sings—ay, ay, O-Linda—and at her leisure goes to the kitchen. At supper she starts again about the movies, the money. She has never complained about her work, but now, displaying her stringy muscular arms, she boasts to Manny and Pepe how tired she is from loading the van. How quick she is with the fi thousan' dollar, tucking the metal strongbox up in a Spanish silk shawl. Dazed, like a child home from a party, Lourdes does not leap to clean up.

"So, Mamma, you gonna be in the movies?" Pepe asks. The boys laugh, but she rises starstruck to put their dirty plates in the sink. Gonna be in movies—the buttons she has sewn on with strong thread, the mended linings and pockets, the cigarette burns she has darned, her very own hash marks and combat ribbons awarded to an officer's coat. That night she does not beseech or strike bargains with Jesus—all has been granted. Lourdes plans: a new toilet, linoleum for Golden Oldies: she will direct partitions to be built and for the window a man and lady mannequin. Carpet and lamps. Cards—a pretty dish of cards will bear her name, Lourdes Perez, along with Mr. Pinkham Strong. No candles tonight. She has spent five thousand dollars twice over by the time she goes out of her dark room to say good night. There's an airplane gleaming on a stretch of private Caribbean beach and an ocean blue and soft, shuffle of marimbas and a woman snakes up out of a wave, a blond woman, large and coarse, not like the angel who follows her this night—Tina, slight as a whisper or the small-boned rustle of a tiny bird.

"Goo ni-i-ide," Lourdes says. She does not pray for Manny. She does not think beyond the miracle, beyond a new tub, formica and red carpets. She does not work the candles and silver or cross herself against the ordinary fears of spring. The weather is nice and now she will have to beg Jesus that Manny not go down on the block, not mess with that woman. But the day has been a dream and Lourdes is sick with happy exhaustion, so tired she slips into a quick enchanted sleep.

• • •

It is after midnight when Manny comes up into Union Square. He takes the wrong way through the sooty park, past derelicts, drugged or sleeping. He is offered anything three times before he finds his way to Fourteenth Street. Anything in a handful of pills, clear plastic bag, syringe. Ludes or what do you want? Nothing. Manny stays clean. This is not his territory, though not unlike his territory of boarded-up buildings and cheap stores. Different, the wide streets, and now he finds his way by the bright beacon of the Con Ed tower. He is afraid. Like any neighborhood punk, big man on the block, Manny is often afraid when he's not on his turf. Manny is abroad in the night. He does not like wide streets or lights. When he ducks into the doorway of a shoe store, Manny sees the police lines set up at the far end of the square. Wooden horses stacked as if to make ready for a riot or parade. That's not to Manny's liking, police lines. Manny is smart—the police have never fucked him over—but not smart enough to know the police will close traffic in the morning at the dead end of this square. It's May Day, that's all, and a few inveterate communists and old-style union officials will assemble to proclaim their rhetoric mostly for each other, to exhort the workers of the world against oppression, continuing and late. Such a small orderly meeting, more a feast day in a quiet parish now. Observance is all—and if the day is fine a few mounted policemen will lend a bit of spirit, turning back cars that try to make the left turn from Broadway.

How would Manny know Union Square as more than a subway stop in his mother's mismapped city, New York in the garbled travelogue of her daily defeats, consoling fancies? Though Manny is smart, he does not know which way to turn and counts the blocks down to Eighth Street scared. He has not imagined so many people out and he is not prepared for their curious looks, as though they had nothing better to do than record the running shoes, blue jeans, black zip jacket, receding hairline of Juan Manuel Perez—Hispanic, twenty-seven or eight, eyes set close, big head like a baby's, no distinguishing marks.

Astor Place is vast, thoroughly exposing Manny, who does not figure the many stop lights and runs across Fourth Avenue, conspicuously dodging traffic. Then he finds it, St. Mark's Place, full of shops and kids. Open all night. It is the first of May and he only knows the street life of his neighborhood, that the barrio stays open but not until it's tropical. In a few weeks his block will go all night, not yet—he is so smart he can call it to the day. He never imagined at this hour, in this cold, record shops open, bars, restaurants serving. A queer place to him and he might like it, the book shops with poems pasted on the windows and ads for lessons in jazz dance and karate. Manny is smart and there was a time some years ago when he might have liked this street, come down to tour, to groove on the last gasp of the Sixties. Now he just curses his mother in a breath, gathers the phlegm in his throat and spits. Smart as he is Manny has never attended to his mother's prattle or he would know that her work is her work: it has no surround. So he has heard of Mrs. Flood's apartment room by room but does not know if the building is old or new, low as a tenement or a high rise, if Mrs. Flood faces dead into an alley or if she has a pleasant outlook. Never having really listened, he does not know his mother's work has no setting, no view. So St. Mark's Place with the chic graffiti, the dubious antiques, Ukrainian Club and unisex enterprises, cop car cruising was never in the picture of Golden Oldies below stairs.

Manny finds the shop down near Second Avenue and walks right by, feels for the key he has taken from his mother's purse. Smart Manny crosses the street, reverses, takes the scene again. The shop is in darkness as far as he can see. He draws on a pair of leather gloves to turn the knob and open the strongbox, a professional touch picked up from countless smart robbers on TV. The gloves make the man and he walks across to the shop as though he owns it. There is one split second when fear runs down his legs like hot piss. The bell over the door. He has forgotten the bell and a soft half tinkle sounds before he stills the clapper. Manny waits. It is smart to wait, get the lay of the land. It is not that dark. The light from the street is absorbed through the big glass windows: it catches at baubles and glitter, flashes bright from every looking glass, travels the stamped tin ceiling. Manny hears breathing—his own and another's. The dull, mechanical snorts of a drunk. His villainous eyes narrow. He waits. The shop comes into focus, rotten and damp as in his mother's stories. He waits, immobile as the hat stand, distracted by a silk opera hat slightly dented. With his black-gloved hand he could touch a gentleman's stiff skimmer or a lady's hat no bigger than a saucer serving a ghostly paper rose.

Manny distinguishes racks of long dresses, dark suits, even scrawled patterns, some color in beach robes, summer shirts that block his way to the counter. He steps sideways across the floor, checking right and left always, a clever move he has observed nightly, the dance of actors playing successful murderers and thieves. He is in the open now, the space left where all the surplus uniforms are sold. Sold to the movies. As his mother told it—the empty racks, empty hangers, but her story has not told that Manny will be exposed to the back of the shop, to the squeak of a bedspring, a sigh, the resumption of the drunk's raspy breathing. Contempt shoots sharp acid up his throat in a stifled belch. Sold to the movies from this junk shop, no better than the voodoo stores with creepy roots and herbs in his neighborhood, and he is quick about his business, seeing the glass case which has been accurately described with the earrings and beads locked in as though they were precious, the wooden tree of bracelets on top (a game of ring toss), his mother's sewing basket with her spools and needles, scraps, other daring devices. Among the folded sweaters and scarves . . . Manny is at the shelf where the strongbox announces its value wrapped in a white shawl. A slippery package, but he has it in hand. The shawl is tied firm, knotted—his mother's primitive idea of security and Manny would laugh out loud but the shawl is fringed and the slithery silk catches on his belt buckle. The silk is strong which Manny should know having watched any number of atrocities committed with silk cord. Then, too, if Manny is so smart in his pursuit of five thousand dollars, he might have figured fringe on a Spanish shawl. The silence is frantic. He tears the box from him in panic, twisting and turning until it breaks loose and in a last quite graceful spin, it looks as though he is holding the box out, handing the money over to Bayard Strong. The box drops in a muffled thud to the floor.

Bayard has heard or sensed someone and come out from behind his screen in bare feet and floppy pajamas with the drowsy, annoyed thought that he has checked the door. It is like a dumb show, what follows, the quiet miming of tragedy, prelude to complicated passions, but the action is simple. Manny, equipped with all the clichés, pulls his blade to scare the kid. Bayard grabs the scissors in the sewing basket and brandishing them like a charging cavalier, slices air. In self-defense, against his own mother's small ineffectual shears, Manny swipes at the boy's throat amateurishly. And then he stabs deep into Bayard's chest, his abdomen—repeatedly, uncontrollably, as he has seen it done. Manny runs, knocking the empty racks so that the hangers ring softly as wind chimes. He sounds the bell above the door loud and clear, but stops to lock up with his mother's key so no one can tell, no one will know.

Know what? Tell what? That Manny is smart. He strolls down St. Mark's Place like a tourist in from Queens, but Manny is not a wide-eyed kid. His skin is gray as cold ash.

He is losing his hair. The waters of nausea flood his mouth and he swallows them back. The sidewalk flutters beneath him. People parking cars, high school girls have nothing to do but look at Manny and laugh, see this fatheaded man with a fringe of white silk shimmering, stuck over his genitals. His mother, in her innocent stories, never said that the block where she works is crawling with queers. At First Avenue he breaks into a run, uptown he thinks, or east—Manny is running scared.

Bayard embraces the strongbox in death. So it seems. So it is chalked out on the cement floor. Body and box in outline. It is a profitless crime. How would Manny know from his mother's tales in which she handles stacks of gold that it was a check he was after. A worthless check—oh, the credit good, but worthless to Manny. Where would a bum like Manny cash Sol's check for five thousand dollars drawn on a California bank? It is a senseless murder. For all Bayard's trials over sixteen years, there is nothing that elevates his death—no martyrdom, no ecstasy. It has been the passion of his life to measure the variable stars, to calculate spheres, our position in the universe—a little beyond his reach, but the boy has wanted only to understand this world, not transcend it.

It is beside the point to figure who set Bayard up—his mother with her injured pride, his father's self-indulgence, Tina's hostile servility to Sol, that sentimental patron who paid five thousand dollars to verify his past, the glories he had seen. Lourdes. Lourdes set up Bayard, her fairy tales garbling the truth, concealing the necessary detail. Suki Moss who dumped him . . . what's the use? His blood was plentiful on the torn Spanish shawl, though the puncture wounds were clean, internal bleeding. Torn shawl: scant evidence. The door was unlocked according to the father who is able to speak precisely, with what ellipses and distortions no one can guess . . . how he thought it was morning hearing the old brass bell and the Spanish woman come, but it was night. Still night. He thought it was earlier in a dream he heard the dreamlike scuffling, the cut, the plunge in flesh. He often dreamt of war . . . but rising, felt the difference. Sober and steady, the useless testimony. By the time Pinkham Strong fumbled with lights and locks, by the time he saw the sole of a long white foot, the striped pajamas . . . or that the mother, arriving in a police car, threw herself like a blotter on the blood stains. It is beyond telling. What is the use—Baby lies dead on the floor.

BRIEF LIVES

Etre un homme, c'est réduire au minimum,
pour chacun, sa part de comédie.

—André Malraux,
First International Congress of Writers for
the Defense of Culture, 1935

THEY HAVE BEEN here a while. The days are long, near the summer solstice. Long because they are busy. Pinky has limed and fed the lawn, fed the trees, too, boring deep holes in the earth, filling them from sacks of fertilizer. There are always the Vermont stones which he hits with his post digger or shovel. No matter what job he sets for himself, he strikes granite and must yield to it, try again. Working out of a manual, he has pruned every branch and small tree. The old shrubs had become thickets drowning in their own sap. Now he has the deadwood out, the weak shoots, and they look shapely—the forsythia, quince, spirea. Air and light will get to them—next year the bloom will be strong. Pinky will not enjoy the fruits of his labor. He will not see if the paint job he has done on the north side of the house survives the winter and Margaret will never know if the steel wool she plugs into cracks and the wire meshing tacked over every visible hole will keep out the mice, the maddening squirrels that roll their nuts in the attic. They have been here nearly two months. The house is for sale.

It must be set in order. They work to that end. Knowing the task can never be complete, they work toward perfection. Margaret has papered an interior corner of the dining room where, though there is no pipe or drain, water had bled uncharted seas. She has mixed the wheat paste, matched the stems and petals of exuberant Eighteenth-Century posies right up the seam. They do everything themselves. The Strongs find that they must drive into town twice a day to the hardware store or the lumberyard on errands. They are familiar figures with their questions concerning paste wax, cedar chips, gutters and downspouts. Good customers, they bless the Yankee reserve of the men and women who wait on them, who never ask about their boy. Perhaps they do not know—Pinky thinks that—these local merchants live by the seasons, hometown events. But Margaret says, "No. Come into the Twentieth Century."

She does not have to elaborate on the sideshow which followed Bayard's death to prove her point. The cameras recording their grief: their grief adjusted for the cameras' cruel remarks. Microphones stuck in their faces. She had no words. But there were words aplenty in the papers, on the news. They had once made good copy, lent themselves to it, now their files were taken out of the morgue . . . clippings that went back to Pinky's First Family, to his days as a minor functionary at this or that agency after the Second World War, back to the Kennedy connection and a cartoon of Pinkham Strong, the saintly fool in white tie and tails, giving the peace sign to druggy kids, an olive branch in his perfect white teeth, a molting dove on his top hat. His disappearance or defection, yes, that, insoluble and unimportant as it was the first time. Margaret's early books: that was a horror to her, the old quotes dusted off, distant cheers for a gullible kid, that girl who thought she'd play with the big boys. She refused to recognize the grinning, posturing figures—Margaret Flood, Pinkham Strong. Then again they were real to her, so real that she understood their second-run celebrity distorted Bayard's death. They were a two-day wonder. The text held great appeal: How the mighty have fallen.

Their misfortune, at least, was fresh, thickened with novel details, a treat for jaded palates. At great cost, Sol Negaly delayed his trip to Spain. He spoke of the Strongs as extraordinary people, survivors of national and now personal disaster. Survivors, maybe, but Sol's statement was a eulogy. They were footage, clips of history. "Amnesia," he said. Movie man as pundit: "We suffer in this country from severe amnesia." His quick take on the Sixties—he remembered them when. It worked nicely into advance notice on the Nazi movie and Margaret forgave him. She always forgave Sol in the end. Not the worst of men, he believed in simple story lines. He was ruthless without knowing for a minute he made use of Bayard's murder. It was his generosity in the strongbox, his five-thousand-dollar check held as evidence that led nowhere. Though he could never begin to see it, Sol was cashing in. The girl photographer, married to a furniture designer in Milan, said the Strongs had been family to her, as though her lusting after Pinky and his cause was no more than a flirtatious signal with a fan—a custom of gentler times. Fred Peach took the opportunity to announce that Margaret Flood was under contract for a book that would blow the lid off the Fifties, hinting at flashy documents, unpublished letters, scandals public and private. "Fearless," Fred Peach said of Margaret.

The Thrift Shop Murder, as it was called, gathered to it a sensational reading of Margaret Flood's medical dossier, a lurid account of Pinkham Strong's activities on St. Mark's

Place. On the whole, Margaret preferred the debauched version of their lives as the estranged couple to the reverent view which embalmed them. But there was no mercy either way. She did not deserve mercy herself or ask it for her husband. Mother and Pinky, a hard act to follow. In those first days she saw the boy constantly, the flop of dark hair obscuring the gleam of high forehead, shoulders squared to put up with their nonsense. She heard him—"Now, Mother . . . ," forbearing and kind. There was no God to forgive her: "Oh, God," she said whenever she found herself alone. "Oh, God," preceded her bone-dry cries, the silent heaving that racked her body. Her scar throbbed continually. No fibrillations or off-beats, none of your warning pain—three or four times a day her heart broke. Let Jack Flood patch this one. There were not enough tears.

The shop roped off, the door sealed—scene of the crime. That is how Pinky finally comes home. She finds him crouched on the floor in Bayard's room, dazed, not sleeping. They look away from each other in pity, but she sees him skeletal, fragile as she's never seen the handsome man. He holds an obscene record jacket in his hands, a dull brass sextant, a school tie. There now, this is real: there will be no more escapades.

"Try me," Margaret says, "try me," and touches his long jaw, thick with white whiskers so that he must look up at her now and see they are locked in this together. They will never move on . . . and she takes him to her bed. From the moment Pinky looked down on his son, he has not wanted a drink. A hypnotist's trick—you will never again need the slug of Scotch; or, like a spell that's broken and the milk, frozen in midair, pours, the cat stretches, the kettle sings. The kiss of death brings Pinky back to life. What a price to pay for mere sobriety. He walks, he talks like a man, though he trembles on schedule. A mechanical quake runs through him on the half hour as he lies next to his wife, she with her hands crossed on her breast, he with his arms pressed flat to his sides, silent as stone, but breathing, still breathing, though they have been reported dead. The curiosity about them ebbs, then flows again on shallow waters —the record of Margaret Flood's mini-arrest in the Chicago riots; Pinky's long-forgotten marriage surfaces and a sordid tale of a Biddle Strong, an apparent suicide in his bath, consequence of stock fraud, 1909.

Lying beside her husband to pass the hours of the night, Margaret cannot tolerate her son's death. For twenty years she has ordered the world, made it accessible, trimmed and fit her stories. More recently, under the trumped-up threat of extinction, she has revised, confessed, approached—well, her version of the truth. For Bayard she has no words. Now she counts herself defenseless, the victim of others' stories—inaccurate, vicious, consoling. Motives beside the point. Her life and Pinky's run off again and again. Mute, diminished, she is no one in the vast audience. Squinting, on the wrong side of the arena, she cannot pick herself out, she cannot heckle. She attends as Bayard's death is turned into cultural commentary, drained of its meaning. Stretched out beside her husband —Lady Margaret and Sir Pinkham, last Baronet Lethe— she is powerless as her son becomes a casualty in the history of their rise and fall.

There is no murderer, not even a suspect, but there are the cameras and a small crowd when they come out of the inquest. And the tired questions about violence at large and do they seek revenge. An old court reporter grabs Pinky and puts it to him about the thrift shop. Ruined, no longer handsome, he stands very grand and tall. He holds Margaret to his side: "Thrift shop implies contributions to the sick and needy. The store on St. Mark's Place helped no one. My wife supported it as she has always supported my interests. There was no thrift, gentlemen, and no write-off. It operated at a loss." That was the old Pinky and they didn't know what hit them, or why they stepped back like shamed children to let them pass.

In Vermont the routine is strict. Early up and out. He runs the dirt road, the crest of their hill. Margaret takes it once slowly and quits, but Pinky builds lap by lap to five miles. He comes back in a good sweat, does leg stretches, head rolls, lifts a couple of twenty-pound weights he leaves by the kitchen sink. They drive to town in the rented car where no one cuts their tires, overcharges, waits upon them with laconic contempt. Margaret says it's as though their television series with the cast of fugitives and hippies was long canceled, another proof they're reckoned with as almost dead. The house, too, is a discarded set. A showplace, never home.

Their assessment of the day: it's gone well if lived through. They fall exhausted into bed and talk, talk endlessly of reasonable plans. Thus they discover they must sell the house only Margaret can afford, as much a plaything as the thrift shop: it is a luxury and they've had enough of that. It should be perfectly presented, ready for an ideal family. The ideal family coming to this place they have misused is painful, so Margaret should dismantle it, sell the furniture off to get a fair price. They talk into the night. Talk: it reminds Pinky of the old days, of the radical meetings that joined each other end to end and he says so—that they are a group of two against the system, talking through maneuvers and contingencies to some degree of sanity in the night.

Run, stretch, caulk, sand, paint. Pinky begins to dig an unsightly boulder out of the back yard. For centuries it has blocked the logical spot where a garden should be as well as the view. For two hundred years farmers have wisely accommodated the boulder; now Pinky will have it out. It is a project demanding great perseverance, greater strength. Each day he digs at the boulder's edges: it bends back the tines of a pitchfork, easily snaps the handle of a spade, doesn't give an inch to the crowbar. The stone is a bastard that spreads deep and wide. Pinky pries at his boulder. He will not admit defeat. Margaret drives off with rabbit ear chairs, Staffordshire china, hooked rugs, to the antique dealers. She gets her price for a pewter tea caddy. As though her life depended on it, she stands firm on the authenticity of a Bennington bowl. Pinky strikes bottom, where the granite seems to rest on a ledge of wet clay. At night they talk of their progress. They see no one. The phone rings until it stops. Heartfelt sympathy, accusations, plain crazy letters follow them to Vermont and they read all of them with equal detachment. The letters are about other people, someone else's son.

Is it that worthless, the material which Pinky has gathered about little old New York of his class and kind? Not as he speaks of it: Margaret sees he has taken hold of some hopeful idea about the failure of a paternalistic society, the formation of an urban aristocracy that was weak from the start but set a mighty high tone. His work he calls it. No, it is not foolish. She cheers him on, knowing his work is a penance at best; at worst, somewhere to put the blame. His work and hers: for the first time leveled in their bed. Now she speaks of Dotty, of Hannah. She tells her husband of the time when she was taken to dinner at the Gideons', brought to be looked over, more likely to admire. That those people had secrets, that she is excluded from whatever it is—merely politics—supposedly deeper and fuller, so damn important, that they lived through. *Hesu*—the sights they had seen. They are not nice people. She no longer believes they are fine—Dotty or Hannah. Max Gideon's editorials crumble at the edges like old sheet music. As for Hannah, Hannah Brandt, she was an enthusiast and plodder, a fateful combination. Heavy Hannah, grinding it out on capital punishment, Hegel, Freud, civil disobedience and in what she must have thought a lighter vein, Valentino, Clare Luce, Krazy Kat. Humorless Hannah, a worker, for all her money, and she managed to stay one step ahead of Max, to outlive him and in her memoirs award him all honors. Really, he is such a dumpling in her memoirs you'd never know Max. A mysterious reputation: Margaret sees Hannah is simpler than she thought, the heiress turned on by radicals, the Bryn Mawr girl who reached beyond her intelligence, the beaky loud woman who competed with her man. The raucous Gideons: and she wonders why it is she still presses her nose to their candy-shop window—envious, greedy and small. As she speaks, Margaret produces the wound—a paper cut or sliver, no more than a grain of anger but it is precious to her—and she knows she will work again, but she doesn't tell Pinky laid out beside her that it's damage control, a hot poultice with the sting of liniment; her work—like lifting weights, increasing the laps. She's improved herself before.

They drive to New York with four valuable quilts. She does not leave Pinky. They are in this together. Any shift, any turning by one or the other, might collapse the shaky structure that sustains them. With all their plots and sensible propositions they are leading a theoretical life. She will not test it. It is June. The apartment is hot. Lourdes keeps it in perfect order. She is scouring and dusting senselessly when they come in. Shriveled and wan, she gives them (still Pingy and Missus Flood) a song—O-Linda, O-Linda—a dirge. The place seems littered with Bayard's artifacts, though they do not open the door to his room. Together they pack up Margaret's papers and tapes. They sell the quilts on Madison Avenue together, checking each other—they are on the buddy system. Were it not for the Strongs' gray hair and the scraped dull look of their eyes, you would think, with their constant touches and whispers, they were lovesick.

Margaret has set a punishing schedule: the quilts, then Dorothy Schwartz and Hannah Brandt all in a day. Pinky drives her to Brooklyn. Twenty-fourth Street is a leafy neighborhood of big two-family houses. The shallow front lawns, no more than a patch, are all as perfect as theirs in Vermont. A solid middle-class street, in order. Between the houses, there resides at least one late-model car. They come to a house, richly green, bigger, better than the others, with swollen white pillars. Margaret panics as she leaves Pinky in the car. It reminds her of home, of her father waiting at the curb outside the doctor's office, waiting for her sick mother and of Ned Lynch waiting patiently outside the high school to drive her home from late rehearsals of *Our Town* and *Sweethearts.* She walks away from her husband, up the cement path, knowing that now he'll be there like Ned Lynch. Behind the scrim curtain, someone is watching, someone comes to undo all the locks and bolts up and down the double front door. It is Dotty Schwartz, brown and lean. Her white hair is cut in the Dutch bob which Margaret remembers from the earliest pictures (Young Communist League), a stern black frame weighting a narrow face . . . before she gussied up with a perm and a pompadour during the war. The white hair, cut in a bell, is becoming—old Village Bohemian, that's Dotty's style. She is done out in hammered silver, a peasant dress.

"Who's that?" she asks Margaret.

"My husband."

"Goodness," says Dotty with a wink, "let's have him in."

Margaret looks to her bag with the notebook, the tape recorder—her work. "Oh, that," Dotty says. "That won't take long."

They sit, all three of them, in the living room with sets of encyclopedias, the bound classics built in around the television screen—lesser books of transient value, Margaret notes hers among them, in cases to the side. Roses, lovely full-blown roses, perhaps to welcome Dotty's visitors, are everywhere. And children, there are photos of children on the mantel, on end tables. Children on sleds, on skis, with tennis racquets and fishing poles, children tap dancing, playing in the sand, holding cats and dogs. A number of Bar Mitzvah boys in new suits and yarmulkes are too much for Margaret and she snuffles and coughs, close to tears.

"It's the roses," Dotty says.

"No, no—" Margaret has been subjected to a blanket of roses over Bayard's casket, tribute of Sol Negaly. They don't make her cry.

"Then why are we sitting here?" And they are made to bounce after Dotty through the dining room (brass menorah, silver ceremonial cup), through the spanking clean kitchen where, among the shining pots and pans there hangs a painting, sharply realistic, of a fair man with sandy eyebrows and a large pendulous nose. The artist has recorded exactly the light freckles of the skin as distinguished from soft brown age spots and the part combed into a few strands of pale hair.

"That's Red Klotz, looking as though he were alive. Come, see his roses."

The back yard is all roses. Roses climbing trellises and fences, standing proudly in their deep loamy beds. No shade, just bright Brooklyn sun. Pinky and Margaret are given the tour of the hybrid teas and floribundas. "Merry Mite, she's a hearty bloomer. Sterling Silver—I never cared for special breeding. I call it eerie, but Red loved that rose. This was his best month with school almost over. He taught English," says Dotty, "at Erasmus Hall High. Take a whiff of this Sarah Van Fleet. I have annuals started back there, petunias I stick in, ageratum, those tawdry dahlias, but this is Red's garden. June was his month."

They sit in metal lawn chairs soaking up the sun. Margaret forgets what she's here for. A big bluebottle buzzes her arm and moves on to Pinky. Dotty Schwartz—Dotty

Klotz, Margaret presumes—addresses herself to Pinky. Laughing and tipping her head to one side, she is a pretty old woman, once an unattractive girl. She takes him round the rose beds again, leading him by her speckled brown hand. You can just see Dotty likes talking to men. Here is how you cut the canes back, eight, ten inches from the ground. Here is where you clip. Here the next bud will form. The white dust is ashes scratched into the earth. "If you have any ashes?" Dotty tilts her head, flutters at Pinky.

"Now then," says Margaret and asks a stupid question she could well answer, "*The New Alliance?* You were on the original board."

"If you say so," Dotty says. "Me and Max Gideon. We were good Marxist kids. Immigrants—the poverty we came from. I speak for myself. We were lucky to have a boiled chicken once a week. My mother supported us. She sucked on the bones."

"The poverty," Margaret says, "led to the commitment."

Dotty stretches in the sun. "You didn't come all the way out to Brooklyn to find out about the Great Depression."

"To find out about you."

"There's nothing."

"You were the smart one, weren't you? The brains behind Gideon?" Margaret has the evidence, the sharp turn of phrase, swift New Yorkese coupled with a stately rhetoric picked up by a girl who revered literature at CCNY, that was the naughty but nice tone of all the pieces signed by Dorothy Schwartz. An original mix, oh, she was certain that was the voice in the good stuff attributed to Max Gideon, the voice of this little old woman flirting with Pinky in the enervating sun. But Margaret has left her notebooks, the tape recorder, in the Klotz living room. She tries it again: "You were the smart one?"

They aren't really listening to her. "We were all smart," Dotty says and taps Pinky. Together, they go to a low metal shed and take out sacks of birdseed. He reaches easily to the birdhouses which hang up on a chain link fence. Dotty points out the ingenious design of each house built by Red Klotz to discourage the pigeons, defeat the squirrels. "We shouldn't feed them in the summer. They should be on their own, but Red had a soft spot for poor city birds."

Margaret can prove *The New Alliance* turned spiritless, academic, the day Dotty walked out. One day in the fifties —and that Max's articles went limp as the memorized homilies of a clergyman hedging his bets. She watches her husband and Dotty. They are a team, talking about song-birds and standard roses at Hampton Court said to be a hundred years old. "They sure have the climate," Dotty says, "but this back yard is close to perfection. We never lose a rose."

Margaret is hot, anxious. She feels decidedly plain. In her gay embroidered dress, Mrs. Klotz is a fiery girl of the people. Pinky escorts her down the garden path. Without hope, Margaret asks, "Tell me about Gideon's work on the Russian novel. Did you write his stuff?"

Dotty laughs. "I take the Fifth." She's leading them back to the house, but first they must take note of a sign, a lacquered slice of pine with the bark left on: *The desert shall rejoice and blossom as the rose* is burned into the wood, the letters charred at random, affecting ye olde. A grandson named Herbert made that for Red.

"The Russian novel?" Margaret asks.

"You've got it," says Dotty. "Max needed a little help."

The house is dark, almost chill. Chillier when Dotty serves them iced tea. They sit under the gentle gaze of Klotz whose pale nearsighted eyes are captured exactly in a muddled stare. Pinky discusses the merits of China tea over Ceylon, a preference Margaret never knew he had. She's longing for the trip to Vermont. Five hours almost alone. She will go through with the Hannah business this evening, but she no longer looks forward to it as bait that will hook her into work. She has gulped air in Brooklyn. Teatime. A guest has no right to ask her hostess if it's true she killed a couple of Falangists in Spain or, pass the sugar, how was it behind bars in Alderson—a country club prison? Up over the refrigerator another plaque, product of Herbert, reads: *The rose that lives its little hour. . . .* She can't make out the rest, cut off by giant boxes of cereal and detergent that do not fit on Dotty's shelves. It is there to remind her of Bayard and the useless broom holder, the tipsy magazine rack he made for her in shop.

Dotty settles two shoe boxes down in a grocery bag—"If you knew how often I wanted to throw these out." *These* are letters, even a couple of diaries that date way back. She looks a dear auntie packing up pound cake and pickles for folks to take home.

"Oh, you can't!" Margaret says. The gift is unexpected, overly generous, more than she came for.

"Whatever use—" says Dotty. "It's all there—the politics and the love letters. I suppose these days all that heavy breathing makes a book. Max was no gentleman, but he did return my letters. Anyway, it's grist for your mill."

They were going. Presented with the grocery bag of secrets, they were dismissed, led through the dim spit-and-polish dining room, to the gallery of sporty children. They are made to observe Sarah, a dancer, Herbie, the craftsman, now in corporate law. "I was nearly fifty when Red married me. Very Old World, old Jewish. His wife died. He needed me to bring up his kids." Dotty Klotz—crinkled, fading. She's a little vague smiling at photographs, a little forlorn in her arty dress. Out on the porch she draws Pinky aside, off by the round pillars where a white wicker sofa and two rockers indicate the leisure of summer nights, watching life on the block. The furniture is chained to the porch. Dotty shows him the arrangement: bolted metal plates, the weight of the chains. "Look here." She speaks exclusively to Pinkham Strong, "Our revolution . . ." Margaret is set aside on the top step. She is meant to eavesdrop, to get this scene obliquely. Given all the Schwartz papers, the full indictment, she is meant to strain for this worn nub of conviction. The rocker does not rock. Dotty kicks her imprisoned couch. "How do you know," she asks Pinky, "who's to say? We couldn't have made things worse."

He sings to himself, driving back to Manhattan. "Wonderful woman," he says, half in love. There is his city. You hardly ever get it in pure sun like this. The long day hangs high and unclouded over the new Wall Street. The World Trade Center looks the glitzy toy it is. The city sits flat on its shelf, impossibly compact. From this angle he comprehends it whole. The low-slung girders of the Williamsburg Bridge do not ruin the sightline. Margaret holds her package with such care you think they would break—old letters. She has her treasure, yet Margaret looks grim. It is because of Brooklyn. With her mission accomplished, Brooklyn becomes the place where her son is buried. They have passed the turnoff to Greenwood Cemetery. Pinky has not forgotten that Bayard lies in Brooklyn. If they stay together, if they mend, every day of his life he must remember not to say Brooklyn, not to say "Bayard lies in Brooklyn with my family."

Hannah. God, in the old days wouldn't she tell about Hannah. Begin, "It was tragic, really—" carry on not missing one detail, until it was hilarious, stop just short of cruelty. Such stories are knocked out of her: "It was tragic," is all she says to Pinky when she gets in the car. He has been waiting down on Park Avenue. She is weary, so weary. Margaret can't wait to get out of the city, to get back to the urgency of talk, busy work, plans—their departure from Vermont. Only now the sun is setting as they head to the West Side Drive, a flat orange cutout sliding down the backdrop of New Jersey. Not the sun, Bayard told her that, a refraction of its upper limb, the sun itself gone below the sensible horizon. It's a hoax but it takes her breath away, bleeding into the Hudson, a proper ending to her evening with Hannah Brandt . . . excuse me, Mrs. Gideon.

That name at the front desk and Max Gideon on a brass plate, like a doctor's office, on the apartment door. Margaret waited at the window as though there was something to see down on the dull block, heavy and expensive as the room behind her. It was all the same, though how could she remember, an impressionable girl. Twenty years ago the people in this room had behaved badly. She had been to the Gideons' again, but then the rooms had been stuffed with customers—one of those fund-raisers for a hapless Democratic candidate, a man who dissolved in public. That night, she and Pinky along with a couple of movie stars, were the draw.

Margaret has been let in by a nurse in trim clothes and gumshoes. On duty. "Just in time," the woman said, but then she had been left in the long dead room. Big canvases done in the fifties hung on the walls—Pollock, de Kooning, Kline (no one obscure) hung among gilt sconces, were rudely bisected by lamps with large pleated shades. Could these paintings have been here? They looked neglected, merely stored, their famous energy drained by velvet sofas, fancy carved cabinets and chairs—American pieces, most probably the Brandts', bought in the thirties for a song. Looking upon the emotional black strokes of an artist's crisis, Margaret turns away: it is an overstatement of troubles long gone. She hears the clipped Brit voice of Hannah Brandt, loud and cantankerous, and turns to find a spindle woman in a wheelchair, eagle head balanced on bones, hair arranged in a honey-blond crest.

This head looks across the room, demands her: "Margaret Flood." Margaret sits where she is told. The nurse pushes Hannah into position, and stands at attention. Her hands remain on the rubber grips of the chair.

"Thank you," says Margaret. She means for letting her come.

"She can't hear you."

Yes, Hannah's ears are plugged with flesh-colored aids not quite hidden by swirls of stiff hair.

"Thank you," Margaret shouts.

"I can't hear you," Hannah says. "Tell this bitch to take her hands off my chair." Her voice is consciously projected, grand lady that was. "I hate the Swiss. They are boring. This one has the usual advantage, being clean. What a culture—neutrality and cows. Ask her how many Jews she refused during the war."

"She's lively," the nurse says. "She's been at it all day."

"Have this woman deported," Hannah says. "There are poor blacks and Hunkies with families to support. She doesn't have her green card. She wants to marry—ask her what she'll pay for an American male."

"It's the excitement." The nurse is a sweet creature, patient and professional—forty, forty-five—with a gold wedding band on the proper finger. She speaks frankly to Margaret. There is no reason to be conspiratorial or coy. "She's thrilled with your visit. We had the hairdresser in and that started her off." The nurse, Annamarie, tucks the old lady into a sweater. Hannah's fingers are blue: her toes peeking out from under a lap robe are puffed and gray. "Take out your tape recorder," the nurse says. "She is at her best when they bring the tape recorders. You give her the little microphone, she won't take it from me."

"Heidi," says Hannah, "eat your chocolate. Drill holes in your cheese."

Annamarie stays calm behind the wheelchair. "Better get started. Pretend you are asking away."

"Do you remember?" Margaret says, "I came to dinner. Do you remember?"

"Love at first sight. Born in 1937. Get that down. I was not born whenever they say, in my parents' house on Gramercy Square, not brought to life by tutors or the magic wand at Bryn Mawr. First steps at a lecture which demolished decadent writers. I heard him, Max Gideon, on the bourgeois adventures of Hemingway and Stein. First love: first love—oh, Hannah, why must you bring home strays, we have Biscuit and Chops, thoroughbred spaniels. I cannot hear myself. I hear their German they thought I could not understand. There is something wrong with Hannah, she can't learn to ride a bike. King Charles spaniels. Get that down. Responsive and bright."

"Ask," Annamarie says at the pause. "Nod. Let her see you write."

"Biscuit and Chops slept in my bed. It was unhealthy, their little warm bodies panting on my stomach and chest. That would come out later. Their warm tongues licked the salty matter from my eyes. Their happy yelps. I have never known such affection. Could not? Let me make the distinction. I would not learn to ride a bike. I want a transcript. I want my lawyer to see this set down. Speak, Hannah. Speak up so we can hear you. That came out in analysis—the murmur and slur. I denied them what I had to say. Max adored Marx. Get that down. Women adored Max. We were anti-fascists. He was a genius. Speak up! You once came here to meet him, Margaret Flood. You came with Philo Pierce who made young women of talent into whores." Hannah taps the mike. She cannot hear the crackle of response. "I can't hear," she says very loud. Her words shatter. They will blur, Margaret thinks, but knows there will be no reason to listen to the tape.

"Speak up," Hannah says. "They often ask me if I loved Biscuit more than Chops. I will never say, never. They were such jealous little pies. Max was allergic. The finest mind of his generation—I speak only of immigrant Jews, Ashkenazi—they clotted his throat. He could not breathe.

He was disgusted by my parents' house. Their linens, banquet cloths, pillow shams of lace. I showed him the cupboards. It was a middling fortune . . . the attic where they kept their trunks and matching Mark Cross cases for our European tours. The nauseating silver vessels. The Bechstein. The phonograph on which they played their bourgeois music, depraved waltzes and two-steps. It is no wonder he could not tolerate Biscuit and Chops. I sold my pearls to buy his magazine. Get that. Get that down."

"Ask," the nurse says. "She's doing fine."

"Why are you sore?" Margaret says softly. "It's all over, Miss Brandt."

"Philo Pierce. I never liked his girls. I never liked smart women. That came out. It was Pierce put Dotty in jail. You have come to find that out. Yes, I bought him the magazine. She was like a midge, a gnat. We were anti-fascist long before Schwartz. Where my husband was concerned that woman knew no shame. Next it was Pierce, your boyfriend."

"Can we stop her?" Margaret asks.

"Then me. That came out. Speak up, Hannah. Talk is cheap, but I spoke it in Yiddish so they could hear me. Shtupp me! Shtupp—Max loved his Yiddish. On linen sheets kept in lavender. Where Max came from they slept three in a bed. I heard the thump of their bodies. It was nauseating, their small bodies scraped, as it were, off the bed. He could not breathe. No wonder—a genius, a Marxist on the rosewood bed with King Charles spaniels. Biscuit and Chops. Both little boys, though not my first set—I was acquainted with death. Their pretty piefaces, always sad, were pitiful. A loyal and scrappy breed, they bit at his shins, leapt back up on the bed to get at his cock. I chose Max. Now hear me. I could not bear for anyone else to love them. I had them put down."

The nurse smooths Hannah's hair, holds her blue hand though she's not in the least upset. A red light on the tape recorder flickers. Margaret hopes the batteries go dead. Why is she in this darkening room listening to an angry old woman who won't give up, her envy a lifeline, but there's no longer any pull, no argument back—Hannah's story told to the Brandt furniture, their money still papering the walls. Margaret has gray hair, a patched heart. She should not be here like a fan, an admiring youngster, a talented whore.

"I want a full transcript."

"She's done nicely. Now the pictures."

"Tell Heidi to bring the pictures. Put a bell on her, she runs like a goat."

Annamarie opens a Philadelphia desk, first-rate, blockfront, original pulls, tasseled key. Behind her an exuberant canvas has gone blank as a cathedral window at night. She brings Margaret a velvet bag. "She won't take it from me."

Margaret obeys. The bag is silky, sacramental, embroidered with gold letters—M.G. She must look at young Gideon with a mustache wearing a seedy double-breasted suit—"a ringer for Thomas Mann," and at old Max, head cropped, clean-shaven, wire-rimmed glasses—"Bertolt Brecht." In both pictures Max looks like Max—coarse, stocky, aggressive. A third picture lives in the velvet case with M.G. It is a photo of a furious little girl, contemptuous from the tip of her patent-leather pumps right up to the taffeta bow in her Orphan Annie hair. She is a plain, uncompromising child with sealed lips, waiting for the cartilage in her nose to pop into a beak, just to prove the world is mean. It's no mistake: this unfortunate child belongs in the bag with the genius M.G., alias Mann and Brecht, whom she has at last made into a German in her final conversion. At ten or eleven, little Hannah will listen to no one. She will have her way. Her story is complete.

"The funeral!" Hannah cries.

"No, no," the nurse says. She steers Margaret to the

door. "Mr. Gideon's funeral is a long one. We'll save that for another day."

"Don't mind me," Pinky says, "have a drink."

They are in a roadhouse, avoiding Bayard's favorite diner on the way back to Vermont. They order Cokes and watch baseball. He explains a difficult call. He is a worn man. In the best of times he had always seemed somewhat wasted, yet easy, so easy with life as it came—First Army staff, dissident, old clothes—life came to him. "You got out of there fast enough," he says to his wife.

"Hannah Brandt was tragic, that's all." Now they are tracking each other again. Margaret says, like it or not, they must have the dealers in for the big pieces, the corner cupboard, the highboy. He says the small tractor rigged with a pulley will unloose his stone. Simon says: Touch your nose, touch your toes, elbow, head, backside, knee. It is a dangerous game: Do this. Do that. Plumbing, painting, tamping, selling, sodding. Working: Pinky makes notes with his old Wahl-Eversharp, carefully refilling its bladder with real ink; Margaret sits over her typewriter but from the sound of it she's not getting much done. He hears her cracked laugh. At times she sings off-key. Bayard, now that they speak of him, they speak as if he's just gone out of the room. Do this. Do that. That. This. So far no one is out. Clap. Simon says clap.

"Goosey, Goosey Gander. Whither do you wander?" That is on Lily Flood's wall. No one has seen it in years. Certainly no one has read it, not even Fay dusting, who sees a yellowed piece of cloth, the edges frayed where they poke out of a cheap frame. The words are crudely embroidered, stitched in a crooked red path that departs from the stamped design. That goose in a straw bonnet is a cooked turkey, its shadow a platter, orange sweet potatoes for its beak and webbed feet, a smudge of cranberry its eye—so Lily thought when she looked at her handiwork, squinting up from her bed she could make it become that—a dressed and roasted turkey. Landlocked, not a Canadian goose resting easy in the salty waters of East Bay. "Upstairs and downstairs and in my lady's chamber." A relic of her childhood, it is the only thing she cares for in her room. Lily would say that if asked, though she has not looked at her embroidery for a long time.

The room is all her mother's choosing, flowers on the sheets and curtains. She could not say what kind. Gold carpet underfoot, the leathery tan of a dry yellow rose. Her window is over the garage and she looks out on her mother and sister turning into the driveway. The car slides along too close to the barberry hedge, then veers toward the lawn. Rose, who is learning to drive, gets out of the station wagon with an officious jangling of car keys and a shiny violet box which she swings by its cord. That will be the white dress, at long last. In the past week they have been to every shop in Baltimore. Lily is surprised they have not driven up to Georgetown for the long white dress. Rose is going to usher at graduation, hand out programs. You'd think she was getting married. You'd think Rose was invited to Annapolis where the midshipmen are in full-dress uniform drifting across the lawn, the music heard down by the towpath where you go if the guy is serious—this all told to Lily as though Rose has been there. Her mother looks pleased walking behind Rose with the famous white dress.

They cannot see Lily above the garage. They would not think to look up through the cherry branches that grow across her window, the bronze leaves pressed against her screen. She would like the tree to grow into her room. When she goes down to the shore in a few weeks the leaves will be almost green, but she has never been home in summer when the fruit is ripe, the tree full of birds pecking. When Lily and her mother and Rose come back after

Labor Day, the roof is stained with a hundred blood clots. The pits have rolled down into the gutter where they lie bleached from the August sun. Her mother says it is a messy tree.

She hears "Lily, are you there?" and does not answer. She is oiling shells in a pie plate, rubbing them up with a soft toothbrush, then they are set on the windowsill to dry, separated out into blue, pink, brown and a pile of perfect whites. She has kept track of the tides, combed the sea wrack and litter, dredged the swamps and marshes of St. Michael's for her shells. Riding off alone on her bike, she has collected her limpets and snails, marginellas and whelks. She cleans them in secret—oil, cotton swabs, soft toothbrush—according to her shell guide. The wooden screen door at the side of the house bangs, then the lid of the trash can, and she sees Fay come round swaying with fatigue, her ankles swollen over the lady pumps she changes into at the end of the day. She will just make it downhill to the bus stop, white sweater folded over her arm though it is hot now in Baltimore, the days hotter in the row house where Fay lives without air-conditioning—by choice. The new buses give her a chill. Lily has taken that bus to get her supplies—jewelry glue, mirrors, boxes—at Hobby World on Thirty-fifth Street. If her mother knew, she would die, not about the bus or even Thirty-fifth Street, but Lily is supposed to be chauffeured in the station wagon, like Rose, wherever she wants, all over town.

Her father is never on time. That would be too much, almost scary, to have him home from the hospital early just because she wants it. There is a parcel on her bed, square and heavy, the size of the atlas or the picture books of flowery houses her mother buys. It is addressed to her father and though it has been sent from San Francisco, Lily knows it is from Yin-Li. The wrapping paper is queer. Where it is ripped a cord is strangely knotted around a

Chinese newspaper. Her mother gets the twitch at any mention of the Chinese doctor. The Chinaman, she says, "your father's pen pal," refusing to learn Yin-Li. So Lily Flood has taken her father's package in the strange paper to her room where it will not be scorned. She has poked at the Chinese newspaper. Something in there is brown. Next door she hears Rose rooting about in the closet and the vibrations of her stereo, the best of old Motown, the going Country Day craze. Then Lily's door flies open and there—surprise, surprise—is Rose in the white dress, tall, steady on high heels. Ruffles and laced bodice of a giant Bo-Peep. Rose is blinded by her importance at this moment and does not see the package, plop in the middle of her sister's bed, hardly sees Lily who admires, as she must, her sister's athletic beauty, though she wouldn't be caught dead in that getup.

A car door slams and it is Jack Flood, for once home on time. Rose runs downstairs, already expert with her long skirt and petticoat while Lily taps on the screen, but he cannot see her in the darkness of her room behind the cherry branches. The heart has gone out of her. It was today the Chinese package came. She had wanted to open it with her father and now Rose is down there showing off. The Bride of Frankenstein. She slams her door so only the pulse of "Baby Love" throbs in her room. She picks through her shells. The scallops, her favorites, are perfect in their classical design; the jingle shells, curled as yellow toenails; the tiny clams and oysters she has chosen are creepy, dead before their time. On Lily's desk there are five jewelry boxes all covered with shells and as many mirrors, shells forming their frames. She alternates her production—mirror, then box, then mirror again—and means to sell them in the summer. When school is out, she can make five bucks a day and save her money. She wants —she is not sure now. The boxes and mirrors look like kid stuff. A boat, her own sailfish is what Lily wanted to buy, to buy it herself, though her parents will get it for her anyway.

Jack Flood comes in the front door. It is hot after the hospital and the air-conditioned car. He pulls his tie down and is halfway upstairs when they call to him. Ginger and Rose stand framed in the arch to the living room. His daughter all in white makes such a picture, his wife seems shoved aside. "Very nice," Jack says. Knowing he must do better, he comes back downstairs and Rose is a sight to behold, taller than her mother, her hair no longer that of a blond child, amber it has become, her eyes steady, lost in the cult of herself—Rose in a white dress. "Beautiful," Jack says. A fatherly kiss never enters his mind. She is too much the portrait. Rose as a milkmaid, only she is so sure of herself and wise. "Yes, that's beautiful," he says. He has forgotten what the dress was for—a dance or a play.

Ginger pokes at a sleeve. She is presenting Rose to her father as an accomplishment, her perfect thing. Fussing over the girl like a maid, she looks completely happy. "Absolutely nothing else," she says, "except my mother's pearls."

"Yes, ma'am," Jack says, "that's the ticket." The hall is oppressive. He can hear the air-conditioner humming in the dining room where he will eat with his girls, not for the last time, but it is near the end. The white dress is spanking clean against the tight scheme of greenish, goldish flowers in the living room. Ginger is on her knees doing something with the hem. He will not leave her. Not tonight, not tomorrow. Perhaps when the term is over. He did not know this when he came in the door. He will leave this woman who is kneeling with pins in her mouth and who is, for the most part, dutiful and kind. She is blameless: that is the gentlemanly position he takes as he showers and eats, watches the news. He is not professionally distracted or once again in love, as a matter of fact it's been a while since he's had anyone on the line, so perhaps this idea of packing up, moving on, started early with the sight of Margaret, or when she went back to her life in New York or later, as late as the boy's funeral. Dr. Flood watches his wife thread a needle, the white dress spilled out on her lap. He is bewildered by the course he sets, but he'll take the blame.

It's late by the time Lily gets hold of him. Her mother and Rose are asleep. She whispers, conspiring over the parcel. It is tea, bricks of pressed jasmine tea, though they do not know that, which have been placed as packing material or camouflage on either side of what they take to be a fan. The fan is silk. It is without a handle, framed in cardboard. Holding it under the light, Jack and his daughter haven't a clue—a mountain scene on one side and black Chinese characters on the other, a number of red devices like emblems. "The gift to the American friend John Sarsfield Flood, M.D., from Doctor Yin-Li (U. of Minnessota)" is printed on a separate piece of paper as though it is a title. Tea and a fan—it takes some time to come up with the answers. Jack scrapes the pressed tea into a pot of steaming water according to the directions of a Chinese intern, Scotty Wong, who has grown up in Boston. At night Lily and her father sit in the kitchen drinking their tea. The four bricks are set up on a counter each stamped with pagoda and tea branches. Across the top it says something they guess at. Something beautiful, Lily says, about jasmines. Something sensible, Jack says—Big Red Chinese Tea Company.

The politics of the house shifts to open warfare. Ginger puts waxed paper under the tea bricks to catch any droppings. Jack and Lily's cups are set aside as though contaminated. He is home most nights and after supper he sorts through the weekend's scratch with Lily. They boil the live specimens and sit at the kitchen table picking out the flesh of dead mollusks. He is a good surgeon, leaving nothing rank behind in the tiniest shell. *Mercenaria mercenaria, anomia simplex*—Lily is thrilled listening to her father read out the Latin names—*mitrella lunata.* When Ginger hears that they have finished, she comes down to the kitchen, puts on her rubber gloves and scours up with Pine-Sol. The fan, as yet unidentified, is placed by Jack Flood in the living room. He moves aside a vase of permanent flowers and sets it up, switching it daily from tranquil landscape to calligraphy—a tan scrap against the ongoing cheer of yellow wall. Nothing is screamed, nothing broken. There is no peace. Rose, taking her mother's part, calls her sister Little Miss Crustacean, a title they have always mocked, handed out to a crabber's child during a touristy summer fair. Rose passes her driver's test, is elected captain of the tennis team—triumph to triumph.

On a muggy day Jack takes his gift from Yin-Li to the Baltimore Museum. It flutters on the seat next to him in the air-conditioned car. The curator, a young woman who has studied at the Fogg, is shocked to see Dr. Flood carries the fan naked, unsheathed. It is a hand-held fan mounted as an album leaf. He must understand, it may be Sung, seven hundred years old. She is prim, so much the lady, but melts before this beauty. Flushed, squinting, she studies the brush strokes through a magnifying glass. Jack can imagine her, myopic and intense in bed. A low hum of continuous pleasure, then her unrestrained cry, "The Imperial Seal!"

"Golly! What does it say?"

The man is a fool. "I don't read classical Chinese. For that we'll have to take it to the Freer. The hand is lyrical, refined, but it wavers." She can't get Dr. Flood: sane enough, professor of medicine—golly, driving around the city with a priceless fan. The usual thing is Nineteenth Century, missionary junk brought in by old ladies who are counting on a fortune. She has learned all the phrases that cover worthless—"a clear example," "family treasure," but she does not know what to make of Dr. Flood's ignorance.

He does not have a plausible story to go with his fan. "It's not the work of a copyist," she says. "It was an unworldly time, overcivilized. . . ." She blushes, lecturing a white-haired surgeon. She can see he is a make-out artist in his linen suit, gold cuff links, Liberty tie.

"The picture?" he asks.

"Elegant, not important—done by an artist of the Imperial Academy. Maybe it is his emperor-scholar under the pine trees." Jack and Lily have seen the small figure of a man looking at mountains, but they have not taken in the mist on the upper peaks or that here and there a tree is in bloom. The bird they have seen, but not the hut in the bamboo thicket. "Ink and light color on silk," the curator says. He has forgotten her name, too late to ask. She is not as young as he thought, virginal thirty-five, not noticeably pretty except as she is aroused by the fan, discovering the last mound of snow in a culvert, the rhythmic repeat of ravines, a plum tree. More than likely a sacred stream. A holograph—her picture on his. She studies a faded red seal: "The three lines of heaven were used only by the emperor."

He hopes he will remember it all for Lily. "Sung?"

"That was a guess. Strictly speaking, we don't have an Oriental department. We'll take it to the Freer." She is barely polite, holding the album leaf away from Jack Flood who doesn't deserve it, the oval fan in the center a thin membrane between them he doesn't understand. "The Sung Dynasty . . . the palace was full of aesthetes, court competitions in calligraphy and verse. It was no wonder they fell to the Mongol hordes."

When Jack leaves, he finds a card in his pocket that tells him he has been talking to Bernice Blau. Dr. Blau. He'll tell Lily how stupid he felt about their fan—Thirteenth Century, an object of daily use, the little bald fellow probably an emperor—and that Dr. Blau, so drawn to her work, so sharp with him, reminded him of someone and he came across it driving home—Margaret. He will say that to Lily as they drink their lifetime supply of that pale perfumed tea.

As a matter of fact, Lily doesn't want her own boat anymore. The shells have become something else. Whether she collects them for their beauty or to listen to her father say *phylum mollusca, conus pura tensis;* whether she sells her boxes and mirrors—it's all the same. She stands free of her mother and Rose. The shells are her money: no purchase in sight, no more immediate use than their value to her and that projects before Lily as miraculous as compound interest. School is almost over. She has done poorly. All spring she has been friendless but happy. On weekends she stands in the saline waters of Chesapeake marshland, combing with her toes for shells. She waits for her father to drive down so they can scrape jetties and pry up stones for live specimens.

At home they work in the kitchen. Her parents never go out. No one comes. The house is hell. Her mother turns out closets and drawers as she does every year, making the rooms perfect for the summer emptiness, drawing shades with a finality so that all her false gardens will bloom on in darkness. They will be going the next day or the next. Her father will not come with them, Lily knows that. He cannot give up his lab or the hospital and come down to the shore.

They sit up late in her room. Is Yin-Li dead? Jack Flood thinks so. He has had no answer to his letters. The old man was tired. Though he was ashamed of his weariness and never troubled his American friend with symptoms, it sounded like congestive heart failure after years of hard labor. Lily thinks he is alive and would look like the old man on their fan if they could see him, one hand raised to his thin beard, thinking about that mountain.

"In a kimono?" Jack asks.

"You know what I mean."

Her father does know, but neither of them figure the translation of the text they have received from the Freer:

In a moment the mist can reform
And the morning make sport.
Last year the wax plum bloomed gladly
And as gladly died.
Today the clouds ring the far mountain
And there is red fragrance and color nearby.
Perhaps we should not thank the God of Spring.

"It's that last line," Lily says, "I mean, why not be thankful? It's a nice day." "*We?*" she asks, "Who's we?"

And every night she asks about the funeral. Their last night together is no different. "Tell me about the music," she says and Jack tells her about the flute and piano duets played by kids from Bayard's school. It is a strange bedtime story. Lily cannot get enough of the red roses, police escort out to the pretty mausoleum among mossy statues, flashing cameras, weeping teachers and students—some of them her age. Nor does Jack Flood know why he likes telling about Bayard. "He was not musical himself, but had just come to love his records, a little later than most. You see, he was brilliant and a mind like that finds its own way. Don't think he was square . . . or whatever you'd say. He was an original. Tall for his age . . ."

Jack's story goes on: Bayard translates into myth for Lily, a prince of a boy she'd never seen, only pictures. Her father was so fond of him. In a way he is her rival, dead and gone. She cannot learn enough about his height and black hair. He knew the planets and stars, completely on his own, the way her father knew Latin when he was a boy. Bayard played soccer. That was his game. Unbelievably kind to his crazy parents. He was a saint, really, when she thinks of it, riding the spooky New York subway down to that shop. Lily has asked her father about the wounds. He has said the shock and the internal bleeding made it quick.

The unsolved murder, that works in Lily's head. Tonight she asks again about the funeral. That was some day she'll never forget. Her father said he was flying up to the funeral and her mother spassed, fell into a kitchen chair like she was gunned down.

"It was cold," Jack says, "cold as the tomb, I guess, and damp. Greenwood Cemetery was like a stone church we'd entered and left Brooklyn behind. Cool that you got used to. We walked single file up a narrow path. Bayard's girlfriend said the vines were melancholy."

"What was she like?"

"A sweet kid—very delicate," Jack says. "She looked about ten years old wearing black."

"I wish I was there," Lily says.

"It wasn't a party."

"I know that." She lays her head down on her pillow. Her face is slack, removed. Jack Flood doesn't leave. He knows this is the last night they will spend together for a while. The girls are going off. He has taken an apartment downtown where they are beginning to doll up whole blocks of old Baltimore. He has loved this city. The hills and the bay remind him of San Francisco—that job at Stanford where the great cardiology went on after he'd left—and the big commercial buildings, red stone and pillars, the old Hopkins Medical School with its domes and spires push him further back to New Haven. What he should have become? Newman—Charlie Newman does all the paperwork for the grants now, does all the science. Dr. Flood signs his name. Newman, the best in twenty years, will have the lab. In the inflated rhetoric that is used these days to recommend students—very good, excellent, best in twenty years—his protégé comes out on top. He would not rank himself. Lily has fallen asleep, but he does not move from where he sits on the bottom of her bed.

Jack has taken a sublet until he decides. He does not think it is a costly move, though this house will stand empty all summer. Full of plans, he thinks of a practice somewhere, not a teaching hospital. A house with an office like the one never set up in New Haven. The simplest kind of arrangement on a street that is quiet and wide, a side street so his patients can park. It is a hopelessly sentimental idea: he is a very good surgeon, still a prominent heart man, but he tells himself that he has failed at fifty and must now heal the neighborhood, live over the store. He would like to see Bernice Blau, read her the text. He has forgotten whether she is fair or dark, but he would like to hear her superior voice—"I don't read classical Chinese." He would like to see her flush with scholarly enthusiasm when he tells her she was on the money about Sung. She knows what she knows.

She had asked: "Do you want an estimate?" He didn't get that. "Do you want to know what the fan is worth when it's taken to the Freer?"

"No," he said.

"The value?" She gave him half a smile. "They always want a price tag."

He will not call the lady curator. He will not move his clothes or books to the apartment until the girls are gone. In the operating room he has always, to the annoyance of his assistants, done the check himself before closing up. Except with Maggie Flood. His daughter's features have suddenly thickened in adolescence. She is not pretty now with braces swelling her upper lip, a blotch on her chin. Her nose and mouth are uncertain, on their way to definition. Little Miss Crustacean, soft as a soft-shell crab. She believes Yin-Li is alive, that Bayard Strong's murderer will be found and thank God for a nice day. He picks up their teapot and cups. Jack Flood is inordinately proud of his daughter's mirrors and boxes decorated with shells and of her collection. Lily has plans. Yin-Li is dead—there is no need for speculation. In Jack's mind he knows that the murder will never be solved. *"We?"* she has asked him,

"Who's we?" He should have answered truthfully that he will never understand the emperor's calligraphy, but why the hell must we thank God when he keeps changing the scene.

Ginger is set to go when Rose comes back with the car. Jack took off for the hospital at dawn. She has put out mothballs and mildew spray for Fay to use as soon as they drive away. She is checking the windows, pulling the drapes across. Jack comes and goes by the front door which locks itself. Like so many doctors she has known, he is not responsible about the house. Lily has been difficult. She would not sit up front with Rose. For the life of her, Ginger cannot see what is so terrible about being driven by your sister. It is very nice of Rose to drive Lily to Country Day where she must clean out her locker which should have been done before exams, weeks ago. An anxious day for Ginger Flood who must remember the prescription medicines, her address book, the new tennis racquets, Cuisinart and clam steamer, though on the weekend Jack will bring what's left behind. It is Thursday, the perfect day to head on down, to beat the traffic to St. Michael's. It is good her parents did not live to see the hordes that drive out from Philadelphia and even New Jersey, trampling their Eastern Shore.

In the living room she puts her vase of eternal iris back where it belongs and whisks the Chinese fan off the mantel as though it were no more than one of Rose's floppy Motown albums which it resembles. She is not angry, not that she knows of, and runs upstairs, up past Fay with the vacuum, the Chinaman's gift in hand. From the door of Jack's room, the room he chooses most often to sleep in, she skims the fan across to his bed with her strong backhand. It whacks the wall and spins down on the floor. The silk is split, thank God not so much on the side with the picture, down through the writing. You can't notice. If it ever comes up, she will say Fay did it, though to Ginger Flood's eyes it can barely be seen.

When she is locking Lily's window, she sees the garbage truck making its way up the street. It is Thursday. Without a thought she sweeps all the shells into the wastebasket. The mess is everywhere. So is the smell. She has them all out the side door, into the trash, by the time the men come to her drive. To Fay she says, "You want to go right up and turn out Miss Lily's room." Southern talk surfaces when Ginger speaks with servants. She does not intend offense, it's just her way. "I do mean it's a bog in there, Fay, all grit, sand and seaweed you wouldn't b'lieve."

Ginger is set to go, just waiting now for Rose to come back with the car. Last night the girls were told to put whatever extra they were taking down in the front hall. Lily lay around drinking jasmine tea. Ginger Flood is not vindictive, not really mean. Such accusations against her scrape bottom quickly, as though tested in the clear tepid waters she loves. The shells—oh, there are plenty more where they came from, the whole summer to find them. Every year Ginger is happy to quit the heat of Baltimore, every year since she was three.

The U.S. Mail car driven by a farmer's wife stops Margaret with a toot as she is driving into town. The mailwoman is a cheerful soul who loves her work, loves driving these hills in all weather and has never lost her enthusiasm for packages—orders filled, surprises, gifts. Mrs. Strong, more accurately Miss Flood, is a favorite who receives any number of important packages when she's in residence on the hill, books and manuscripts, a common annoyance to Margaret, but to the farmer's wife it would seem Christmas every day. She gets out of her car and takes letters and a soft bulky package to Margaret who hands over a big envelope she's sending off, a friendly exchange.

The mailwoman says, "I'm real sorry you're moving

away." And she is, her Yankee shrug shows it's too bad. It's been something of a thrill these years. Aside from the many packages, there's been inflammatory folders to read and what looked like opened mail, now the many letters of condolence which, though the boy's been dead for weeks, she still delivers to the Strongs each day.

"We must move on." That seems impersonal to Margaret, but may be a protective phrase, useful as they take their leave. She squashes her package to her breast and waves the mail car off. The handwriting is perfect, therefore anonymous. It's not books or papers that have found her this time on top of the hill. She's curious and snaps the string. The paper springs open and there is Bayard's Irish sweater. She cries out, sitting alone in her car by the side of the road. The moment has come. She weeps into the rough wool and keens loudly. Ground birds flutter up from their cover of fern and laurel. She damns their silly flight. She would like to strip the trees above her that won't keep the sun from her scalding eyes.

The sweater smells of its animal life. It is small, made for a growing boy. The designs are beautiful. Mrs. Grogan's note is in a sleeve. A long while passes before Margaret can read it—something about not wanting her fee, something Irish—the bad fairies would be after her, charging for a shroud. *May the earth's pity cover him with kindness.* The lad she calls him. "Give it up," Margaret cries to Mrs. Grogan. "Give it up with the Irish talk, you harpy. I know that game." Her breastbone aches against the steering wheel. "You will not get me with your blather from a doomed island in the North Sea. You have your share of martyrs. Give it up." Mrs. Grogan has written it's a cruel world, indeed, he's well out of it—as though Bayard were a fisherman's boy. *Lad. Lad.* Margaret mocks Mrs. Grogan's lilting brogue. This stuff could break your heart. Jaysus, the throubled toimes. *God will look after the world when the both of us are gone,* Mrs. Grogan has written.

The sun beats down on the windshield. Margaret is exhausted and says to Mrs. Grogan, "Won't that be fine."

Tina is bopping down the Ramblas. Ticket to L.A. via N.Y.C. in her Spanish leather jeans. She has left Sol Negaly und hiss zieg heil moofie—kerplotz. The vurst—mit extras these Tex Mex guys look nothing, nothing like Chermuns. Call in the cavalry. Like Navahos are supposed to be these Bavarian waiters and pass for Schutzstaffel, SS.

On the Ramblas, the birds are singing in their cages, the flowers blooming on their stalls, also these wacko tape decks, cheap, FM radio—cheap, cheap—Rocka Rolla chili music made in Taiwan. The birds are tweeting like it is morning in *Snow White.* Whistle while you work. Sing the merry tune. All high and trembly, singing to rabbits and chipmunks. On the Ramblas, cages and cages, bargain birds. How often do you need a bird? All its life one song. Tina's got it together, high—but not outside. One *hora* till she grabs a rapist cab to take her out to TWA Fly American. Tina is going home to White Bread. And the passport, her first, *Tina Negaly,* like she needed that name. Take a break, needed crawling around these rocky cliffs, nothing, nothing like Chermuny. In the dark, 5 AM, taking Sol's notes on this angle you could shoot a castle looks like Taco Bell. Tina moves fast into a café, back out of sight. No more Señorita see Spanish dance, see gypsies, see bulls. What is she supposed to do with the blond hair? Put a sack on her head? Jerk off *en español.*

One *hora* to go. One airline bag, that's it. What does she want from Sol—the house in Bel Air, pool, Jacuzzi, Mercedes? *Gracias,* no way. And her name off the movie. The haircuts wrong, uniforms, furniture all wrong. Car wrong—Himmler drove a black coupe. Tina is drinking Coca-Cola in this funny wineglass, bitter like they got the secret formula from Mars. Baby (that's Tina), you got to sacrifice a little awethenticity. Like this actress is ten years too old for the part. Big star. Tiny tits. Practice the nude scene with Sol, be Tina's guest. Achtung, Tina is crew. *Gracias,* no lottery. Tina wants out of the country where her luck runs bad. Coming down from this motel in the Pyrenees where they are shooting, the bus is out of gas. She can believe it—like the Santa Ynez Pass, you got thirty latinos paid up and you don't check the tank. Yah, Hitler said Spaniards were dumb, no fear. It is the way this actress treats Tina like a waitress or kid in the beauty shop sweeps up her hair. Dry rust hair, damaged. And already Sol and this guy are rewriting the script—she can't *feel* the lines. Without three hours' eye contact with Sol and a case of dago red to build the interior motivation. Build Mr. Sol Hollywood. Awethentic—feel the goods. All Tina ever wanted was the movie made right. Tina knows show biz, but doesn't take shit. The Nazi dog's name and even the dog don't make it with Bel Star, this Bette Davis bitch. *Fritz,* it *feels* German, *Fritz.* So goodbye Blondie, goodbye authentic Alsatian pup, goodbye Leningrad, goodbye Rommel—whee! So long footage of Eva Braun romping at Berchtesgaden. Goodbye Negaly. Well, let her say this —Tina has never been INVOLVED WITH THE POLICE and a spooky basement murder before she entered the matrimonial state. And weirdo Mr. Strong. He was sweet, unreal, like tripping on *Fantasia.* The music starts. You want to see Tina at her worst, crying over a Coke. She is not even high, not really, sobbing at the nothing flamenco beat. Tina is going home to White Bread. It is yesterday in California. By tomorrow she will be trading guitar leads, blistering, hands on. Authenticity is for the birds. Pulverized hard funk in the atmospheric lights. Tina will wear her iron cross and killer glasses. *Gracias,* no Valium, no poppers, no gypsies. Tina runs out on the Ramblas. She is boogying on down to the cab stand when she is nabbed by Sol Negaly and the Barcelona police. *Muchas gracias,* his little wife.

Pouting in the Porsche. Sol has bought her roses. Sol has bought her this blue-and-green tiny bird, cocks its head—tweet-tweet—like Tina is Snow White in the morning dusting up the dwarf mess. They are driving up this pass like California.

"The actress is gone. All right?"

"All wrong," Tina says. "Too old."

"All right! We get your epaulets, black coupé, blond soldiers. We get a girl with no name . . ."

Tweet-tweet.

". . . but don't work me over on Leningrad and the damn chronology."

"Mock-u drama," Tina says.

"A little give and take, baby."

"I'm cool. I'm cool." Tina smells her roses: "Back to the old script?"

"Believe me," Sol says, "I know how to make this picture."

Tweet. Tweet-tweet. Tina waves her finger in the cage. The little bird shakes its tail and winks. It has only one song.

The house will soon be empty. The house is sold. Pinkham Strong is plagued by flies, out back working a crowbar around the edges of his rock. It moves. Maybe it is the sensation of leverage, he can't tell, or wishful thinking. He swats his neck and arms. Swats. Real estate agents showing the property had always paused, made a point of their honesty acknowledging the oozing trenchlike scar he has dug around the boulder. It is nearly six o'clock. The sweat on his body chills. The flies stick to his clammy skin and he swats. It is going to be one of those Vermont nights when the temperature falls suddenly, a good twenty degrees. Then Margaret will put the boy's sweater on. She has started that—she smells it, plucks at its stitches, wanders off in her head. He would like to burn the thing along with his rakings and the last of the New Left magazines, old papers, the residue of vital facts that drove him to high principles and his dishonor a few years back. Walking to the downside of the boulder, he tries the earth again, strikes a soft spot. The crowbar sinks deep. The strain grabs at his back and thighs. A give, a little give, he can't be sure. The house is sold, yet he still hopes to accomplish the removal of this massive stone. He has made the back yard unsightly, but he cannot stop. He takes off his sweaty shirt and swats.

Margaret has gone to the dealer who is buying the remaining corner cabinet, the sideboard, the very chairs they sit on and their high carved bed. He was working at his desk when she came up behind him quietly, not to interrupt. Off to the dealer's. They have no phone. Back when they—when she—first bought the house it was impossible to get the local workmen to come out on a job—a month, six weeks' wait. Now they are leaving, a man in a trim uniform has driven off with their phone a week early. Margaret is glad of it. And he can cut off from the world: he's had a go at that in the cellar on St. Mark's Place. He calls himself the Former—Former Socialite and Sportsman, Former Activist, formerly attached to headquarters and hindquarters, Former Single Agent, over-the-counter spy. Former Platform Personality. Margaret will not hear such talk though it's a great relief to him. "With that boulder you'll be former," she says. "You'll have a first prize hernia if it doesn't kill you."

She's still a contender: he feels that. It is only at night when she pulls on Bayard's sweater that she wanders off. Though she is in sight, picking at the wool, tucking her gray head down to smell a sleeve, he worries she has left him. He has no right to feel lost. He walked out. Mostly they do all right but now she has been gone longer than he likes. To the dealer's. Margaret loves to close a deal. Three thousand for the Connecticut sideboard and she'll get it. He was hopeless with the old clothes. Like most of the Strongs he is arrogant about money and one thing he can't forgive himself, one thing among many, is the shoddy commercial cover he dreamt up in that basement. Not facing Margaret, he made his son an emissary—tell her . . . he'd thought of a phrase the kids use—tell her I've dropped out. Unnecessary, it was all unnecessary. Properly speaking, he was passing through, that was not his war. The boulder does move. Very slightly tips toward him. His arms tremble with the effort. A small legacy for those who come after. The view will be improved.

Three thousand dollars. "It's a signed piece," Margaret said. "Wait till you see what I get for the pineapple carvings on our bed." She has seemed close to happy—that's not the word—at least happily occupied as she heads to the post office to mail off her work. Typing like the old days. "Bits and pieces," she said, sealing the envelope. "The grand design emerges. Plot thickens. We last saw Dotty in the arms of two-faced Max." Yes, he would say his wife has been pleased—considering—if not happy in the execution of her contracted work.

Muddied, shuffling his notes, Pinkham Strong waits at his desk where he can see Margaret drive up the hill. He has no right to feel abandoned. He drinks a can of sweet lime soda. For the first time since Bayard's death, he wants a beer. A misty photo from the Bettmann Archives looks up at him. It is the Italianate façade of a housing project built by young Harrison Bidwell, the grandfather on his mother's side. Apartments for immigrants, prescribed as the workingman's dream: interior courtyard as playground, balconies, the most advanced sanitary refinements. And a reading room—the catalogue of books provided has been found in the family papers: Shakespeare, Milton, Emerson, long works by Fenimore Cooper, the collected poems of Longfellow and James Russell Lowell—for Italians and Germans who could barely make themselves known in English. For greenhorns who, if they could read, were more interested in Boss Tweed's shenanigans at Tammany Hall. Episcopal tracts and the King James Bible for Roman Catholics and Lutherans. For Jews. For anarchists. Pinky is much taken with his grandfather's assigned reading list: The scientific essays of Herbert Spencer, of Huxley and Darwin, so that men and women who worked twelve, fourteen hours a day could read up on the survival of the fittest. Bidwell Gardens had no boiler, no furnace. You could clean them up and educate them but it was not your Christian duty to keep them warm. And it was never meant to be a handout, on the principle that the poor are best off paying for their self-respect. A principle not tested in this case: Bidwell Gardens with its airy enlightenment was unaffordable, inhabited by the American-born who had made it to the middle class: a stop on their way out of town to the suburbs, for twenty years it paid well, before a fire in the dead of winter burned it to the ground.

Today Pinky has worked on that grandfather, a tall stick figure, thin and gray as himself, who he remembers stalking a Fifth Avenue apartment, dressed for business, no business to go to in the thirties. A solemn show of reading the newspapers. British murder mysteries stacked by his wing chair, three or four of the same next to the crystal water jug on his night stand—*The Secret of Hearthsdale Hall*—Bertie and Lady Clive, Maybelle, the Brighton tart, *Terror at Tattersall Park*. He had tried the old man's mysteries, but they bored him as much as the pastel mints and ginger ale his grandmother served as a treat.

When Harry Bidwell died, Pinkham had been given a glass of sherry and the privilege of looking through, which meant taking what he'd like of his grandfather's books. He wanted nothing. He was not a reader. At Princeton he suffered through the necessary Shakespeare and gave a passing nod to the likes of Henry Adams and Thoreau in

American Political Thought. He wanted nothing off the library shelves—the library being a paneled room with club chairs pulled up to the big radio in a modern Tudor cabinet, copies of *Country Life, Vogue, The New Yorker. The Saturday Evening Post* was the only magazine that ever looked read. He had poured himself a second sherry, then a third, while his grandmother, a corseted woman in new black, disapproved of his indecision. Knowing he must please her, he grabbed three or four volumes, he couldn't remember the titles except that they were gilt-edged, leather bound, one was Twain. That was all he wanted, to make the gesture, thank his grandmother formally. She took in his kind words—a good woman whose intolerance of sin had never allowed her to bob her hair. He remembered her as a large pillar decorated always with carved jade and yellowed ivory. She was of missionary descent, sweet and cold as the Schrafft's lemon sherbet she invariably served with one cream wafer for dessert. On the window seat which overlooked the courtyard of the Frick, she had already gathered the piles and piles of British murder mysteries (her husband's great weakness) to give to St. Luke's hospital where she would fill out Harry Bidwell's term on the board. The classics Pinkham thanked her for had nothing to do with the grandfather he had known. He did not want that baggage. It was 1941. He was about to go to war.

Pinky waits for Margaret. Only now, as it edges toward seven, do the trees and lawn soften. The feathery shadow of a Japanese maple dusts the barn. A tree of Margaret's choosing, it has prospered. The farmers laugh no more. The new owners of the house—corporate, retired—who aim to set their tax base in Vermont, are mad for the Japanese tree. It reminds them of the dwarf cut-leaf in their condo garden at Hilton Head where they will go in the winter. A continuity of maples. Pinky thrives on continuity and likes the fact that these vigorous people, aging beautifully, are coming up from Carolina in pursuit of their best interest, from the very swamp that one of the Strongs went to during Reconstruction. A spinster, teaching the freed slaves to read. Not accepting her twenty dollars a month from the Freedman's Bureau, writing home for clothes, soap, beans, tea to give to her scholars who shared one bowl, one spoon. Her letters were a catalogue of torment—rattlesnakes, wood ticks, mosquitoes. She slept on a pallet of moss with a hammer at hand to kill any man who pushed in the door. Even in her shortest notes Christ was invoked—that He will sustain—that she will embrace her hardship for the merciful Lord. Her "nig school" was taken from her by the whites returning to their land and they laughed at Miss Bella Strong who taught on the beach where her children drew their letters with sticks in wet sand. The Carolina summer was the punishment she'd come for, until her father made the long trip south to bring her home, home to Twelfth Street, a defeated revolutionary. There is not another word to be found on Miss Strong though she lived into her eighties. He is fond of that woman and works up her dead end life, one of his parables. As he gets out his maps of Greenwich Village, Grace Church parish, he looks anxiously downhill for Margaret and thinks of the new owners, slick and no more greedy than most people, who are leaving the air-conditioned condo for the chill mercurial nights and black flies of Vermont.

The continuity appeals: the Carolinas, plague of insects, ornamental maples. It wavers in front of him, perceptible as the coming of evening which he can't quite hold. The damp shirt stuck to his back; Pinky stuck in the chair to be sold from under him. He wants a beer, but his life does not depend on it. On Margaret, though he is not entitled, and on these maps and half-written pieces of his family making sense. *Pro bono,* for the good of the Republic, that was the honorable affliction of the Bidwells, Bayards,

Strongs—"the lot of them" his wife would say, the lot with their good works. Bidwell Gardens with its lofty arches and its interior courtyard would have looked to poor immigrants the unwelcoming fortress of a prince. Built up near Central Park on the outskirts of the city, far from the sweatshops and foundries, they could not afford the daily carfare, never mind the rent. *Pro bono*—what a vision, the reading room like a nick off the Society Library where Harry Bidwell paid his dues but never read. They could eat their garlic and noodles then come down to the public rooms, Giuseppe and Moishe, to partake of the forest primeval, the murmuring pines and the hemlocks. Or Poe, maybe they would be improved by *She was a child and I was a child in our kingdom by the sea,* grieving patrician verse, a singsong downer for comfort while their own children's dying, unsung, remained a daily sorrow.

Pinkham Strong's mind is not nimble. He works hard at the simple (and to him overwhelming) ironies. It has been an effort to come up with the lines from *Evangeline* and *Annabel Lee,* lines from childhood, from the schoolroom that was mostly a trial. He sets aside the hours each day to come upon hard thoughts which he writes like a boy with ink-stained hands. He is amazed when a sheet of paper is covered with a pattern of words. It is that difficult, a strict theme, spelling out tales which can only be of his family, only of old New York. These are not rules of composition but there is such a wealth, he cannot imagine needing ever to go beyond it. The texts of his forgotten speeches, even his communiqués (First Army) and manifestos (pacifist), were in some part committee efforts. Now Pinky is on his own.

Margaret cheers him on. He cannot bear to tell her that his tales, each with its moral closing, are written only for himself. So, he has learned that his grandfather Bidwell's generosity—the palazzo for immigrants—paid off as though the money had been invested at what was then, given the Gilded Age and inflation, a neat 16 percent. That—and collecting the fire insurance, along with the rising value of uptown land, was *pro bono* for sure. And Miss Bella May Strong, spinster, had gone to teach black children in good enough faith with the healing Republic—but also to save her soul, for the eternal reward. The continuity: maples, the Carolinas, self-interest, the trust funds that thrive on national disaster. He knows every federal house, brownstone and solid apartment his family has lived in and could conduct a walking tour of the city charting their naiveté, their crafty self-deception and at the end there is a giant finger, like an old advertising sign, that points to a ramshackle structure, Pinkham Strong. The Former. He would like that on his grave.

In Greenwood Cemetery he had looked in amazement at his grandfather's headstone, arched like a miniature entrance to Bidwell Gardens, its angel head eroded to pit eyes and thinning curls so soon that it must have been carved of inferior stone. Harry's name vanishing. Solve the mystery—Pinky has thought of this: one of his continuities, that the old man's head, full of ingenious clues picked up by country squires, of motives that cross class lines between cockney maid and duchess, the hundreds of entertaining riddles old Harry solved waiting for the Depression to be over, would be no help in the matter of Bayard's death.

He sets out cold chicken and salad. They eat simply. The sun blazes in the kitchen window which faces west. It is seven-thirty and no Margaret. He fears it is her heart or that she has worn that damned sweater and cannot remember the road home. Then he hears, so high and mighty, Margaret Flood's professional laugh, confident, stagy—a laugh he has not heard in a number of years, and she enters the kitchen with a little man in checks, like a bun in a picnic napkin, a basket coddling his head.

"Look who has found us," Margaret says.

Pinky does not remember Fred Peach. There are only two chairs. They lean at various angles, propped by the refrigerator, sink and stove. Two portions of boiled chicken and wilted salad set the limits.

"No, really! No," says Fred Peach. "I'm staying down at the Inn." He lounges against the electric stove. It is only later they will discover that he has switched the front burners on with his delectable rump and the elements gleam behind him, spiral red eyes in the spook house. Later, they laugh at Fred Peach like bad children—at his bun-basket hat and country-mouse attire. They laugh to cauterize the wound as the orange sun wipes its fire down the windows and Margaret, who aches with mirth, calls his visit The Great Swap.

Pinky stood against the refrigerator in his work shirt—strong male smell mingling with Peach's eau de cologne. The poor salad, oh, their visitor could not hide his contempt for the watery leaves weeping their last in the bottom of the bowl. Thank you, he was at the Inn and to woo them, trying too hard, he emitted shrieks of pleasure at the empty house and what he called, after one squint at the bloody sunset, their view. "So idyllic," Peach said. "You have no phone." Right, no phone, so he was always ha-ha-ha, catching up with Margaret Flood and . . . a nod to Pinkham, her family. "Here we are," he said, flapping an envelope, "your little pieces."

"Yes?"

"They are very charming—Dorothy and Hannah—all of that, but I did have something else in mind."

Margaret could answer that. Ha-ha, Peach cut her off, "After what you have been through, my dear. The sorrow. A mother's sorrow." All the while pressing the stove buttons with his precious behind.

Pinky got wind of it like a sweet stink of rubbish burning, and said, "We were just about to eat our supper." So he had learned something about rot, clearing the yard, or about corruption from the story of another disgraced Bidwell, bilked out of his land by the great railroad crook Jay Gould, and he would maintain that Fred Peach festered in front of their eyes. It was Margaret who didn't see it, smell it, and had actually said, "Supper can wait."

"What I have in mind," the editor said. Should remain unspoken: his obscenity seeped out in the lurid orange light. Later, Margaret will not even think of what he had in mind, but laugh at The Great Swap—the moment in which she gave Fred Peach a check for the full amount of her advance on the important book—wonderful, scabrous, blow the lid off the Fifties—and took from him the envelope with her final words on Dotty, Hannah and Max. They were out on the front lawn by this time. Pinky had removed the fellow bodily from the house, that is how Margaret remembers it. The back of his countrified shirt was singed like a potholder and the little man had turned blue, whether it was cold or his bloodless rage they hardly cared, watching him step lively in his spanking-white sneakers, hearing his last injured screech as he ran down the hill.

"Weasel. I know how people weasel out of contracts." Folding Margaret's check, Peach had stamped on the lawn in a muffled tattoo. "I know it was trash you gave me—that you have already gone elsewhere with your story for big money. This business is—"

"Full of whores," said Pinky, and then he had done the John Wayne clutch at the holster, spat in the grass. "Get off my land."

The burners were red hot when they went inside and they laughed, defenseless and uncontrolled as little kids, at the waddling scorched backside of Fred Peach in his tight new jeans. Pinky claimed he never spat, but Margaret saw him. Yes, he gathered the yellow bile of anger in his throat and took professional aim.

Touch your nose. Touch your toes. Margaret got her price that day for the sideboard: it wasn't easy. What the editor had in mind they did not speak of. As soon as the sun went down and gave them darkness they went upstairs, stripped and stood forth in slight moonlight. Lean, gray, worn, they lie on the four-poster. Do this. Do that. Entwined for dear life, they look as though they have leapt upon each other. Just so, they have come together in great need since their reunion on St. Mark's Place. Their want is terrible. It cannot be satisfied, only spent. They ride each other in urgency, not entirely sure they will become a man and a woman again. All they can take is scant pleasure, the feel of their limbs in the maze, breast to breast and the thrill—they note and record it—that their bodies still differ. But tonight, a miracle of the flesh, they come alive and are blindly lost, their history silenced in unconscious cries.

Margaret covers him up. The last quilt. The half-light is gone. She hears the rough draw of his breath. It is not late. He wants the end of days: sleep comes to him quick. When she leans to him he smells of sweat and their boiled chicken. His frontier swagger on the well fed lawn was ridiculous, outdated. The Handsome Man. She turns from him and pulls herself out of their warm nest by the carved bedpost. The wood is silky. She runs her hand up the tapered flutes. She won't miss any of it. Listen, she thinks as though she's talking to Pinkham, but talking easy, not their life-support babble of downspouts and screen doors . . . listen, I've lived in empty houses before. I've divested. Suicides, did you know, often give things away, get ready. Not me. I can unload the furniture, but I don't travel light. The floorboards are cold as she feels for her discarded clothes. Two Irish sweaters lie side by side. She puts on her own.

Absorbed by her plans, three nights to go on the Chippendale bed; the last night, mattress on the floor like a crash pad. When will she wash their spermy sheets? This teakettle is better than the one in New York. She gathers papers and letters, seals them in a box. Listen, I'm not sure about the typewriter. 1954. It was secondhand in New Haven, a present from Jack Flood. Two plates, forks, knives. She had once fed an army in this house during the Children's Crusade. The sweet cloud cover of pot while they ate cookies kneeling about the floor. High Mass. Pinky their defrocked priest. Those were not squirrels writing violent speeches in the attic. The new owners were never told that history. A few years missing among so many. A necessary gap. She carries the sealed box downstairs. Listen, she has something to say about leaving—not opening the new can of coffee, finishing off the heel of bread. And Margaret is not about to drive Baked Beans Old Fashion Style and half a box of Gorton's codfish into New York. She turns to the kitchen, these pressing matters of available rations, and there's the evidence, her checkbook and Peach's envelope like leftovers that have not been eaten up.

What the editor had in mind comes to her mind fully. No laughing matter, with her sorrow, a mother's sorrow. With her talent, her name. Their-ah-reputation (mouse sniff at Pinky). Her disease even (tiny paw tapping, high and outside, the rodent heart). In sum, the tragedy. She must write about the murder on St. Mark's Place. Others want her story. They have ha-ha no phone so he has come to Vermont, agreement in hand, to offer her more money. More money, of course. Who cares? (Flip of the envelope containing Dotty, Hannah, Max.) Really, with a mother's sorrow she is not committed to old contracts or, ha, old Commies. Pinky makes his move while Fred Peach is still saying what he has in mind: Sell him the death of her boy.

Now, at the kitchen table, she finds that he has left behind the new agreement, and the money proposed, bless his wizened heart, is handsome. Is as does. She tears it.

Though, listen, don't you know that what this man proposes is no worse than what I've done? I want to be damned for my sins, but why compound it. I want to be damned for the past. Sure, recoil at the horror, well the devil has been in this kitchen. No wonder he did not feel the heat of the stove. *Hannah, Dotty, Max,* etc., are there just as she has written and mailed them from Vermont. There is no editorial comment: she would like to be able to say her words have never been read, that they remain entirely private, that she's her only audience. Now, as the days peel off and she's down to the last bean and one potato, two potato and the next to the last night in the Chippendale bed, she can rig this one like a game of her childhood . . . one potato, two potato, three potato, four. In which Margaret wins, counting everyone out—

MAX

Gideon was born in Russia. He claimed it was so, though a male child was delivered of a Pearl Gydonsky at the Lying-In Hospital on Mercer Street on the given date of Max Gideon's birth. The size of the infant, the head in particular, is remarked upon in the proceedings of the Medical Association, City of New York. Max Gideon was hard on women, so the hospital account in which he enters the world outsized, difficult and with some notoriety, while not verified, is more likely true.

The Russian story most probably dates from the early Thirties when he became enamored of Soviet culture, but it is curious, for though Max had a strong personality, he did not have a strong or inventive mind. Often he was heard to shout, "I was born in Nizhni Novgorod during a pogrom," and that ended any argument in which Max's authority on matters Russian had been called into account. When he became a rich man, he wore a fur hat from the first cold day, his Moscow hat, in which he was a most convincing Russian.

Max was studying to become an engineer, when, in his twenty-fifth year, already married to the widow of a covered-button manufacturer and with prospects in that market, he pushed a fellow student away from a water fountain up at City College. Thus a rude gesture (his hallmark) launched his public life. It was said that this small girl was a terrier who worried him to love. But it was surely a mutual passion since he left the widow with nothing more than a suitcase and the Ford car she bought him to live with Dorotska Schwartz in what was called free love. Free to Max.

Dark as a Mongol, broad, with a pebbled skin, he appeared a massive peasant, but one who got the better of his masters. He cultivated his abusive tongue and was much admired by clever women whom he openly called snatch and cunt. An animal among the civilized radicals who were planning the future, he was their darling. He wrote with difficulty, an agitprop pidgin. To the surprise of some comrades he was set up with a magazine. Gideon's charm remains a mystery, but in all accounts it is mentioned—how he would drink with poets and, finding them bogus or just bourgeois, break a table, a chair. How he would bait a professor to get him going on that flibbertigibbet Trotsky or the Byzantine politics of an international congress and then fall loudly to sleep. That he believed his fate was allied to the Party, I have no doubt.

Max was a man who knew when to move on. And so married, in a civil ceremony, Hannah Brandt. She was a great supporter of the arts. When red-baiting was over in the Fifties, he lectured widely proclaiming Russia the great and thrilling experiment, still worth watching as a show, bringing his legends of the Popular Front and the old radical days to the universities where he enjoyed, most notably, a new generation of eager girls. Max was a man who never got caught.

Much taken with fine dress, it is rumored that this gigantic man had his clothes made one size too small, here and there patched, that he might appear stuffed into a Sabbath suit, a worker out of the fields or the pit. I myself heard the long rip of Max's seams punctuate the conversation like a lyric fart. Coarse kosher salt, he was able to melt the strict party line of Dorotska, the frigid glaze of Hannah, into smoldering female hearts. His detractors say that if he had stayed with covered buttons he would have voted for Dewey, Eisenhower, Nixon. Yet, it would seem he was loyal to the cause and died on the eve of the next revolution, being fitted for a Mao jacket. Two tailors could not pry this fallen giant off a bolt of raw silk.

DOTTY

The Dorothea with its many pink blossoms is the rose her husband named for her. As far as I know it is the only miniature floribunda propagated under fluorescent light in a Brooklyn cellar. It is appropriate to Dotty Klotz, being both lively and bright.

"Do you want to talk?" the federal agents asked her. She was enormously intelligent, therefore envied by both men and women alike. Her modesty was real as well as theoretical. Many dazzling articles, reviews, translations were not signed with her name. "Do you want to talk?" they'd ask. She believed that to be true to her convictions her considerable talents must be thrown in the common pot. Like a girl who takes the veil, vows poverty, humility—but not chastity. Not our Dot. Faithful comrade, passionate friend—her mind was supple, more intense than those she worked with, still it was Dotty with a sweet nature and all her reservations about dogma who went to prison in the end. For the middle-class Red Crossy mission of helping the wounded in the Spanish Civil War. "Do you want to talk now?" he asked her. This time it was a big ape who followed her into Macy's. She laughed in his face. Says Dotty to the Fed, "Speak, monkey, speak." Heroics of a sort when you think of Dotty's size. It had been reported that she meant to change the world. What did they want to know? Who changed the bandages? Who downshifted the ambulance bouncing up a Catalonian hill?

In the finest anti-bourgeois tradition, she had little interest in her own adventures.

I remember she told me that in 1937 she met Red Klotz, an anti-fascist schoolteacher from Flatbush. Yes, with the Lincoln Brigade and he got shot in a skirmish. Tracer bullets overhead, shells screaming, she found him in a parched Spanish stream attempting to wash the corpse of his friend, the little grocer, Bloch. The back of Red's neck was fiery as a boil. The Mediterranean sun was merciless to his fair skin. She rubbed him with green olive oil. He smelled, poor man, like he was frying. Theirs was a love story. She married him many years later and lived in happy exile. In Brooklyn she never let Red out in the garden without the protection of a large straw hat.

HANNAH

Her parents, longing for a son, were given an only girl. Hannah, who wasn't pleased about it herself, did her best. All sinew, straight as a board, she became an imposing figure. Among her accomplishments, it should be noted that she was hostess to the great. In speaking kindly of Hannah, many would say that she earned her ravaged face or might quote Francis Bacon—"There is no beauty that hath not strangeness in the proportion." Her style was crusty, vulgar to the end, in repudiation of what she might have been. She might have been a lady.

During most of her adult life a student of Freud's picked at Hannah's head, straining to discover that her parents, longing for a son, were only given a girl. The expensive puzzle was not solved when she met and married a poor but ambitious man. By then her addiction to the doctor was complete and she endlessly played with the fascinating (to her) one-sided Moebius strip of her childhood. It inspired and continued the contempt which she felt for the money and haut bourgeois culture of the Brandts. This basic text which she drew on daily never failed her. I can guess it was a vigorous disdain that led her to drink too much Neirsteiner at her family's table and proclaim that the people will rise and serve the middle classes up as *trayf*. The ugly Yiddish word was offensive to the Brandts; still they could afford Hannah's politics better than her tantrums.

By then she had her backup, she had her Max. She was so pleased to be married, to be radical. The German cousins were delighted with Hannah's behavior and said that, in fact, the Brandts were no longer disappointed in their daughter once she became a card-carrying intellectual which was, after all, one fulfillment of their European dream.

In her own essays and memoir, a career she forged, Hannah appeared as a political figure, that is to say a politician soliciting my vote. More often than not I'd give it to her no matter what the argument, for she wrote a surprisingly graceful, even genteel prose. She always stood for something.

Once, in the early Sixties, I saw her throw a drink at a clergyman who spoke against her husband's by then fashionable magazine, with never a thought to her Balenciaga dress. She was brave like that and loyal. A testimony from a hostile source carries some conviction; that she was a sore loser, but Hannah was merely scrappy, loved a fight, whether it be over her property line in Truro or her defense of Max Gideon's tunnel vision—hanging in there with Joe Stalin, despite the Moscow Trials.

And it must never be forgotten that with all her efforts, Hannah Brandt remained an innocent, a rich girl buying favors. Her life was, given the case history, heroic as she wrote it and extended that glory to Max. He should never have died before her. The apartment on Park Avenue became his shrine with all-but-votive candles.

But in the old days which are sorely missed, she was fine sitting at the head of the Brandts'—it was Sheraton that table—toasting the fabled company, so grand it would seem that aside from her sharp tongue, Hannah greatly resembled her mother. She was much honored, palmed and plumed as a survivor and in the end it can be said she achieved her life. She was counted with the men.

PHILO PIERCE

Editor. Born 1901. Son of Hugh Waldo, pastor, the Congregational Assembly, Greenwich, Conn. Yale, B.A., Scroll and Key, Elizabethan Club. Later—University, Knickerbocker, Grolier, Century, Players and Ballywynde. Married Edith Pugh who wisely kept to the country. Set his tone after the successful Max Gideon. Though far from handsome, women were an easy prey. Politically astute. Purveyor of talent. Hail fellow well met. In the long run: Children, Dogs, Stone Farmhouse. Died haying in notorious red suspenders, 1970. A pamphleteer and sometime critic, Pierce did little harm.

The light in the kitchen flickers as the pump in the cellar switches on. After all the expense Margaret's gone to, the electricity remains temperamental. Local workers will rewire once more for the new owners, honest men knowing it is pointless, that the electricity will bounce around the valley, glance off hills making its mischief. Margaret sits at the kitchen table in her soiled Irish sweater. It is cold, dim as candlelight. In a while she gathers her few papers, torn contract included, and wanders upstairs. She tosses them in with the last local bills and the most recent letters of condolence. It is altogether too dramatic to throw her trick chronicles away. Who knows?—some day she may want to look back, but she thinks not.

She will never want to use Hannah or Dotty. She has laid them to rest. Mighty Mouse with his peachstone for a heart: her cute editor called it: she wrote in bad faith, distracted, even amused herself. Boiled down lives until they were bittersweet, frothy. As she saw fit, condemned or absolved and as always, had the last word. Dotty was right—"our revolution" she said to Pinky, cutting out Margaret. Oh, Dotty had her number—it was all material for Margaret Flood, grist for the mill. She sees Peach in country gear pursued by Br'er Rabbit, a jointed paper doll, he is running downhill with a six-figure offer, three miles to the Inn. Margaret has closed the deal, written her way out of the contract, an old gambit—to save her soul and not known it. Has she learned it? That she cannot dispose of other people's facts. Listen, she says, beginning her discourse with Pinky, they were grand figures in their day so let them remain curiosities. Let the myths accrue, gather. My feet are like ice. She shivers by the bed, then carefully crawls in. So—let them stay heroes. What's the difference to me and what's the difference in the end.

For Lourdes it is pure tragedy, not like the devastation of her village by torrential rain, huts floating on mud pastures, or the sad smell of useless herbs burning against disease—events inevitable as market day or Corpus Christi, accepted and observed. Tragedy without precedent has been visited upon her. Now she is like the madwoman with one unproductive hen, her cock picked off by wild dogs, who begged at the well with her desolate story, or the girl with crossed eyes, San Pedro's curse, no man would marry. It has been done to her, decreed, taken place. Lourdes now wears a black kerchief. She has given up hats and the wig. The dull cotton cloth is pulled tight over her bristly gray head as she travels underground. She goes to Missus Flood, to the empty apartment. There is nothing to do. Ay—it is awful and she cleans what is already clean. A thick layer of silicone wax with lemon scent has built up on all the furniture. Brass and what's left of the silver gleams. The neglected plants now thrive on the front windowsills, a trim and miniature tropics facing the lush summer in Central Park.

She opens and shuts windows, vacuums to no purpose. Pingy has given her the direction to clear out Bayard's room. That she has done, or rather Pepe has hauled it off

—furniture, books, record player—in one hour with the help of a friend. Pepe can only help Sundays now he is managing Exxon, but he has cleared and painted the room. She did as she was told, only she has got Pepe two gallons of pink. Is sooo beaudiful, she thinks, but more important it will never remind them of their boy. Pink is for a girl. Yet she kisses her thumb and crosses herself before entering the room. It glows around her, still and empty. Pepe has hung a white paper window shade which she keeps drawn. Quiet like someone is sleeping. In the closet is left (Lourdes crosses herself twice) a tripod, a telescope, two globes—one of the earth with its blue oceans, the other a transparent ball, presumably the universe. Help me, Jesus. These objects she will not touch, but she brushes the sleeve of a worn Trinity blazer which hangs by itself. It is the emblem with gold words "Lux et Labore" she cannot dispose of—already badness, too many curse.

Lourdes' days, never complete without their omens, are now fearsome morning to night. The subway stalls in darkness: there are pebbles among the black beans; a slick of oil in the sink after Pepe washes forms a figure or face. Watching her, following her to the door of the Acme Bodega, the little black girl in filthy overalls, a top-heavy child with a round bush of wire hair, skinny arms with dappled sickly skin and, what is worse to Lourdes, worn sneakers with no laces. "Go. You go," she says in English. The child retreats no more than a step. In the morning she is already out there, an urchin sucking her thumb on the curb. Something moves behind Lourdes' new magenta curtains, not just the wind and it is not just the sun that wakes her at dawn sweating and fearful in her bed.

Then one day the bird comes. She is airing Missus Flood room. The sheets and summer coverlet are folded back as though someone has slept in the bed. The closet door is flung open and Lourdes is shifting bottles of evaporated cologne around the dressing table when she hears the ruffle of its wings. The bird preens on the windowsill, invites itself in, strutting across the carpet, a white bird mottled with soft brown markings, tail feathers tipped with lavender. Lourdes knows it is a New York pigeon, but sees it as a dove, a spirit. Is so high up, so high. Where Missus Flood live are no birds. She kisses her blessing thumb. Sooo beaudiful.

The bird is calm in his purveyance, as though this bedroom with its furniture legs, wastebasket, chintz drapes is his as well as Central Park. His glassy red eyes remind Lourdes of the roundheaded pins she used in the shop, so nize, to fix a blouse or scarf on display. His shaded feathers are exactly the same as the trim on a pillbox hat she was to repair on that very day. "Ay," she says to the bird. The pigeon swells out its throat and coos, settles under a bureau in the shade. Coo-coo.

The day it took place she arrived to find the police sealing the shop door. She asked in the thinning crowd and the crowd answered to left and right, "They got the boy," a tragic chorus. For drugs or money. Quantities of blood are described. They stabbed a boy. Lourdes' face, so placid, so evasive, withers in pain and she moves away from Golden Oldies, a little dried apple doll, running back to her subway. Later, she is able to show the key with Pingy and Missus Flood looking on. What do the policemen think? Sure, she have her key to the shop which they now take away. Here the edges blur—the shop and her son are gone all in a day. Even as the policeman asks her address and members of her family, she counts Manny dead and does not give his name. Pepe, Help her Jesus, is at Exxon. God has punished Missus Flood and Lourdes. Is terrible, terrible—ay, Jesus, she complains, at least they have the funeral, the body. It would be hard to say how much Lourdes knows, but she knows she can only cry in public for another woman's son. She is profligate with tears for

Bayard who was smart like Manny though too young to go to college. She's right, Manny is smart. He took only ten bucks from her wallet and see, the key was in her purse where it belong.

In the kitchen she finds stale crackers which she crushes and brings to the bird. He is delighted and gives her the glassy eye. Coo-coo. He eats out of her hand, his quick pecking tingles her palm, then the pale bird flies away just skimming a vase which teeters and falls off the sill. Not broken. It is a sign and Lourdes takes heart at this magic invasion. She vacuums the crumbs. She is singing. The vase, once favorite of Missus Flood, is chipped not broken. She has told how at this apartment there were thieves who stole silver, broke and entered, yes, and scratched the door. She has told of all the queer and assorted people who come to the shop, revealed their motives and that now and again she herself sews a false label, jacks up a price. In a full confession Lourdes told a bilingual cop that on the day it happened she was about to disguise the molting feathers of a hat under a bit of illusion veil. She does not say that in her heart, here, the heart she points to, she knows she will never see Manny again.

Why does she sing? Why is her burden lighter, now the common pigeon has come? O-Linda. O-Linda. She ties on her black kerchief at the end of the day. The subway car is new. She sits under a fan. Why is Lourdes happy when her contractual arrangements with Jesus have gone awry? Candles, photos, silver, wig, prayers she gave Jesus. But she could not give up the fashion business, therefore Jesus took Manny away. He drives a hard bargain, so why does she buy yams tonight, guava jelly, pork chops, a coconut? And why does Lourdes cry out in wonder, a high piercing scream, and cross herself when she opens the door to find the filthy child in overalls sitting at her kitchen table.

"Mamma," Pepe says. "Cut it out, Mamma. How long you want to play stupid? This is Felix, Manny's kid."

"Pobrecito," she sighs.

"Yeah, *pobrecito.* The woman cut out with Manny."

But Lourdes doesn't hear this. The apparition of the child has already entered the realm of miraculous cures, stigmata, holy birds, blessed waters, virgin births. She touches the child's face, takes up a sticky hand. Its delicate shoulder bones hold up frayed suspenders. It wears no shirt, no underclothes under the greasy overall and she can see down past the frail rib cage and dark sunken belly, past the last shred of her incredulity, to the very small penis. "Felix," she says in adoration. That is the name of a boy.

Now Lourdes is singing—phew, she has put Felix in the tub and he bites when she washes his hair, just like Manny. His little thing stands up when she dries him, thank you, Jesus. She creams the discoloration on his arms and cuts away at his hair. "How old?" she asks in Spanish, then in English. Felix, who has not spoken a word, holds up four fingers. Like his dead father, so smart.

After supper they watch, well, not Lourdes, she sits on the couch and prays. A low black car drives along a cliff; below, a beach, palm trees, a pink building which enters her mind as the Governor's palace, popgun shots. The child, drugged with food, lists to one side as though he might come to rest on Lourdes. Now that she has trimmed his puffball, she sees the head itself is wide. Cleaned up he is more golden. She does not think Felix has been scrounging off neighbors and Pepe for weeks, a four-year-old kid, sleeping and peeing in hallways, surviving, evading the authorities. Like father, like son. The boy has come to her perfect, thank you, Jesus, as though on a bed of straw.

Pepe has cracked open the coconut with his tools. Lourdes scoops out a quarter moon of the white flesh and offers it to the boy with a pink shimmer of guava jelly. Tonight there will be candles, photos of the living and dead, prayers for Pingy to get well, for Missus Flood sin and ecstasy in an extended litany of Thank yous. She has given up her wig, her hats, the Lexington line, all pleasure in the fashion business: Jesus has come through with Felix. His woolly head rests in her lap.

The house takes to its emptiness. Floors stretch out comfortably in the void. The windows, stripped, look wide-eyed but indifferent at the road and hills, the minor changes over the years of electric lines, foundation planting and the patch of seasonless green—a tennis court. Clean grates, corners exposed—it is a self-contained, well-proportioned house that never needed furniture or people. At its back door two cartons sealed and marked—Books, Kitchen Bowls. Margaret says, "What do I want with kitchen bowls? It's a throwback." She leaves it at that. In New York she has more kitchen bowls than she will ever need. Pinky, who has climbed halfway up Mount Everest in his sporting days, knows what is unnecessary. It is their last night and too late to rethink the kitchen bowls. At the front door a dozen cartons from the best shops in Hilton Head await the new people.

Eating odds and ends, Pinky and Margaret each drink a glass of wine. He proudly recorks the bottle, good stuff they will leave behind. But not his twenty-pound weights which are already in the car. It is amazing what he has accomplished between elbow and shoulder and more generally the upper pectorals during the past six weeks. Their talk—as to clearing out of Vermont and the friendly bearers in Nepal who led him from Katmandu up to the first station in the Himalayas—has run out. The house underscores their silence with creaks and yawns. Margaret chews on a chicken bone, the leg which she has always preferred, in particular the smooth white cartilage at the joint—round, slick, opaque. It will ruin your teeth they told her. She had never listened, too eager to know and dead sure that something of value lay inside. It gives to her bite, tasteless as always. She is no longer disappointed, no longer the perversely hopeful child. It is going to rain. Margaret knows. Her chest incision aches; it is absolutely accurate in its predictions.

Their departure from a house they have toyed with for fifteen years doesn't trouble them. They have sworn off sentimentality, any displaced emotion which they could easily wring from the touching detail that they first came up here when Bayard slept in a canvas basket on the back seat of the Corvette. But separately they know that fifteen years, ten years, next year—then and now—are irrevocably altered, their calendar changed, forever to be reckoned from a central date. When it is finally dark they go outside, leaving the near perfection of their last cleanup behind. Margaret, enveloped in her Irish sweater, follows Pinky.

"A lot of hoopla," he says.

"They better get on with it." Heavy cloud cover to the north, but they look down to the valley as though facing a proscenium arch. It begins: at first a gentle ak-ak, ground fire, then a rocket that shoots up with a tremendous blast, pink sharpening to yellow and brightest white, then crackling off in fragments against the night. It is the Fourth of July and the town, like many that have never afforded fireworks, has gone all out with flags and banners, high-steppers announcing the Republic's been around two hundred years. There have been villagers dressed as Minutemen, a Betsy Ross, a fellow playing the flute with a bandage on one eye, a small parade of Vets and Scouts led by the high school band—not seen or heard by the Strongs from their vantage point. Now the display. Pinwheels, geysers, a dazzling rocket followed by dandelion bursts to left, to right—high, higher still, comic in that they finish off and come again like a vaudeville turn—one more, just one more time. "Oh," she says, "Ah," at a streak of popping green light turned lyric waterfall. She cries out at the finale, a giant gold chrysanthemum that begets buds and in full flower overwhelms the sky: its last petals fall softly, fade, turn loveliest to die. The show is over. Pinky moves to go inside.

"I'll be fine," she says. She cannot see his face in the dark. He puts his arm around her and they stand together. Margaret sees them, the well-preserved protector and his little woman going graceful white, trim, radiant with vitamins and the best medical care, posed to face whatever— They have signed a binding agreement: the absurd comfort that they will profit by each other's death. They must never let the payments lapse. Insurance, her father's trade in limited liability, extended coverage, all these years for Mutual of Omaha, Hartford Accident and Life.

"Leave me," Margaret says.

Pinky is crazy to go inside. She can tell. He is cramming, a wayward student catching up. Today, he has constructed from his note cards a remarkable story. That one, De Lancy Jerome, scion of an old distinguished family—which, in some system elaborate as trunk lines or jacquard weave, is always Pinky's family—that this Jerome who founded a Utopian summer colony up near Amenia—wood huts, spring water, sketching and songfests, mathematics and moral lectures—that this same gentleman, as Jerome De Lancy, frequented a "house" in the Tenderloin where girls without bloomers played leapfrog over his nude body, three dollars a head. Margaret can tell he's mad to get to it. What went on in Amenia where the high-minded Jerome copied out in his commonplace book: "As souls unbodied, bodies unclothed must be to taste whole joys."

It's in the cards. Fan them out and play. Pinkham Strong searches for correspondences: they are marvelous and true. Then and now. She envies her husband's archives: scraps of romance, family tales that linger in black and white, of treachery and self-deception, of naive realism. If in the past, then in the future . . . Turn up the two-faced Jack: De Lancy or Jerome reads out both good and bad. If his sins have been forgotten, then mine, then ours. From this we learn, we gather that early as San Juan Hill personal valor was obsolete, thus we see that cavalry charge at machine gun scatter . . . and so forth. Listen, Margaret walks the lines of the tennis court, history is a dodge, but it buys time. What wouldn't she give for the safety of a parallel, words to live by. Listen, what she wouldn't give to be up there with Pinky manipulating facts that reveal, predict. Reshuffle: now as opposed to then. Half card shark, half gypsy—deal a royal flush, call it luck. She knows that route, it's a magic trick and Margaret has no aces up the sleeve of her Irish sweater. Not now. Perhaps never again.

She walks the perimeter of the house and barn, then back to Pinky's rock which is, praise be, out of the ground. Tomorrow they will roll it into the undergrowth before they take off. To the back rooms and sun porch, to the kitchen window they leave the legacy of an unimpaired view. The hole has yielded nothing. He had only hoped for something recent and small—a hand-cut nail, an arrowhead, bone button. But the stone is older than all that, kicked there by a mastodon, maybe a pebble flung out of the sky. Bayard might have answered that one in time—as to Late Cretaceous origins or a speck of dust from some imploded star, but Bayard has done enough. He has saved his father. In the best family tradition he has left a little something in trust: the news of his death has brought Pinkham Strong, that name, back to light, so when Pinky goes into the city he will resume a career, take up one or another offer to do good works.

Margaret sits by the stone. Her breastbone aches. The clouds move in, but over the town where they have watched the fireworks the sky is still clear, indeed, the stars are bright. The flat reddish moon rides low, incomplete, and though it is a miracle she does not oh or ah, that's for a lot of hoopla, the razzmatazz of holiday fare, impermanent art. She understands the fireworks to be like Greenwood Cemetery, formal and celebratory to keep reality at bay. She has discovered that by thinking Greenwood Cemetery she contains herself. A noble place, hill and dale, the contrivance of land for privacy, repose. Cedar Grove and Vista Hill—the rich block out their neighbors.

Greenwood Cemetery, that gilded, carved, pilastered, domed and gabled fantasy which overpowered death. They had not been up to it—crypts, obelisks, funereal urns, the marble-and-rose stone elaborations on weeping willows, sorrowful nymphs . . . hooded sleeping figures, Niobe, a languid unrepentant Magdalen. Dante—it was Dante at the last turn as they wound up and around the mausoleums, little palaces and follies, each architectural gesture competitive and distinct. It *was* the poet with quill pen, the big Italian nose. A crown of laurel held the draped hanky on his head. Paradiso in Brooklyn. Bayard will lie with the illustrious—Horace Greeley, Louis Comfort Tiffany, Civil War generals, Lola Montez. They came in their cortege of hired limousines unprepared for this grandeur, this somber show. A museum of sorts. And the names, the names polished, incised, gleamed out of the shadows, immortal graffiti.

Pinky did not have to choose Greenwood Cemetery, the family plot. She would be forever grateful. The line of black cars came to a halt and when they stepped out, the ancient trees spread above them, a bright tent of early leaves, the ivy and moss, cool green in May. All was settled: here nothing was new or raw. They climbed steps that might lead to an English garden. The Bidwells had shrunk Monticello, fanlight and all, in tawny limestone, inscribed with high ancestral name. It sat on its own little lawn no larger than Margaret's big living room rug. So they arranged themselves around the border. The bronze doors stood open. Inside the flash of red roses on the bier, Sol's Hollywood touch. When she runs off Greenwood Cemetery, Margaret edits the assembled company: Jack Flood, her own father (neat old man in a black suit who never met her boy), Sol Negaly with the good sense to leave Tina in the loft, a clump of schoolchildren struck dumb, led by Suki Moss in widow's weeds, an Episcopalian clergyman in a Roman collar whom they have never seen, will never see again. And the soldier. Out on the grass with the mourners, the soldier stands lifesize among them, creamy as a tusk and perfectly detailed—his musette bag, canteen, officer's cap, down to the fussy buttons on his marble puttees. This visionless kitsch stands guard, ready to serve. When they file away in a true recessional, branches close behind them, as in a dark wood, thick and strangely consoling. I dreamt I dwelt in marble halls—that's Greenwood Cemetery. You do not believe it has been there with vassals and serfs at your side.

Then there is always life, the tick of it going on, so that when they returned to the apartment, pursued by the media, Ned Lynch, Sol, Dr. Moss and Suki, all of them upstairs among too many flowers, driven back to the excess of food essential to our mourning, there was Lourdes in her dress whites. Having placed all the delicacies which Margaret had ordered herself carefully to the side, Lourdes stands at attention over the dining room table where she offers towering, God-given peaks of rice and beans.

"What shall we do with the ink?"

"*Your* ink," she calls up to Pinky. He is up at the window in their empty bedroom. Last night they slept like kids, mattress on the floor.

"My ink," he says. "What shall we do?" The light is far behind him and he appears to her in profile, a silhouette looking her way, his features cut so skillfully the character of the man is revealed. He is a man of character to Margaret now, but she cannot read the blank interior. As always, there is something she misses in Pinky. "Forget the ink," she says. "It would be a disaster."

There is a pause in which he hovers, will not leave her. "I'm coming," Margaret says, "believe me, it's about to rain." A major catastrophe, if the ink spilled on his cards crossing out all those dates and names with their illuminating tales. But Pinky is blessed, always pulls through. *Annuit Coeptis,* thinks Margaret—oh, come on, where have you seen it? No, she's not being fancy. Where have you seen it?—*He has favored our undertaking.* And she knows for sure Pinky is favored, if not by God as it says on the dollar bill, at least this time he is working ahead from reliable sources. She hopes he never reaches his own story.

Margaret waits, sits on: the moon is going, going, finding its way through the clouds. Bayard, with his extensive knowledge of the heavens, might have left, gone there. He had that option. "The heart . . ." says Margaret. She has stayed out here for a final tryst—the last frame, stone to her back. Don't sit on the cold ground, the cement steps. "The heart must weigh . . ." Will you listen, it's bad for your kidneys, your bowels. She had never listened, always sat out late. Now, of course, she knows that she has kidneys and bowels, a rackety heart and that the heart must weigh the stone it earns. What's more, though it is not good for her, she's angry. She did not die: she did not remain alive. Faked out death: it found her. She would like to slit the world like a hollow rubber ball, turn it inside out, reverse the hemispheres and hand it to her son as a better thing. Listen, she says, talking to Bayard, what I wouldn't give for some undertaking. Goods, not words. Retail business. I'd sell old furniture, old clothes. Sharp trade, but this time harmless.

The moon's gone. The first splat of rain strikes her forehead. She gets up, turns and does a pratfall into the gaping hole, a clownish spill but with the snap of a joint that's painful. She cannot stand. There she lies in the mud. A thorough rain, but gentle, no thunder, no lightning. She cannot play Lady Lear: "There's hell, there's darkness, there is the sulphurous pit." No, she's in her senses. It's a wonder how the Irish sweater sheds water. Oh, Lord, using the Lord's name Margaret laughs, they will identify the body as Moran. They'll not have an easy time of it—I'm Flood, I'm Strong, born Lynch.

She can turn and twist, but she cannot get her leg straight. She cries out from her hole, "Help me. Help me, Pinky," but he is burning the midnight oil. She envies his prospects. Pinky is up there waiting for the next America. She cannot stand. The hole claims her. She is finished. How will she make it to New York, a purgatory in summer? How will Margaret go on pilgrimages, walking the city streets with Pinky from Old Trinity Church to Central Park? How will she kneel at each station of the cross, each family shrine? The pain is real, less real than her memory of pain. Now she'll never wave and smile after the double somersault. It is the end, the final take. She is through and so forth—Margaret with no words, little drama. Until, using her wits, she hugs the stone. It will not roll back on her. Watch as she hoists herself out of the abyss, crawls over the perfect lawn toward the light. Dead reckoning: no instruments, not even stars to guide her. She's got spunk—a little rain must fall. Listen, Margaret Flood had wanted to be Madame Lulu, the human meteor, shoot sixty feet to the top of the tent. (It's done with springs, not gunpowder, despite the convincing blast.)

Now it is possible that Margaret has no more words beyond a summary text directed to the innocent reader: "This note is legal tender for all debts, public and private." But she is not up to her old tricks. Listen, if she writes again—and we know her to be incurable, a repeated offender—she will tell about people who bury their dead in plain sight of each other, in flat land by railroad tracks at the edge of the city. About a smart girl who prayed for a two-wheel bike and got it. Lives without incident—almost. Wet and numb, she is happy to reach the back porch. Oh, one last time—

This one's for you, Baby: They could never call her in. Her mother who was sickly would come to the screen door or call from her bed, her voice filtered through starched white curtains, distant and fearful, calling, "Margaret—come in, come in." She would not go, defiant, then dreaming on in the dangerous night air. Too smart for her own good. Star gazing, she could not show you the Big Dipper, the North Star, just the dumb glory of it all and that the universe could not contain her yearning. "Margaret," they called, but she took her chances. She would not go in.

It is like her to sit on the cold granite steps. The shower is past. She searches the sky for the returning moon and it appears like the flick of a coin. Listen, they could never call me in. It was my choice, my predilection, my habit—a silly girl in short summer dresses, the rough cement on her bare bottom and I laugh at her still. Still, though night hangs in shreds around her, she will not go inside.

ABOUT THE AUTHOR

MAUREEN HOWARD is the author of four previous novels —*Not a Word About Nightingales, Bridgeport Bus, Before My Time,* and *Grace Abounding*—and an autobiographical book, *Facts of Life,* which won the 1978 National Book Critics Circle Award. Her articles have appeared in the *New York Times,* the *Washington Post,* the *New Republic, Vogue, Vanity Fair* and the *New York Times Book Review.* Ms. Howard is a Guggenheim Fellow and a Fellow of the Radcliffe Institute and has been nominated for a National Book Award and a PEN Faulkner Award. She teaches at Columbia University and is currently at Yale.